GETTYSBURG

The Civil War Battles Series
by James Reasoner

Manassas
Shiloh
Antietam
Chancellorsville
Vicksburg

GETTYSBURG

James Reasoner

CUMBERLAND HOUSE
NASHVILLE, TENNESSEE

Published by
CUMBERLAND HOUSE PUBLISHING, INC.
431 Harding Industrial Drive
Nashville, Tennessee 37211
www.cumberlandhouse.com

This novel is a work of fiction. Names, characters, places, and incidents either are the
product of the author's imagination or are used fictitiously. Any resemblance to per-
sons, living or dead, events, or locales is entirely coincidental.

Cover design by Bob Bubkis, Nashville, Tennessee.

Library of Congress Cataloging-in-Publication Data.

Reasoner, James.
Gettysburg / James Reasoner.
p.   cm. — (The Civil War battle series ; bk. 6)
ISBN 1-58182-220-0 (alk. paper)
1. Gettysburg (Pa.), Battle of, 1863—Fiction. 2. United States—History—
Civil War, 1861–1865—Fiction. I. Title.
PS3568.E2685 G4 2001
813'.54—dc21   2001037131

Printed in the United States of America.

1 2 3 4 5 6 7 8 9 10—05 04 03 02 01

For Ed Curtis,
with thanks

GETTYSBURG

Chapter One

THE MEN TRUDGED ALONG in the cold rain, slogging down a seemingly endless road that was slick with mud. Their clothing, thin and ragged to start with, was soaked. Chills ran through their bodies. Some of them stumbled, caught themselves, then forced their legs to move again. Some stumbled and fell and could not get up again. Using the bayonets attached to the muzzles of Springfield rifles, guards in slickers prodded the fallen to their feet and forced them on. Everywhere up and down the mile-long column of prisoners, men shuddered from wracking coughs and hugged themselves against the cold, but there was no escape from it. No escape, and for these men, nowhere to go.

All those hellfire-and-brimstone sermons he had heard in the First Baptist Church of Culpeper had been wrong, thought Titus Brannon as he shambled along the road. Hades wasn't hot and full of eternal fire. It was cold and wet, and Titus knew this was hell because he was right in the middle of it.

"Move along . . . move along," the Yankee guards called constantly, their voices a weary drone. This northward trek was probably hard on them, too, but Titus didn't give a damn about that. He hated them, and they could all come down with the grippe and die, as far as he was concerned. Of course, a lot more of the Confederate prisoners were going to suffer that fate. Already quite a few of them had died from exposure to the elements of this brutal winter.

Was it still December? Or had New Year's come and gone already? Titus had lost track of the days. He knew the battle of Fredericksburg had been on December 13, 1862, because he had been there, crouched behind the stone wall at the base of Marye's Heights, pouring lead from his Sharps rifle into the onrushing Yankee horde as fast as he could load and fire. He had felt the savage satisfaction of the Sharps kicking against his shoulder, had reveled in the clouds of powder smoke that stung his eyes and nose, had listened keenly to the screams of dying men, the roar of artillery, the rattle of musketry—all the sounds that made up the music of war.

Then, like a damned fool, he had left the safety of the wall and rushed out at the head of a small party of Rebels who were determined to smash a group of Yankees who had gotten cut off from their fellows.

It had been the Confederates who were crushed instead when Union reinforcements showed up at just the wrong time. Titus was pretty sure that all the men who had gone with him were dead. Somehow he had survived and been taken prisoner. His mother, devout churchgoer that she was, no doubt would have said that God had watched out for Titus and shielded him with His hand.

Titus knew himself too well to believe that was true. If anyone had saved him, it was the devil.

One of the other prisoners stumbled heavily against Titus's shoulder. Acting out of instinct, Titus put a hand on the man's arm to steady him, as he had done numerous times before during this nightmarish march. Nathan Hatcher coughed a couple of times. "Sorry, Titus. Guess I wasn't watching where I was going."

"Forget it," Titus mumbled. He knew that Nathan was exhausted and little more than half-conscious. It wouldn't do any good to get mad at him for being clumsy. Nathan had always been pretty much useless anyway. He never would understand what his sister, Cordelia, had seen in him.

Nathan and Titus were both from Culpeper County. The Brannon farm, which had been in the family for years, was a few miles from the town of Culpeper, sometimes known as Culpeper Court House.

Nathan had lived in town and worked as a law clerk. A slim, studious young man, he had been ostracized by the community when he refused to join the Confederate army and fight for the Southern cause. Instead, on principle, Nathan had gone north and enlisted with the Yankees.

That hadn't stopped him from winding up in the middle of a bunch of Confederate prisoners. Titus had heard the story several times and still found it hard to believe. Fleeing back into the town of Fredericksburg when the Yankee attack on Marye's Heights collapsed, Nathan had been jumped by a Confederate deserter and knocked unconscious. The man had switched uniforms with Nathan so he could pass unmolested through the Union lines, leaving Nathan behind clothed in Rebel gray. The Yankees who had grabbed Nathan during the retreat across the Rappahannock hadn't believed the seemingly wild yarn he told them about being a member of their army. Nathan's captors saw the Confederate uniform, and that was more than enough for them. He was a prisoner of war of his own army.

He and Titus had wound up in the same group of prisoners. Titus wasn't the pitying sort, but he knew Cordelia had a soft spot for Nathan, so he had tried to explain to their captors that, despite the Virginia accent, Nathan really was on their side.

They hadn't listened to him, either, of course.

After that, the whole thing struck Titus as sort of funny. Nathan had gone to such lengths to avoid being a Confederate and wound up one anyway. The two of them had been together ever since.

He wasn't sure where they were bound. He knew it would be some Yankee prison camp. After being taken across the Potomac with Gen. Ambrose Burnside's retreating forces, the prisoners had been put on a train. For several days they had ridden the rails, hundreds of men packed into cramped, cold, nearly airless freight cars. Men who were unlucky enough to have been wounded in the battle were given no medical care, so each time the train stopped and the doors were rolled back and the prisoners were allowed a little exercise, some of them were dead. Yankee soldiers dragged the bodies to the open doors and tossed them out like bags of potatoes. Titus would never forget the soggy thumps as the dead men hit the ground.

He had figured they would ride the train all the way to the prison camp, wherever that might be, but after a few days the captives had been herded out of the cars while the train was stopped on a siding in the middle of some winter-desolate farm country.

"It'll be shank's mare the rest of the way for you boys," one of the guards told them. "Abe Lincoln needs this train for something more important than carrying Rebel scum like you."

Since then they had been marched through the rain along some seemingly endless, narrow lanes. There weren't enough guards, and some of the prisoners probably could have made a break for it, if they had not been so sick and dispirited.

But that would mean fighting, and they had all had their fill of that. All but a few.

Titus wished he could get his hands on a gun again. He wouldn't mind dying if he could just kill a few more Yankees first. Killing was the only thing that had kept him alive—since Polly . . .

Best not to think about Polly, he told himself now as her image floated up in his memory. She was beautiful, sure, and most men in his situation would cling desperately to memories of their wives. But that was not the case. If it weren't for Polly, he never would have been at Fredericksburg in the first place.

She had made her choice. She had picked her father over him. Titus supposed he couldn't blame her. He was just a farmer, not penniless but certainly not rich, and Polly's father, Duncan Ebersole, owner of the plantation called Mountain Laurel, was the wealthiest man in the county. When the inevitable clash came and Polly sided with her father, Titus had left Mountain Laurel and gone home to the farm. He never should have left there in the first place, he had thought many times since. He should have known better than to marry Polly. But pride and ambition and lust had convinced him otherwise.

MORE SOLDIERS came out from the camp to meet them. Any chance the prisoners might have had to break away from their captors was gone now. They stumbled along between rows of well-armed blue-uniformed Union soldiers. The Yankees stared at them with hatred and disdain, as if these gaunt men in gray wool and butternut homespun were less than human. A few of the Confederate prisoners, Titus among them, returned defiant glares, but most of the men were too tired and sick for that. They kept their eyes on the ground, careful not to stumble or fall.

They were marched in through the gates. Guards were everywhere. The gates closed behind them and a bar was lowered into place.

"Form into ranks! Damn it, form up!"

The new prisoners numbered a couple of hundred. Slowly, they shuffled around until they were standing in rough ranks in front of what Titus took to be the administration building. They stood there for several minutes, and now that they were no longer moving, the icy rain seemed even colder.

A door in the wing to the left of the main building opened. Several men came out. One of them wore the uniform of an officer, and he was accompanied by an orderly who carried an umbrella over his head to keep the rain off him. Two guards with rifles trailed the officer and the orderly.

The little party came to a stop in front of the prisoners. The officer put his gloved hands behind his back. "At ease, gentlemen," he called in jovial tones. "I'm sure you want to get out of this miserable weather, so I won't detain you for long. My name is Captain Floyd Morton, aide to the commandant, and I want to take this opportunity to welcome you to Camp Douglas on behalf of myself and the commandant, Colonel Tucker."

Welcome? What the hell? thought Titus.

"I regret the necessity of imprisoning you poor lads," Morton went on, "but this is, after all, war. It is my fervent hope that your stay here will be short and not too unpleasant."

The captain was a short, stocky man with a curling brown beard. He didn't look like much of a soldier, which was probably why he'd wound up as the aide to a prison camp commander, Titus thought. Too soft to even stand out in the rain without somebody holding an umbrella over his head. If Titus had been a Yankee, he wouldn't have wanted to go into combat behind an officer like Morton.

From beside Titus, Nathan whispered, "He doesn't make it sound too bad. Maybe the rumors were wrong."

No sooner were the words out of Nathan's mouth than Morton's right hand shot up. "What was that?" he asked. "Someone talking in the ranks? I didn't give permission for anyone to speak." Morton looked back and forth along the rows of men, but all the prisoners were silent now. "Ah, well," the captain went on, "I had not yet explained all the rules, so I'll make allowances for that. You see, there is no talking in the ranks without permission. Absolutely no talking. So I must ask . . . who just broke that rule?"

Silence from the prisoners. All of them kept their eyes trained on the ground.

"Come, come," Morton said. "Due to the circumstances, the punishment will be mild for this infraction. But there *was* an infraction, so punishment must be carried out. Now is the time to speak, lads."

Still no response. After a moment, Morton shrugged and turned to one of the guards. "Very well. Pick anyone at random."

The guard grinned, stepped forward, and grabbed the collar of one of the men in the front row. The prisoner let out a frightened yell as the guard jerked him forward and flung him to the ground. Mud splashed up around him from the puddle in which he landed.

"I think ten lashes will be sufficient under the circumstances," Morton said.

Titus and Nathan were four rows back in the formation. Titus sensed Nathan stiffening beside him and guessed that

Nathan was about to step forward and take responsibility for breaking the rule rather than let another man be punished in his place. Titus caught hold of Nathan's wrist and clamped down hard on it. Nathan looked over at him, and Titus gave a tiny shake of his head. The fellow up front had had some bad luck, but Nathan couldn't help things now without making them worse for himself.

Nathan's eyes bored into Titus's. Titus saw the guilt and horror there. Once again, he shook his head, just enough so that Nathan could see it. Nathan took a deep breath, let it out in a long sigh, and relaxed.

The guard selected to dole out the punishment reached down and hooked his fingers in the waistband of the prisoner's butternut trousers. He pulled them down, baring the man's buttocks. Then the Yankee straightened and took off the broad leather belt that was fastened around the waist of his uniform jacket. He doubled it, bent over, raised his arm, and brought the belt down in a slashing stroke across the man's buttocks.

The prisoner let out a cry of pain and tried to scramble forward on hands and knees in the mud to get away from the lashing belt. Another guard stepped up and slammed the butt of his rifle into the prisoner's back, between his shoulder blades. The blow drove the man facedown in the mud. The second guard put his boot on the back of the man's head and held it there while the first guard continued the whipping.

Titus couldn't see very well, but he could hear the mud-choked screams, the grunts of exertion, and the sharp inhalations of breath from the other prisoners every time the belt fell. The fleeting glimpses he caught of the scene showed flashes of blood. The rain fell harder and washed the blood away almost as fast as it seeped from the broad welts on the prisoner's buttocks. The screaming stopped after the fifth stroke.

Titus couldn't help keeping count in his head as the blows fell. Morton had ordered ten lashes, but the guard gave the prisoner twelve before stopping. He stepped back, took a rag from his pocket, and wiped the blood from his belt. Then he fastened it around his waist again. Morton either hadn't noticed the extra lashes or didn't care, because he nodded in satisfaction.

"Very good. Now let that serve as a gentle reminder that the rules must not be broken. There will be punishment for each offense, although at times it will be tempered with mercy, as on this occasion."

Never once had Morton deviated from the mild, friendly tone he had taken from the start. The man was a lunatic, Titus thought, if he considered what had just happened to be merciful.

The guard who had used his foot to hold down the prisoner's head looked at the man. "Uh, Cap'n, he don't seem to be breathing. Must've swallowed too much mud."

Morton glanced down. "Is that right? Oh, well, what a shame. Tend to the burial, will you?"

Titus glanced over at Nathan, who was staring at the ground. His hands were fists, clenched so tight that trickles of blood came from his palms where the nails were digging into them.

"Now, then, where were we?" Morton went on. "Oh, yes. The rules. Each of you will be assigned to a barracks. You will remain in the vicinity of that barracks at all times. If you stray more than fifty yards from it, you will be severely punished. There is a deadline of sixty yards. Go beyond that without supervision and you will be shot. You will be fed twice daily. If you require medical care, report to the sergeant of the guard at morning roll call. Congregating in large groups is forbidden. Loud talking is forbidden. Any assault on a guard will be punishable by death, to be administered on the spot. Any attempt to escape will be punishable by death, to be administered on the spot. Remember, you are our guests. Comport yourselves accordingly. That will be all. Sergeant of the guard?"

One of the soldiers who had come out of the administration building with the captain stepped forward.

"Right face! Follow me!" he ordered. "Anybody who breaks ranks gets a whippin'!"

The prisoners shuffled toward the cluster of barracks in the northwest corner of the wretched compound, leaving behind the body sprawled facedown in the mud. Titus saw Nathan glancing back and risked hissing, "Forget it." Over the tramping of feet and the pounding of the rain, no one could hear him except Nathan.

Nathan swallowed hard and nodded. There was nothing else he could do now.

Titus knew him pretty well by this time. He knew that Nathan would blame himself for the man's death and torture himself with guilt. Well, to be honest about it, thought Titus, Nathan was partially to blame for what had happened. But none of them could have known at the time just how crazy Morton was. He had seemed pretty reasonable at first.

Titus hadn't trusted him, of course. He was never going to trust any Yankee, no matter how friendly they might act.

The sergeant of the guard took the prisoners to one of the long wooden buildings that was set a foot off the ground on heavy blocks. The crowd of men who were already in the camp parted to let the newcomers through.

The sergeant turned. "Halt!" When the prisoners had come to a shambling stop, he went on, "This is Barracks Twenty-three. This is your home from now on. Like Cap'n Morton said, don't let us catch you more'n fifty yards from it, or you'll be damned sorry."

He was already damned sorry, Titus thought. But he had sense enough not to say it.

"Fall out!" the sergeant bawled.

He and the rest of the guards moved back, letting the prisoners break ranks. The newcomers moved in a mass toward the barracks, but before they reached the three wooden steps that led up to the open door, several men appeared in the doorway. If anything, they were even more gaunt and haggard than Titus and his companions, but there was determination on their faces as one of them said, "You ain't gettin' in here."

"What?" asked one of the newcomers. "But we're assigned to this barracks."

"I don't give a goddamn where you're assigned," the man said. "There's already 176 men in this barracks, and there ain't but bunks for 120. So you ain't comin' in."

"Then where are we supposed to stay?"

The man shook his head. "That ain't our worry."

Angry muttering came from the newcomers as they stood in the rain. Other men stood in the mud, seemingly resigned to that fate. The new prisoners weren't and surged toward the steps. For a moment Titus thought there might be a riot. Then a new voice came from inside the building. It demanded in the sharp tone of command, "Sergeant Cartland! What's going on out there?"

The spokesman for the men occupying the doorway turned and said over his shoulder, "Nothin', Colonel. Just some new boys come in, and we're givin' 'em the lay of the land."

"Not trying to keep them out in the rain, are you?" A couple of the men in the doorway moved aside, making room for a tall, slender figure who limped up, leaning heavily on a rough piece of wood that was used as a cane. His uniform was tattered and filthy, but the gold braid of a colonel was still visible. With his free hand, he motioned to the newcomers. "Come in, boys, come in. Welcome to Barracks Twenty-three."

Cartland scowled but stepped out of the way, unwilling to cross the colonel. The new men ascended the steps and filed into the barracks. The colonel shook hands with some of them as they passed.

"Colonel Thaddeus Newberry of Kentucky," he introduced himself as he took Titus's hand. "Formerly a member of the staff of Major General John C. Breckinridge, captured at the battle of Shiloh. I'm the senior officer in this barracks."

"Titus Brannon. I'd say I'm pleased to meet you, Colonel, but I reckon I ain't pleased about any part of this."

Newberry smiled. His face was hollow-cheeked with hunger and weakness, but he stood as straight as he could for a man with a game leg. His long mustaches, which no doubt had been waxed and curled when he was still serving on the general's staff, now hung limply past his wide mouth. Beard stubble covered his angular jaw and chin.

"I know how you feel, Private Brannon. It is Private Brannon, isn't it?"

"Yeah, but rank don't hardly matter anymore, does it?"

Newberry drew himself up even straighter. "Military discipline always matters, Private Brannon."

The colonel's eyes burned with intensity and possibly fever as he fixed his gaze on Titus. After a second, Titus looked down and muttered, "Sorry, Colonel." Something about Newberry just wouldn't let Titus argue.

"Quite all right. An understandable reaction. Move along, Private Brannon. I'd tell you to find yourself a bunk, but I'm afraid you'll have to settle for a piece of floor."

The barracks was crowded, all right. Every one of the rough bunks had at least three men sitting on it, and Titus didn't see any empty floor, either. He worked his way through the crowd, ignoring the hostile glances that were thrown his way, and finally found himself next to one of the walls. He turned and put his shoulders against it. This was his spot, he told himself, and he wasn't going to be budged from it. The barracks was unheated, so it was still cold in here, but not as chilly as outside. And the rain wasn't falling on his head now. The smell of unwashed men was almost enough to make him gag, but he figured he could put up with it.

Somehow, Nathan found him. Titus had lost track of him in the crowd. Nathan moved up alongside him. "This is really bad, isn't it?"

Titus couldn't help it. He started laughing. Nathan stared at him in amazement, and Titus said between laughs, "I'll say one thing for you, Nathan—you got one hell of a grasp of the obvious."

Chapter Two

WITH THE HEAVY OVERCAST, night fell early over Camp Douglas. The prisoners were not allowed candles or matches, not even steel and flint, for fear that they would set fire to the buildings and try to escape in the confusion. So Titus stood against the wall in near darkness and tried to ignore the feelings of fear that wiggled around in his belly like snakes.

He didn't like the dark, and he didn't like the way men were pressed in all around him. All he had to do was let his thoughts run wild a little, and he could imagine that he was lying down instead of standing up, and that the weight of all the other prisoners was instead the weight of the earth pressing down on him in his grave. Here and there in the barracks, men whimpered and moaned, and to Titus's ears those sounds were the gibbering and chattering of the imps of hell. From time to time, someone cried out, and the screams were the screams of the damned. He bit his lip and wanted to take a deep breath, but he couldn't because of the stench in the air. If he sucked down too much of it, he would be sick. He was sure of that.

Out of the darkness, a hand touched him. It grasped his thigh and moved slowly upward.

A fierce gladness surged through Titus. At last, a threat he could deal with. His hand shot down, and his fingers clamped like iron around the wrist of the man. The wrist was very thin, and Titus could feel how fragile the bones inside were. He heard a gasp of surprise and pain somewhere close by.

Through clenched teeth, Titus said, "Get your hand off me, you son of a bitch, or I'll break your wrist right now."

The fingers left his thigh. Titus could imagine the hand splaying out in panic as its owner reacted to the threat.

"I'm gonna let go of you now," Titus said. "If you ever touch me again, I'll kill you. I don't give a damn what the Yankees do

27

to me, and I ain't scared of anything your friends might do to me, if you got any friends. All you got to know is that you will be one . . . dead . . . bastard."

He let go of the man's wrist.

A second later he heard a choked sob. Nothing else happened. Titus leaned back against the wall, relishing the satisfaction that the brief moment of violence had brought him. The other men around him must have overheard him, but no one responded to it. Titus crossed his arms and lowered his head. He was exhausted, and he dozed for a little like that, head down and chin on his chest.

When he awoke, his head came up with a jerk. The muscles in his neck were painfully stiff. He turned his head from side to side and rolled his shoulders as much as he could, trying to loosen the stiffness.

"Nathan? You still here?"

"I'm here, Titus," Nathan said from beside him.

"When do you reckon they feed us in here?"

A voice said, "They ain't going to feed us. Not tonight."

"What?" Titus scowled. "They got to feed their prisoners. It's the law."

Another man gave a soft hoot of derisive laughter. "The law don't mean nothing to these Yankees. About half the nights they don't bring us no supper. They never feed us when it's rainin' hard like this. Can't be bothered."

"Or if it's too cold," another man chimed in.

"Or if they just don't feel like it," added a third.

Titus grimaced. No wonder the fight had gone out of a lot of these men. Two meals a day wasn't enough to start with. If the Yankees refused to feed them, starvation took care of any unrest. Their captors were executing them, as surely as if they had been put up in front of a firing squad. These Yankees just liked to take their time with their killing, that was all.

They wouldn't beat him down, he vowed, wouldn't knock the fight out of him or starve it out, either. It didn't matter how tired or scrawny he got, if the Yankees gave him a chance, he'd spit in their faces and kill them all. Just let them try to break Titus Brannon and see how far they got.

Far in the back of his brain, a tiny voice warned him that if he kept thinking like that, he would go mad.

That was all right, Titus told himself. Maybe there were times when it was better to be crazy.

—m—

SOMEHOW DURING the night he slid down the wall to the floor, so that he woke up the next morning huddled there in a ball, surrounded by other men who had collapsed into exhausted slumber. Some of them were stirring, and everyone woke up when the door to the barracks was jerked open and a loud voice yelled, "Grub! Grub, you Rebel maggots!"

Shaking off sleep, the prisoners scrambled to their feet and crowded toward the door. Titus had no choice but to go with them. He looked around but didn't see Nathan.

The prisoners filed out of the barracks and lined up to receive their breakfast. Under the rifles of half a dozen watchful guards, the inhabitants of Barracks Twenty-three shuffled past a burly sergeant who took loaves of moldy bread from a burlap sack and tore off a hunk for each of the men. When it was Titus's turn, the piece of bread he was given barely filled the palm of his hand. "Is this all we get?" he asked.

"Be glad you get that much, Johnny," the sergeant sneered. "'Tis more'n ye deserve."

Titus bit back the angry response that he felt. Nothing he could say would do any good. He moved on and found himself a place to stand while he ate. What with no supper the night before, his stomach was empty and growling. He looked at the bread. It was not only moldy but soggy, and it had insects crawling in it. Titus's stomach lurched at the sight. He wanted to throw down the bread and demand something decent to eat, but he had been a prisoner of war long enough to know better than that. No matter how bad it was, you ate what they gave you and were grateful for it, because it was the only thing keeping you alive.

That, and the hatred you felt for your captors. He lifted the hunk of bread to his mouth and took a big bite.

Swallowing the bread, bugs and all, was easier than he'd thought it would be. A few bites and it was gone. That was enough to blunt the savage hunger in his belly. Soon enough it would be back, gnawing on his insides with its sharp fangs, but for now he felt a little better. With the pressing need of his hunger alleviated, he became aware that his bladder was full. He looked around and said to the man standing next to him, "Where do you take a leak around here?"

The man pointed with a grimy thumb. "Latrine's down yonder at the end of the barracks."

Titus made his way through the crowd of prisoners. The rain had stopped during the night, and there were gaps in the clouds that let some pale, watery sunlight shine through. The wind was colder than ever, though. Crusts of ice were beginning to form on some of the puddles around the prison grounds. If the rest of the clouds cleared off before nightfall, it was liable to get really cold by the next morning, Titus considered.

He reached the latrine and saw that it was nothing more than an open ditch dug along the ends of all the barracks on this side of the cluster. It was also the source of much of the stench that filled the air. The heavy rain of the day before had made it overflow. A small lake of human waste lay there. Breathing shallowly, Titus relieved himself as quickly as he could, knowing he was adding to the problem but knowing as well that there was nothing else he could do.

When he turned away from the latrine, buttoning up his trousers, he almost ran into Nathan. "Wondered where you'd got off to," he said.

"I was talking to Colonel Newberry," Nathan said. "It turns out he was a lawyer before the war."

"Discussin' legal strategy, were you? Maybe you're going to bring a lawsuit against the Yankees?" Titus grinned.

"As prisoners of war, we do have some rights, you know." Nathan was holding the piece of bread he had been given for breakfast. "This food isn't fit for hogs. They're supposed to feed us better than this. We're supposed to receive humane treatment. Having that man whipped to death yesterday was nothing less than murder. After the war, I intend to see that Captain Morton answers for his crimes."

Nathan sounded like he really meant what he was saying. Titus shook his head. "You're dreaming. Fellas like that always get away with it."

Like Duncan Ebersole, he thought. Ebersole sat there at Mountain Laurel like an ugly spider, making everyone's life miserable, but he was still rich and powerful. He was living proof that there was no justice in the world. Titus had learned that you couldn't rely on everything turning out all right in the end. The best you could hope for was revenge on those who had wronged you.

"You'll see," Nathan mumbled. "It'll be different—"

"Better eat that while you got the chance," Titus said, gesturing toward the bread in Nathan's hand. "Otherwise, somebody's liable to take it away from you. Might even be me."

THERE WAS nothing to do in the camp but shuffle back and forth in the allotted area. That was what the men did all day long. At one point during that first day, Titus found himself with Thaddeus Newberry. The colonel moved slowly, leaning on his makeshift crutch. Titus would have gone on past him without speaking, but the colonel spoke to him. "It's Brannon, isn't it?"

Titus slowed down so that he could stay beside the colonel. "That's right."

"Where are you from, Private Brannon?"

Titus didn't particularly want to share his life story with Newberry, but on the other hand, he didn't have anything better to do right now. "Culpeper County, Virginia," he said.

"I've never been there, but I've heard that nearly all of Virginia is beautiful country. The Old Dominion, they call it. A name from colonial days, I believe."

"I don't know about that. I've just always called it home."

"Farming man, are you?"

Titus nodded. "Yes sir."

"Do you have your own plantation?"

Titus laughed and said, "Not hardly. It's just a farm my pa took up, back a long time ago. He's been gone for a good many years, but my ma is still there."

"What about brothers and sisters?"

"There's a passel of us, all right. Five boys and a girl. My sister, Cordelia, is the youngest, and I'm in the middle of the boys, two older and two younger than me."

"What are their names?" Newberry asked.

Titus wasn't sure what it was, but something about the colonel made him want to answer. "My oldest brother is Will. William Shakespeare Brannon."

"Your parents must have been admirers of the Bard."

"Just my pa," Titus said. "Ma never cared for it much, but he got his way when it came to namin' us kids. My next oldest brother is MacBeth. We call him Mac."

"Let me guess," Newberry said with a smile. "Your full name is Titus Andronicus Brannon."

Titus had to laugh. "You got that right, Colonel. My little brothers are Cory and Henry, Cory bein' short for Coriolanus."

"What a literary family."

"Not really. I ain't read a book in years. My pa was the big book reader, though I reckon Mac and Henry like it some, too."

"Your brothers, are they all in the army?"

"All but Henry. Will's a captain in the Stonewall Brigade. He signed up first out of all of us. Then Mac, he got on with General Stuart's cavalry."

"Ah, Jeb Stuart," Newberry said. "I've heard great things about him. The cavalier of the Confederacy."

"My brother Cory got in the fightin', too, some places out west. Shiloh was one of 'em."

"Really? Your brother was at Shiloh?"

"That's what his letters home said. Before that he was at those two forts the Yankees captured. I don't recall their names."

"Henry and Donelson?" suggested Newberry.

Titus nodded. "Yeah, that's them. I remember now. Cory always was one for winding up where the trouble's thickest."

They had reached the limit of their area and turned around. Newberry asked, "What about you?"

"Fredericksburg was my first battle. And my last, from the look of things now. But it was hot while it lasted. I killed me a bunch of Yankees that day."

Newberry nodded. "Yes, there's been a lot of killing on both sides. Regrettable. So regrettable."

Titus frowned. "No offense, Colonel, but I don't regret a one of them Yanks I killed. I'll kill a lot more if ever I get the chance."

"Of course. You're a loyal soldier. So am I. But I wish this war had never come. Cooler heads would have prevailed if given the opportunity."

Titus thought about that for a second and shook his head. He wasn't going to argue with the colonel, but he didn't believe what Newberry said. From the moment the Northern states had decided that they could impose their will by force on their Southern neighbors, the war had been like a runaway train. Nothing could have stopped it.

He shambled along in silence. After a moment, Colonel Newberry started talking to one of the other prisoners. Titus was left with the memories of home that their conversation had stirred up. He wished he could be there now, sitting in the dining room with the smell of his mother's biscuits drifting in from the kitchen. Putting up with the way she and the rest of them fussed at him because of Polly and his drinking and his no-account friends would have been worth it just to pour molasses over one of those biscuits and sink his teeth into it.

Titus sighed. Before he could ever experience such things again, he would have to get out of here, and right now that didn't seem too likely.

But his chance would come, he told himself. Sooner or later, it would come.

JUST AS Titus expected, the temperature plummeted that night under clear skies and light winds. He woke up the next morning with his teeth chattering from the cold. A few men in the barracks were lucky enough to have blankets, but most didn't, including Titus and Nathan and the other newcomers. Titus was glad that he at least had shoes, although there were large holes in them. They were better than nothing. Even at that, he could barely feel his toes this morning.

He sat up, hugged himself, and rubbed his hands on his arms in a vain attempt to generate a little warmth. When the call came for breakfast, men struggled to their feet all over the barracks. A few didn't get up. Titus heard somebody say, "That's it for old Ned. Poor son of a bitch must've died during the night."

When they stumbled outside and roll call was taken, it turned out that four men had died in the barracks during the night. Some of the guards hauled out the bodies and unceremoniously dragged them away.

"What'll they do with 'em?" Titus asked one of the other prisoners.

The man shrugged. "They got a big ditch on the other side of camp they fling 'em in. When it fills up, I reckon they'll cover it up and dig another one."

Titus repressed a shudder. The thought of winding up in a mass grave like that made him almost as cold inside as he was on the outside.

The sun was shining brightly this morning, but there was no warmth in it. The puddles that were left from the rain were frozen solid now, forming sheets of muddy ice on the ground. Titus's shoes slipped on some of the slick stuff as he lined up for morning grub.

He wasn't quite as hungry this morning as he had been the previous one, because the prisoners had been fed supper the night before. True, it was only another hunk of moldy bread and a piece of rancid meat, but it was sure better than nothing, Titus thought.

Water had to be dipped up by bucket from a mossy cistern, but since it was frozen over this morning, the guards rolled out a water barrel and passed around a dipper. When Titus's turn came, he had sucked down barely half the water that was in the dipper when a hand grabbed it and jerked it away from him, spilling what was left. "Gimme that," a rough voice growled. "You done had your turn."

Titus looked around and saw a tall, heavy-shouldered man with a broken nose and a bullet head covered with hair like rusty nails. The sleeves of his uniform shirt had been torn off sometime in the past, leaving his arms bare even in this frigid weather. Goosebumps stood out on the pale, freckled skin.

"Outta the way," the man said, then put his hand on Titus's shoulder to shove him aside and get to the water bucket. But Titus braced his legs and resisted the shove. He didn't move. The prisoner's rugged features twisted in anger. "Dammit, I said get out of my way."

"Go to hell," Titus said, "just give me that dipper back first."

"I'll give you the dipper—"

With no more warning than that, the man slashed at Titus's face with the dipper. That was enough, though, to alert Titus to what was coming. He swayed backward and dropped his left shoulder, and the dipper missed him by several inches. Thrown off balance by that, the other prisoner stumbled forward a step. Titus brought up his left fist and buried it in the man's belly. The man grunted in pain. Titus threw a right and caught him on the jaw, staggering him even more. But the man didn't go down. He stayed on his feet, moving back out of reach and shaking his head.

Titus had put most of his strength behind those blows. If they weren't good enough to drop his opponent, then he was in trouble—big trouble.

With a roar of rage, the man dropped the dipper and threw himself forward, his hands reaching for Titus's neck. Titus managed to knock the man's arms aside and keep him from getting a stranglehold, but the man still crashed into him and knocked him backward. Titus would have fallen if someone hadn't caught him.

"Fight! Fight!" The cry that always rang out at moments such as this sounded through the area around the barracks. Many of the prisoners turned to watch, but some of them ignored the commotion, sunk so low in despair that nothing could engage their attention now.

The same hands that had caught Titus and kept him from falling shoved him toward the rusty-haired man. He saw a punch coming his way and tried to get his arms up to block it, but he was too late. The man's fist sledged into Titus's left cheek, cutting it. He felt blood start to trickle down his face.

He threw a wild right that skidded off the left side of his opponent's face. It caught the ear, though, tearing the lobe a little and drawing a shout of pain and anger from the man. He swung a looping left that Titus ducked under. While he was down low, Titus drove forward in a tackle, wrapping his arms around the man's waist and butting him in the stomach. The man was bigger and heavier, but he wasn't expecting such a move from Titus and hadn't set himself. Titus knocked him backward, off his feet.

This time the other prisoners got out of the way, so that the rusty-haired man fell onto his back with an impact that must have knocked the breath from his body. Titus landed on top of him and came down with his knee in the man's groin. The man tried to scream but didn't have any air. Titus hit him in the throat, then slammed his knee into the man's crotch again.

The brutal blows were enough to end the battle. The man's eyes rolled up in his head. He swept an arm around and knocked Titus off him, but then he turned onto his side and curled up in a ball on the frozen ground, clutching his ruined testicles.

Titus scrambled to his feet, just in case he needed to keep fighting, but one look at his whimpering, mewling opponent told him that the fight was finished. He grinned then grimaced as something slammed into his back and knocked him forward. He landed facefirst on the ground and was rocked from side to side by the kicks pounding him.

"Stupid Rebel bastard!" someone shouted. "There's no fightin' here!"

Titus cried out in pain and jerked his head around. He saw blue uniforms all around him. The Yankee guards had noticed the fracas and closed in, and now Titus bore the brunt of their anger. He tried to shrink away from the kicks, but they had him surrounded. All he could do was absorb the punishment.

It was fairly short. "That's enough," the same voice said. "Get him up."

Hands caught hold of Titus's arms and hauled him to his feet. He stood there unsteadily with a pair of guards holding him. The sergeant of the guard moved in front of him, glaring at him. Titus returned the hostile gaze through slitted eyes.

"What's your name, Reb?" the sergeant demanded.

"Brannon." Titus tasted blood in his mouth and spat. "Titus Brannon."

"Well, Brannon, I don't know who started this fight, but you're going to be punished for it." The sergeant looked at the other guards. "Get his pants down."

Titus started to thrash. He knew that nothing good had come of any discipline he had seen administered in the camp, especially when a prisoner had dropped his trousers for the guards. He didn't know whether they intended to whip him or inflict some other indignity on him, but he was sure that he didn't want his pants taken down.

There were too many of them. The two who had hold of him twisted his arms until it felt like they were going to pop out of their sockets. Other guards grabbed hold of his trousers and yanked them down around his ankles. He didn't have any underwear, so for all practical purposes he was naked from the waist down.

"Sit," the sergeant commanded.

Titus blinked in confusion. *Sit where?*

A hand shoved down on his shoulder while somebody kicked the back of his right knee. His leg buckled, and the left one went with it. He was on the ground, and as his bare skin came in contact with it, he realized he was sitting on one of the frozen puddles. His buttocks were pressed directly onto the ice.

The cold went through the lower half of his body like a knife. He gasped and leaned forward, trying to push himself up. A rifle butt hit him on top of his right shoulder, numbing it. "Stay down there, damn you!"

Titus began to shake. The sergeant of the guard loomed over him and grinned. "Maybe that'll cool you off so you'll think twice before fightin' again, Reb. You sit there until you're given permission to get up."

"I . . . I c-can't," Titus said through chattering teeth.

"Sure you can. And if anybody tries to help you, they'll get the same treatment." The sergeant glared around at the other prisoners. "Understand?"

No one spoke up, and most of the men looked away. There wouldn't be any help coming from them.

"Don't worry," the sergeant said. "You won't really freeze 'em off. That's just an old saying." He started to laugh, and the other guards laughed with him.

Titus sat there on the ice and shook, feeling the cold become fire and the fire burn deep into his soul.

Chapter Three

AFTER SITTING THERE ON the ice for an hour, the lower half of Titus's body was numb. The blood that had trickled down his face from the cut on his cheek was frozen. He felt it pulling at the skin every time he grimaced.

The heat of his body, meager though it was, had been enough to melt the ice a little, but the cold air refroze it so that now he was stuck to it. It was like touching a cold metal pole with your tongue, he thought. The sheer ludicrousness of having his butt frozen to the ice struck him as funny in a way, but he was in too much pain to smile about it. When he was finally allowed to get up, he was liable to leave a large chunk of his hide behind.

The other prisoners milled around, a few of them giving him pitying glances, most ignoring him. No one spoke to him. This sort of punishment must be something that had happened before, because no one seemed shocked by it. Titus lowered his head, clasped his arms around himself as tightly as he could, and hung on, hoping that he could survive until it was over.

One thing was certain. He wouldn't beg for mercy. Not from the Yankees.

More time dragged by. Titus never knew how much. Finally, a voice called out, "Oh, my God! Titus!"

A few seconds went by before Titus was aware that someone was speaking to him. He lifted his head a little and saw Nathan Hatcher standing there, an appalled expression on his slender face. Nathan dropped to his knees beside Titus and reached out to him.

"Let me help you—"

"Don't!" Titus hissed through his frozen face. "Get away from me, Nathan! Dammit, get back!"

"What?" Nathan stared at him, confused and puzzled. "I just heard about what happened to you. I came to help you—"

"You c-can't help me," Titus said through chattering teeth. "You'll just g-get yourself in trouble."

Newberry limped up behind Nathan and touched the young man's shoulder. "He's right, Private Hatcher," the colonel said, a note of desperation. "Please come away before it's too late."

Nathan twisted his head around to look up at Newberry. "But—"

"You there! Reb!"

Titus groaned in despair as he heard the harsh shout. He knew what was going to happen next. Prisoners fell back, hurrying to get out of the way and open a lane for the sergeant of the guard, who came striding through with his long blue overcoat flapping around his knees. His strong-jawed face was flushed with anger under the blue cap.

"On your feet!" he bellowed at Nathan as he came to a stop and rested his fists on his hips.

Nathan scrambled to his feet as several more guards came up behind the sergeant, brandishing clubs. Titus looked at the heavy bludgeons and almost licked his lips. The desire to get his hands on a weapon flared within him.

"This man is being punished!" the sergeant of the guard shouted at Nathan. "Are you trying to help him?"

"I . . . I didn't mean to interfere," Nathan said. "It's just that Titus and I are friends—"

"Friends, is it? Then you won't mind sharin' his punishment, will you?" The sergeant turned his head and bellowed an order. "Get his pants down!"

Nathan was too shocked to put up a fight as the guards swarmed around him, jerked down his uniform trousers, and forced him to the ground. He cried out as his scrawny buttocks hit the ice.

"Sit there for a while and you'll learn not to interfere with a prisoner's punishment," the sergeant said.

Nathan bit his lip to keep from crying out again. Tears ran down his face. He was pretty ignorant about real life, Titus thought, but even he had to know that arguing wasn't going to do any good now.

"The rest of you Rebel scum understand?" the sergeant shouted to the other prisoners. "Stay away from these two!"

The prisoners backed off even more, leaving a bare space around Titus and Nathan. Before striding away, the sergeant cuffed them both for good measure—ringing, open-handed blows that made Nathan gasp in shock and pain. Titus endured the assault in stoic silence.

When the sergeant and the other guards were gone, Nathan groaned through his chattering teeth. "God, I can't stand this. What are we going to do, Titus?"

"Sit right here, I reckon," Titus replied in a low voice. He gave a grim chuckle. "After a little while, you won't have much choice. Your ass'll be froze to the ground."

Nathan whimpered. "How can they d-do this?" His teeth were beginning to chatter. "They're such s-savages."

Titus finally allowed himself to feel a little anger, but it wasn't directed at his captors for a change. "You mean how can them noble Yankees, those high-minded folks who say they're just fightin' to abolish slavery, treat us worse than nearly every plantation owner in the South ever dreamed of treatin' his slaves? How can they be a bunch of torturin', brutalizin' murderers when they're on what you thought was the right side?" He spat in disgust. "Just shut up your mewlin', Nathan. I ain't in no mood to listen to it right now."

LATER, AFTER another unknowable stretch of time had passed, Titus found himself getting sleepy. That was a bad sign. It was even worse when he realized he wasn't cold anymore. In fact, he was warm, just like he was snuggled under a thick goose-down comforter.

He realized that he was on the verge of freezing to death.

Nathan hadn't tried to talk to him anymore, but the young man couldn't stop the occasional groans and gasps from escaping his lips. Everyone else stayed well back, although Colonel Newberry stood the closest, watching them in silence, lines of sympathy etched on his haggard face. If the colonel could do anything to help them, he would. Titus knew that. But the only ones who could save them now were the Yankees. If he and Nathan were left out here much longer, they would die. Titus didn't doubt that for a second.

He wished he had been killed in the fighting at Fredericksburg. How much better it would have been to go down in the bloody midst of combat, dealing out death to the hated Yankees, than to survive only to be subjected to this cruel, humiliating existence in prison. Many nights since his capture he had dreamed of dying in battle, and now, as he slipped closer and closer to death, the images came back to him. He felt hot blood flowing in his veins, felt the heat of the rifle barrel against his hands as he reversed the weapon and used it as a club. Felt the heat of an exploding shell that knocked him off his feet . . .

Felt the burning, searing touch of hot water puddling around his frozen hindquarters.

For the first time during this whole ordeal, Nathan screamed. Pain unlike any he had ever known filled him and became his entire world. Steam rose around him.

Close by, Nathan screamed, too, as another Yankee came up behind him and sloshed a bucket of hot water onto the ground where he was sitting. More guards closed in behind Titus and Nathan and grabbed their arms, jerking them upright. The hot water had melted the ice enough so that they came free from it without peeling away huge sections of skin. Only in places had their skin stuck, so that their buttocks were now dotted with small, raw wounds where blood seeped out.

The sergeant of the guard strode up. "Pull your pants up, Rebs." He waited until Titus and Nathan reached down with trembling hands, grasped the trousers bunched around their ankles, and slowly pulled them up. The sergeant grinned. "I hope you boys have learned your lesson. If not, we can do this again tomorrow, and the day after that, and the day after that, as long as you want." He stepped closer, reached out and grabbed Nathan's chin, and wrenched the young man's head to the side. "How 'bout you, Reb? You learned your lesson?"

Nathan was crying and trying not to whimper. "I . . . I won't do it again, Sergeant. I promise!"

The sergeant let go of his chin and slapped him, a hard enough blow to jerk Nathan's head back the other way. "That's good, Reb."

He stepped over to Titus. "How about you?"

Titus wanted to tell him to go to hell, but he knew what would happen if he did. There would be more punishment, and Titus was all too aware how close he had come to dying a few minutes earlier. His pain-wracked body couldn't take anything else right now. He had to rest some and get over what had been done to him.

"You gonna behave?" the sergeant of the guard prodded.

Titus swallowed. His tongue felt thick. All he could do was mutter the words, "Yes, Sergeant. I'll behave."

"Good." The sergeant looked past Titus and Nathan. "You! Newberry! Take care of these wayward sheep."

The colonel limped forward. "Yes, Sergeant. We'll see that they're tended to properly."

With a jerk of his head, the sergeant led the other guards away, and Newberry and several of the prisoners hurried forward to grab the arms of Titus and Nathan before they collapsed.

"You boys are lucky to be alive," he told them in a quiet voice. "I've seen Sergeant O'Neil leave men out here on the ice until they froze to death."

"D-damn near did," Titus said. He was starting to shiver again, now that the shocking heat had worn off. His trousers were wet, and the frigid wind was trying to freeze them onto his legs.

"Let's get the two of you inside," the colonel ordered.

They were taken into the barracks. There were no dry clothes to give them, but at least they were out of the wind. Newberry found them a place to sit against the wall. Titus leaned back and closed his eyes. He felt someone tucking a blanket around him and opened his eyes long enough to see the colonel leaning over him.

"The blanket is merely on loan," Newberry said with a faint smile. "But you need it right now more than its owner."

"Tell him I'm m-much obliged," said Titus.

Newberry had another folded blanket under his arm. He moved over to wrap it around Nathan, who was shivering and weeping at the same time.

As Newberry straightened from that task, Titus inquired, "Colonel? . . ."

"What is it, Private Brannon?"

"That sergeant, you said his name is O'Neil?"

"That's right. Why do you ask?"

Titus leaned his head against the wall and closed his eyes again. "Just curious," he said. *Because one of these days, I'm going to kill that son of a bitch, and I wanted to know his name.*

THE NEXT day Titus hurt so much he could barely hobble out of the barracks for breakfast. Nathan, weaker to start with, was in even worse shape. He refused at first to get up, and it took Colonel Newberry to prevail on him the need to do so. "You have to eat, son," Newberry told him. "You have to keep up your strength. Otherwise you're letting the Yankees win."

Nathan finally hauled himself to his feet and staggered out with Titus and the colonel. Titus and Nathan hadn't gotten anything to eat the night before, on orders of Sergeant O'Neil. Titus tore eagerly into the hunk of bread, forgetting his pain for the moment. Nathan took his time, nibbling small bites of his food and whimpering in pain between chews.

After they had finished breakfast and paid a visit to the latrine, the three of them walked around the barracks, just as so many of the other prisoners were doing. Staying active was the only way to keep warm.

"I'm afraid that you two are on Sergeant O'Neil's bad side now," Newberry told the two Virginians. "And he tends to hold a grudge. I've seen him punish several men until they died."

"Always by making them sit on the ice?" Titus asked.

Newberry shook his head. "Not at all. He metes out all sorts of punishments. When there is snow on the ground, he likes to make men stand at attention in it, in their bare feet. They leave many a bloody footprint behind when they're finally allowed to come in. And then there's the Mule."

"What in hell's name is that?"

"The guards set up a pair of wooden supports with a board fastened between them, narrow side up. Prisoners are forced to sit on it for hours at a time. The board is too high for their feet to reach the ground, so they have to balance themselves on that narrow edge. If they fall off, they're given more hours as punishment." Newberry shook his head. "Sometimes the guards tie weights to the men's feet to make it even more painful and difficult. The sergeant calls it 'giving them spurs.'"

"Son of a bitch," Titus breathed.

Newberry nodded. "He is a truly brutal man. And there is no one to stop him. Colonel Tucker turns a blind eye to everything that Captain Morton and Sergeant O'Neil do."

"Morton," Titus repeated. "He's another one I'd like to get my hands on."

"Be very careful, Mr. Brannon. He is a man perhaps even more evil than Sergeant O'Neil. At least the sergeant's brutality is honest and in the open. He hates all Southerners and doesn't care who knows it. Captain Morton, on the other hand, is an ardent abolitionist and a very religious man. He believes he is doing the Lord's work by dealing out harsh punishments to those who enslave their fellow man."

"I never owned any slaves," Titus muttered. "Damned few folks I had anything to do with ever did. The one fella I know who owns a bunch of slaves—" He was thinking of his father-in-law, Duncan Ebersole. "—is a gold-plated bastard."

"Nevertheless, in the eyes of Captain Morton, those of us who have aligned ourselves with the Confederacy are nothing less than minions of Satan. He thinks we should all be exterminated. That's why he can stand by and watch a man being beaten or kicked to death and believe that he's being merciful. Because he's on the side of the Lord, you see, and therefore anything he does is God's will."

Nathan had listened in silence. Now, after a moment, he said, "I used to feel the same way."

Newberry stopped in his tracks. "What?"

"I believed in the Union," Nathan said. "I opposed slavery."

Titus's hand shot out and closed over Nathan's arm. "Hush up!" he said in a low, urgent voice. "You don't want these other boys to hear that."

Newberry leaned closer, a concerned look on his face. "Private Brannon is right, Private Hatcher. You can trust me, but if the others found out . . ." He shook his head. "They would make things harder on you than even Sergeant O'Neil can manage."

Titus doubted that, but he knew if Nathan went around proclaiming his support for the Yankees, he would be dead within days. The other prisoners would find a way to kill him.

Nathan looked at Titus and Newberry. "I said, 'I used to feel that way.'" He shook his head. "I don't anymore."

"Well, I'm certainly glad to hear that," Newberry said. "Perhaps sometime, when the circumstances are better, you can explain what you mean."

Nathan shrugged. "I'm not sure what I mean. I'm not sure of anything anymore."

Titus understood that feeling. Only the simplest emotions made sense these days, and the simplest emotion of all was hate. That was enough to keep him going.

—⟋⟍—

DESPITE THE fact that Sergeant O'Neil held a grudge against them, for the next two weeks Titus and Nathan managed to blend into the pitiful mass of Confederate prisoners at Camp Douglas. Snow fell for several days, dropping nearly a foot of the cold white stuff on the camp. The prisoners stayed inside more, except for those who were unfortunate enough to cross one of the guards. Whenever that happened, Titus witnessed another of O'Neil's favorite punishments. Just as Colonel Newberry had said, barefooted prisoners were forced to stand at attention for hours in the snow. Guards checked them often to see that they hadn't been moving around. When they were finally allowed to come inside, some of them screamed with each step. More than one man lost toes to frostbite.

No one, however, wanted to go to the camp hospital, even when the damaged toes turned black and began to rot off. The camp surgeon would hack the toes off, but loss of blood or infection from the crude surgery might prove to be even more dangerous in the long run.

"Stay out of that pesthole if you can," one man warned Titus. "That sawbones has killed more of us Rebs than a whole damned Yankee brigade."

The temperature dropped lower and lower, many days not climbing above the freezing point. And the guards, led by Sergeant O'Neil, conducted raids on the barracks, confiscating any blankets they found.

"Once we boil all the lice out of these blankets, we'll ship 'em off to our boys at Falmouth," O'Neil explained with a grin. "They need 'em more than you filthy Rebs."

That told Titus the Union army had gone into winter camp at Falmouth, a short distance up the Rappahannock from Fredericksburg and on the opposite side of the river. He wondered how Will and Mac had come through the battle. Wondered if they were even still alive. Somehow he was confident that they were. Brannons were survivors. Despite his current condition, he was living proof of that.

Nathan hadn't said anything more about supporting the Union, and Newberry hadn't asked about it. But one day, when the weather was a little warmer than it had been and more of the men were outside, the colonel motioned Nathan over to the corner where he sat by himself. Titus saw what was going on and followed Nathan. The boy had a big mouth, thought Titus, and somebody had to watch out for him.

"Sit down and join me for a spell, men," Newberry invited them. He glanced around, saw that no one was looking, and slipped a hand inside his tattered coat. When he withdrew it, he was holding something that made Titus's eyes widen with surprise. It was a small, dirty biscuit.

"One of the guards dropped this this morning and didn't bother to pick it up since it fell in the mud," Newberry said. "I was the only one who noticed, so I was able to get hold of it later. I'll share it with you."

"We're obliged for that, Colonel," Titus said. He watched, his mouth watering, as Newberry tore the biscuit in three pieces. The colonel handed one to each of them. Titus stuffed the entire piece into his mouth so no one else would notice he was eating. The Yankees had turned them into something no better than animals, he thought. But still he chewed slowly and carefully, so the motion wouldn't be so obvious.

When they were finished, Newberry said in a half-whisper, "I've been wondering about what you said, Private Hatcher. About supporting the Union."

Nathan looked down at the filthy planks of the floor. "I fought for it," he said, his voice hushed. "I was in the Union army at Antietam and Fredericksburg."

"Good Lord!" Newberry uttered beneath his breath. "You're a Yankee? Then how on earth did you come to join us in these calamitous accommodations?"

Titus chuckled. "You won't believe this, Colonel."

Nathan shot him an angry glance, then turned back to Newberry and explained what had happened during the Federal retreat through the ruined streets of Fredericksburg. "No one would ever believe me," he concluded. "I was wearing a Confederate uniform, so to them I was just another Rebel."

Newberry nodded. "And how do you feel about it now?"

"About what?"

"The war. The cause each side is fighting for."

"As much as I've seen of it, there isn't any cause in this war anymore except killing," Nathan said bitterly. "Whatever else might have started it, nobody cares about anything else now. They just want to win and kill as many of the enemy as they can while they're doing it."

Titus rubbed his bearded jaw and chuckled again. "Sounds good to me," he said.

Newberry's expression was serious as he studied Nathan's face. "I'm asking you about this, Private Hatcher, because I'd like to think that I can trust you. You may hear many things said in here that could curry favors for you if you repeated them to the Yankees."

Nathan shook his head. "What's the old saying, Colonel, about not liking either side?"

Titus surprised both of them by quoting, "A plague on both your houses. They have made worms' meat of me." He grinned. "It's from *Romeo and Juliet*. I heard my pa recite damned near the whole play from memory. Reckon I'm startin' to understand it. I've felt like worms' meat a bunch of times here lately."

After a moment, Newberry said, "I take that to mean you no longer support the Union, Private Hatcher?"

"The only side I'm on is my own," Nathan said. "But I owe you and Titus. I wouldn't ever betray you."

Newberry looked at Titus. "What do you think, Private Brannon? Can we trust Private Hatcher?"

Titus shrugged. "I reckon. I never thought much of him, but I never heard him tell a flat-out lie, either."

"Very well."

"What's this about, Colonel?"

Newberry lifted a hand. "Later, my friends, later. Right now, we have to focus all our attention on surviving the winter. But remember this: It won't always be winter. Sooner or later, spring will come."

He wouldn't say any more, and for a while Titus puzzled over what he had meant. But that night, as he dozed fitfully with men crowded against him on all sides, he thought about how spring would mean better weather, and how better weather meant it would be easier to travel through the countryside.

His heart began to pound in his chest. Maybe he was wrong, but suddenly he had the feeling that Colonel Newberry had been talking about getting out of this hellhole. In the middle of winter like this, escape might be possible, but getting home likely wouldn't be. Once spring arrived, though, any prisoners who got loose would at least have a chance.

It was a hell of a long way back to Virginia, he told himself, but he could make it. He *would* make it, by God!

Titus drifted off to sleep with the word looming large in his mind, offering him the first comfort he had felt for a long time.

Escape.

And wouldn't the rest of the family be shocked when he showed up at home?

Chapter Four

I DON'T KNOW," WILL BRANNON said quietly as he stood in the warm spring sunshine and watched Cordelia kneel beside the headstone. "It just doesn't seem right to me."

"It's a comfort to Ma," Mac said as Cordelia placed a small basket of freshly picked flowers on the grave. "I suppose it makes her feel closer to Titus."

"Maybe so," Will said, "but he's not here. We don't know where he is."

In the bloody chaos of the battlefield between the town of Fredericksburg and the long ridge known as Marye's Heights, nothing had been certain except that death had walked there on that cold December day. Ever since Will had joined the Army of Northern Virginia in the spring of 1861, scene after scene such as that had imprinted itself on his memory so that he would never forget them. Manassas, Kernstown, Seven Pines, Manassas a second time, Sharpsburg . . . the names of the places all ran together in his head so that he sometimes had trouble remembering what had happened where.

But the consequences of what had happened at those places . . . the sprawled bodies frozen in awkward positions . . . the wide, staring, sightless eyes . . . the mouths open in cries of agony that would resound through eternity . . . and most of all the blood, God, the blood, Will had never known there could be so many shades of it, from the pink tinge that it had given to Antietam Creek downstream from Burnside's Bridge, to the bright red flow that spurted from a man's neck when a saber was dragged across it, to the brackish black that the puddles of the stuff turned as the flies feasted on them . . .

Will looked down at the uniform he wore. Not to mention the ugly brown stains that never quite came out of a man's clothes once they dried there.

Cordelia's head, its thick red-gold hair bright in the sunlight, was bowed in prayer. She murmured, "Amen," and stood. Mac stepped forward to take her arm. She smiled. "Thank you, Mac. Do either of you have anything you want to say?"

Will frowned. "Nothing *to* say."

"A word of prayer wouldn't hurt," Mac said. With his free hand, he took off the gray hat he wore. "Lord, we ask that You grant our beloved brother Titus the rest and comfort in death that he never knew in life. In Your Son's name we pray, amen."

"Amen," Will said. As Mac had pointed out, it couldn't hurt.

Will wasn't convinced it was going to help much of anything, though. Might make Mac and Cordelia feel a little better. It wasn't going to do anything for Titus, because he was beyond any help now.

Chances were they would never know where his body lay buried, other than that it was somewhere on the battlefield at Fredericksburg. The group of soldiers he'd been with had been wiped out, shot full of holes by the Yankees, and what was left had been hacked to pieces by sabers and bayonets. The unrecognizable shapes that once were men had been interred in a mass grave. Maybe Titus was among them; maybe he was somewhere else, in one of the other holes in which corpses had been dumped.

When he and Mac had come back to Culpeper after the battle, they had told the truth about Titus's death, except for one thing. Neither of them had been able to stand the idea of telling their mother that Titus hadn't had a proper burial, so they lied. At the time, Abigail Brannon had seemed to accept the lie.

But when they returned to their home county again following the massive clash of armies at Chancellorsville, they found that Abigail had ordered a headstone made for Titus and set up in the cemetery behind the First Baptist Church, in the plot where John Brannon lay and where someday she would rest when she had gone to her reward. After the war, she said, they would see to it that Titus was brought home from Fredericksburg. In the meantime, this empty grave gave her a place to go and pray and feel closer to her lost son.

His mother said more nice things about Titus now than she'd ever said while he was still alive, Will thought bitterly as he walked with Cordelia and Mac back to the wagon that had brought them into town. He limped from the leg wound he had received a month earlier at Chancellorsville. The injury had healed, but it left his leg a little stiff.

Mac helped Cordelia climb onto the wagon seat then stepped up beside her to take the reins. Will climbed into the back so that he could stretch out his leg. He reckoned he was getting old. Nigh on to thirty now. A decade older than his pretty redheaded sister. And the past two years had aged him beyond the normal passage of time. In the early days of the war, he had bounced back more quickly from injury.

Mac flapped the reins and called out to the mules, and they did what he asked them to do. Animals always cooperated with him, even mules.

Will had marvelled for years at his brother's knack for getting along with critters. But he had never seen anything like the bond that existed between Mac and the huge silver gray stallion he rode as part of Fitzhugh Lee's cavalry brigade.

The stallion belonged to Mac, not to the army. Like most Southern cavalrymen, he had provided his own mount when he joined up. Mac had caught and tamed the wild stallion after Will had enlisted, and Will swore sometimes that the two of them could read each other's mind. That horse was smarter than a lot of men he had met. In unguarded moments, Mac would admit that he thought there was something almost supernatural about the animal. A ghost horse, he called it. Sometimes Will came close to believing that himself.

The wagon rolled down the main street, and Will felt a pang inside as he looked at Culpeper. So many of the buildings were boarded up now, empty of life. The tide of war had swept close enough to the town on several occasions during the past year that people had moved out in droves, seeking a safer place to live. Without the majority of its citizens, there wasn't much reason for Culpeper's existence anymore. Not only that, but the town and the surrounding area, like most of the rest of northern Virginia, had been pretty much stripped of supplies, all of them gone to feed and outfit the army.

As the wagon bounced along the rutted road in front of what had once been Davis's Emporium, Will thought about all the time he had spent sitting there on the porch of the general store, swapping lies with Michael Davis, the proprietor. He'd heard that Davis had left Culpeper once all the shelves in the emporium were empty with no prospect of getting more merchandise to sell. Will had no idea where his old friend was now.

Just down the street was the courthouse. Will had worked there first as a deputy and then as county sheriff, and he had been a good lawman, even if he thought so himself. It had been his feud with the ne'er-do-well Fogarty brothers, brought on by his job as sheriff, that had influenced him to join the army when he did. That and the desire to do what was right for the newly formed Confederacy.

The Confederacy was more than two years old now and struggling for its very life. Its army had won more than its share of battles and cost more than one Yankee general his command, but still the North sat there with its seemingly never-ending supply of men and guns, and times grew more and more desperate in the South. Will had heard that the British were thinking about getting into the fight on the side of the Confederacy. Something about turning for aid to the very oppressors whose yoke the country had battled out from under eighty years earlier rubbed Will the wrong way, but that might be the only thing that would save the South.

"I'm so glad you boys got to come home for a little while," Cordelia said as the wagon left the settlement and headed for the Brannon farm. "How long do you think General Lee will stay in camp?"

"There's no way of knowing for sure," Mac told her. "It all depends on what he decides to do next. We all needed a rest after Chancellorsville, though."

It had been the most stunning victory for the South so far—and perhaps the most costly in the long run. General Lee, with the more than capable assistance of Thomas J. "Stonewall" Jackson, had done the unthinkable and split his army in the face of a much superior force. Thanks to the daring leadership of Jackson, the bold gambit had worked, and the Yankee army under Joe Hooker had been soundly whipped.

But Jackson had gone down, wounded by his own men while reconnoitering in the dark, and after lingering for a few days and seeming to rally, his injuries had cost him his life. Will and Mac had both been nearby when the general was wounded as well as when he died. It was a tragedy neither of them would forget.

Now General Lee had gone off to Richmond for a council of war, with President Jefferson Davis and the other leaders of the Confederacy, to decide what to do next. In the meantime, the Army of Northern Virginia was in bivouac near Culpeper, which meant that Will and Mac were able to go home once again.

Virginia was uncommonly beautiful in the late spring, Will thought. Although the fighting had come near here, it hadn't actually touched these green, rolling hills and flower-dotted meadows. If he hadn't known better, he would have said that they rode through a land at peace.

A short time later, as the wagon rolled past one of the Brannon fields, Mac noticed another vehicle on the road. "Who's that? Looks like the Ebersole carriage."

In the back of the wagon, Will twisted and saw the carriage parked beside the road up ahead. It was impossible to mistake the black carriage with the fancy silver trim. It belonged to Duncan Ebersole, all right, but one of Ebersole's slaves wasn't at the reins of the matched pair of grays hitched to the carriage. Instead, Ebersole's daughter, Polly, was perched on the seat, and she was talking to Henry Brannon, who had left his plow in the field and come over to rest his hand on the carriage as he looked up at Polly.

Mac brought the wagon to a stop beside the carriage and tugged on the brim of his cap as he nodded to Polly. "Good afternoon," he said.

"Hello, Polly," Cordelia added.

Will didn't say anything.

Polly gave them a wan smile. "Hello. It's good to see you again, Mac. You, too, Will."

Will just grunted. Polly Ebersole was blonde and beautiful, even in dark mourning clothes, but she was still Duncan Ebersole's daughter, and Will didn't have any use for the man or anything having to do with him.

Polly Ebersole *Brannon*, that was the girl's name, he reminded himself. She'd been married to his brother Titus over the violent objections of her father and the less vehement disapproval of the rest of the Brannon family.

For years Titus had mooned over Polly Ebersole. Dancing with her at a party had gotten him a beating from some of Ebersole's overseers. But eventually, Titus had worn down the opposition, and Polly had agreed to marry him. Will hadn't been at the wedding—he was already off with the army—but he had heard all about it. One of the fanciest get-togethers ever at Mountain Laurel, the Ebersole plantation. After the wedding, Titus had gone there to live rather than bring his bride home with him, the way any respectable groom would have done. That should have been a warning sign right there.

Will had no idea what kind of wife Polly had been to his brother, but he knew that the time had come when Titus left her and moved back home. Something had come between them, something that Titus's stubbornness couldn't overcome. And then Titus had gone off to join the army and get himself killed at Fredericksburg . . .

"Polly just stopped by for a chat," Henry said, smiling up at her. His sleeves were rolled up, and his dark hair was wet with sweat. He'd been walking behind a mule and wrestling a plow all afternoon. Keeping the farm going in the midst of the war was quite a chore, especially since Henry now had to do most of the work by himself. Will felt guilty about that, but there was nothing he could do to change things. Maybe, with any luck, the war would be over soon, and he and Mac could get back to farming.

"It's such a pretty day," Polly said. "I didn't feel like being cooped up in that old dark house. So I decided to go for a drive."

"Why don't you come on up to the house with us?" Cordelia suggested. "You can sit and visit for a while."

Will knew for a fact that his sister didn't like Polly very much, but Cordelia was always polite. And maybe she felt a little sorry for the other girl. Maybe the marriage between Titus and Polly hadn't been the best, but still Polly had suffered a loss too when Titus was killed. She was a widow now, and Will had to admit that she had acted with the proper decorum since Titus's death. Her mourning might even be genuine—or she might just be putting up a front. Rich folks were good at that.

"Thank you, Cordelia, but I'd better be getting on home," Polly said. "I wouldn't want my father to worry about—"

She broke off at the sound of hoofbeats approaching, and Henry muttered, "Speak of the devil."

Will turned his head and looked back up the road. He saw a rider coming toward them and recognized the man as Polly's father. Ebersole was riding a fine black horse, and despite the heat he wore a black suit and a flat-crowned, wide-brimmed black hat. Henry was right, Will thought: Ebersole did look a little like the devil.

Ebersole drew rein and said sharply to Polly, "I've been lookin' for ye, girl. What're ye doin' over here?"

"Just visiting the Brannons, Father," Polly replied.

Ebersole looked at them, eyes narrow in his lean face. He sported a closely trimmed gray beard, and long reddish-gray hair fell nearly to his shoulders in the back.

"Get on home wi' ye," he snapped. "I'll see ye there later."

"Cordelia just invited me up to the house for a visit," Polly said. Her chin lifted, and there was a note of defiance in her voice. She had been about to refuse the invitation to the Brannon farmhouse, but now that her father was demanding that she return home, her own stubbornness was coming into play.

"Ye'll have to have yer visit some other time," Ebersole said. "I need ye at Mountain Laurel."

Cordelia spoke up. "Please, Mr. Ebersole. Polly and I are sisters now. I'd like to talk to her."

Will saw a muscle in Ebersole's jaw twitch as the plantation owner looked at Cordelia. Ebersole thought all the Brannons were nothing more than white trash, but he had been raised to be polite to females.

"Another time perhaps, missy," he said. "Besides, the vows Polly took wi' yer brother said until death do they part, and beggin' yer pardon, Titus is sure enough dead. My daughter ain't no relation to you now."

Cordelia paled so that the scattering of freckles on her face stood out more than ever. Will dropped down from the wagon bed. "That's enough, Ebersole. No call to be insulting."

"I'm just speakin' the truth," Ebersole said. "Polly, get that buggy movin'."

Polly hesitated. Will and Ebersole locked eyes; Will was aware of the revolver holstered on the plantation owner's hip. For a moment, the threat of impending violence hung over the hot, dusty road. Will was unarmed, his pistol and saber were back at the farmhouse, but he figured that if he had to, he could get his hands on Ebersole and pull the man out of the saddle before Ebersole could draw his gun.

It wasn't going to come to that. Polly acquiesced, "All right, Father. I'll see you at home." She snatched up the whip from its holder and flicked it at the rumps of the horses as she tightened her grip on the reins with her other hand. The carriage lurched into motion. Will stepped out of the way and let it roll past him.

"Come back and see us, Polly," Henry called after her.

Ebersole shot him a glare then turned the horse and heeled it into a trot. He followed the carriage down the road, away from the Brannon farm.

"What a son of a bitch," Henry said into the silence that fell on the departure of Ebersole and Polly.

"Henry Brannon!" Cordelia said. "Don't you talk like that around me."

Henry grimaced. "Ah, you're gettin' as stiff-necked as Ma, Cordelia. Are you denying that Ebersole's every inch what I called him?"

"I'm not saying anything."

Mac took up the reins and tried not to smile. "We'd better get going," he said. "Will, climb in."

"No, you and Cordelia go on," Will told him. "I'll stay here and give Henry a hand for a while."

Henry shook his head. "You don't have to do that, Will. I know your leg still hurts you some."

"What my leg needs is some good hard work to loosen it up." Will stripped off his uniform jacket, tossed it into the back of the wagon, then started rolling up the sleeves of his shirt. "Go on, Mac. I'll see you later."

"Well, if you're sure . . ." Mac got the wagon moving again, and he and Cordelia drove away.

As Will and Henry started out into the field, Henry said again, "Will, you don't have to do any of this. I can handle plowing this field."

"Go right ahead," Will said. "What I really want to do is talk to you."

Something about Will's tone of voice made Henry shoot him a wary glance. "About what?"

"About Polly Ebersole."

For a moment, Henry didn't say anything. Then, in an even more cautious tone, he asked, "What about her?"

"What was she doing here?"

"Visiting, like she said," Henry replied with a shrug.

"Looked to me like the two of you were having a fine talk. Lots of smiling and laughing going on."

"I was just telling her about how balky this old mule is. Nothing wrong with that, is there?"

"Didn't say there was anything wrong with it."

"Yeah, well, you sounded like you thought there was. I don't see why you're gettin' all upset about me havin' a talk with our sister-in-law."

Will's voice hardened. "Ebersole was right about one thing. Polly's not our sister-in-law anymore. Not with Titus gone."

"Hell, Will, you know what I mean—"

"I know one thing for sure," Will broke in. "It's a damn-fool mistake for you to be flirting with that girl."

Henry stopped short and glared at him. "Flirting? Have you gone crazy, Will? I wasn't flirting with Polly!"

"Looked like it to me," Will insisted. "And it seemed like she was flirting right back at you."

"Now I know you're crazy! Polly's still in mourning. Besides, she's older than me."

"It's been more than six months since Fredericksburg. Maybe not enough time for a widow woman to start having gentleman callers again, but plenty of time for her to start thinking about it. And Polly's less than a year older than you. That's not enough to matter."

Henry shook his head. "I never heard such foolishness. I've tried to be nice to Polly, that's all. She was hurting after Titus died, just like the rest of us. It's a fella's Christian duty to be comforting in a time like that."

"You sure that's all there is to it?"

"Of course I'm sure!"

"Then maybe you'd better tell that to Polly," Will said, "because she wasn't looking at you just now like some sympathetic former brother-in-law. And you've got to know that you're just asking for trouble from Duncan Ebersole if it ever turns into anything more than that."

"I didn't notice you backin' down from Ebersole. It looked to me like you were getting ready to haul him off that horse and whale the tar out of him."

Will shrugged. "Ebersole's always figured that he can push around everybody else in the county whenever he feels like it. I never cottoned to being shoved, and he knows it. That's why him and me don't get along."

Henry stalked over to the plow and gripped its handles. "Well, you don't have to worry, big brother. Polly and me are just friends, that's all. And that's all we ever will be."

"I hope you're telling me the truth," Will said. "Now, step aside and let me do some of that plowing."

"I can do it—"

"I know you can. It's just that after following the army for a couple of years, the back end of a mule doesn't seem near as ugly a view as it used to."

—◊—

POLLY WAS furious as she brought the carriage to a stop in front of the big plantation house. One of the slaves hurried up to grab the horses' halters and promised, "I'll take good care of 'em, Miss Polly."

"Thank you, Luther," Polly said as she stepped down from the seat and started taking off her black leather gloves. "Is my father back yet?"

Duncan Ebersole had galloped past the carriage on the way back to Mountain Laurel. Polly didn't see his horse in front of the house, but that didn't mean anything. He could have gotten back to the plantation long before her so that the animal could have been unsaddled and put away in the stables.

"Yes'm, Marse Duncan's here," Luther answered. "I done put up his hoss my ownself."

Polly nodded curtly and went toward the massive front door of the house. She opened it and stepped inside.

It was always dark inside Mountain Laurel now. The curtains were kept tightly shut twenty-four hours a day. Duncan Ebersole was prone to headaches, and he claimed the light made them worse. But it hadn't seemed to bother him, Polly thought, when he was out riding around the countryside, looking for her so that he could embarrass her.

All she'd been doing was talking to Henry Brannon. There was nothing wrong with that. Henry was a sweet boy. He had been broken up about his brother's death, but his own grief hadn't stopped him from being concerned about her.

Polly was well aware that most of the Brannons didn't like her. The old woman, Abigail, was so self-righteous and unbending that she didn't even like her own children that much, let alone the woman she regarded as a hussy, the woman who'd had the gall to marry one of her sons. And Cordelia had always been cool to her, although she would at least put up a front of being polite. Will had never gotten along with Polly's father, and his dislike for the father spilled over onto the daughter. Mac was more friendly, but while Mac was nice to just about everybody, he didn't really care that much for people. He liked animals a lot better.

No, Henry was the only one of the Brannon family who really treated her decently, Polly thought. Since that was the case, she would be better off just forgetting about the whole family. There was no reason she had to have anything to do with any of them.

But the alternative was staying shut up here in this mausoleum all day, every day, and Polly couldn't stand the thought of that. Sometimes she just had to get out, and if the only real friend she had left was Henry, she would go see him—and anybody who didn't like it could go to hell!

"Polly! That ye, girl?"

She grimaced as the harsh voice came down the hall from her father's study. She should have closed the door more quietly when she came in, she told herself. She could ignore him, but if she did, he would just come looking for her. She'd had quite enough of that today.

He was sitting in his favorite armchair in front of the cold fireplace, his legs thrust out in front of him. As Polly came into the room, she answered, "I'm here, Father. What do you want?"

He had one hand clasped over his forehead. "This poundin' in me skull is nigh to drivin' me mad! Gi' me a glass o' brandy."

Polly went over to the sideboard, took off her black hat with its small veil, and set it aside. She picked up a crystal decanter and a heavy glass and poured the drink for her father. When she carried the glass over to him, his hand shook as he reached for it.

She watched impassively as he gulped down the liquor then slumped back against the cushions of the chair. The glass would have slipped out of his hand and fallen to the floor if she hadn't reached down to catch it.

Ebersole sighed. "That's better. I'd take it kindly if in the future ye didn't make me go gallivantin' all over the countryside lookin' for ye."

"You didn't have to look for me. I was perfectly all right."

Ebersole glared up at her. "Don't ye know there could be Yankee patrols in the area? The damn bluebellies ain't that far away, ye ken?"

"You're not worried about the Yankees," Polly said. "You're upset because I was visiting the Brannons."

"Not all of 'em!" Ebersole's fist thumped the arm of the chair. "You were over there a-battin' yer eyelashes at that boy!"

"Henry? My God, Father, what are you accusing me of?"

He pointed a finger at her. "I know ye, gal. I know how ye're natured. Ye canna be trusted around a man!"

Polly turned away from him. "I'm not going to stand here and listen to this," she said in an icy voice.

Ebersole surged up out of the chair and lunged to grab her wrist. He jerked her back around to face him and leaned close to her. "Ye've had one o' the Brannons," he said. "Don't tell me ye're not thinkin' about takin' another of them!"

He wasn't much taller than she, and their eyes were only inches apart. Polly's fingers tightened on the heavy glass. She fought the impulse to smash it into the side of his head. But if she did that, she knew she would hit him again and again and again until he went away and could never look at her like that ever again.

Instead of giving in to what she really wanted, she forced herself to be calm. "If you don't want me to go over to the Brannon farm again, then I won't," she said. "I didn't mean to upset you."

"I've yer word on that?"

Polly nodded. "I give you my word. Now, please let me go."

For a second, she thought he wasn't going to do it. Then he winced as a fresh twinge of pain went through his head, and the fingers that were digging cruelly into her wrist released her. "I need another drink," he muttered.

"Sit down and I'll get it for you." She would be glad to fetch him drinks for the rest of the afternoon. If she did that, he would go to sleep in the chair and she could retreat to her room.

She filled the glass from the decanter and carried it back to him. He threw the brandy down his throat and sighed as the warmth spread through him and the pain in his head eased. Polly smiled in grim satisfaction as her father's eyes closed.

Lord, let us not run out of brandy before this war is over! she prayed silently.

Chapter Five

WILL HEARD THE DOGS barking while he sat in the parlor that evening and read a two-week-old newspaper from Richmond. A moment later the sound of hoofbeats came from outside. The horse was walking slowly, not galloping, so this late arrival probably didn't represent any sort of danger. Will stood up and dropped the newspaper in the chair. He stepped over to the fireplace to take down the rifle that hung above the mantel. His years as a lawman had taught him it was best to be prepared when greeting night visitors, even when you weren't expecting trouble.

Besides, with a war on, everybody was a little more cautious, a bit more nervous.

Will was the only one in the house still up. Everyone else had gone to bed, but as usual, he found himself not really all that sleepy. His leg was aching some, and there were other small pains in various places around his body, souvenirs of previous wounds suffered in battle.

As the hoofbeats came to a stop outside, Will blew out the lamp and walked over to the door, trying not to limp. He eased the door open but didn't step onto the porch, remaining instead in the shadows. He peered out and saw that the visitor wasn't riding a horse after all, but rather a mule. The man was bareheaded and wore a linsey-woolsey shirt and a ragged pair of trousers. The dark skin of his face told Will that he was a slave.

"Stay right there," the former lawman called softly, the rifle cradled in his arms. "Who are you, and what do you want?"

"Mister Will?" a familiar voice asked. "Mister Will, is that you?"

Will stiffened in surprise as he recognized the voice. "Roman?" He stepped onto the porch and lowered the rifle. "Roman, what are you doing here?"

73

"It's Massa Yancy, Mister Will," the slave replied. "He's in a bad way, and I . . . I don't know what to do for him no more."

Will went down the steps and walked over to the mule. "What do you mean, in a bad way? Is he sick?"

"The way he's drinkin' these days, I think I'd call it a sickness, sure enough. Earlier this evenin' he was ragin' all over the house best he could on those crutches, knockin' portraits off the walls and turnin' over furniture and bustin' up the family crystal. I never saw him like that before, Mister Will. I thought he was goin' to hurt himself if he kept on."

"What happened? Is he still at it?"

Roman shook his head. "Not unless he woke up and started in again. When I left, he was passed out cold on one of the couches in the parlor."

Will frowned. "If he's had so much to drink that he passed out, he probably won't wake up again tonight. Why don't you go on home and keep an eye on him, and I'll ride over to Tanglewood tomorrow and have a talk with him."

"I'm mighty worried he's goin' to hurt himself."

"I know," Will said. "But I'll see if I can't get him to listen to reason."

"I sure hope so. Massa Yancy, he always was one to get fired up by spirits. Ever since he come back home from Richmond, it's been worse than ever."

"I've been meaning to get over there anyway," Will said, smiling up at the anxious young man. "You still owe me a rematch from the last time we played chess. I sure thought I had you that time."

Roman relaxed a little and smiled for the first time. "Yes sir, I miss them chess games we used to have, too. You're just about the only white man I never worried about gettin' a whippin' from if I beat 'em, Mister Will."

"You always won fair and square," Will said with a laugh. "Go on back to Tanglewood now and watch over Yancy. I'll be there in the morning."

"Yes sir, Mister Will." Roman turned the mule, banged his heels against its flanks, and got it moving. He rode out of the yard between the farmhouse and the barn.

Will turned back to the house and started up the steps to the porch. He saw movement at the door. His mother's voice called out, "Who was that?"

Will stopped, a little surprised that Abigail was there. He'd thought she was sound asleep in her room upstairs. "Roman," he said. "Yancy Lattimer's boy."

"Land's sake, what did he want at this time of night?"

"He knows that Yancy and I are friends, and Yancy's having problems these days. Roman got scared and thought maybe I could help."

"Problems," Abigail repeated under her breath. "Whiskey problems, you mean."

Will shrugged. "I'm sure he drinks some. To forget." *To forget that in the prime of his life, the life of a healthy young man, he had left his right leg behind in the bloody chaos of a field hospital, not far from the battlefield along Antietam Creek, near Sharpsburg, Maryland.*

A Yankee bullet had shattered Yancy's knee during that battle. Roman had been with him, willing to go into combat and risk his life to stay with his master, and he and Will had been able to get Yancy off the battlefield. Roman had taken him to the field hospital, where a doctor had amputated the right leg at the middle of the thigh in order to prevent the spread of gangrene. Even without the threat of gangrene, Yancy never would have been able to use the leg again with the knee destroyed as it was.

Will had visited Yancy a few times during the aftermath of that bloody confrontation between the Army of Northern Virginia and the Army of the Potomac. Not surprisingly, Yancy had been bitter and withdrawn over the loss of his leg, and he had taken little if any comfort from the awkward words Will had spoken. Then Yancy had been sent to a hospital in Richmond to recover as best he could, and Will had moved on with the army to the next battle and the battle after that. When he had come back here to Culpeper County, he had thought about going to Tanglewood, the Lattimer plantation, to pay a visit to Yancy, but so far he hadn't gotten around to it.

Deep down, he supposed he didn't really want to. Remembering Yancy the way he had been, the daring, dashing, fearless young officer, Will didn't want to see him the way he was now. It was unfair for him to feel that way and he knew it, but he couldn't help it.

Funny how war brought people together and changed them, Will thought. Before the great conflict that now gripped the land, back when he'd been the sheriff of Culpeper County and Yancy Lattimer was the scion of a wealthy family and master of his own plantation, they hadn't been friends. They had barely known each other. Then the war had come and both of them had wound up captains, leading their troops into battle, sometimes fighting side by side. A bond of friendship had sprung up between them almost immediately.

He couldn't turn his back on that bond of battlefield brotherhood, Will told himself. If there was anything he could do to help Yancy, he had to try.

"Instead of turning to the bottle, that young man would be better off turning to the Lord," Abigail announced, breaking into Will's thoughts.

"That's easier for some people than others, Ma," Will said.

"Nonsense. It would do Yancy Lattimer a world of good if he would just drop to his knees and—" She stopped short and put her hand to her mouth. "Oh, dear. I'm sorry, Will. I shouldn't have said that."

"You were just speaking your mind, Ma. Nothing wrong with that."

And nothing unusual about it, either, Will added to himself. No one had ever accused Abigail Brannon of hiding her light under a bushel. When she had an opinion on something, she voiced it, regardless of other people's feelings.

"Are you going over there to see Yancy?" she asked after a moment's silence. "You haven't been to Tanglewood since you got home."

"I thought I would. I promised Roman I'd ride over in the morning."

"I think that would be a good idea. If you're going to do that, you ought to go on upstairs and get some sleep."

"That's just what I'm about to do, Ma," Will promised. When she turned to go back into the house, he followed her and went into the parlor to replace the rifle on the pegs over the mantel. The lamp was already out, so there was nothing stopping him from going up to his room.

He knew it would be awhile before he dozed off, though. There were just too many hurts in this world, both physical and spiritual, to let a man who'd been to war rest easy.

TANGLEWOOD WAS southeast of Culpeper. Will saddled up the rangy lineback dun he had ridden into battle so many times and rode over to the plantation the next morning, skirting the camp where the army was resting from the battle of Chancellorsville. The Confederate forces had won that battle, but even victorious, they had emerged from the conflict bloody and battered, and all were grateful for the opportunity to rest and recover from their wounds.

When he reached the plantation, Will found that slaves were still working in some of the fields, although without their white overseers, all of whom were now in the army. It would have been easy for them to walk away and never come back, but loyalty to Yancy kept them at Tanglewood, along with the fact that they really wouldn't have any place better to go.

The place wasn't as well kept up as it had been, Will noted, especially the lawns and the area around the plantation house itself. He didn't see any horses or cows or pigs or chickens. Army foraging squads would have commandeered all the livestock and drained the plantation of most of the rest of its supplies. Trying to maintain a semblance of normalcy was almost impossible under the conditions that now gripped Virginia and the rest of the South. Everything that hadn't been destroyed by the war went to support it. As he looked around, Will realized how lucky his family had been. Although times were lean on the Brannon farm, at least conditions there were something like they had been before the war.

No one came out to take care of Will's horse as he reined up in front of the house. He swung down from the saddle and tied the dun's reins to an iron ring attached to a post. A single step led up to a broad, columned gallery that ran along the front of the house for its entire width and then down the sides of it as well. Will walked over to the large mahogany front door and used the big brass lion's-head knocker to announce his presence. When no one responded, he pounded on the door with a fist instead.

A moment later, hurried footsteps sounded, and the door swung open. Roman looked out at Will. "Thank the Lord you're here, Mister Will," he said. "Massa Yancy's gettin' an early start this mornin'." He stepped back to let Will come into the house.

"You mean he's drinking already?" Will asked as he moved into the dim foyer.

Roman shut the door. "That's right. That no-account Israel Quinn rode by this mornin' and dropped off a jug. Massa Yancy's been buyin' his whiskey from him."

Will frowned. Israel Quinn was a cousin to the Fogartys, a family of thieves, ruffians, and murderers who had been a particular thorn in Will's side when he was sheriff of the county. Will had long suspected that Quinn was part of the Fogarty gang.

Of course, there was no Fogarty gang anymore. Will himself had gunned down Joe Fogarty in Davis's store when Joe drew on him, and Joe's older brothers, George and Ransom, had died at the battle of First Manassas. The war had effectively ended the feud between the Fogartys and the Brannons.

But even in the midst of war, there were still sundry crimes, and Will suspected that whatever mischief was going on in Culpeper County, Israel Quinn probably had a hand in it. That, however, was none of his business now. He had to see about Yancy instead.

"Where is he?" Will asked.

"In the library."

Roman led the way down a long hall and opened a door. The moment Will stepped into the big, dark room lined with bookshelves, he smelled the unpleasant mixed stench of whiskey and unwashed flesh.

"You got a visitor, Massa Yancy," Roman said. "It's Mister Will Brannon."

"Will?" The thin, reedy voice came from an armchair in a corner of the darkened room. "Tell the sorry bastard I don't want to see him."

"Too late," Will said as he took a step into the room. "The sorry bastard's already here."

A grim chuckle sounded from the armchair. "I'd apologize," Yancy Lattimer said, "but I don't really give a damn."

Will stepped farther into the room. Thick curtains were drawn over the windows so that they admitted no light. The big desk on the other side of the room, where Yancy had sat and kept the plantation's accounts in better days, was nothing but a looming shape in the shadows. The fireplace near the armchair was cold. The air was thick and heavy with musty smells as well as the obnoxious odors of hard liquor and human decay, as if it hadn't been freshened in here for weeks.

Roman moved toward the windows. "Massa Yancy," he said, "why don't I pull these curtains back so you can get some light in here?"

The shape in the armchair, which to Will looked like a bundle of sticks, jerked forward. "No! Leave 'em drawn. I don't want any light, you stupid darky."

"Be better if you get some light, maybe a mite of fresh air—"

Yancy's arm drew back and then snapped forward, and an earthenware jug sailed past Roman's head to smash against the desk. The reek of raw whiskey in the room suddenly grew stronger as the contents of the jug splashed over the desk and the rug in front of it.

"Damn you!" Yancy screamed. "Damn you all. Get away from those windows!" He struggled upright, balancing himself on his good leg and the pair of crutches he snatched up from the floor beside the chair. Hobbling forward awkwardly, he threatened his manservant. "I'll whip the sorry black hide off you, you insolent son of a bitch!"

Roman stood stock-still, clearly willing to take whatever Yancy wanted to dish out. Will wasn't that tolerant. He moved to intercept the raging Yancy, gripping the arm of his friend. "Stop that! Have you lost your mind, Yancy?"

"My mind?" Yancy repeated. Now that they were closer, their faces only inches apart, in fact, Will could see the drawn, haggard lines of Yancy's bearded features. "It's not my mind I've lost. Have you forgotten so soon, Will? It's my *damned leg!*"

"I haven't forgotten," Will said. "I don't reckon I ever will."

This close, Will could not only see Yancy better, he could smell him better, too. Yancy stunk to high heaven of filth and liquor and something else. Decay, that was it, Will realized after a second. He could smell putrefying flesh.

"Yancy, sit down. I want to take a look at your leg. Roman, open the curtains."

Yancy started struggling in Will's grip. "Dammit, no!" he cried. "I said no!"

"Do it, Roman," Will snapped as he forced Yancy back toward the armchair.

Yancy was no more than a shadow of what he had been. All the vital strength that had filled his body had wasted away by now. Although he struggled, he was no match for Will, who picked him up and shoved him into the armchair. The crutches slipped out of Yancy's hands and clattered on the hardwood floor of the library. Will hated treating his friend like this, but Yancy wasn't giving him any choice.

With a rasping sound, the curtains slid back. The light that slanted in through the big windows was blinding for a moment. Will squinted against the glare as his eyes adjusted. Yancy clapped his hands over his eyes, shrieking, "Shut them, damn you! Shut them!"

Will motioned wordlessly for Roman to leave the curtains as they were. As Yancy huddled in the chair, his shoulders began to heave with sobs. He kept his hands over his face.

In the light from the windows, Yancy was a pathetic figure. His hair was long and tangled, his beard matted. He wore a white shirt that was open at the throat and brown trousers. Both garments were dirty and wrinkled, as if he had been living in them for days, maybe even weeks. Will suspected that was the case.

The right leg of the trousers was pinned up, and the area around the stump was heavily stained. Will bent over and took the pins loose. Yancy started batting at him. "Get away from me! Leave me alone!"

The blows were weak and futile. Will ignored them. "Let me take these off of you," he said, "or I'll cut 'em off."

Yancy slumped back, sobbing. As gently as possible, Will worked the trousers off of him, exposing the stump of the right leg. It was an ugly sight, covered with ragged scars where the doctor in the field hospital had done a rushed, patchwork job of pulling the flaps of skin together and sewing them into place. Many men died from such hurried amputations, which often caused the very gangrene they were supposed to prevent.

The area at the end of the stump was a mottled red. Some of the scars had burst open, bled, and scabbed over. Thick greenish-yellow pus seeped from the sores. Will's face hardened at the ugly sight.

"What did he do to himself?" he asked Roman. "His leg can't have been festering like that ever since he was wounded. It would have killed him a long time before now."

Roman's voice trembled a little as he explained, "About a week ago, when he'd been drinkin' heavy, Massa Yancy said he was goin' to throw away them crutches. Said he'd get around without 'em. So he got down on his left knee and that stump and started tryin' to run all over the house. He kept fallin' down, but he'd get up and try again. I finally had to wrestle him into his bed and nearly tie him down to get him settled. But by then he'd tore himself up pretty bad. I cleaned him up and said I'd go for the doctor, but Massa Yancy said he'd throw me off the plantation if I did." Roman's voice shook even more as he added, "Said he'd sell me to Massa Ebersole."

Will grunted. That was an effective threat, all right. Duncan Ebersole was well known for the harsh treatment handed out to his slaves at Mountain Laurel. He would have been perfectly capable of buying Roman from Yancy and taking the young man away from Tanglewood at gunpoint if necessary.

"But you came to see me last night," Will said.

Roman swallowed. "Had to. I can't stand seein' him this way no more. Somebody's got to help him."

Yancy let out a groan. "Nobody can help me," he said. "Can't you idiots see that? I'm dead already!"

"No, you're not," Will said. "You just need a doctor and something to treat this leg, and you need to stop getting jugs of whiskey from Israel Quinn."

"Whiskey—" Yancy gave a hiccuping sob. "Whiskey is all that I've got left."

"The hell it is." Will turned back to Roman. "I'm going to get a doctor and send him over here. There are surgeons at the camp who can take care of a problem like this."

Yancy sat up, furious. "No! It was an army surgeon who did this to me!"

"He was trying to save your life." Will put a hand on Yancy's shoulder and pushed him back into the chair. "And that's what I'm doing. Roman!"

"Yes, Mister Will?"

"Keep an eye on Yancy. I'm trusting you to keep liquor out of his hands and to do whatever the doctor tells you when he gets here. Can you do that?"

Roman nodded. "Yes sir, Mister Will."

"I'll sell him!" Yancy cried. "I'll sell the uppity bastard!"

"No, you won't," Will said. "You're not of sound enough mind right now to conduct any business affairs, and that includes selling slaves."

"By God, you can't tell me what to do with my darkies!"

"I just did." The hard tone of Will's voice made it clear that he wasn't going to budge on this argument.

Yancy slumped lower in the chair. "Oh, God," he said miserably. "I'm too tired for this. I don't care what you do. Just draw those damned curtains and let me sleep."

Will motioned for Roman to draw the curtains. As the young man did so and shadows filled the room once more, an audible sigh of relief came from Yancy.

Will stepped to the door of the library. Roman followed him out into the hall. "I'll get a doctor over here today," Will said. "You're going to have to be strong for Yancy right now, Roman, because he can't do it for himself. Can you handle that?"

"You won't let that Massa Ebersole buy me?"

"Don't worry about that. I'll see to it that Duncan Ebersole won't come near here."

"All right. I'll do whatever I can for Massa Yancy. You know that, Mister Will."

Will clapped a hand on Roman's shoulder. "I know that," he said with a nod. "Yancy doesn't realize it, but he's a lucky man."

Roman frowned. "Lucky?"

"He has you for a friend."

———✄———

WILL RODE to the bivouac area and up to the large hospital tent. Since he wasn't wearing his uniform but wore civilian clothes, he was challenged briefly when he dismounted and started inside the tent. The soldier on picket duty recognized him and let him pass.

He found a doctor and explained the situation to the man. "I remember Captain Lattimer," the doctor said. "He's been mustered out of the army because of his wound, though. I'm not supposed to treat civilians."

"Yancy was hurt fighting for the Confederacy," Will said. "Seems to me like the only decent thing is for the Confederacy to see that he doesn't get worse."

The doctor thought about it and shrugged. "Well, since you put it that way . . . I'll ride on over to the captain's plantation and see what I can do for him. From the way you describe his injuries, a poultice might help."

"Thanks, Doctor. Do the best you can."

With that errand out of the way, Will turned his attention to another task that had occurred to him. The loss of a leg wasn't the only problem Yancy had. Wallowing in liquor was another. But maybe Will could do something about that, too.

The Fogarty clan included several families named Quinn and Paynter. Will wasn't sure how all of them were related. In all likelihood, with all the inbreeding that went on, they weren't certain, either. But Will knew where to find them, especially Israel Quinn, who had taken over nominal leadership of the bunch following the death of the Fogarty brothers. Quinn had a cabin west of Culpeper, handy to the Blue Ridge Mountains so that he could make a dash for safety if the law ever got after him.

Will rode up to the cabin that afternoon. It was set in a clearing and had a weedy garden patch next to it. Three scrawny hounds came loping out to bay at him and his horse. As Will reined in, he saw several filthy-faced children dashing around to the back of the cabin, obviously frightened by him. The windows in the cabin had no glass in them. A woman's face peered out at him for a second, her pinched features framed by lank blonde hair. She disappeared, and a moment later the front door swung open. Israel Quinn stepped onto the rickety porch, a shotgun tucked under his arm.

Quinn was tall and slender, almost scrawny like the hounds. His graying hair was cut short, and his face was mostly planes and angles, like the blade of an ax. His thin lips smiled, but his eyes were cold. "Why, howdy there, Sheriff. Ain't seen you up here in a coon's age."

Will stayed on his horse. "I'm not the sheriff and haven't been for a long time. You know that, Quinn."

The man's narrow shoulders rose and fell in a shrug. "Reckon there ain't no real law in Culpeper County now 'cept the army." Quinn pursed his lips. "Say, I was mighty sorry to hear 'bout Titus. That boy was a good friend of mine."

Will felt his jaw tightening. Despite the enmity between the families, there had been a short time when Titus had run with Quinn. And Quinn had provided the whiskey that kept Titus drunk most of the time, Will suspected. Now Quinn was at it again, only with Yancy Lattimer this time.

"I didn't come to talk about Titus," Will said. "I'm here about Yancy Lattimer."

"Cap'n Lattimer? What about him? Poor fella's a war hero, ain't he?"

"You've been selling whiskey to him. I want you to stop."

Quinn looked surprised. "No law 'gainst sellin' whiskey that I know of. And the cap'n's money spends as good as any."

Will didn't know what Quinn was spending money on. There was nothing left in the county to buy. But to a man like Quinn, hoarding coins was probably an end in itself. He had always been a petty thief.

"I told you, I'm not the sheriff. I'm not talking about the law. I'm talking about a friend of mine who's going to drink himself to death on your damn 'shine. That's why I want it to stop."

Quinn's face hardened as he stepped down from the cabin's porch. "You got no right to come on my land and tell me what I can and can't do, Brannon. You run off an' joined the army 'cause you was scared of my cousins, so don't you come 'round here givin' orders." A sly smile plucked at the corners of Quinn's mouth. "I don't see no gun on your hip today, Brannon."

"I don't need a gun to deal with the likes of you. I'm telling you, Quinn, stay away from Yancy. If I hear about you taking any more whiskey to him, I'll come back here and give you the thrashing of your life."

Quinn started to lift the shotgun. "Why, you dirty son of a—"

Will's heels sent the dun plunging forward. The horse's shoulder slammed into Quinn and knocked him spinning off his feet before Quinn could bring the scattergun to bear. In a flash, Will was out of the saddle and on the ground. He jerked the shotgun out of Quinn's hands, broke it open, and let the shells fall into his hand. He tossed them one way and the now-empty shotgun the other.

Quinn was cursing him from the ground. Will shut him up by saying coldly, "You remember what I said, Quinn."

"Dammit, you ain't even gonna be around here! You'll be off with the army—"

"The war won't last forever," Will said. "And I'll make a special point of surviving so I can come back and deal with you."

He caught the dun's reins and mounted. As he turned the horse to ride away, Quinn sat up on the ground and shouted, "I hope the Yankees kill you, you bastard! I hope they shoot you full of holes!"

Will didn't look back as he called out, "Remember what I said." He heeled the dun into a trot so that the thudding of its hoofbeats drowned out the shrill curses that followed him.

Chapter Six

MAC RAN THE BRUSH over the sleek, silver gray hide of the big stallion. The horse was in a stall by himself in the barn. He couldn't be put in the corral with the other horses and the mules because he got too high-spirited and caused trouble when he wasn't out running for miles each day. He was the perfect mount for a cavalryman, never tiring, steady of nerve even when guns and artillery were crashing around him and possessed of a seeming sixth sense that warned him of danger.

Other than his brothers, this horse was the best friend he'd ever had in his life, Mac thought.

He still wasn't sure what stroke of luck had brought the stallion to the Brannon farm a couple of years earlier. All he knew was that as soon as he had seen the horse rearing up defiantly in the moonlight, he had known that the two of them were meant to be together. The stallion had made it difficult, because it had taken Mac months to catch and corral him. Once that task was finally accomplished, however, the horse had never given him a bit of trouble.

The only trouble had been with certain people—like Maj. Jason Trahearne.

Another cavalryman in the First Virginia, Trahearne had had his eye on the stallion for a long time. He had threatened to confiscate it and use it for his own mount, but Mac's friend and commanding officer, Gen. Fitzhugh Lee, had put a stop to that. Mac was convinced that Trahearne had even tried to steal the stallion, a plan that had resulted in the death of a fellow officer who had been one of Trahearne's friends.

Mac told himself to put Trahearne out of his mind. Trahearne was with the rest of Jeb Stuart's cavalry in the encampment near Culpeper, on a hilltop overlooking a creek known as Mountain Run.

And that corps of cavalry was larger than it had ever been. Stuart's three brigades under Fitz Lee, Rooney Lee, and Wade Hampton had been augmented by two more brigades, one brought from the Shenandoah Valley by Gen. William E. "Grumble" Jones, the other a band of bold North Carolinians under the command of Col. Beverly Robertson. Robert E. Lee, the commanding general, had ordered this consolidation of the Confederate cavalry in the East after seeing how successful the massed Union cavalry under Maj. Gen. George Stoneman had been. Stuart now had almost ten thousand men at his disposal, and Mac knew the general was eager to get back into action against the Yankees.

That would have to wait until Robert E. Lee determined what the next action was to be. In the meantime, Mac and the other men whose families lived in the area of the bivouac had been allowed to visit their loved ones.

The stallion turned its head and nudged Mac's arm, breaking into his thoughts. Mac grinned and finished the brushing then patted the horse on the flank. "Maybe tomorrow we'll get out for a run," he told the stallion. "I reckon you're about as eager to smell powder smoke again as General Stuart is."

The stallion snorted.

Mac left the barn and started toward the house. He saw a match flare on the porch, and in its brief light he saw his brother Will's face as the flame lighted the bowl of his pipe. Will shook out the match as Mac came up the steps.

"Mind if I join you?" asked Mac.

"I'd like that," Will said. He sat in a rocking chair with a wicker bottom and puffed contentedly on the pipe. Mac figured he'd been brooding about Yancy.

Mac sat down on the top step, dug out his own pipe and tobacco pouch, and started packing the bowl. The two brothers sat there in companionable silence until Mac had his pipe lit and the air held a smoky haze. Will surprised him by saying, "I'm worried about Henry."

"How so? You think he's liable to try to enlist?" It was one of Mac's main concerns that his mother and Cordelia not be left alone on the farm.

Will grunted. "Not as long as Polly Ebersole's around."

"Polly? What do you mean?" Mac asked with a frown.

"You saw for yourself the other day."

"All I saw was the two of them talking."

"He's sweet on her, Mac," Will said. "The same sickness that wound up killing Titus has got hold of Henry now."

Mac sat up straighter. "Wait just a minute. Are you saying that Polly is to blame for what happened to Titus?"

"He wouldn't have enlisted and gotten himself killed at Fredericksburg if it hadn't been for her."

"You don't know that for sure," Mac said. "We don't really know what happened between them."

"We heard enough about it from Ma and Cordelia. Titus left Polly, and it was after that he signed up."

"Maybe so, but that doesn't mean she's entirely to blame. And I don't see how you can think the same thing's going to happen to Henry."

"Maybe not exactly the same thing," said Will, "but he's in love with that girl, and no good can come of it."

For a moment, Mac didn't say anything, then he laughed.

"What's so funny?" Will asked, sounding surprised.

"You. You're starting to sound like Ma. Never thought I'd see the day."

Will puffed heavily on his pipe, and the glow from the bowl lit up his face for a second. "That's not it at all. I just know how those Ebersoles spread trouble behind them."

"I won't deny you're right about the old man. Polly's not like that, though. I always thought she was a mite stuck-up, but she seems different somehow since her marriage to Titus and his death. Maybe it didn't work out, but I think he did her some good, anyway."

Will didn't say anything to that.

After a couple of minutes of silence, the front door opened, and Abigail Brannon stepped out onto the porch. She wiped her hands on her apron and took a deep breath. "My, isn't the night air sweet."

"Be a nice night to take a walk under the stars with a beau," Mac said with a sly smile.

"Hmmph. I wouldn't know about that. Such things are the concern of young people."

Will leaned back in the rocker and lifted his legs to rest his booted feet on the porch rail. With a grin he said, "From what I hear, it's not just the young girls who have gentlemen callers." He paused. "Has the preacher been out here lately, Ma?"

"You hush, Will Brannon," Abigail snapped. "I don't have the slightest idea what you're talking about. Reverend Spanner is a fine, decent, God-fearing man."

"Never said he wasn't," drawled Will. He and Mac looked at each other and chuckled.

"Oh!" Abigail said. "You two!" She turned and went back into the house, letting the screen door bang shut behind her.

Cordelia came out a few minutes later. "What did you say to Mama?" she asked. "She looked as mad as if somebody just asked her to dance!"

"We were just teasing her a little about Reverend Spanner," Mac said. "Looks like what you told us is true, Cordelia. Those two are sweet on each other."

"I knew it! I don't know how many times I've come into the parlor when the reverend was visiting, and they're both of them blushing fit to beat the band!"

"The good reverend's been stealing kisses, more'n likely," Will said, a look of mock solemnity on his face.

"We shouldn't be sitting out here gossiping about our own mother," Mac said.

From the doorway, Henry asked, "Why not? She's laid down the law to us often enough. I think it's sort of funny she's got her a beau, even if it is that preacher man."

Mac looked around. He hadn't been aware that Henry was standing there. "Where is she?"

"Don't worry, she went on upstairs. She was muttering something about insolent young pups, so I figured she was talking about you and Will." Henry came out onto the porch and moved to the top step to sit beside Mac. Cordelia perched on the railing near where Will was resting his feet.

Mac puffed on his pipe and thought about how good it felt for the four of them to be here together like this. Of course, it would never be the same since with Titus gone, and Cory way off in Tennessee or Mississippi or somewhere beyond the Shenandoah. Cory moved around so much it was hard to keep track of him. But considering that they were in the middle of a war, to have four of the Brannon siblings sitting on their own front porch on a warm, peaceful summer night was a rare blessing indeed.

True, supper had been pretty skimpy because of the dwindling supplies in the county. The front lines were close now so that if Union and Confederate pickets happened to blunder into each other, the Brannons could have heard the resulting gunfire.

But the night was quiet except for the chirping of insects and the soft sigh of the breeze in the tree branches.

It was odd that at this moment, the topics of discussion on the front porch had been matters of the heart rather than the clash of great armies, thought Mac. The times they were living through doubtless would go down in history and might still be studied a hundred or more years from now. But those of them who were experiencing that history were more concerned with mundane things. Mac wanted the Confederacy to win the war, but the hopes and dreams of his family mattered more to him than the South. Battle had a way of concentrating a man's mind, focusing it down on one hard, simple truth: the instinct for survival. But let the guns fall silent, let the night breeze blow away the powder smoke, and his thoughts turned again to those other, greater truths.

Without family, Mac concluded, the war meant nothing.

Moments like these were why the men of the South fought so hard to defend their homeland.

Cordelia laughed. "My, you're all quiet tonight."

"Just thinking, I reckon," Mac said.

"About the war?"

Mac shook his head. "Nope. The war's the farthest thing from my mind right now."

—m—

MAC, WILL, and Henry were just inside the open doors of the barn the next day, bending over the plow where the blade had come loose, when hoofbeats sounded in the yard. Mac glanced up and saw a large, bearded, affable-looking young man riding toward the house. The newcomer wore a soft gray hat with a plume on it and the uniform of a brigadier general in the Confederate cavalry.

"General Lee!" Mac exclaimed as he snapped to attention.

Fitzhugh Lee reined in and turned his horse toward the barn. He smiled as Will also came to attention and saluted. Henry just straightened up and stared goggle-eyed at the dashing young cavalry commander.

Lee lifted a hand to his hat brim and sketched a salute. "At ease, Captain Brannon. You, too, Captain Brannon," he added with a chuckle. He looked at Henry and asked, "Are you another Captain Brannon?"

"No sir," Henry said. "I mean, I'm a Brannon, but I ain't a captain. Or anything else in the army."

"This is our little brother Henry, General," Mac explained. "He's been taking care of the farm while Will and I are gone."

"A vital job in itself," Fitz Lee agreed. "Is it all right if I dismount?"

Mac started forward with a jerk. "Yes sir. Sorry we forgot our manners. Please, come into the house."

"Quite all right," Lee said as he swung down from the saddle. He handed the reins to Henry, who hurried forward behind Mac. "I reckon you didn't expect to see me here."

"No sir, not really," Mac admitted.

Lee pulled the gauntlet off his right hand and offered it to Will, who had been a little slower coming out of the barn. "Good to see you again, Captain."

"Good to see you, too, sir," Will said. "I hope there's no trouble with the army."

"No, we're all still catching our breath and waiting for Uncle Bob to get back from Richmond."

It was strange to hear the commander of the Confederate army referred to as "Uncle Bob," but to Fitz Lee, that was who he was.

Lee continued, "General Stuart's not content to rest on his laurels, though. You know Beauty, Mac. Always got to be doing something. He's decided to have another grand review of all the cavalry. You're going to have to report back to camp tomorrow."

Mac nodded, accepting the news without particularly liking it. He had known this visit home couldn't last forever. But a few more days would have been nice.

Something else was puzzling him. "Begging your pardon, General, but . . . you rode over here just to tell me that?"

A grin stretched across Lee's bearded face. "That . . . and to sample some of those biscuits of your mother's that I've heard you talking about. It's been a long time since I've had a home-cooked meal."

"Well, we'll sure try to oblige, General," Mac said, hoping that there was enough flour on hand for a suitable batch of Abigail's biscuits.

"Oh, and since I knew I was riding out here—" Lee reached under his coat and brought out a folded piece of paper. "I took the liberty of calling at the post office in Culpeper to see if you had any mail. The postmaster was a little leery of letting me deliver this letter, but I guess he decided he could trust me."

Lee handed the paper to Mac, who recognized his brother Cory's distinctive scrawl. "It's from Cory," he said, excitement growing inside him. It had been awhile since the family had heard from Cory.

"Let's take it inside so Ma and Cordelia can hear it, too," Will suggested. "Come on, General. There's some fresh buttermilk down in the cellar."

As the four men went inside, Henry hurried on ahead, calling, "Ma! Cordelia! We've got company, and you'll never guess who it is!"

Fitz enjoyed the attention, but he downplayed it. "You folks don't have to make a fuss over me."

Will chuckled. "Too late for that, I'd say, General."

The Brannon women came out of the kitchen as Will and Mac ushered Lee into the parlor. "My goodness!" Abigail exclaimed when she saw the general's uniform. She started wiping her hands on her apron. Cordelia followed suit, trying not to gape at Lee as she did so.

"General, this is my mother, Mrs. Abigail Brannon," Mac said. "And my sister, Miss Cordelia Brannon."

"It is my great honor to meet you, ladies," Lee said with a charming smile as he took their hands.

Mac half-expected him to bow and kiss the hands of the Brannon women. Stuart would have. Lee stopped short of that, however. His smile was sufficient to fluster both women. Cordelia began to blush as he held her hand for a moment longer than absolutely necessary.

"Ma, Cordelia, this is Brigadier General Fitzhugh Lee, my commanding officer."

Lee held up his left hand. "Not today, Captain. Today I'm just a friend and a hungry man in search of a good meal."

"Could be I've bragged too much on your biscuits, Ma," Mac said with a smile of his own.

"Well, I'll certainly be glad to whip up a batch," Abigail said. "It would be my pleasure, General Lee."

"The general brought this from town," Mac went on, holding up the piece of paper. "It's a letter from Cory."

"From Cory?" Cordelia repeated, excitement in her voice. "Let me see it."

Mac knew that Cordelia usually read aloud any letters that came, so he handed the paper to her. Abigail meanwhile offered Fitz a seat.

Lee hesitated. "You're sure I'm not intruding, ma'am?"

"Of course not." Abigail turned back to her daughter as Fitz Lee sat on the sofa. "Read the letter, Cordelia."

While the others took seats around the room, Cordelia broke the wax seal on the letter and unfolded the paper. She said, "It's dated May 12."

Less than a month earlier, Mac thought. That was mighty efficient for mail delivery in these hectic days.

"'Dear Folks,'" Cordelia read, "'I put pen to paper to share with you the happy news that I have now entered the holy state of matrimony.'" She looked up. "Cory's married!"

Mac saw tears spring up in his mother's eyes as Abigail coached, "Yes, yes, go on, dear."

"'Lucille and I were married two days ago here in Vicksburg, finally accomplishing our long-delayed nuptials.'"

"This letter is from one of your sons, Mrs. Brannon?" murmured Fitz Lee.

"Yes, my son Cory," Abigail said.

"And he's in Vicksburg?"

Cordelia said, "We know the Yankees have their eye on Vicksburg, General. Cory has told us in previous letters about his involvement in efforts to protect the city."

"Let us pray they're successful," Lee said. "Vicksburg is vital to the South. I fear that devil Grant won't stop until he's taken it."

"'I cannot tell you what a beautiful bride Lucille made, nor how happy I am to finally be her husband,'" Cordelia resumed reading from Cory's letter. "'We were married in the cellar of her aunt and uncle's house as Federal gunboats on the river continued the bombardment of this fair, unfortunate city.'"

Abigail put a hand to her mouth. "Dear Lord. A bombardment during their wedding . . ."

Mac looked at Will. They had heard plenty of artillery in the past two years. Still, they hated to think of their younger brother, his new wife, and her family having to undergo such an ordeal.

"'Everyone says things will get much worse before they get better, but I cling to the hope that such will not be the case. Regardless of what comes, I know that I will be strong, for my beloved is by my side.'"

Henry said, "Cory always did have a way with words."

"'I hope this letter finds you all in good health,'" Cordelia read. "'You are all in my prayers daily, and Lucille says for me to tell you that she prays for you as well. She is looking forward to meeting all of you when this terrible war is over. I know you will love her every bit as much as I do.

"'I must close now, and I do so with fondest wishes and much love, your son and brother, Cory.'" Cordelia's voice caught a little as she finished reading the closing words.

"Boy ought to be home, not wandering halfway across the country," Will said, the gruffness of his voice trying—and failing—to hide the love and concern he felt for his brother.

Mac blinked away a tear of his own. "One of these days, he will be home. We all will be."

"God willing," Abigail said.

"Amen to that, ma'am," Fitz Lee added.

Abigail got to her feet and used the hem of her apron to dab at her eyes. "Well, I've got to get busy on those biscuits," she said briskly. "Come along, Cordelia."

—m—

CONSIDERING THE circumstances, Abigail outdid herself, providing a meal of hamhocks, greens, biscuits, and molasses. She must have been saving the molasses for just such a special occasion, Mac thought, because he had believed they didn't have any more of the sweet, sticky stuff.

Fitz Lee exclaimed over the biscuits and complimented Abigail on the delicious meal, causing her to flush with pride.

"I have to be getting back to the camp," he said when supper was over. "Although I certainly hate to leave such pleasant surroundings for the squalid hubbub of a military encampment."

"Do I need to go with you, General?" Mac asked as he stepped out onto the porch with Lee.

"No, you can report tomorrow morning, Captain. That will be sufficient."

Mac snapped to attention and saluted. "I'll bid you good night then."

Lee returned the salute. "Good night, Captain." He put on his hat and descended the steps.

Henry had already fetched Lee's horse. The general took the reins from him, swung up into the saddle, and with a wave to the rest of the family that had followed Mac onto the porch, he rode out.

"My, he's such a dashing man," Cordelia said in a hushed and quiet voice.

"I'll bet he's a terror in battle, though," Henry said as he came over to the porch to join the others.

Mac nodded. "He's a good officer. I'm glad he took me under his wing and made me his aide. I reckon everything I know about war I've learned from Fitz Lee."

"I wish none of us had to know anything about war," Abigail said with a sigh.

"Ma," Will noted, "before the war started, you were as big a fire-eater as anybody."

She gave him a hard look. "Things were different then. All I knew was that the Yankees were trying to tell us how to live our lives, and they had no right to do that. They still don't. But . . . it was different then."

She didn't have to say anything else. Mac knew she was thinking about Titus's death, about Cory huddled in a cellar as artillery shells burst overhead, and about the dangers he and Will had faced during their time in the army. Mac knew his mother, knew that she believed as strongly as ever in the Confederacy, but now she knew firsthand the costs of war. She was right. That made all the difference in the world.

—∿—

A COUPLE of weeks earlier, Jeb Stuart had held a review of his troops, but at that time, his command had consisted of only three brigades. Since then Grumble Jones's and Beverly Robertson's brigades had come into the fold, and a review of the combined brigades promised to be quite an impressive spectacle. Stuart sent word of the grand review to Robert E. Lee, hoping the commander would be able to attend. Lee, however, busy with his plans to assemble his entire army at Culpeper and then march north into Pennsylvania, had to decline.

Such a disappointment was not enough to faze Stuart. The grand review of all five brigades would go ahead as planned on June 5, 1863, at Brandy Station, north of Culpeper.

When Mac rode through the town on June 4, on his way to the hilltop encampment nearby, he was surprised to see how busy Culpeper had become in such a short time. Wagons and buggies were parked all along the main street, and the boardwalks were packed with pedestrians, most of them civilians. A train was pulling into the station, and as Mac rode by he saw dozens of passengers disembarking from the cars. Many of them were women in expensive traveling gowns and held umbrellas to shade themselves from the hot sun. Mac spotted the huge figure of Heros Von Borke, the Prussian soldier of fortune who served on Stuart's staff, striding along, and he hailed the foreigner.

Von Borke, who stood several inches over six feet tall and weighed at least 250 pounds, stroked a finger over his sweeping mustaches and said in a thick accent, "Ah, Captain Brannon! You haf returned."

"To something I didn't quite expect," Mac said as he reined in the stallion. "Why is Culpeper so crowded today? Who are all these folks?"

"Friends and family of General Stuart und his commanders und a few politicians. Zey haf come from all ober ze South for der grand review," Von Borke said. "Zat ist alzo de reason fur mein splendid new accoutrements." He made a sweeping gesture with his right hand, indicating the new uniform he wore.

It was an eye opener, all right, thought Mac. A dark green jacket with a red sash draped diagonally over it, a brilliant white shirt with plenty of frills and lace spilling from its bosom, tight tan trousers, high-topped boots of brown calfskin, a belted saber and holstered pistol, and a gray hat with the left side of the brim pinned up and a tall, bright red plume attached to it. The green and red colors and Von Borke's great height made him look a little like a tree decorated for Christmas, Mac decided, but he kept that opinion to himself.

"You must report to your brigade," Von Borke went on, "zo dat you, too, can be outfitted properly, Captain."

Mac's gray uniform and black campaign cap were all right with him, but he supposed if he was ordered to wear a new uniform, he would obey the command. He just hoped that in that case, the garb wouldn't be as gaudy as the Prussian's. He knew he would never feel comfortable decked out like that.

"Thank you for warning me, sir," Mac said, drawing a chuckle from Von Borke. He saluted then rode on through the town toward the encampment.

It was amazing how much Culpeper had changed overnight. Mac saw several of the townspeople standing in the doorways of their homes, dazed by the constantly arriving crowds. He trotted the stallion around the wagons clogging the street and was relieved when he finally reached the edge of town. He thought that maybe it wouldn't be so crowded out here.

He was wrong, he saw right away. A steady stream of wagons and buggies and carriages rolled toward the hill where the Confederate cavalry camp was located. Extra tents had been pitched, especially near the large tent that marked General Stuart's headquarters. Those new tents would be for the general's guests, Mac supposed. He shook his head and thought that no one had ever accused James Ewell Brown Stuart of doing anything halfway. It was all or nothing with the general known to his friends and former classmates from West Point as Beauty.

Mac found the tent that served as the headquarters of the brigade commanded by Fitzhugh Lee. He swung down from the saddle, handed the stallion's reins to a soldier who stepped forward to take them, and spoke to the guard standing at the tent's entrance. "Is General Lee inside?"

"Yes sir," the trooper replied.

"Captain Brannon, reporting as ord—"

He stopped at the sound of a sudden commotion behind him. A voice said, "Give me those reins, soldier!" and hard on the heels of the words came the shrill whinny of an angry horse. Mac knew the sound of that animal as well as he knew his own voice. He whirled around in time to see Maj. Jason Trahearne rip the stallion's reins out of the hands of the soldier to whom Mac had given them. Trahearne had a quirt in his other hand, and he raised his arm, ready to slash the quirt across the stallion's nose.

Without even thinking about what he was doing, Mac tackled Trahearne from behind, slamming him to the ground.

Chapter Seven

A RED RAGE GRIPPED Mac, blurring all thoughts of rank and propriety. He and Trahearne rolled over and over on the ground. The major managed to tear free from Mac's grip and threw a punch that grazed the side of Mac's head. The blow half-stunned Mac and stopped his attack for the moment. Trahearne made it to his feet first, and as Mac started to rise, Trahearne kicked him in the jaw.

The kick exploded like a rocket in Mac's face, catching him off balance and driving him backward. As Mac sprawled on the ground, Trahearne snatched up the quirt, which he had dropped when Mac had tackled him. Looming over the stunned man, he began lashing him with the quirt.

Mac caught one of the slashes across his left cheek. It felt like a line of fire had been drawn down his face. Blood sprang out from the welt and dripped, hot and wet, on Mac's throat. He rolled to the side to protect his face and flung up an arm to block the quirt. His forearm banged against Trahearne's wrist and knocked the quirt out of the major's hand.

Mac kept rolling until he came up on his hands and knees. He lunged forward, wrapping his arms around Trahearne's knees. Again Trahearne went down. Mac crawled up the major's body, punching hard as he went. He drove a couple of blows into Trahearne's belly, and then he was kneeling atop the major's torso, slamming punch after punch into Trahearne's face. Trahearne tried to jerk aside to escape the brutal punishment, but Mac had him pinned. There was nowhere for him to go.

Throughout the fracas, Mac was aware that other men had surrounded the two brawling combatants. All were shouting, some in excitement, some in dismay, some in outrage. To him, however, the sound was muffled, the voices vague. He didn't realize he was being ordered to stop the fight until strong arms caught him from behind and hauled him up and off of Trahearne's semi-conscious battered form.

"Dammit, I said stop, Mac!" Fitz Lee bellowed in his ear. The general, who was taller and heavier than Mac, still had trouble dragging him away from Trahearne. The fury of a temporary madness had filled Mac with unusual strength.

The red mist in front of Mac's eyes began to clear, however, and the terrible pounding inside his skull eased somewhat. He stopped struggling in Lee's grip and belatedly realized what he was doing, as well as what he had done. A cold shudder ran through him.

"If I let go, are you going to stop fighting?" his friend and commander asked.

"Yes sir," Mac said, his voice sounding strange and hollow to his ears. The blood was still roaring in his head, although not as loudly as it had been a few moments earlier.

Lee released Mac and stepped back. "See to Major Trahearne," he snapped, and several officers from the group that had been watching the fight hurried forward to lift Trahearne to his feet and lead him away. Trahearne was groggy, only half-conscious, and without the men supporting him, he would have fallen. "Take him to the infirmary," Lee added.

He turned to Mac and scowled. "The infirmary's where you need to be, too, Captain, but I want to keep you and Major Trahearne apart for the time being." Lee took a handkerchief from his jacket and pressed it into Mac's hand. "You're getting blood on your uniform."

Mac took the handkerchief and held it to his face to stem the flow of blood from his cheek. The injury stung and burned badly now. In the heat of battle, he hadn't noticed it so much. He muttered, "I'm sorry, General—"

"Sorry?" Lee cut in. "Sorry for attacking a superior officer and beating him senseless?" The general's tone was caustic.

"I realize there's no excuse for my behavior, sir." It was soaking in on Mac that he might be in serious trouble. No matter what the provocation, what he had done was a court-martial offense. He took the handkerchief away from his face and saw that it was very bloody. "Sorry, general. I seem to have ruined your handkerchief."

"That's the least of my worries right now," Lee snapped. "You're my aide, Mac. What could make you jump Trahearne like that?"

"He was after my horse again, sir." That reminded Mac of the stallion. He looked around for the horse and saw it standing off to the side, watching him. One of the troopers approached and reached out for the reins, but the stallion flared its nostrils in a threatening manner and backed off a couple of steps. Clearly, the horse was unwilling to let anyone handle him except Mac.

Lee shook his head. "That stallion's a mighty fine mount, and I know you've had trouble with Trahearne over it in the past. But that's still no excuse for what you did."

"No argument, sir."

Suddenly, the men around them came to attention, and some of them moved back to open a path for another tall, bearded officer, resplendent in a new gray uniform with a bright yellow sash. Mac recognized General Stuart.

Like the others, Mac and Lee came to attention and saluted. Stuart stopped in front of them and returned the salute. "At ease, gentlemen." He looked at Mac. Most of the bleeding from the cut had stopped, but Mac figured his face was still a gory mess. "Was there a battle I was unaware of? I don't recall seeing any Yankees 'round here today."

"No battle, sir," Lee said. "Just a . . . private matter between two officers."

"Two officers of equal rank?" Stuart's eyes bored into Mac's. "Captain Brannon? I take it from your injury that you were one of the combatants?"

"Yes sir. Major Trahearne was the other."

Stuart's expression hardened quickly. "And where now is Major Trahearne?"

"I had him taken to the infirmary, General," Fitz Lee said.

"So he came off the worse in the fracas, despite the injury to Captain Brannon here?"

"Yes sir, I'd say so."

Stuart nodded. He studied the gash on Mac's face for a moment. "I think that cut's going to need to be sewn up, Captain, or else you're going to have a nasty scar there. I'll have my personal surgeon take care of it."

"Yes sir. Thank you, sir."

"I'll speak to Major Trahearne concerning the incident, of course, but since I'm here now, I want to hear your side of the story, Captain."

Before Mac could respond, Lee said, "You know what it's about, General. Trahearne has had his eye on Mac's horse ever since Mac joined up. He tried to take it again."

"And when my horse resisted, Major Trahearne threatened to strike it with a quirt." Mac lifted his left hand and gently touched the cut on his cheek. "He took the quirt to me instead."

"So this is nothing but a squabble over a horse that deteriorated into a brawl?"

The stallion wasn't just any horse, not by a long shot, Mac wanted to say, but he couldn't bring himself to do so. Stuart would never understand. No one could. No one but him.

"I deeply regret what happened, General—" Mac began.

One of the officers standing nearby spoke up, interrupting Mac's apology. "I saw the whole thing, General Stuart. This captain launched an unwarranted attack on Major Trahearne. Worse yet, he hit the major from behind."

The man was a colonel, a member of Wade Hampton's staff, and Mac recognized him as a friend of Trahearne's. Mac knew he wasn't going to get any sort of help from that quarter.

"Is that true, Captain?" Stuart asked.

"I grabbed Major Trahearne from behind and threw him to the ground to keep him from attacking my horse," Mac said. "The only blows I struck came from the front, sir."

"That hardly matters," the colonel said coldly. "It was still a treacherous attack on a superior officer."

Stuart grimaced and looked very displeased. With all these witnesses around, he couldn't very well sweep the incident under the rug, even if the general had been so inclined. Mac doubted that Stuart would have done such a thing, anyway. For all his flamboyance, Stuart was a conscientious soldier.

He looked at Mac with cold, narrow eyes. "You know that a grand review is scheduled for tomorrow, don't you, Captain?"

"Yes sir," Mac said.

"We have a great many ladies and other important visitors in camp, and more will be arriving shortly. This is *not* the right time or place for such a disturbance as you've caused. For the time being, consider yourself under arrest, Captain."

"Yes sir." There was nothing else Mac could say.

"You will be confined to this camp, and you will not leave it except under the direct orders of either General Lee here or myself. Do you understand?"

"Yes sir."

Stuart's head jerked in a nod. "I assure you, we'll get to the bottom of this. But I will not allow it to interfere with the grand review. Nothing will interfere with the grand review. Do I make myself clear?"

Fitz Lee said, "Very clear, General. And I give you my word that Captain Brannon will appear for any proceedings that may take place following the grand review."

"Of course he will. I expect no dishonor for any man who rides with me." Stuart glanced at Mac again. "I'll send my surgeon," he said again, then clasped his hands behind his back and turned to walk away, followed by the members of his staff who had accompanied him to see what the commotion was.

Fitz Lee waited until Stuart was out of earshot, then blew out his breath in a long sigh. "You've let yourself in for a lot of trouble, Mac," he said quietly. "Beauty doesn't want anything messing with the show he's putting on."

"I'm sorry, sir." In truth, Mac regretted the problems he had caused for Lee and Stuart, but he wasn't a bit sorry about laying into the annoying Trahearne. The major had had a thrashing coming for a long time.

And it had felt *so* good to smash his fist into Trahearne's face. Mac wasn't a violent man by nature, but he would long remember the satisfaction he'd felt as that impact shivered up his arm.

"Go to your tent, Captain," Lee said. "I'll send General Stuart's surgeon to you when he arrives."

"Thank you, sir."

Lee shook his head. "Before this is over, you may not be thanking me, Mac. I'll do what I can for you, of course, but it may not be much."

"Sir, before I go to my tent, I think I need to take care of my horse . . ."

Lee waved a hand. "By all means. From the looks of him, he's not going to allow anyone but you to get near him." Lee dropped his voice so that only Mac could hear and added, "It's a damned shame he didn't rear up and bust Trahearne's head open with a hoof."

"Yes sir," Mac agreed. "A damned shame."

—∞—

IT HURT like blazes when the surgeon cleaned and then stitched up the gash in Mac's cheek. Mac gritted his teeth and refused the flask of whiskey the surgeon offered him, "strictly for medicinal purposes, of course."

"Lucky for you I'm good at what I do, Captain," the physician said as he pushed the needle through Mac's cheek and drew the sutures after it. "You'll have a small scar, but it won't be a bad one. What happened, somebody take after you with a side knife?"

"No sir," Mac replied between tightly clenched teeth. "It was a quirt."

"Oh, ho," the surgeon said. "You're the fellow I heard about on the way over here, the officer who got in a fight over a horse. The whole camp's buzzing about you, Captain."

That wasn't good news, Mac thought. He wasn't particularly proud of what had happened, and he didn't like the idea of the story going all over camp. If nothing else, it would ensure that sentiments were running against him when it came time for his court-martial.

He was convinced it would come to that. Trahearne would insist on it, and so would Trahearne's friends. Stuart would have no choice but to put Mac on trial for striking a superior officer.

The surgeon tied off the last suture and left Mac there in the tent with his face throbbing in pain. As the day dragged by, the discomfort eased until there was just a dull ache in Mac's cheek. He didn't feel like eating, knowing it would be agony to do so.

The camp was in an uproar as preparations for the grand review proceeded. Mac lay on his cot and listened to the tramp of feet, the thudding of hoofbeats, the rattle of wagons and buggies, and the laughter of ladies. Although happily married, Stuart greatly enjoyed female companionship. There was nothing really improper about it; the general simply liked to be surrounded by attractive women. In keeping with his personality, though, he was always a gentleman.

Late in the day, Mac dozed off, and so he didn't hear the footsteps that stopped just outside his tent, didn't know that he had a visitor until the entrance flap was thrust aside and a tall, muscular figure stepped into the tent.

"Mac!" Will Brannon said sharply. "What's this I hear about you getting into a fight with a major?"

Mac sat up with a jerk, the sudden motion making his wounded cheek start throbbing again. He winced at the looming figure of his older brother. "Hello, Will."

He swung his legs off the cot as Will drew up a three-legged stool and sat down. "Not back in camp even a day, and you've already raised a ruckus," said Will. He was upset, but there was also a grin lurking around the corners of his mouth. "What happened? Was it Trahearne again?"

"How did you know?"

"I figured he's the only fella on our side who could get you riled up enough to take a punch at him."

Mac nodded. "It was Trahearne, all right. He tried to take a quirt after my horse."

Will let out a little whistle. "He's lucky you didn't beat him to death, the way you feel about that stallion."

Mac smiled humorlessly. "I thought about it."

"What the devil made him think he could get away with a stunt like that?"

"You saw for yourself how busy the camp is." Mac waved a hand to indicate everything that was going on outside the tent. "I suppose he thought that in the confusion, he could slip the stallion in with his own mounts. I was on my way into General Lee's headquarters tent and would have been occupied with that for a while. Trahearne made his move too soon, though, while I could still hear what was going on."

"The man's a damned fool and a disgrace to the uniform. You told me what happened at Fredericksburg. He's nothing but a coward."

Mac's mind went back to that cold December day when he had come across the Confederate officer begging for his life in front of three Union soldiers along an isolated brook that ran into Massaponax Creek. The incident had taken place in a small pocket of the battle that swirled up and down the two-mile length of the Rappahannock River near Fredericksburg. No one had seen the confrontation except Mac, and when he had gone to the aid of the Confederate officer, who had turned out to be Jason Trahearne, Trahearne himself had later tried to kill Mac. Trahearne claimed that he had mistaken Mac for one of the Yankees, but Mac knew better. Trahearne wanted to conceal the evidence of his cowardice, and the best way to do that was to make sure Mac died.

Mac had survived, of course, and Trahearne's fears must have eased when Mac didn't tell anyone what he had witnessed. The only other person who knew the story was Will. With the return of Trahearne's confidence had come a renewed desire to own the silver gray stallion. If anything, Mac knew that Trahearne wanted the horse more than ever.

"I don't have any higher an opinion of Trahearne than you do," Mac said, "but that doesn't change what happened. I attacked a superior officer, and I'm under arrest and facing a court-martial."

Will smacked his right fist into his left palm. "It's not fair, damn it! Rank shouldn't matter in something like this."

"Rank always matters."

Will couldn't argue with that. He and Mac weren't professional military men, but even citizen soldiers such as themselves were aware of the rules.

"What are you doing here?" Mac asked after a moment of silence. "Don't tell me they're talking all the way over in the Stonewall Brigade about what happened between Trahearne and me."

Will grinned. "You're not quite that notorious yet, little brother. I just came over to see you after reporting back in myself, and I heard about the fight as I came through camp." He became more serious. "If there's a court-martial, you'll need someone to represent you."

"I'm sure General Lee will see to that."

"I plan to be there and speak in your behalf."

Mac started to protest that that wasn't necessary, but then he changed his mind and nodded in gratitude. It would be good to have somebody there on his side.

At worst, he thought that he might be cashiered out of the army if the court-martial found him guilty. While his offense was serious, he hadn't deserted or committed treason or anything that would warrant a firing squad. It would be a disgrace to get booted out of the cavalry, but he would survive.

"When do you think this is going to happen?" Will asked.

Mac shook his head. "I don't know. The review's tomorrow, and General Stuart isn't going to let anything interfere with that. I imagine he'll want to dispose of the matter as soon as possible afterward, though. Maybe as quick as the day after tomorrow."

"If you hear anything, can you send word to me right away?"

"Sure." The subject wasn't something Mac wanted to dwell on, so he changed it by asking, "Have you heard what the army's going to be doing next?"

"The word is that as soon as General Lee—General Robert E. Lee—has all our forces concentrated, we're going to march north again."

"Another invasion?" The last Confederate invasion of the Union had ended in a stalemate, if not outright defeat, at Antietam Creek in Maryland.

Will shrugged. "We had good reasons for going north before, and they still apply. Virginia—hell, the whole South—is just about drained dry. The folks up in Maryland or Pennsylvania or wherever we wind up, they helped start this war by answering Lincoln's call for an invading army. It's only fair that they feed us for a while."

"So it's to be nothing more than a glorified foraging expedition?"

"Call it what you will, I'll bet that in a month or two we'll be tramping around on Yankee ground." Will grinned. "That'll draw Hooker and his army after us, sure as shooting. I know what's in the back of Lee's mind. We whipped the Yankees at Chancellorsville. Give us one more good shot at them, and we might just wipe them out."

Mac knew what that would mean. If they could destroy the Union army, the war would be over. The Yankees would have no choice but to accept an offer of peace from the Confederacy. Then, at last, the killing could stop.

Mac stretched out on the cot and put his hands behind his head, lacing the fingers together. "If that happens," he said, enjoying the daydream for a moment, "do you think we'll go back in the Union?"

"Not a chance," Will said. "The Confederacy is here to stay. We've come too far, lost too much, to give it up now when we have a chance to run our own affairs without the North trying to tell us what to do. But there's no reason we can't be good neighbors if the Yankees will just realize we won't be dictated to."

"I hope that's the way it works out."

Will stood up and stepped over to the cot. He leaned down to pat Mac on the shoulder. "Best leave all that to the generals and the politicians. For now, let's just worry about getting you past that court-martial."

Mac nodded in the gathering dusk. For him, history had to wait while he fought his own personal battle.

FITZ LEE came by during the evening, after Will had left, and told Mac that the brigade would be riding up to Brandy Station the next morning. "I want you with us, Mac," he said, "and you can consider that the direct order General Stuart said was necessary before you could leave the camp."

"Thank you, sir. I was afraid I'd be confined to the camp and would miss the review."

"Not a chance," Lee said with a grin. "You're part of the First Virginia Cavalry Brigade. We won't leave without you. I'm not worried about offending Trahearne, either." He stepped closer and studied Mac's face by the light of the single candle burning in the tent. "Looks like the surgeon did a good job on those stitches."

"Yes sir."

"I'll bet they hurt, though."

Mac allowed that they had.

Lee put his hat on. "Well, I'm on my way into Culpeper. Beauty has taken over the town hall and is throwing a ball there tonight. We'll be dancing long into the night." He hesitated. "It probably wouldn't be a good idea for you to attend the ball, Mac. The review is one thing, but . . ."

"It's quite all right, sir," Mac said. "I'm not in much of a mood to dance anyway, and besides, my family's Baptist. I don't think I'd want my mother to hear that I'd been sinning."

Lee threw back his head and laughed. "Good night, Mac. I'll see you first thing in the morning."

Mac didn't sleep well; the cut on his face was too uncomfortable for that. It was almost a relief when dawn came up over the Virginia landscape the next morning. He left his tent early and had a cup of coffee and a little mush for breakfast. Eating hurt, just as he thought it would, but his belly was too empty for him to ignore it any longer.

He hadn't been given a new uniform, so he wore his old one as he saddled the stallion and got ready to ride along with the rest of the brigade. He had brushed the tunic and trousers as best he could and shined his boots, but there was nothing he could do about the bloodstains on his collar. In a way, he was glad they were there. He considered them something of a badge of honor.

The regular members of the brigade pulled out first, heading up the Orange and Alexandria railroad toward Brandy Station. As a member of Fitzhugh Lee's staff, Mac would leave later, as part of the commanders' entourage, with Lee and Stuart and the other brigadiers and their staffs. This group would not proceed to the reviewing area until the full body of horsemen were in position.

Mac was aware that people were watching him and whispering behind his back as he took his place with the other members of Lee's staff. The story of his fight with Trahearne had spread all over the camp and among the civilians as well as the soldiers. He sat stiffly in the saddle and stared straight ahead, his campaign cap pulled down so that the bill was low on his forehead, shading his eyes.

Lee moved his horse up alongside Mac's. "Good morning, Captain" the general said quietly.

"Morning, sir."

"I know this is rough for you, Mac. You're handling it well. Don't let any of it get to you."

"Yes sir."

The officers' party assembled, with Stuart's being the last to join it and looking magnificent in a new uniform. A cape lined with red silk was fastened around his shoulders and billowed out in the early morning breeze. He looked around to make sure that everyone was there, and his eyes paused for a second on Mac. Then he lifted his hat, waved it over his head, and called, "Forward, gentlemen, forward!"

The horses stepped out smartly, almost prancing as the sound of bugle calls filled the air. Stuart had sent buglers on ahead to clear a path through the massive crowd of civilians that had gathered to watch the festivities. Men cheered and waved their hats in the air. Women sighed and fluttered lace handkerchiefs. Girls carrying baskets of flowers ran along in front of the horses, strewing blossoms in their path.

Mac had never seen anything quite like it.

The ride to Brandy Station took more than an hour. The civilians trailed along behind the officers, some on foot, most in wagons and buggies. In addition, trains were being dispatched from Culpeper to Brandy Station so that passengers could watch the review from the cars. This was the largest gathering ever of the Confederate cavalry, and it was probably the largest concentration of civilians to watch a military maneuver since the battle of First Manassas.

Stuart led the way to a knoll west of the rail line that would serve as a reviewing stand. As the riders came into sight at the top of the hill, a salute from the Horse Artillery boomed out. Mac drew rein with the others and looked down the slope at the assembled mass of the cavalry. The line of gray-clad horsemen stretched for more than a mile, and as they caught sight of

Stuart, the cavalrymen snatched off their caps and plumed hats and waved them in the air, cheering and shouting accolades at the top of their lungs.

Mac felt a tingling sensation. This was an awe-inspiring sight. Almost ten thousand men were arrayed on the plain at the base of the knoll, all of them eagerly saluting their leader, the man they would follow into battle anywhere, anytime. Stuart doffed his own hat and gestured expansively with it, and though Mac would not have thought it possible, the roar of the cheers grew even louder.

Suddenly, he sensed a presence beside him and looked over to see the bruised and swollen face of Maj. Jason Trahearne. Trahearne gave him an ugly smile and said so that only Mac could hear, "Enjoy it while you can, bastard."

Then Trahearne wheeled his horse and rode to the other side of the knoll, leaving Mac to stare stonily after him.

Chapter Eight

AFTER THAT EXCHANGE, ALL the pomp and spectacle of the review took on a hollow, bitter air for Mac. Trahearne's presence had been a blunt reminder that very soon he might no longer be a member of the Confederate cavalry.

But if Trahearne had cast a pall over the day for Mac, the same could not be said of the rest of the multitude assembled at Brandy Station. As the cheers rang out, Stuart began the festivities by galloping down the hill to pass in review of his troops. The hurrahing never slacked off as he rode up and down in front of the assembled cavalrymen.

When he came back to the top of the hill, he turned his horse and gazed down in satisfaction as the Horse Artillery passed by. Then, one by one, the companies of cavalry peeled off from the line and rode in front of the hill at a fast trot and circled around to the rear of the assembly. Several carriages full of ladies had pulled up next to Stuart, and he was his usual charming self as he identified each company to his guests.

The next part of the review was a mock battle. Again the horsemen passed in front of the makeshift reviewing stand, but this time they went at a gallop, with sabers drawn and flashing in the sun, shouting the Rebel yell. Artillery pieces had been set up around the field, and they boomed loudly as they fired powder charges at the "attacking" cavalrymen. From where he sat on the stallion, Mac saw more than one woman swoon from the sheer excitement and grandeur of the display.

His mouth twisted grimly. He had seen enough battles, heard the roar of enough cannons that weren't firing just smoke, to know that there was nothing grand about the real thing. Maybe cavaliers such as Jeb Stuart and Fitz Lee found some actual glory in battles; Mac just wanted to live through them and get them over with.

When the review was finally finished, Stuart announced that his headquarters would be moved to this hilltop immediately. That came as something of a surprise to Mac, but not too much of one. If the rumors Will had mentioned were correct and the army would soon be marching north, establishing a headquarters at Brandy Station would give the cavalry a jump over the rest of the Confederate forces down at Culpeper. And Mac knew that no matter what the army was doing, Stuart liked to be out in front.

Teamsters would bring all the tents and supplies to the new camp, so there was nothing for Mac to do the rest of the day. With so many civilians on hand, the convivial atmosphere continued even after the grand review was over.

It was a day-long party, and it continued on into the evening. Stuart ordered large bonfires constructed and lit so that there would be plenty of illumination for the dancing that followed. Military bands played civilian music rather than martial airs and marches. Smartly uniformed officers swept around the open area with brightly dressed ladies in their arms. Long tables were set up and filled with food, in what might be the last great feast of the war.

Down on the plain at the foot of the hill, away from the headquarters area, the enlisted men had set up their tents, and fires were scattered among them, too. The scraping of fiddles and the wailing of mouth harps drifted up the hill as the enlisted men followed the example of their officers and celebrated. Jugs of whiskey and rum were passed around, but although there was much hilarity, the festivities never deteriorated into drunken debauchery. Stuart's grip on his men was too tight for that. Above all, a cavalryman was always a gentleman.

Mac spent some time brushing the stallion then strolled among the tents and enjoyed the music. Despite the ugly wound on his face, several ladies flirted with him, and he knew they wouldn't mind if he asked them to dance. He disengaged from the conversations as politely as possible.

Tiring of the celebration, he headed back toward the part of the camp where Fitz Lee's staff was quartered. Before he could get there, however, he overheard a voice from behind. "There he goes, my dears. The brawling simpleton who'll soon get his just comeuppance."

Mac stopped and turned. Even though the voice was thick with drink, he had recognized it as Jason Trahearne's. The major stood there with several friends and three lovely young women, who giggled as Mac faced them.

Trahearne leered at Mac. "How does one feel to be court-martialed, Brannon?"

Mac knew that the smart thing to do would be to ignore Trahearne and go on to his tent, turn in, and perhaps get a better night's sleep than he'd had the previous night. He had always been the sort to follow the prudent course of action.

And what had it gotten him? he asked himself suddenly. Mac thought himself to be a reasonable, peaceful man, and yet he was in as much trouble as if he'd been the most rash, hot-headed firebrand in the cavalry.

As he looked at Trahearne's bruised, arrogant, and gloating face, Mac's jaw tightened in anger. The tension made the wound on his cheek twinge, and the painful reminder of his situation just made him more furious.

He took a step toward Trahearne, not knowing what he was going to do but not caring either, but before he could reach the major, a figure moved smoothly between them.

"Good evening, gentlemen," General Stuart said. "Enjoying the festivities?"

Mac stopped short. He knew that it was sheer luck that the general had come along just as he was about to confront Trahearne again. Stuart was much too involved with his party to have been keeping an eye on Mac. Still, he was willing to accept this stroke of good fortune. He took a deep breath and brought his raging emotions under control.

"Yes sir," Mac said. "It's a fine party."

"Wonderful, General, just wonderful," Trahearne said, smiling now and ignoring Mac.

Stuart put a hand on Mac's arm. "Under the circumstances, Captain, I think it would be best if you came along with me. I've prevailed upon your old friend Corporal Hagen to do a little jig for us, and he should be just about ready to begin."

"Thank you, General," Mac said. Not fully trusting himself, he didn't look in Trahearne's direction again as Stuart led him toward the huge tent at the center of the camp. But Mac was convinced he could feel Trahearne's hate-filled gaze boring into his back.

"It's lucky for you I came along when I did, Captain Brannon," Stuart said quietly, echoing what Mac had been thinking a few moments earlier. "Unless I miss my guess, you were about to square off with Major Trahearne again."

"No sir, I—" Mac stopped short. "I don't really know what I was about to do, General. The major baited me, and I'm afraid I was rising to it."

Stuart nodded, his bearded face serious in the light of the bonfires. "Captain, I know that you're a good soldier, and I know that Fitz Lee depends quite a bit on you. However, we simply can't have our officers brawling with each other, especially officers of unequal rank. Now, if you had challenged Major Trahearne to a duel, instead of simply attacking him, we might have been able to accommodate that. An affair of honor and all, you know. The way things are now . . . ," Stuart shook his head. "I have no choice but to bring you before a board of court-martial. Major Trahearne has his supporters among the general staff, and they will accept no less."

"Yes sir," Mac said, forcing the words past the lump in his throat. "I understand."

"The trial will convene tomorrow morning. The board will consist of myself, General Jones, and General Hampton."

Mac hesitated. "Begging your pardon, General, but Major Trahearne serves in General Hampton's brigade."

Stuart's voice was chilly and his eyes narrowed as he asked, "Do you believe that will prevent General Hampton from serving in a fair, unbiased manner?"

"No sir, not at all," Mac responded quickly, realizing he had made a dangerous misstep. "I have full faith in General Hampton's fairness."

"Good, because I do, too. He's a fine soldier."

"Yes sir." There was nothing else Mac could do except agree with Stuart.

They came up to a big tent, where Stuart was greeted with shouts of laughter by the group of officers and civilians gathered there. Corporal Hagen, a bearded giant of a man who was even larger than Heros Von Borke, stood waiting for the general to arrive before he began his dance.

Mac knew Hagen fairly well and had gone on several scouting missions with him. The big corporal was one of Stuart's particular favorites.

"Resin up those fiddles, boys!" Stuart called to the waiting musicians. "I want to see some dancing!"

Grinning, the fiddlers launched into a jig. Hagen clicked his heels together and began to dance with a grace and agility that was surprising in such a large man. The officers and guests clapped along with the music. Stuart sat down on a bale of hay, stretched one leg in front of him, and joined in the clapping. He looked up at Mac, who stood beside him, and said, "Don't worry about tomorrow, Captain. It'll bring whatever it brings. Just enjoy tonight while you have it."

"Yes sir," Mac acknowledged, summoning up a smile and beginning to clap along with the others.

It was all an act. The court-martial loomed in front of him like some sort of gigantic specter. There was no escaping the potential for disaster.

Tonight might be his last night in the cavalry.

THE STRAIN and lack of sleep finally caught up to him, and Mac was almost out on his feet by the time he stumbled into his tent and sprawled on his cot later that night. He fell into a deep, dreamless sleep and didn't awaken until dawn was breaking the next morning.

Stumbling out of the tent, he went over to a cook fire and claimed a cup of coffee and a piece of hardtack. The so-called Army Bread was so tough he had to let it soak in the coffee for a while before he could eat it. Even so, chewing still hurt his wounded face.

Despite the aggravation, the skimpy breakfast made him feel somewhat better. When he was finished, he walked over to Fitz Lee's tent and found the general already up and about.

"General Stuart has the court-martial set to convene this morning, sir," Mac told him.

Lee nodded. "I know. Have you sent word to your brother?"

"No sir. I never had a chance last night."

Lee waved a hand. "Well, don't worry about it, because I've already taken the liberty of doing so this morning. I know Will wants to be there."

"Yes sir. Thank you."

"As your commanding officer, I can't represent you, but I'll be making a statement in your behalf," Lee went on. "I know that some other officers will be, too. But Trahearne has his own friends and supporters. And I'm afraid the facts of the situation are fairly inescapable. You *did* strike a superior officer. We have to hope that the board of court-martial finds that Trahearne's actions were a sufficient provocation to justify what you did."

"In other words, sir, the only thing I can do is throw myself on the mercy of the court?"

Lee grinned. "That's about the size of it, Captain. Now, why don't you sit down and have some coffee and bacon with me before we go over there?"

Mac was about to refuse and say that he'd already had breakfast, but he decided he might as well go to his fate well fed.

"Thank you, sir," he said as he sat down on one of the logs that had been dragged up around the fire.

It was a beautiful late spring morning, warm and fair, a harbinger of the summer that was soon to come. Mac loved this time of day, and ordinarily he would be pleased to walk around the camp and feel the breeze and watch everything come to life for another day.

Today, however, might as well have been cold and rainy, to match Mac's mood. For over a year now, Trahearne had been a thorn in his side. Now, the major was finally going to get what he wanted. Mac was sure that if he was convicted and cashiered out of the cavalry, the stallion would be confiscated as part of his punishment. Once he was gone, Trahearne would have no trouble talking himself into ownership of the horse.

Suddenly, Mac wondered if that had been Trahearne's plan all along. Trahearne's last attempt to take the stallion had been clumsy, and his brandishing of the quirt where Mac could see him was like waving a red flag in front of a bull. Trahearne was smart enough to know that. The more Mac thought about it, the more he was convinced that Trahearne had known exactly what he was doing.

And he had played right into Trahearne's hands, Mac thought. He cursed himself for that, yet he knew that he could not have done anything else. Seeing the stallion threatened, he'd had no choice but to react as he had.

"You're looking mighty solemn, Mac," Lee said. "I suppose I can understand why."

"Yes sir," Mac replied, even though he was convinced that Lee had no idea what he was thinking.

Lee put his hands on his knees and pushed himself to his feet. "Well, I suppose we'd better get on over to General Stuart's headquarters." He extended his right hand. "Good luck, Mac. You have a lot of people rooting for you today."

"Thank you, sir," Mac said as he shook hands with Lee. "I hope all of you aren't disappointed."

Lee chuckled again, put on his hat, and led the way to the large tent in the center of the encampment. Stuart's headquarters tent was perched at the very top of the hill, giving him a commanding view of the countryside all around. To the west were more hills, gradually rising and becoming more rugged until they turned into the Blue Ridge Mountains. To the east was the plain where the grand review had taken place the day before, as well as the railroad line and beyond it, open fields alongside the winding, tree-lined Rappahannock River. It was a lovely panorama, Mac thought as he and Fitz Lee climbed the hill. It was too bad that nothing good waited for them at the top.

A table had been set up already, and the three members of the board of court-martial were seated behind it. Stuart was in the middle. To his right was Gen. William E. "Grumble" Jones, a balding, dour-looking man with a full beard and piercing eyes. Mac knew that Stuart and Jones could barely stand each other and that Jones's brigade had been assigned to Stuart's command over the objections of both men. Robert E. Lee wanted his cavalry consolidated, however, so Stuart and Jones had had no choice except to put their personal animosity aside and try to get along. So far it had been difficult. Mac supposed that Stuart had picked Jones for this board of court-martial so that there would be no question of its fairness. No one who knew both men would ever think that they could conspire together about anything.

The third member of the panel, to Stuart's left, was Gen. Wade Hampton from South Carolina, commander of the Hampton Legion. With his dark, wavy hair and full beard, he would have been a handsome man had it not been for the deep pouches in which his eyes sat and the pronounced lines of strain around his nose. He had a reputation as a fine commander and a man of great moral fortitude. The fact that Trahearne served under him was worrisome to Mac, but he knew Stuart was right: Hampton would be fair above all in his findings.

Flanking and behind the table where the three generals sat were dozens of other officers from their staffs. Mac saw Trahearne standing off to the side with some of his cronies. He also spotted Will leaning against a tree and felt a little better at the sight of his brother. Will gave him a grin and a reassuring nod.

An unloaded pistol lay on the table in front of Stuart. He picked it up and rapped the butt on the table. "This board of court-martial is now convened," he said loudly, and all the talk among the men gathered on the hilltop ceased. "We are here to consider the charge of striking a superior officer that has been brought against Captain MacBeth Brannon of the First Virginia Cavalry Brigade. Captain Brannon, have you a representative to speak for you?"

Mac stood at attention in front of the table. "No sir."

"Very well, then. Major Benjamin Reed of Colonel Robertson's staff will do so."

Reed stepped forward from the group of officers. He was young, no more than twenty-five, with sandy brown hair. Mac was acquainted with him, but only slightly. Reed gave Mac a curt nod, and Mac could tell that Reed was not too happy with being assigned to defend him. Stuart would not have picked him, though, if he hadn't thought Reed would do a competent job, Mac told himself.

It was too bad Nathan Hatcher wasn't here. Nathan had been studying to be a lawyer, and Mac was inclined to believe he'd be a good one. But Nathan's conscience wouldn't let him support the Confederacy, and he had gone off to join the Union army. Mac had no idea what had happened to him since then. He might not even be alive anymore.

"We'll begin by hearing from some of the officers who witnessed the incident between Captain Brannon and Major Trahearne," Stuart announced. "Major Crowe, are you ready?"

One of the officers who had been standing with Trahearne stepped forward and nodded. "Yes sir, quite ready. We call as our first witness Captain James Hughes."

For the next half-hour, Mac stood and listened grimly as a parade of witnesses condemned his attack on the major. All of them had been present when he attacked Trahearne. When Major Reed took his turn questioning them, he got them all to admit that Trahearne had threatened Mac's horse with the quirt. That made Trahearne flush with anger, but Mac didn't know how much good it did with the court-martial board. All three generals were carefully expressionless.

Finally, though, after just such an exchange, Grumble Jones snapped, "It don't matter why Captain Brannon did what he did. Fact is, he did it."

Mac's spirits sank even more at the blunt remark. Jones was right, of course.

Stuart, however, observed, "There are such things as mitigating circumstances."

"Only in the determination of punishment," Wade Hampton added. "Not in the determination of guilt or innocence."

Stuart nodded.

Mac could only stand by silently, hands clasped behind his back, trying to keep his roiling emotions from showing on his face. He was almost at the point now where he just wanted the affair to be over, no matter what the outcome.

Finally, Trahearne himself was called to testify by Major Crowe. "Major Trahearne," Crowe said, "you've heard the testimony of your fellow officers. Is it correct?"

"Yes, it is," Trahearne said steadily.

"Even the part about your raising a quirt as if you were about to strike Captain Brannon's horse?"

"I had a quirt in my hand, and I raised my hand," Trahearne said. "But I was not about to strike the horse. I was merely reacting to threatening gestures on the part of the animal. Captain Brannon would have seen that for himself if he had refrained from attacking me."

Reed glanced at Mac. It wasn't a good thing that Trahearne was getting to put his own interpretation on the story, Mac gathered. But there was nothing they could do about it.

"Why were you trying to take Captain Brannon's horse?"

"I wasn't going to *take* it. It's a beautiful animal. I just wanted a better look at it."

Crowe looked around and said, "No further questions."

Before Reed could step forward, Stuart interrupted, "You tried to buy that horse from Captain Brannon in the past, didn't you, Major?"

Trahearne's features tightened. "Yes sir. Captain Brannon refused to sell it."

"So you were already quite familiar with the animal?"

"I hadn't seen it close up in a while. I wanted to see how Captain Brannon was taking care of it."

The response sounded limp to Mac's ears, and he thought from the look on Stuart's face that the general didn't believe it, either. Again, though, would it really matter?

Reed began his cross-examination. "After Captain Brannon refused to sell his horse to you, you attempted to commandeer it, did you not, Major?"

Trahearne flushed. "Brannon was not a captain then. He was just a private. It was my belief that only an officer ought to ride such a fine animal as that. My actions were based on what I thought was best for the cavalry."

"I see," Reed said. "What about a later attempt that was made to steal Captain Brannon's horse? Do you know anything about that?"

Trahearne's face turned an even darker red. "By God, sir, I'll have satisfaction for that remark!"

Stuart snapped, "That's enough! You can deal with your wounded pride later, Major Trahearne. Please answer Major Reed's question."

Tightlipped, Trahearne said, "Yes sir. I know nothing about any attempt to steal Captain Brannon's horse, and for the record, I deeply resent the major's implication."

Hampton said, "Noted, Major."

Reed wasn't going to get Trahearne to budge from his denial, Mac thought, and to be honest, there was no proof that

Trahearne had had anything to do with that particular incident. Mac was certain that Trahearne had been behind it, but that wasn't evidence.

Reed shook his head and murmured, "Nothing further."

"We have nothing else," Crowe said.

Stuart looked at Reed. "We'll hear from the defense."

"Yes sir. The defense wishes to call first Brigadier General Fitzhugh Lee."

Lee gave Mac a grin as he stepped forward. With no prodding from Reed, he told of how he had stepped in to put a stop to it when Trahearne tried to commandeer the stallion. He testified as well that Mac had later become a member of his staff and served with courage and distinction as his aide. The praises he sang were effusive, and Mac felt a little embarrassed.

Grumble Jones put a stop to Lee's testimony. "It don't mean a thing. A good soldier can still be guilty as sin."

And that was exactly the case, Mac thought. He was guilty as sin.

Lee looked coldly at Jones. "The general is right, of course."

There was nothing else he could say, no other defense he could mount for Mac.

That left only Mac to speak in his own behalf, and he wasn't sure what to say. *He was about to hit my horse.* That was the sum total of his defense, and Trahearne had already denied that. Everyone who had been present knew that he was lying, yet there was no way to prove it. It was his word against Mac's—and Mac was only a captain, while Trahearne was a major. That was a card Mac could never trump.

"I've got something to say here."

Mac's head jerked around at the sound of his brother's voice. He saw Will stride forward, limping still from his Chancellorsville wound.

"Who are you, Captain?" Hampton demanded in answer to this sudden interruption. "And why are you here? You're obviously not a cavalryman."

"No sir," Will said as he came up to face the table where the generals sat. "I'm a member of the Thirty-third Virginia Regiment, from the Stonewall Brigade."

Stuart introduced him to the court. "I believe this is Captain William Brannon."

"Another Brannon, eh?" said Grumble Jones. "The brother of this'n?"

"Yes sir," Will said. "Mac's my little brother."

Crowe spoke next. "We object to this officer's testimony. Not only is he related to the defendant, but he was not present at the time of the attack on Major Trahearne."

"I've heard all about it," Will said sharply. "And I know my brother better than anybody else here. If he says Trahearne was about to take a quirt to that stallion, that's what happened. Where I come from, when a man's about to whip another man's horse, if he gets a beating he's got it coming."

Will's blunt statement was like setting a match to blasting powder. Trahearne's friends tried shouting him down. Crowe objected again. Finally, Stuart rapped the gun butt on the table. "Settle down!" he commanded.

Quivering with anger, Crowe addressed the court. "This officer has no right to be here, General, let alone to make such statements. They have no bearing on the charges against Captain Brannon."

Will ignored Crowe. "You gentlemen do whatever you want, but it just doesn't seem right to me to punish a man for handing a licking to a damned coward."

His comments started the chaos all over again. Trahearne lunged at Will, but a couple of his friends caught his arms and held him back. "Let me have my saber!" Trahearne raged. "We'll settle this here and now!"

"Major!" Stuart shouted. "This is a legal proceeding. We'll have no duels fought here today!" His eyes were glittering with fury as he swung his gaze back to Will. "Your statement is reprehensible, Captain."

"Begging your pardon, sir, but it's the truth." Will looked over at Trahearne, who was still shaking with anger. "Ask *him* what happened at Fredericksburg."

Mac jerked like he had been hit. He stepped forward and said, "No!"

Trahearne paled.

Mac caught hold of Will's arm. "Damn it, Will," he said in a half-whisper, "I told you about that in confidence."

"I don't care," Will said. "I'll be damned if I'll stand by and see you run out of the army on account of what you did to a man like Trahearne." He paused. "Hell, it never even occurred to you to bring that up, did it?"

As a matter of fact, it hadn't, Mac realized. The cowardice Trahearne had demonstrated at Fredericksburg had nothing to do with the current situation. Besides, there was something so ugly, so . . . dishonorable . . . about using something like that in his own defense.

Mac looked at the generals. "Sirs, I appreciate my brother's speaking in my behalf, but I disavow his statement—"

"Not so fast, Captain," Stuart cut in. "A very serious charge has been leveled here. I, for one, would like to get to the bottom of it."

"So would I," growled Wade Hampton, and even Grumble Jones nodded.

"Captain Brannon, what happened at Fredericksburg pertaining to you and Major Trahearne?" Stuart asked.

Before Mac could answer, Crowe interrupted. "General, I object! This isn't relevant—"

"This isn't a civilian court, Major. What's relevant is what we say is relevant." Stuart looked at Mac. "Captain?"

Mac swallowed. "Sir, I very respectfully decline to answer."

Will drawled, "You tell 'em or I will."

"Hearsay!" Crowe shouted. "It's not admissible."

"Again, Major, this is not a civilian court," Stuart said, ice in his voice. "One of you Brannons explain this."

Fitz Lee came up beside Mac and gripped his arm. "Whatever it is, you'd better tell them, Mac," he said quietly.

Mac looked over at Trahearne and saw the mixture of naked fear and blind hatred on the man's face. He hesitated a moment longer. "It's really nothing. During the battle, I saw the major surrendering to a number of Federals."

"There's nothing dishonorable about surrendering when you're outnumbered," Stuart pointed out.

"No sir."

"Tell it all," Will said, ignoring the look Mac gave him. "Tell them how you came across Trahearne while he was crying and begging for his life. Tell them how you went to his aid and how after you killed those Yankee soldiers, Trahearne tried to kill you to cover up his cowardice."

Mac looked down at the ground and didn't say anything. After a moment, Stuart prodded, "Captain?"

"That's . . . pretty much the way it happened, sir," Mac said. "Major Trahearne said that in the confusion he mistook me for one of the Yankees, and that was why he shot at me. But the Yankees were all dead by then."

"Killed by you?"

"Yes sir . . . Well, actually, I just killed two of them. My horse kicked the third one in the head and busted his skull."

"That horse again." For the first time since the court-martial had begun, a hint of a smile played over Stuart's lips. It vanished abruptly as the general looked over at Trahearne. "Major?"

Mac and all in attendance looked at Trahearne now and saw that he was standing more or less alone. The many men who had been clustered around him a moment before had pulled away now, retreating a few steps. Every one of them looked on Trahearne, their former friend, with expressions of regret and revulsion on their faces. Mac's words had had the ring of truth, and everyone here knew it.

"It . . . it's all a damned lie," Trahearne said. "I would *never* try to surrender to any number of Yankees, no matter how badly

I was outnumbered." His voice grew stronger, and his chin lifted in defiance. "It's a damned lie, I tell you!"

Wade Hampton leaned forward. "I think it *is* a damned lie that you tell us, Major. You're right about that, anyway."

After a moment, Stuart said, "Is there anything else? If not, the board will retire to its deliberations."

No one said anything as the three generals got to their feet and withdrew into Stuart's tent. Flanked by Fitz Lee and Will, Mac walked off a short distance to stand staring down the hill and breathing deeply. Major Reed followed them.

"Is all that true, Captain?" Reed asked as he came up alongside Mac.

"Yes sir," Mac said.

"Trahearne begged for his life to only three Yankees then tried to kill you because you witnessed the incident?"

"Yes sir."

"And one of the Yankees had an empty rifle," Will put in.

Fitz Lee said, "You should have told me about this, Mac. I'd have spread the word, and Trahearne would have been drummed out of the cavalry."

Mac looked at Lee. "Why would I do that, General? For all his faults, Trahearne's not a bad soldier. As far as I know, he's served honorably except for that one time."

Lee frowned and shook his head. "Blast it, Mac, you're as stiff-necked as my Uncle Bob."

"Considering that you're referring to General Robert E. Lee, sir, I take that as a great compliment."

Lee looked at Reed. "Does this change anything?"

Reed just shrugged. "Who can say? We won't know until they come back with their findings."

That didn't take too long. Less than half an hour later, Stuart thrust aside the flap of the headquarters tent and strode out, followed by Jones and Hampton. They went to the table and sat down as the large group of officers who had been awaiting their decision gathered again at the top of the hill.

Trahearne stood alone, except for Major Crowe, who didn't look too pleased. Mac was surrounded by people now. He had more supporters than when the proceeding had started, that was for certain. But as he looked at the grim faces of the three generals who sat at the table, he wasn't comforted. If their expressions meant anything, the decision had gone against him.

Stuart didn't have to rap the gun butt on the table to get everyone's attention this time. A tense silence hung over the hilltop. Stuart cleared his throat, looked one more time from right to left at Jones and Hampton. "It is the finding of this board of court-martial that Captain MacBeth Brannon is guilty of the charge of striking a superior officer."

Mac's jaw tightened. The decision was what he expected, but it hurt to hear it. He glanced over at Trahearne, who visibly relaxed. Trahearne was still upset that his act of cowardice at Fredericksburg had come out, but at least he had won his long-sought victory over Mac.

Stuart went on, "In accordance with the rules and regulations of the Army of Northern Virginia, we hereby levy the following punishment on Captain MacBeth Brannon. Captain Brannon?"

Mac forced his muscles to work and took a step forward. "Yes sir?"

"You will be assigned extra duties, said duties to be determined by your commanding officer, for a period of one week." Stuart banged the gun butt on the table. "This board of court-martial is concluded."

Mac stared at the generals, unable to comprehend for a moment what he had just heard, and when the meaning of the words soaked into his stunned brain, he was barely able to believe it.

Trahearne seemed to grasp the implications immediately, because he exclaimed angrily, "No! Damn it, no!"

Stuart, Jones, and Hampton were getting to their feet. Stuart turned toward Trahearne and said sharply, "Major, these proceedings are over. Therefore, I can speak off the record as one officer to another. The best thing you can do for yourself and for the cavalry is to tender your resignation."

Trahearne shook his head, looking so stunned that he was on the verge of passing out. "No, I . . . I can't." He stared at Wade Hampton. "General, you know I'm a good officer."

"You were," Hampton said. "That's what makes this so regrettable. Like all men, you have moments of weakness and temptation, Major. Unfortunately, you give in to them." He turned away, clearly dismissing Trahearne from his thoughts.

Fitz Lee and Will came up beside Mac. Will pounded him on the back. "It's about time somebody saw things straight around here," he said.

"Let's not lose sight of the fact that you were convicted, Mac," Lee added. "There *will* be extra duties for you, in accordance with the finding of the board. You can count on that."

"Yes sir," Mac said. "I'll accept whatever you decide."

Lee put out his hand. "That said, I never thought I'd be shaking hands with an officer who'd been court-martialed, but put 'er there, Mac."

Mac looked past Lee as he shook the general's hand. If it was possible, Trahearne was more alone now than ever. Even Major Crowe had drifted away, leaving Trahearne to stand by himself. Trahearne's face was flushed and his chest rose and fell rapidly from his labored breathing. He looked as if he were on the verge of apoplexy.

Instead, he suddenly jerked his saber from its scabbard and bellowed, "Brannon! Damn you! Let's settle this, man to man!"

With that, he charged at Mac, the saber upraised.

Will stepped forward, his hand undoing the flap of the holster on his hip. With practiced ease, he drew the Colt Navy and looped his thumb around the hammer as he brought it up. The revolver came to full cock as he leveled it at Trahearne's chest.

Mac was too surprised to move. He stood there staring as Trahearne stopped short. Trahearne was no more than eight feet away. At this range, Will couldn't miss.

"Plenty of witnesses this time, Major," Will said. "If you're determined to try to murder my brother, well, I reckon I'll just have to shoot you in defense of his life."

Trahearne stood there, quivering, torn between his insane desire for revenge and the preservation of his own life.

From the headquarters tent, Stuart snapped, "Major Trahearne! You have two choices: Leave this camp immediately and never return, or be placed under arrest and clapped in irons. It's up to you."

For a long moment, Trahearne made no response. Then, slowly, he lowered his saber. The steel of the blade rattled against the scabbard as he replaced it. Trahearne looked more sick than angry now. He looked around at the officers still gathered there, but none of them would meet his gaze. Surrounded he might be, but he was also utterly alone.

He turned and began to walk down the hill. His pace was slow and rather awkward. He did not look back.

As Mac watched him go, Will observed, "Good Lord. You feel sorry for the son of a bitch, don't you?"

Mac shook his head. "Not a bit. He got what was coming to him."

But Will knew Mac all too well. There was a small part of him that did feel sorry for Trahearne. As Hampton had said, Trahearne had been tested, as all men are from time to time, and he had failed by giving in to his fear and greed. That failure tainted all the other times Trahearne had passed the tests. The bad, as always, outweighed the good.

And someday, Mac knew, the test would come that *he* would fail. No man left this world without that bitter taste in his mouth at least once.

Fitz Lee put a hand on his shoulder, breaking into those bleak thoughts. "Well, I'm glad that's over," Lee said. "Now we can get back to our real business: fighting Yankees!"

Chapter Nine

ALTHOUGH THE PRESS OF military affairs had prevented Gen. Robert E. Lee from attending the grand review on June 5, on June 7 Stuart received a message from Lee saying that he would be pleased to review the cavalry the next day.

It was short notice, but Stuart was not going to pass up the opportunity to parade his troops before the commanding general of the Army of Northern Virginia. All the civilians had gone home, so this would be much less of a spectacle, but Stuart was confident Lee would be impressed by the Confederate cavalry and therefore impressed with him.

Earlier in the spring, following the great and unexpected victory at Chancellorsville that had been tempered by the death of Stonewall Jackson, Stuart had expected to be given command of Jackson's division. Instead, Lee had reorganized his army into three corps commanded by Gens. James Longstreet, Richard S. Ewell, and A. P. Hill. Those close to Stuart knew how upset he was by Lee's decision and how he felt that the command that had gone to Hill should have gone to him instead.

Stuart was adaptable, however, and his ambition was leavened by his devotion to duty. True, he had been passed over, in his mind unjustly, but there would be another day and another decision to be made. He would show Lee just how outstanding the Confederate cavalry really was, and when the next opportunity for promotion arose, surely Lee would do the right thing and select Gen. James Ewell Brown Stuart.

So the orders went out through the five brigades, commanding the men to prepare for yet another review. This event would be staged in the same location, at the foot of Fleetwood Hill, overlooking Brandy Station and the Rappahannock River.

Mac was surprised when he heard the news, but not too surprised. As much as he admired Stuart, he knew the man would never pass up a chance to show off.

Mac brushed the stallion on the morning of June 8 in preparation for the review. As he did, he thought of Jason Trahearne, who, just as Stuart had suggested, had resigned from the cavalry and departed the camp.

Before Will returned to his company, he had warned Mac, "You'd better keep an eye on your back from here on out. Trahearne's the sort to turn bushwhacker."

Mac didn't believe that was going to happen. Trahearne was gone for good, too humiliated to ever return and risk facing his former comrades in the cavalry.

As Mac saddled the stallion, he heard several muttered complaints from the men about having to stage another review so shortly after the first one. "Old Beauty's just interested in putting on a show," one of them said.

"It's sure a waste of horseflesh," another agreed.

Mac understood why the men felt this way. These reviews accomplished nothing militarily. As Fitz Lee had said, the cavalry's real business was fighting Yankees, and parading up and down had nothing to do with that. But Stuart had issued the order, so everyone would obey.

By midday, all was ready. Robert E. Lee arrived on his famous horse, Traveller, followed by his staff. Stuart rode out to greet the commanding general with garlands of flowers draped around his neck and around the neck of his mount. Mac had been hard put not to laugh when he saw the way the general was decked out in blossoms. He noticed several other men looking down to hide their amusement.

Fitz Lee came up beside Mac in a carriage accompanied by several young women who were either relatives or friends of relatives. He grinned at Mac and slapped the thigh of the leg he had stretched out in front of him.

"Rheumatism's acting up in the knee this morning," he said. "I had to ask Tom Munford to lead the men in my absence." Suddenly something caught his attention, and he pointed over Mac's shoulder. "Look over there . . ."

Mac turned and saw what appeared to be a wall of gray coming along the river toward Fleetwood Hill. "What's that?" he asked, startled.

"Looks like a whole blasted infantry division," Fitz Lee said. "At least they're on our side, judging by those uniforms. Go find out about it, Mac."

"Yes sir," Mac said. He heeled the stallion into a trot that carried him down the hill and across the fields toward the oncoming newcomers.

As he came closer, he saw rank after rank of Confederate soldiers marching toward him. A group of officers rode in front. Mac came up to them, reined in, and saluted. He said to the tall, erect man who seemed to be in charge, "General Fitzhugh Lee's compliments, sir. He sent me to assist you." He was shading the truth a little, but this was a general he was talking to. Mac couldn't very well ask the man who he was and what he was doing here.

The general returned Mac's salute then announced, "Please return my compliments to General Lee, Captain. He invited us here today for the show."

"Sir?"

"Please tell him that John Bell Hood and his men are honored to witness this review of General Stuart's cavalry."

"Yes sir." Mac had heard of Hood. Although not a Texan by birth, Hood had served there in the regular army before the war, and since resigning his commission to join the Confederacy, he had been given command of a hard-fighting brigade of Texans, all of whom, it appeared, were with him now.

Mac turned the stallion and galloped back. "General Hood sends his compliments, sir. He says you invited him and his people to the review."

Lee's eyes widened in surprise. "I meant for him and his staff to attend. I didn't expect his entire division!"

"Well, it appears they're here, sir, so I don't know what we can do about it other than make them welcome."

For a moment, Fitz Lee looked angry, but then his natural good humor took over and he threw back his head and laughed. "You're right as usual, Mac," he said. "Make sure they have a good spot to watch the party."

Hood's division settled down along the river while the five cavalry brigades formed up in the fields at the base of the hill. When everything was in readiness, Robert E. Lee and Stuart rode side by side in front of the assembled cavalry. Lee nodded his satisfaction and from time to time spoke to Stuart, who appeared pleased by what his superior had to say. Once they had completed their pass in front of the troops, they returned to the hilltop, where they sat as the brigades paraded one by one in front of them.

The only calamity was a minor one. Grumble Jones's brigade, thinking that the review was finished when Stuart and Lee returned to the top of Fleetwood Hill, had fallen out, dismounted, and were taking their rest in a nearby field. Stuart spotted this problem in time to have an aide rush to the spot and order Jones's men back into line. Jones lived up to his nickname, grumbling complaints the whole time, but he got his men back where they were supposed to be before Robert E. Lee noticed that anything was amiss.

Mac heard about that incident later and chalked it up as one more example of the friction between Stuart and Jones. It was possible that the mistake had been an honest one, but Mac doubted it. Jones probably had wanted to embarrass Stuart in front of the commanding general.

Finally the review was over, and rumors began to fly. The most common story was that Lee had told Stuart the army was moving northward to invade Yankee territory. Remembering the discussion he'd had with Will about strategy, Mac believed the rumor. It made perfect sense.

As the afternoon went on, everything began to indicate the truth of the speculation. Stuart ordered that camp be broken. His headquarters tent was taken down. It and everything it contained were loaded onto wagons that rolled off in the direction of Culpeper. Only a small tent remained at the top of Fleetwood Hill, and that was where Stuart would spend the night.

In the meantime, orders for movement went out to the five cavalry brigades. Mac packed his gear and rode with the First Virginia as they headed up the Rappahannock River to a new camp at Oak Shade Church. They were the northwesternmost unit; the other brigades were strung out to the southeast along the river: Rooney Lee at the little community of Welford; Grumble Jones and the horse artillery near St. James Church and Stuart's former headquarters at Fleetwood Hill; Beverly Robertson's North Carolinians on the Botts farm; and finally, at the other end of the line more than ten miles from Fitz Lee's new camp, the Hampton Legion under Wade Hampton. When the order came to move north, as Mac was sure it would, the five brigades could cross the Rappahannock and present an impressive front.

After Mac had his tent pitched that evening, he went to the headquarters tent to make sure Fitz Lee didn't need him for anything. "Feeling better, General?" he asked. Lee was sitting at a small folding table, studying a map by the light of a lantern.

For one of the few times since Mac had known him, Lee seemed depressed. His ready smile was nowhere in sight. "This knee really is acting up, Mac," he said. "I thought staying off horseback today would help it, but it hasn't. Can you go find Tom Munford for me?"

"Of course, sir," Mac replied. He sketched a quick salute and departed in search of Col. Thomas Munford.

He found Munford's tent and brought the colonel back to Lee's headquarters.

"Good evening, Tom," Lee said when they came into the tent. "You did a good job leading the troops while I was, ah, incapacitated at the review this afternoon."

"Thank you, sir," Munford said. "It was my honor and privilege to be placed in command, even temporarily."

"Well, you still are, at least until this blasted rheumatism goes away. Make a note of that, Mac. Colonel Munford has assumed temporary command of the brigade."

"Yes sir."

Munford shook hands with Lee. "Thank you, General. I won't let you down."

"I know that." Lee smiled. "Better go get a good night's sleep. That goes for you, too, Mac. I reckon when we move, we'll move hard and fast, and the order could come at any time."

Mac went to his tent and stretched out on his cot. The past few days had been exceedingly hectic. He had barely had time to think, so he hadn't had much opportunity to brood about Tra-hearne or the court-martial or anything else. The court-martial, despite its outcome, would be a stain on his record, and he would have been more worried about that if he intended to remain in the army after the war was over.

But that was the furthest thing from his mind. He enjoyed the friendships he had formed with Fitz Lee and some of the other cavalrymen, but when peace finally returned to the South, Mac would go back to the farm and spend the rest of his days there, hopefully to never take up arms or put on a uniform again. Some men took naturally to the military life; Mac thought that Will, in many ways, was one of them. But not him. At heart, he was a civilian and always would be.

He went to sleep thinking about the farm and his family.

EXCITED SHOUTS jolted him out of his slumber. Mac jerked upright and swung his legs off the cot, grabbing for his pistol and saber as he did so. He came to his feet and lunged out of the tent. A trooper ran past, yelling, "Yankees! Everybody up! Yankees!"

Mac listened but didn't hear any artillery or rifle fire. He grabbed the soldier's arm to stop him. "Where?" he asked. "Where are they?"

"Downriver," the man replied, his voice high-pitched with excitement. "They hit Grumble Jones's bunch a little while ago! A galloper just got here with the news!"

The night was very dark around the camp, but when Mac glanced toward the east, he saw a faint gray lightness in the sky. It was after four o'clock in the morning, he judged. It would be dawn in an hour, maybe less.

He let go of the trooper's arm. "Keep spreading the word." Then he stepped back into the tent to pull on his boots and tunic and clap his cap on his head. He buckled on his holster and scabbard as he hurried toward Fitz Lee's headquarters.

Colonel Munford was outside Lee's tent, snapping orders. He saw Mac. "Glad you're here, Captain. See that the horses of the staff officers are saddled and brought up as quickly as possible. We're moving downriver to the aid of General Jones."

"Yes sir," Mac replied with a quick salute. He would have preferred getting his orders from Fitz Lee personally, but for the moment Munford was in command.

By the time a quarter of an hour had passed, the men were ready to move. Mac swung up onto the stallion's back and rode over to his usual spot, near the commander. Lee's absence made Mac a bit ill at ease. It was foolish to be superstitious, he knew, but he believed in Lee's ability to lead the cavalry to victory against almost any odds.

Munford ordered the brigade to advance downriver. The cavalrymen moved out at a brisk trot through the predawn gloom. As they rode along at the head of the column, Munford said worriedly to Mac, "I don't know how many men the Yankees have on this side of the river. The messenger wasn't clear on that. But I expect it's a good-sized force."

"Yes sir, probably," Mac replied. He didn't know what Munford wanted from him, blind agreement or an actual discussion of the situation.

"Well, no matter," Munford said. "If all five of our brigades come together again, the Federals won't stand a chance."

Unless it was the whole blasted Army of the Potomac streaming across the Rappahannock, thought Mac. But surely that was impossible. All the scouts said that Hooker was still somewhere near Fredericksburg.

A thick mist hung over the river and the adjoining fields, making it hard to see very far in advance. The brigade hadn't gone far, however, before the sound of cannon fire came to them. As the roar of artillery grew louder, they knew they were going in the right direction. "Ride to the cannons" was an old adage in the cavalry.

The horsemen picked up the pace as they neared the battle. Well ahead of the main body of the brigade, Munford, Mac, and a few more officers galloped up a long rise and reined in when they reached the crest of the hill. The sky had lightened and the mist had thinned so that they could see what was going on down below. The steeple of St. James Church was visible in the distance to the right. The river was to the left, and straight ahead was another small ridge with a stone wall running along the top of it. Hundreds of men were clustered behind that wall and fired toward the area between the river and the church. Their horses were gathered in a huge mass behind them.

"Who's that?" Munford snapped at Mac.

Mac brought out his telescope, squinting as he tried to locate a guidon. After a moment he found one and recognized its markings. "Those are General Rooney Lee's men, sir."

Munford nodded. "They've moved down in support of General Jones. We'll do the same. Order the men up to the right of the line."

The orders were passed back to the waiting troopers, who boiled over the hill and streamed down the far side. It wasn't a classic charge, because they weren't riding head-on toward the enemy, but the advance had something of the same feeling. Mac was caught up in the press of galloping horses and riders. The brigade surged up the second hill and found themselves looking down at a narrow road that led from the river to St. James

Church. That road, however, was clogged with blue-clad cavalry and infantry trying to reach the church and the camp of Grumble Jones. Mac's first impression was that the Yankees had penetrated Jones's pickets and reached almost as far as the camp, but now they were being forced back slowly.

More gunfire came from the far side of the Union salient. That would be either Beverly Robertson or Wade Hampton, up from the southeast to lend a hand to Jones, just as the other two brigades had hurried downriver from the northwest. Both Robertson and Hampton might be over there, Mac thought. In that case, the Union thrust across the Rappahannock was probably doomed.

But if all five brigades were together, that left other fords open and exposed to a Federal advance.

The cavalrymen piled off their horses and found what cover they could, even if it meant stretching out on the dew-wet ground at the top of the ridge. Their carbines began to bark as they opened fire on the Yankees. Mac didn't dismount; he wheeled the stallion around and hurried over to Munford, wondering if he ought to suggest that he locate Stuart and find out what else was going on downriver.

Mac didn't have to make the suggestion. Munford saw him.

"Captain Brannon, carry a message to General Stuart! Tell him we have moved into position to support General Rooney Lee and push back the Yankees!"

Mac snapped a salute, acknowledged the order, and heeled the stallion into a run. He pointed the horse straight at Fleetwood Hill, where Stuart had remained overnight following the second grand review.

As he raced through the fields, it struck Mac as strange that less than twenty-four hours earlier, this had been the site of that review, and a few days before that, the earlier one with all its pomp and splendor. If the Yankees had been able to strike them then, unsuspecting as they were, the results could have been disastrous. As it was, both sides seemed to be in for a stiff battle, and instead of music from the military bands and laughter from the ladies, the air was filled now with powder smoke and the blasting of artillery.

The stallion pounded up the hill toward the small tent that still stood there. Mac saw a lone figure standing in front of it, bareheaded in the early morning. He reined to a halt and saluted General Stuart.

"Compliments of Colonel Munford, sir, in temporary command of General Fitzhugh Lee's brigade!"

"Speak your piece, Captain Brannon," Stuart said calmly. He lowered the field glasses he had been using to study the battle spread out below him.

"We're in position to support General Rooney Lee, sir." Mac ventured to add, "It looked to me like the Yankees were just about stopped in their tracks."

"To me, too, from what I could see of the conflict," Stuart agreed. "I take it that Fitz is still indisposed if Tom Munford is still in command."

"His bad knee is acting up, sir."

Stuart nodded. "Tell Colonel Munford that I've sent Colonel Robertson downriver to watch the other fords. We have four brigades here; that should be plenty to take care of the Yankees."

"Yes sir."

"And keep an eye on your backs," added Stuart. "Occasionally one of those Federal commanders will try something clever to cross us up."

"Yes sir," Mac said again. There was always the danger of a flank attack, especially in the early morning like this when the light wasn't as good and it was harder to keep track of the enemy's movements.

He wheeled the stallion and rode back to Munford's position, passing along Stuart's orders when he arrived. The brigade, of course, was already executing just what Stuart had ordered it to do, which was to pour its massed fire into the Yankees on this side of the Rappahannock.

The sun rose and began to burn off the mist that cloaked the river and the fields. As the fog dissipated and the sun climbed higher in the sky, Mac could see that the Yankees, despite heavy losses, were clinging stubbornly to the ground they had gained on this side of the river. By midmorning, the Union cavalry fell back, but the Yankee infantry moved up to take its place.

The guns of the horse artillery, located primarily near St. James Church, continued a steady fire. From where he sat on the stallion, Mac could see the shells bursting among the Union lines, flinging Yankee soldiers into the air and tearing them to pieces. Although infinitely more hardened to battle than he had been when he joined the cavalry, Mac still felt a bit sick when he saw the human destruction on what should have been a glorious morning.

Several times during the morning, Munford dispatched him to ride along the line and bring back reports of casualties, which had been light so far among the brigade. As midday approached, Munford spotted Stuart and his staff riding down from the top of Fleetwood Hill. He pointed out the party to Mac and dispatched him to see what the general was up to.

Mac nodded. He rode in a large half-circle, skirting the battle so he could intercept Stuart's group near the church. As he trotted up to join them, the general grunted a greeting.

"You boys are making a good account of yourselves," Stuart said. "Fitz should be proud."

"I'm sure he is, sir, and I'm sure he wishes he could be here as well."

Stuart made no objection, so Mac rode along with the group. When they reached the church, which was cloaked in a cloud of powder smoke from the cannons, they encountered a courier.

"General Stuart!" the man called out as he reined in. "I have a message from General Jones!"

"Let's have it," Stuart snapped.

"We have word from Colonel Robertson, sir, that a Federal column is on its way here from Kelly's Ford."

Stuart didn't appear worried as he heard the news. "All right, son," he told the courier. "Ride back and tell General Jones to attend to the Yankees in his front, and I'll watch the flanks."

"But sir—"

"Get going, Lieutenant."

"Yes sir." The courier turned his horse and galloped off toward the front.

"If the Yankees came across at Kelly's Ford, Robertson is there to deal with them," Stuart said as much to himself as to any of his companions.

That wasn't the way the message had sounded to Mac. The courier had made it sound as if the Union column had gotten past Robertson and was now bearing down on Brandy Station and Fleetwood Hill. But he was only a captain and Stuart was a general, and Stuart didn't seem concerned.

After a while, though, as the fighting between the church and the river entered a lull, Stuart began glancing to the rear. Finally he looked at Mac and crooked a finger.

"I left my adjutant, Major McClellan, back on top of the hill. Why don't you ride up there, Captain, just to make sure that he's all right."

"Of course, sir," Mac agreed. He already had the stallion's reins in his hand. Mac mounted and rode toward the top of Fleetwood Hill, passing a single cannon at the base of the slope.

When he got there, not seeing anyone around the tent where Stuart had spent the night, he rode on past and headed toward a large red-brick house a short distance down the far slope.

The house belonged to a family named Barbour, he recalled, and it had been taken over the night before by Robert E. Lee and his staff. Mac spotted Maj. Henry McClellan, Stuart's adjutant and a cousin of the famous Yankee general, standing near the Barbour house and looking toward Brandy Station through a pair of field glasses.

Mac looked in that direction, too, and shocked at what he saw, he pulled the stallion to an abrupt halt. A thick dust cloud rose from the hooves of a large Union cavalry force riding hard and fast toward Brandy Station. They would sweep past the depot within minutes, and nothing stood between them and Fleetwood Hill.

McClellan heard the hoofbeats and looked around at Mac. "Captain, the Yankees are almost upon us."

"Yes sir. Can we hold the hill?" Mac suddenly felt like a tiny pebble in the face of an onrushing tide.

"I have only a few men and General Lee and his staff," McClellan replied, casting a nervous glance at the house.

An idea came to Mac. "Major, there's a cannon down at the bottom of the hill. If we could get it up here in time . . ."

McClellan seized the thought. "Were the gunners nearby?"

"I believe so, sir."

"Get them up here, Captain, as quickly as you can!"

Mac wheeled the stallion and galloped over the ridge, back toward the place where he had seen the field piece. It was still there, along with the gun crew assigned to it. Mac spotted the man in charge, a young officer. "Lieutenant, move this piece to the top of the hill and commence firing on the Yankees on the other side!"

The gunners looked shocked to hear that the Yankees were that close, but they sprang into action. "I've only got a few rounds," the lieutenant said to Mac as the mules attached to the cannon began pulling it up the slope.

"Whatever you've got, it'll have to do," Mac replied.

His heart pounded hard in his chest. If the Yankees took Fleetwood Hill, not only would they be in position to utterly destroy the Confederate cavalry with their artillery, but they would probably be capable of capturing Robert E. Lee as well. That could prove to be a death blow to the Confederacy. The slender line at the top of the hill had to hold off the Union column at all costs.

As Mac and the gunners were getting the field piece up the hill, a courier from McClellan galloped past, going the other direction. McClellan had sent the man to warn Stuart of the dangers, Mac guessed.

"Get that gun in position and open fire whenever you're ready, Lieutenant!" McClellan ordered as Mac and the others arrived at the top of the hill.

"I'm mighty low on ammunition, sir," the lieutenant said.

"Then fire slow and steady and make your shots count," McClellan advised. He looked at Mac. "I've just sent a rider to General Stuart, Captain, but I want you to go, too. He'll be more likely to believe two couriers than one."

Mac hesitated. He wanted to stay on the hill and do what he could to hold back the Yankee advance, but he might be able to do more good if he could convince Stuart to meet this new threat. He nodded and acknowledged the order.

Stuart did not look happy when Mac raced up to the general's position near St. James Church a few minutes later. He just glared at the courier dispatched earlier by McClellan.

Clearly, the messenger had delivered the news, but the general was either unwilling or unable to accept it. He turned to an aide and ordered him to verify the situation. "Ride back there and find out what all this foolishness is about."

"General—!" Mac said, daring to interrupt. But before he could go on, a booming report came from the top of the hill. The lieutenant and his men had gotten their lone cannon into action.

"What in the world!" Stuart exclaimed. "Captain Brannon?"

"This fella's right, General," Mac said, gesturing at the first courier. "By now the Yankees are in Brandy Station and bearing down on the hill."

Stuart stared toward the top of Fleetwood Hill, and in his eyes Mac saw the bleak knowledge that Lee was up there.

"I want four more artillery pieces up there—now!" Stuart barked. "Have General Jones pull two of his regiments out of the line and send them up the ridge as well."

Aides sprang into action to carry out Stuart's orders. The general turned to Mac. "Your brigade is in position to support the right side of the hill if need be, Captain. Tell Colonel Munford I said to do so."

"Yes sir!"

Mac rode as hard as he could toward the ridge where the brigade had been when he left it. He found it still there. As he galloped up, Colonel Munford called out, "Captain, where have you been?"

"With General Stuart and on Fleetwood Hill, sir," Mac replied somewhat breathlessly. The stallion was holding up fine, and he was thankful for that. "A Yankee column is bearing down on the hill, sir. We're to move into position to support the defenders. General Stuart's orders, sir."

Munford signaled for his horse. "Very well. Get up there and let whoever is in charge know that we're coming."

"Yes sir!"

So Mac was off again, the wind in his face, holding his cap on with one hand while the other gripped the reins. He started up the hill and saw more cannons being wrestled into position. The regiments that Jones had sent to the relief of the defenders were almost at the top. As Mac rode closer, Jones's men swarmed over the crest. A handful of heartbeats later, Mac heard a loud, clashing noise as the two cavalry forces crashed together. The rattle of small-arms fire, the ringing of sabers, the heavy thud of horse against horse. Mac reached the top of the hill and stopped short at the sight of the grim spectacle spread out before him.

This was no grand review, no mock battle. This was the real thing, a confusing array of blood and smoke and death. The Union and Confederate lines had slammed together no more than fifty yards from the crest of the hill.

Mac glanced at the Barbour house. It was safe for the moment, far off to the side of the fighting. But the battle could spread in that direction at any moment. He saw the sun reflect from something in the cupola atop the big house. Field glasses, perhaps. It might well be that Robert E. Lee himself was watching the battle that could decide his fate and the fate of the South.

Mac looked around for Major McClellan but didn't see him. At that moment, the line of resistance thrown up by the men from Jones's brigade crumbled and collapsed. Howling like madmen, sounding more like Rebels than Yankees, the Union cavalry swept on toward the hastily erected artillery pieces. The gunners met them with revolvers and handspikes and sponge staffs, fighting desperately as the positions were overrun.

Mac had no choice but to join the battle. The enemy was in his face now. He drew his pistol and emptied it into the line of blue-clad horsemen, shoved the gun back in its holster, and pulled his saber from the scabbard. With a yell he drove the stallion forward and began slashing at the Federal cavalrymen.

As always at moments such as this, Mac's sense of reality disappeared, leaving only the battle and the instinct for survival. He hacked and slashed with the saber, brutal man-to-man fighting at quarters so close that a trooper lucky enough to escape injury still found himself covered with blood as it splattered from the wounds of his enemies.

Mac leaned in to run his blade through a Yankee then ripped it free as the stallion danced back, seemingly as light on its feet as a cloud. Turning in the saddle, Mac swung hard at another Yankee and felt the jolt in his hand as the saber sheered the man's arm at the elbow. The Yankee screamed and fell off his horse, and that was the last Mac saw of the man.

He found himself pressed forward, Union cavalrymen all around him now, but they were retreating. For a moment, they had taken the top of the hill, but the timely arrival of Colonel Munford's reinforcements had driven them away from the crest. Still fighting, Mac was near the bottom of the hill before he knew what was going on.

A Federal artillery battery had been set up there, and the Yankee gunners were about to get the cannons into action. Mac lunged among them, riding like a daredevil. He thrust his saber through the neck of one man, cut down another with a sweeping slash, broke the jaw of a third with a kick. Then he shoved his foot back in the stirrup and wheeled the stallion. The big silver gray horse moved so fast it seemed as if all the other men and animals around it were stock still.

Mac's saber chopped into the neck of another man, then the stallion sprang aside as a pistol cracked right behind them. The bullet whined past Mac's ear. He twisted and brought the saber around, raking it across the belly of a Union rider so that the man's intestines spilled out through the horrible wound.

Mac drove his heels into the stallion's flanks and sent the horse back up the hill, out of the bloody melee. When he reached the crest, he saw that Stuart himself had arrived to supervise the defense. Mac turned to look back down the slope. The Yankee officers had stopped the retreat from turning into a full-fledged rout. In fact, they had gathered their forces and seemed to be readying for another charge up the hill. A moment later, that was exactly what happened. The Union cavalry charged, and forces from Jones's brigade that had survived the initial clash countercharged.

This time, Mac stayed back, looking for Colonel Munford. He found the colonel. "I'm afraid I never got the chance to tell anyone that you were on the way, Colonel," he said.

"From the looks of you, Captain, you probably got the message across," Munford said.

Mac glanced down at himself. His uniform was splashed with blood, but most of it seemed not to belong to him. He had only a few cuts and scrapes, nothing serious.

He sat there on horseback and watched the ebb and flow of the battle, charge and countercharge, advance and retreat. More men arrived, diverted from the battle around the church, and the tide began to turn against the Yankees. Mac shifted in his saddle to look toward the river, and he saw a flanking maneuver by the Yankees blunted by a breakneck charge from some of Rooney Lee's men.

By now it was past the middle of the afternoon. Time never moved normally in battle, Mac knew. Hours could fly past like minutes, and minutes could drag on like hours. In the midst of combat, nothing else existed, only life and death and the furious struggle to separate one from the other.

Finally, when the Union forces had been pushed back to Brandy Station, they began to withdraw, not only on that side but back across the river on the other side as well. The Confederates had retained their grip on Fleetwood Hill. Stuart ordered a defensive line along the southeastern side of the hill, just in case the Yankees came back and tried again, but that seemed highly unlikely. They'd had enough for one day.

Almost. In the distance, Mac saw the dust of another skirmish and found out later that it was another Yankee division being engaged and driven off by three Confederate regiments that had swung around to the southern flank just in case the Federals tried to slip up on them from that direction. Once those Yankee soldiers withdrew, the battle was truly over.

Mac dismounted and led the stallion by the reins when a carriage rattled up beside them. Fitz Lee brought the team to a halt. "Climb on up, Mac. I'll take you wherever you want to go."

Exhausted and grimy with powder smoke, Mac wasn't going to argue. He tied the stallion to the rear of the carriage and clambered up beside Lee. "Is your leg better, General?" he asked.

"Some. But, blast it, I missed all the fun today."

"Yes sir," Mac said. "We had plenty of it."

"I hear the boys did well."

"That they did, sir."

Lee flapped the reins and got the team moving again. "You didn't tell me where you wanted to go," he said.

Mac was fighting to keep his eyes open. "Home would be nice," he said drowsily. "Yes sir, mighty nice."

Fitz Lee looked at him, saw that Mac's eyes were closed now and his head tipped forward on his chest. Lee clucked to the horses and kept them moving, heading northwest away from Brandy Station.

Chapter Ten

FROM BONE-NUMBING COLD TO blazing heat: That was how conditions seemed to go at Camp Douglas. One day Titus was freezing, the next he was baking under the suffocating heat that settled down over the camp in the late spring of 1863.

Of course, he shouldn't complain too much about being hot, he reminded himself. For the greater part of the winter, he had been convinced that he would never live to see warmer weather.

He shuffled along just inside the deadline, Nathan beside him. Both young men were little more than skin and bone and hair. Even mild-mannered Nathan looked like a wild creature with his long, matted hair and tangled beard, his eyes sunken in and burning above hollow cheeks. Titus knew that he looked just as bad or worse.

They had no shoes, but the soles of their feet were so thick with calluses that they were like leather. Their uniforms were nothing more than rags. The only ones in the camp who were any better off were the recent arrivals, and Titus knew it was only a matter of time before they looked just like the rest of the men confined in this hellhole.

Nathan stumbled, but Titus's hand on his arm steadied him and kept him from falling. Nathan was closer to the deadline, and if he had tripped and gone sprawling on the ground, he might have fallen on the wrong side of the line. In that case, there was a good chance one of the Yankee guards stationed around the compound would shoot him before he could get back up. Titus had seen it happen before. Only a week earlier, a middle-aged sergeant from Mississippi had accidentally taken a half step over the line. Titus had been standing nearby and had seen the unfortunate man jerk as the bullet hit him in the side of the head and burst out the other side of his skull with a spray of brains and blood and bone fragments. The poor bastard probably died not knowing what had happened.

In the commandant's office, Capt. Floyd Morton would mark the dead man's name off the roster with the notation that he had been killed trying to escape. Another evil, godless Rebel gone. Titus could just see Morton smiling and nodding in satisfaction. If Morton could get away with it, he would exterminate every prisoner at once. That would look bad, however, so he had to settle for getting rid of them one or two at a time.

Titus and Nathan had walked around their barracks twice. Nathan's breath was labored. "That's all I can do."

Titus nodded. "We'll go inside and check on the colonel."

They were getting weaker and weaker. The terrible food and the exposure to the elements were taking their toll. Soon both Titus and Nathan would be like the oldtimers—living skeletons who lacked the strength or the will to move any more than absolutely necessary.

That meant their time was short. If they were going to escape, it had to be soon.

Thoughts—no, dreams—of getting out of here had been in Titus's head from the day he'd arrived at Camp Douglas. He had considered and discarded dozens of escape plans. Even though he had yet to come up with a scheme that had a chance of working, he knew he couldn't give up. To stay here was to die. He was convinced of that. And if he was dead, he couldn't kill any more Yankees.

He wasn't the only prisoner who harbored thoughts of escape. During the winter, some men in another barracks had actually tried it. They had taken up the floorboards and started a tunnel, digging with their bare hands all night and then replacing the boards the next morning so the guards wouldn't discover what they were doing. The barracks was fairly close to the outer fence, and although it had taken them weeks, the men finally succeeded in tunneling underneath the fence. They were noticed by a watchful guard when they made their break, and all but one were shot down as they raced for the distant trees outside the prison.

A few days later, the body of the one man who had gotten away was brought back to the camp and slung into one of the mass graves. He had frozen to death.

Titus had known then that he would have to wait until warmer weather to escape. Now spring was here and summer wasn't far away. It had to be soon.

He and Nathan climbed the steps into the barracks then clambered over the floor joists as they looked for Colonel Newberry. The actual floorboards had been pried up after the escape attempt, so that any more tunneling would be seen immediately by the guards. That left only the heavy beams that had supported the floor, with dirt a foot and a half below them. When the weather was rainy, as it had been quite often this spring, water ran under the buildings and turned the dirt into mud. But that was the only place the men could sleep, and at least they still had a roof over their heads.

The two Virginians found Colonel Newberry with his back against one of the beams that formed the foundation of the barracks. They dropped down beside him and perched atop one of the floor joists.

"How are you feeling, Colonel?" Nathan asked.

Newberry summoned a weak smile. "A bit better, actually," he said. "It's kind of you . . . to be concerned."

Titus heard the rattle and wheeze in the colonel's thin chest as he breathed. Newberry had suffered a bout of pneumonia in the late winter, and Titus had been convinced that the man was going to die. Newberry, however, had pulled through somehow, summoning up reserves of strength that he shouldn't have had remaining to him. But the illness had damaged his lungs, and he would never be the same again. Like everyone else in the camp, he was growing weaker, but the pace of Newberry's deterioration was even faster than the others.

Titus hadn't given up on getting the colonel out when he and Nathan escaped. That was another reason they couldn't wait much longer.

But so far he hadn't been able to figure out a way.

"I heard some . . . interesting news," Newberry said, struggling for breath between the words. "Some of the . . . new prisoners told me . . . that our boys beat the Yankees . . . at a place called Chancellorsville."

"Really?" Titus said. "Beat 'em bad?"

Newberry nodded.

"I've heard of Chancellorsville, but I don't reckon I've ever been there," Titus said with a grin. "It's good to know the Yankees got whipped again. You'd think they'd get the idea sooner or later that we're not goin' to give up."

"I'm afraid all the news . . . wasn't good. General Jackson . . . was killed in the fighting."

"Stonewall?" Titus exclaimed, startled. "Damn, that's bad. He was quite a general."

"Indeed," Newberry agreed. "The army will be . . . hard put to recover from his loss."

Titus wondered if Will and Mac had been involved in the battle. If they were still alive, they were probably in the thick of it, he thought.

Right now, though, the only war news he would have been interested in was if the war was over. That would mean the prisoners were going home. Since that seemed highly unlikely, he turned his thoughts back to the issue that consumed them most of the time.

He looked around the barracks. It was mostly empty. Anyone who could get up and move around was outside. The heat was bad, but at least the air wasn't quite as stuffy as it was inside the building. Leaning closer to Newberry and keeping his voice down, Titus said, "Colonel, we need to talk about a plan."

"What . . . plan?" Newberry asked. "I thought . . . you didn't have one."

"I don't. That's the problem. Colonel, we've got to get out of here." Titus heard the note of desperation edging into his voice but couldn't stop it.

Newberry smiled. "You, perhaps . . . my young friend. I fear I'm not going . . . anywhere."

"We're not going without you, Colonel," Nathan said.

Titus glanced at him and saw the determination on Nathan's haggard face. He understood how Nathan felt. Colonel Newberry had been a good friend to them, and back in the early days, right after they'd arrived at Camp Douglas, they might not have survived without the colonel to show them the ropes and warn them what could and couldn't be done.

On the other hand, despite his fondness for Newberry, Titus didn't want to promise that they wouldn't make the escape attempt unless the colonel could accompany them. The most important thing was to get out of here and get back to the business of killing Yankees. Everything else had to come behind that objective.

"You're our strategist, Colonel," Nathan went on. "Titus and I don't know anything about escaping."

"I appreciate . . . the sentiment, Mr. Hatcher . . . but at the moment I fear my brain . . . has nothing to offer. If those . . . poor devils hadn't dug their tunnel . . . back in the winter . . . I would suggest that approach." Newberry waved at the bare joists and the dirt floor of the barracks. His hand was so thin that light shone through it and outlined the brittle bones. "Now that would appear . . . impossible."

"If we had some sort of diversion," Titus thought out loud, "we might make it to the fence and get over before they could stop us."

Newberry shook his head. "You'd be . . . shot down before you got . . . a dozen yards."

"Well, we have to do *something.*"

"Be patient," Newberry murmured. "Patient . . ."

To hell with patience, thought Titus. The only thing being patient got a man in a fix like this was dead.

LATER IN the day, when they were outside again, making another endless shuffling walk around the barracks, Titus turned to Nathan. "Am I makin' a mistake by trusting you?"

Nathan stopped short and looked at him. "What do you mean by that?"

Titus picked a louse off himself as it crawled out of his beard onto his bottom lip. He looked at the ugly little thing for a second before crushing it between his thumbnails. As he flicked it away, he said, "Once we finally figure out what we're going to do, how do I know you won't tell Sergeant O'Neil all about it?"

Nathan glared at him. "I thought that's what you meant. After all this time, you don't trust me, Titus?"

Titus tugged on his tangled beard. "I want to," he said after a moment. "I really do. I know you say you ain't got no more use for the Yankees. But I can't help but remember that you went off to fight for 'em."

"That was a long time ago."

"Less than a year," Titus pointed out.

"And more than half that time has been spent in here." Nathan gave a hollow, humorless laugh. "Any sympathy I might have had for the Yankees is long gone, Titus. I despise both sides in this war now. I will never fight again—except for my own freedom."

Nathan's words had the ring of truth to them. Titus nodded. "Sorry I doubted you."

They resumed their walk, only to stop again a few minutes later. "Look there. Something's going on," Nathan noted.

Titus looked toward the long double row of barracks that formed the west side of the large, square parade ground behind the administration building. A group of Union soldiers had come around the corner of the barracks. They were marching toward the cluster of barracks where Titus and Nathan were housed. As they came closer, Titus saw that the soldiers formed a loose square around a smaller group in the center. The smaller group included several officers, a couple of men in civilian clothes, including black stovepipe hats like the ones Lincoln favored, and a woman in a dark gray dress and hat.

Titus's heart thudded heavily in his chest. He hadn't seen a woman in over six months. He had no interest in what this one looked like; he just wanted her to keep getting closer to him. She could be as ugly as mud, and he wouldn't mind a bit as long as she was female.

But she wasn't ugly at all. Titus could only catch glimpses of her past the soldiers that formed the group's escort, but he saw enough to tell that she was pretty. Curly dark red hair spilled out from under the hat she wore. The hat had a veil attached to it, and the woman had lifted a handkerchief and covered the lower half of her face—protecting her senses from the stench surrounding the barracks. Her skin was as fair as milk.

"My God," Nathan breathed.

"Yeah," Titus agreed.

Other prisoners had spotted the woman also. They hooted and called out lewd comments. One of the officers accompanying the civilians snapped an order, and the soldiers stopped and leveled their rifles at the Confederates. Titus recognized Capt. Floyd Morton, the commandant's aide. The threat of the rifles was enough to make the prisoners lapse into a sullen silence.

One of the other officers spoke to Morton, who in turn ordered the soldiers to lower their rifles. The Yankees held the weapons ready for instant use, however.

Morton signaled to Sergeant O'Neil, who was also with the group, and the brutal sergeant of the guard stepped forward and bellowed, "Fall in! Fall in, the lot of you! Everybody out of the barracks! Fall in for inspection!"

Inspection by whom? Titus wondered. The civilians? Maybe the men in the stovepipe hats were from the Yankee War Department or some other part of the government. Maybe they had come to see for themselves just how bad conditions were at Camp Douglas. Titus didn't hold out much hope that would be the case, but he supposed it was possible.

"We'd better get the colonel," Nathan said quietly. "He'll need help if we have to get in formation."

Titus nodded. He started toward the barracks with Nathan.

"Brannon!" Sergeant O'Neil shouted. Titus stopped and turned around. O'Neil was striding toward him, face flushed with anger. "Where do you think you're goin'?"

"To get Colonel Newberry, Sergeant," Titus replied, being careful not to let his hatred come through in his voice. For the most part, he had successfully laid low and avoided O'Neil's wrath since his first days in the camp, but that didn't mean he would ever forget the agony and humiliation of being forced to sit bare-assed on the frozen ground.

"I issued the order loud enough for everybody to hear. If Newberry don't come out and fall in formation like he's supposed to, it's his lookout, not yours."

"Sergeant, he's sick—" Nathan began.

O'Neil stepped closer and lowered his voice. "I don't give a damn if he's coughin' up what little guts he has left," he hissed. "If he don't get out here on his own, he'll be punished once these damned civilians are gone. And if you two don't fall in right now, it's the Mule for you."

They had no choice. Neither of them wanted to endure the terrible punishment of the Mule. They walked over and joined the rough ranks that were forming in front of the barracks.

That brought them closer to the visitors. Titus looked directly at the woman. He couldn't take his eyes off her, which he suspected was true of most of the other men. As he watched her, a flush slowly rose into her cheeks, what he could see of them past the handkerchief she held over her face.

Titus heard a stirring in the ranks behind him and glanced over his shoulder to see Colonel Newberry coming out of the barracks. The colonel's movements were slow and stiff and painful to watch. Several men started to go to his assistance, but O'Neil barked again. "Back in the ranks, Rebs!"

Titus felt his teeth grinding together as he watched Newberry hobble into the formation. He looked at the redheaded woman and saw that she was watching the colonel, too. He hoped what he read in her eyes was sympathy, but he couldn't be sure about that. She seemed to be trying to keep her face expressionless.

Finally, Newberry reached the formation. He came all the way to the front row of prisoners and took his place at one end of it. His withered body straightened. He squared his shoulders and pulled them back so that he was standing at attention as he stared straight ahead. One by one, the other prisoners followed his example. The colonel was one tough bastard, Titus thought.

The Yankee soldiers spread out so that the officers and the civilians could get a good look at the prisoners. Captain Morton stepped forward, his round face as bland and cheerful as always.

"Gentlemen," he said in a loud voice, "thank you for your cooperation. As you can see, we have some visitors today. This is Colonel Albert Chambers—" Morton indicated one of the officers. "Colonel Chambers is one of the army's chief medical officers. We also have Mr. Wallace Dunlap and Mr. Stephen McChesney of the War Department in Washington, D.C., honoring us with their presence, and Miss Louisa Abernathy of the Benevolent Society of Friends in Philadelphia."

So she was a Quaker, Titus thought. He had heard of them. They were a religious group that opposed the war, but they also acted as monitors on prison camp conditions in both North and South. The idle thought he'd had a few minutes earlier was actually coming true. These people were here to inspect the prison camp and see for themselves just how deplorable conditions were.

"Our visitors are going to talk to you," Captain Morton went on, "and I want you to speak freely with them. All they ask is that you tell them the truth, and I expect you to cooperate fully with them."

Morton stepped back and motioned for Chambers, Miss Abernathy, and the two men from the War Department to approach the prisoners.

Behind them, where the visitors could not see, Sergeant O'Neil drew a long, heavy-bladed knife from his belt and ran his thumb along the edge. The look he gave the prisoners made it quite clear what he expected from them—and what they could expect if they didn't go along with what he wanted.

Chambers came along the line first, performing a cursory examination of some of the men. He looked at their hands, had them open their mouths, and tapped their chests. He frowned steadily and nonstop.

The two War Department men came next. "Have you been mistreated?" "Do you get enough to eat?" "Do you get any medical attention?" The prisoners grunted noncommittal answers. When pressed, they glanced at O'Neil and the other guards and lied, saying that they received sufficient rations and that they had medical attention whenever they needed it.

Titus hoped they wouldn't ask him any questions. He wasn't going to lie just because O'Neil wanted him to, even though it would doubtless mean more punishment later.

The woman came last, tentatively approaching the men and staying farther back than her male companions had. "Have you been punished unjustly?" she asked, and the sound of her voice twisted something inside Titus. This was the closest he had been to a woman since leaving Polly. He stared down at the ground, unable to bear the torture of looking at her any longer.

Suddenly, he heard her voice right in front of him and saw the skirts of her gray dress swishing lightly over high-buttoned shoes. "You there," she said. "Please look at me."

Titus lifted his head. His eyes photographed her and his lips drew back from his teeth in a grimace.

Miss Abernathy caught her breath and took a half step backward. Titus knew that, to her, he must have looked like some kind of rabid animal.

"Have you . . ." She had to swallow hard before she could go on. "Have you been punished unjustly since you've been here at Camp Douglas, sir?"

Titus thought about the beatings, about the long hours of being forced to stand at attention in the snow, about how it had felt when the skin tore off his bare buttocks from being frozen to the ground. In a raspy voice, he said, "I've been punished, ma'am. Whether or not it was unjust, I reckon that's up to your Yankee friends."

The woman caught her breath, and beside Titus, so did Nathan Hatcher. Nathan knew that Titus's answer was going to mean trouble. Titus knew it, too. He saw the scowl on Sergeant O'Neil's face.

Miss Abernathy swung her gaze to Nathan. "What about you, sir?" she asked. "Have you been punished unjustly?"

"Ma'am, I . . . I'd prefer not to answer . . ."

"That's all right," Miss Abernathy said. "I'm sorry." She looked at Titus. "I'm very sorry."

So she knew what her questions and their answers had caused, Titus thought. Why the hell did she come to places like this, knowing that she was either going to be lied to, or, if the prisoners answered her honestly, they were letting themselves in for more torture? What sort of good was she doing by putting them in this position?

Miss Abernathy moved on. When she was farther down the line, out of easy earshot, Sergeant O'Neil stepped up to Titus. "You're going to be sorry for that, you Rebel son of a bitch."

"I'm already sorry I'm here, Sergeant," Titus said. "I don't reckon you can make me much sorrier."

O'Neil's eyes lit up. "You know, Brannon," he said. "I love a challenge."

The sergeant turned to walk away, and as he did so, something made Titus glance along the line of prisoners. He saw Miss Abernathy looking in his direction. Had she seen the exchange with O'Neil and guessed what it was about?

When the inspection was over, Chambers stalked over to Captain Morton. "Captain, I've seldom seen a more pitiful-looking bunch of prisoners. You're supposed to hold them in custody, not starve them to death!"

Morton's eyebrows raised, and he looked genuinely surprised and offended. He sounded that way, too. "I assure you, Colonel, that's the furthest thing from my mind! True, there are few amenities here, but these men have a roof over their heads and plentiful rations. I'll be glad to show you the records proving just how well we feed them."

"I'll want to see those records," Chambers said. "And I'll want to speak to Colonel Tucker, too."

"Of course, sir. He's expecting you in his office." Morton ushered the visitors toward the administration building.

Titus saw Miss Abernathy glance back at them one more time as she left.

"Fall out!" Sergeant O'Neil shouted when Chambers and the civilians were gone. Then he added, "All but you, Brannon, and you, Hatcher!"

Titus was expecting that. He stood there, his back stiff, with Nathan beside him. O'Neil walked over to them. The sergeant's eyes, deep-set in pockets of gristle, gleamed with hate and maybe even a little madness.

"I'm going to make you two bastards wish you'd never been born," O'Neil said. "We'll start out with six hours each on the Mule! With spurs!"

Nathan made a strangled sound in his throat. Titus felt like cursing, but he remained silent and stared straight ahead at O'Neil. The sergeant's face was mottled with fury.

Six hours on the Mule, with weights attached to his ankles, would crush a man's testicles to jelly. He would never be a real man again, even if he survived the ordeal.

Had it been worth it to cross O'Neil? Suddenly, Titus didn't think so. The damage this punishment would do to him was bad enough by itself, but he'd probably wind up in the infirmary, which in most cases was a death warrant. He would be likely to die of an infection before he ever got out of there. And if he lived through it somehow, he would be laid up for so long that he would never have a chance to escape. He had thrown all that away for a moment of bravado—and without even really telling the truth about how things were here in Camp Douglas.

"Well, Brannon?" O'Neil prodded with an ugly grin. "Ain't got so much to say now, do you?"

Before Titus could respond, a new voice called out for the sergeant's attention.

O'Neil jerked around and came to attention as he saw a lieutenant hurrying toward him. "Sir?" he asked.

"Colonel Tucker wants you to bring these two men—" The young officer indicated Titus and Nathan. "—as well as Colonel Newberry to his office immediately."

O'Neil's eyes widened with surprise. "But, sir, I was just about to discipline these men—"

"It'll have to wait, Sergeant. Colonel Tucker wants to see them right away."

Titus heard a small grinding sound and knew it was O'Neil's teeth clenching in frustration. There was nothing else he could do unless he wanted to disobey a direct order. He looked at Titus and Nathan and snapped, "You two stay here while I get the old man."

Titus and Nathan stood there as O'Neil went to fetch the colonel. Other guards were close by, glowering at them and holding clubs ready to strike if either of the prisoners tried to attack them or escape.

In a half-whisper, Nathan asked, "What do you think this is all about?"

"I don't know," Titus replied, "but I'm mighty glad we're going to the commandant's office right now instead of having to ride the Mule!"

O'Neil came back a few minutes later, gripping Newberry's arm and hurrying the colonel along. Newberry gave Titus a quizzical look. All Titus could do was lift his shoulders in a half-shrug. All three prisoners were hustled toward the administration building by O'Neil and the other guards.

O'Neil jabbed Titus in the back with his club as they walked along. "You got lucky, Reb," the sergeant grated, "but you got to come back out here sooner or later, and when you do, I'll be waitin' for you."

Titus had already thought of that. He knew this was only postponing the inevitable. Still, he would take any reprieve he could get.

He had never been inside the administration building before. It felt strange to be in a building with clean floors and paint on the walls. They marched down a hallway, and the lieutenant who fetched them opened a door at the end. The commandant's office, Titus thought.

The three ragged men found Colonel Tucker waiting for them, along with Colonel Chambers, the medical officer, Dunlap and McChesney, *and* Miss Louisa Abernathy.

Chapter Eleven

TITUS STOPPED SHORT AT the sight of Miss Abernathy. Here in the administration building, she had lifted her veil, and she was no longer holding a handkerchief to her mouth and nose. As she turned her head to look at the three prisoners, he got a good look at her face and saw that she was lovelier than she had looked to him on the parade ground. He saw that her eyes were green, and she had a cluster of faint freckles spilled across her nose and cheeks.

Colonel Newberry drew himself to attention and saluted the two Union officers in the room. A wracking cough shook him, but he held the salute until both Tucker and Chambers had returned it.

Colonel Tucker responded, "Stand at ease, sir." He glanced at Titus and Nathan. "That goes for you two, as well."

"Thank you, sir," Newberry said. "What can we do for you?"

The medical officer spoke up next. "You should instead be asking what we can do for you, Colonel. Don't you know that you have pneumonia?"

Newberry smiled thinly and coughed. "I did have pneumonia, sir. I have recovered."

"The hell you have," Chambers said, adding to Miss Abernathy, "Pardon my language, ma'am."

"That's quite all right, Colonel," she said. She turned to Newberry. "You need proper medical attention at once, sir. Colonel Chambers and I intend to see that you get it."

Tucker spoke up. "Captain Morton assures me that all the prisoners get adequate medical care—"

"Colonel, I have never seen a more wretched cesspool of humanity in my life," Chambers interrupted. "And from what I have seen of him, your Captain Morton is both a bloodthirsty monster and a certifiable lunatic."

Tucker's face flushed. He leaned forward and rested his knuckles on the top of his desk. "How dare you, sir!" he demanded. "You were sent here to inspect this camp, not to slander my officers!" He waved a hand at the three prisoners. "Do you think it's easy dealing with these treasonous animals? They are the enemy, Colonel! Have you forgotten that?"

Miss Abernathy responded, "Have you forgotten that they're human beings as well?"

Tucker glared at her, but he didn't answer her question.

One of the War Department men tried to settle things. "All right, let's all calm ourselves. Colonel Tucker, we're aware of the problems you face in dealing with the Confederate prisoners. To tell the truth, they don't receive an abundance of sympathy in the War Department. As you point out, they *are* the enemy."

Tucker nodded, clearly pleased with what he was hearing.

"On the other hand," the man from Washington went on, "the citizens of the United States don't like to think of themselves, or their military, as cruel. We have to provide humane treatment for Confederate prisoners." He glanced at the three men. "No matter how much we may despise them personally."

Titus kept his face expressionless as he looked at the man. From the sound of things, these visitors might actually take steps to improve conditions at the camp. He didn't want to ruin that by revealing that he despised the Yankee official every bit as much as the man despised him.

"What would you have me do?" Colonel Tucker asked, his voice stiff.

Chambers pointed to Newberry. "We're going to take the colonel with us and see that he's placed in the hospital."

"And I want these men to come along as well, so they won't be unfairly punished for speaking to me," Miss Abernathy added, nodding toward Titus and Nathan.

Titus's heart began to thump with hope. If he and Nathan could get out of the camp, even for a little while, their chances of escape would improve tremendously.

Tucker began, "Begging your pardon, Miss, but I can assure you—"

"I saw the way that sergeant was looking at them, Colonel."

Tucker's jaw tightened. "We must have discipline. I'm sorry, Miss Abernathy, but I cannot allow you to interfere with that."

"Colonel—"

Tucker shook his head. "Absolutely not." He looked at Chambers. "And you can't authorize their removal from the camp on medical grounds, either, Colonel. You can see for yourself that they're perfectly healthy."

"Starved half to death and covered with lice," Chambers said then shrugged. "But other than the usual illnesses of men in cramped quarters, I suppose you're right."

Miss Abernathy said, "Colonel, I appeal to you—"

"If you want these prisoners, Miss, you're going to have to appeal to a higher authority. I won't release them."

Titus's spirits sank. For a brief second, freedom had been so close he could almost taste and smell it before it was snatched away. He tried not to show his disappointment, but he could feel the tension in his face.

"Very well, Colonel," Miss Abernathy said in a subdued tone. "But I assure you, I *will* be returning to the camp to check on them."

"You will be welcome at any time, of course."

She looked at Titus and Nathan and gave a brief shake of her head as if to say she was sorry for failing them.

Newberry spoke up, addressing Chambers, "Colonel, I'm sure there are . . . men in this camp who are . . . in worse condition than myself. You should . . . take them instead."

"I don't think so, Colonel," Chambers replied. "I know that a good officer hates to leave his men, but in this case you have no choice."

Newberry looked at Titus and Nathan, torn between his loyalty to them and his ill health. Finally, he said, "I'm sorry, boys. If there was . . . anything I could do . . ."

"You get well, Colonel," Nathan said. "We'll be fine."

"Yeah, Colonel, don't worry about us," Titus forced himself to say, even though jealousy gnawed at his insides. In a way this might make things easier, he told himself. When the time came to make a break for it, they wouldn't have to worry about the colonel slowing them down.

"There's one thing more I want, Colonel Tucker," Miss Abernathy said.

"If I can oblige, I'll be happy to," Tucker said.

"Have Captain Morton and that sergeant of the guard come in here. I want to hear you order them that these men are not to be punished for speaking freely to me."

"Miss, again, that's interfering with a disciplinary matter—"

"They were promised that they could speak freely. I insist that that promise be honored."

In frustration, Tucker blew his breath through his mustache. "Very well," he said. "Bring Captain Morton and Sergeant O'Neil in here."

A couple of minutes later, Morton and O'Neil came into the room and saluted. "Captain . . . Sergeant," Tucker began. "I have orders for you regarding these two prisoners." He indicated Titus and Nathan. "They are not to be punished for anything they might have said to Miss Abernathy here. Do you understand?"

"Of course, sir," Morton replied without hesitation. "They were told to speak freely. We would never punish prisoners for obeying orders, sir."

Colonel Chambers made a small noise of disbelief and contempt. Morton ignored him but a red flush appeared on the back of O'Neil's neck.

"All right, that's all," Tucker said.

Morton and O'Neil turned to go, but before they could leave the room, Miss Abernathy stopped them. "Gentlemen!" she said. "I hope you really do understand, because I intend to come back to this camp and check on the welfare of not only these two men but all the other prisoners."

"Yes, ma'am," Morton said. "We'll take the best care of them that we possibly can."

"I hope so, Captain. I sincerely hope so."

She didn't say anything else. Morton and O'Neil filed out of the room.

"Is that all?" Colonel Tucker asked. He looked at Chambers, Dunlap, and McChesney and got nods of agreement from all of them. "Miss Abernathy?" Tucker prodded.

"That's all, Colonel," she said, sounding reluctant to leave.

"Very well." Tucker looked at his aide. "See that the prisoners are taken back to their barracks. Colonel Newberry, is there anything you want to take with you?"

Newberry smiled and spread his hands. "These days I carry . . . all my earthly possessions . . . with me, sir."

The lieutenant ushered Titus and Nathan out of the office. As they left, Newberry lifted his hand in a gesture of farewell. Nathan saluted, but Titus just gave the colonel a curt nod.

O'Neil and several more guards were waiting in the corridor. The sergeant glowered at them. Titus thought about taunting him but suppressed the urge. No point in pushing his luck, he told himself. Besides, he wasn't convinced that O'Neil wouldn't find some way around the order not to punish him and Nathan.

O'Neil indicated as much by saying quietly as he fell in behind them, "I don't care what that Quaker bitch says, you Rebs'll pay for what you did."

"We didn't even tell her the truth," Titus said without looking around. "Not anywhere close to it."

"It don't matter. You better not look cross-eyed at me, Brannon, or sure as you do, you'll be up on the Mule. Just give me a reason, any reason at all."

"Whatever do you mean, Sergeant? We'll be the best little prisoners you ever saw. Ain't that right, Nathan?"

Nathan Hatcher didn't say anything. He just trudged along, head down, probably wishing that Titus would just leave him out of this.

When they returned to the barracks, several men crowded around, asking questions. "Where's the colonel?" "What happened?" "Did you get to see that redhaired woman again?"

Nathan explained that the colonel was being taken to a hospital. "That's really all that happened," he concluded

"How come you and Brannon ain't up on the Mule, like O'Neil said?"

Titus grinned. "That Quaker gal laid down the law to O'Neil. Said he couldn't punish us for speakin' up. She fussed at Colonel Tucker until he gave her what she wanted."

"Son of a bitch!" one of the prisoners exclaimed. "And O'Neil went along with it?"

Titus looked around and saw that the sergeant had withdrawn about fifty yards. He stood there with his arms crossed, glaring at the little cluster of prisoners, a club dangling from his wrist by its leather strap. The expression on his face was dark and murderous.

"For now," Titus said. "He went along with it for now."

"So you did see the woman again?" A man asked, plucking at Titus's sleeve, an eager desperation on his gaunt, whiskery face. "You was in the same room with her?"

"Yeah," Titus said with a nod, and as he thought about Miss Louisa Abernathy, he felt the familiar empty ache deep inside him. Miss Abernathy hadn't looked anything like Polly, but being that close to her, just hearing a woman's voice again, had brought back too many memories of his wife. He thought about how Polly's mouth had tasted when he kissed her and how warm her body had been when he put his arms around her and how her hair had smelled and felt when he ran his fingers through it . . .

Damn, he thought, *some things hurt a man even worse than the Mule.*

"OH, MY," Polly said in breathless surprise. "Oh, my."

Henry pulled away from her, appalled at what he had done. Words tumbled out of his mouth. "I'm sorry, Polly. Oh, Lord, I'm sorry. I don't know what got into me, I had no right, I'm so sorry—"

"Stop it," Polly said sharply, causing him to fall silent and stare at her. "You don't have to pitch a hissy fit, Henry. And you don't have to apologize. In fact . . . I liked it."

He knew he was gaping at her like an idiot, but he couldn't help himself. "You . . . you did?"

"Yes," she said. "I did."

And then she put her hand on the back of his neck, came up on her toes, and kissed him just as he had kissed her a moment earlier, albeit with more passion than Henry had ever known.

They stood in the shade of a grove of trees next to one of the fields on the Brannon farm. Henry had been walking through the field, checking on the progress of the corn growing there, when he saw the buggy parked on the road nearby. He had recognized it right away, and when he walked over to it, he had been pleased—but not surprised—to see Polly sitting there in a dark blue dress and bonnet.

"Hello, Henry," she had said. "How are you today?"

"Why, just fine," he'd replied, glad that he hadn't been doing any heavy work so far this morning. His shirt wasn't soaked with sweat like it sometimes was by this time of day. "And how are you, Polly?"

"All right," she'd said. "A little bored. I thought I'd take a drive around the countryside." An appealing little laugh came from her. "I've been over here so much I suppose this old horse knows the way by now."

It was true: Polly had paid quite a few visits to the Brannon farm over the past couple of months, since the weather had started getting better with the arrival of spring. Now, in early June, it was not uncommon to see her over here.

And each time he saw her, the terrible knowledge grew stronger in Henry's heart: He was in love with his brother's wife.

His brother's widow, he reminded himself. Titus was dead and gone. Henry would always miss Titus, would always mourn him, but things had changed. Even before Titus went off and joined the army, he had left Polly. Divorce was uncommon but not unheard of. It was possible that had he remained at home, Titus would have divorced Polly, or vice versa. There was no way of knowing what would have happened.

Still, every time he looked at Polly and felt the warm tightness in his chest caused by her beauty, Henry also felt a twinge of guilt.

He supposed he would just have to learn to live with it.

During her visits to the farm, Polly always stopped by the fields to talk to him. Today was no different. Sometimes she didn't even go on to the house to see Abigail and Cordelia, just chatted with him for a while, then turned the buggy around and drove home. On many a dark night, staring sleeplessly at the ceiling of his room, Henry had asked himself if it was possible she was coming over here just to see him. Did she feel anything for him even remotely like what he felt for her?

Henry didn't know, but each time those questions went through his head, he resolved to find out. The next time he saw her, he told himself, he would ask her just what was going on between them. He would bring it out into the open and be done with it.

And every time she'd visited, he had failed to do so, letting his fears get the better of him. He was terrified that if he spoke of his true feelings, she would slap him and storm away outraged. Worse yet, she might just laugh in his face. After all, she *was* older than he, although not by much. But she was . . . experienced. She had been a married woman. She knew all about love. She probably thought of him as just a boy, nothing more than a little brother by marriage.

He told himself, in those agonies of indecision, that he would rather have her around as a friend than not have her around at all. At least that way he could bask in the light of her beauty and thrill to the sound of her laugh. So he justified his inaction to himself.

Until today.

Today Polly had suggested that they walk over into the shade of the trees to get out of the heat, and Henry had agreed. Once there, she had untied the strings of her bonnet and taken it off.

Even in the shade, her blonde hair had shone like the brilliance of the sun to Henry's eyes. It was pulled into a bun at the back of her head, but several strands had escaped, and without thinking about what he was doing, he reached up to touch one of them. As he did so, his fingers brushed her cheek, and she smiled up at him. He leaned closer to her and kissed her, and she didn't jerk away and slap him, or laugh, or any of the things he had feared. Instead her lips were soft and warm and sweet against his, and he had lost himself in the sensations for several moments before the awful realization of what he was doing crashed down on him.

He was kissing his brother's wife.

And judging by the fact that now she was kissing him back, even more passionately than before, she *liked* it.

Henry's arms went around her, and she came eagerly into his embrace. He had kissed only a few girls in his life, so he knew he was still a little awkward about such things. For some reason, though, he didn't worry about that now. Polly made all his fears and worries go away. It was the most natural thing in the world to hold her and press her body to his as their mouths worked against each other. Even through the stiff fabric of her dress and the undergarments beneath it, he could feel her softness. He had never felt anything more exciting in his life, never tasted anything more intoxicating than the sweetness of her mouth.

The moment had to end, and both of them were breathless when it finally did. Polly put her other arm around his neck and laced her fingers together behind his head. She smiled up at him. "There now. That wasn't so bad, was it?"

"Bad?" Henry repeated, his voice hoarse with strain. "That . . . that was . . . I never knew . . . I never felt . . . Oh, Polly, I—"

"Don't," she said, her face suddenly growing serious. "Don't say it, Henry. Not yet. Just kiss me again."

He hesitated. The feelings inside him were so strong, so eager to burst out, that he felt as if he might explode if he didn't express them. But he didn't want to do anything to offend her, and since she had asked him to kiss her again, he supposed it would be the gentlemanly thing to do if he obliged her.

So that was what he did. Several times.

Polly became more breathless, her face more flushed each time Henry kissed her. Finally, she took her arms from around his neck, placed her hands on his chest. "I . . . I have to go."

She didn't push him away, just rested her hands on his chest, but he stepped back anyway, putting a small distance between them. His heart was already tripping along a mile a minute, but sudden terror made it pound even harder. "Polly, if I've offended you—"

"No, silly," she said with a smile. "I already told you. I'm not offended, and you don't have to apologize to me."

"What I did was improper—"

She stamped her foot on the ground. "Now you just stop that, Henry Brannon! Can't you get it through that thick head of yours that I wanted to kiss you every bit as much as you wanted to kiss me?" She rolled her eyes. "Probably more. Lord knows it took you long enough to catch all the hints I've been dropping."

"Hints?"

"Well, of course! A young lady can't just come right out and tell a young man that she wants him to kiss her, now can she?" Polly reached out and rested her hand on Henry's arm for a second before pulling it back. "But you came around. I knew you would."

He felt a little lost, and the earth was unsteady under his feet. He remembered once, when he was a small boy and learning to swim in the creek called Dobie's Run, how he had drifted into deep water. The panic he'd experienced then as the creek closed over his head was something like what he was feeling now.

But he had been able to kick his feet and flail his arms and swim back to the shallows, and after that he had never been quite as afraid of deep water.

"Polly, I've never known a girl as sweet and pretty as you."

"I could listen to you go on like that all day, Henry, I really could, but I've got to get home."

"You do? So soon?"

"I'm afraid so," she said. "But I'll come back to see you again. You can be sure of that."

Again she stepped closer to him, and again she lifted herself on her toes. Her lips brushed across his, and her hand tightened on his arm. Then she turned and was gone.

Henry stood there, feeling as stunned as a poleaxed steer. He watched as Polly ran back into the corn field and hurried across it toward the road, where the horse waited patiently with the buggy.

When she was almost to the road, she turned and waved to him, and the sudden motion made her hair come loose from the bun. It fell around her shoulders, spilling over the dark blue dress like liquid sunlight.

The bonnet, Henry thought. *She doesn't have her bonnet.*

He looked around, frantic. The bonnet was on the ground a few feet from where she must have dropped it when he first kissed her.

He scooped it up, lifted it, and straightened to call to her. "Polly . . . !"

It was too late. She had already climbed into the buggy and picked up the reins. She flapped them against the horse's back and sent the vehicle rolling down the road, away from the field. Henry stood there for a moment, the hand holding the bonnet still upraised, then he slowly lowered his arm.

He hadn't waved back at her as she left, he realized. Had she noticed? Was she angry with him because of it?

He looked down at the bonnet in his hand and rubbed the fabric of it between his fingers. He brought it to his nose and inhaled, smelling the clean scent of her hair.

It was wrong and he knew it, but God forgive him—he knew he loved her!

ON A wooded knoll a quarter of a mile away, Duncan Ebersole sat on his horse, his broad-brimmed hat pulled down to shade his eyes. With a curt, savage motion, he closed the spyglass he had been using and slipped it back into his saddlebag. In the distance along the road, a plume of dust curled into the air, and he knew it came from the wheels of the buggy his daughter was driving.

He had seen it all, and the sight had filled him with a purple rage unlike any he had ever known. Fate had intervened and saved his daughter from one of those white-trash Brannons, he thought, and now Polly was throwing herself right into the arms of another one. She was precious to him, but he knew she had always allowed her baser nature to rule her emotions.

Not this time, Duncan Ebersole vowed. Henry Brannon would never have her. He would put a stop to this.

Whatever it took.

Chapter Twelve

THERE HAD BEEN PLENTY of times in his life when he wished he had been wrong, Will Brannon reflected, and this was one of them. Just as he had suspected, the Army of Northern Virginia was on the move again, and this time it was headed north.

Part of the army, anyway. So far, the corps commanded by Gen. Richard S. Ewell was the only one that had pulled out from the camp near Culpeper. The preparations for departure had been hurried, the orders having come hot on the heels of the news about the massive cavalry confrontation near Brandy Station. Tents had been struck, the few supplies on hand were gathered, and by the afternoon of the day following the battle, Ewell's corps began marching toward the Blue Ridge Mountains. Ewell himself traveled at the head of the column in a buggy. This was his first real command since he'd lost a leg in battle nine months earlier. The leg had been replaced with a wooden one, so that he could ride a horse if necessary, but most of the time he traveled by buggy, especially during large-scale movements such as the one that was underway now.

Will rode alongside his company. The men were moving smartly despite their tattered uniforms and the fact that some of them had no shoes or boots. Their rifles were shouldered and their steps were crisp. Their faces, which should have been pinched and gaunt from hunger, were instead smiling and full of anticipation. Sgt. Darcy Bennett, one of Will's old adversaries from his time as sheriff who had become a staunch friend and ally, had no trouble keeping the men moving along at a fast pace. When Stonewall Jackson was alive, he had referred to the men of this brigade as his foot cavalry, because no other unit in the army could cover so much ground so quickly.

Rumors were running rampant concerning the army's ultimate destination. Right now they were heading for Chester

Gap, which would take them through the Blue Ridge and into the Shenandoah Valley, an area that had already seen a great deal of fighting during the war. Will had traveled the length and breadth of the Shenandoah with Jackson, dealing out misery to the Yankees. He was convinced, however, that the coming campaign wasn't going to be just a series of raids like that. The Shenandoah Valley was going to be the first step in a larger objective. Once it was firmly in Confederate hands, the way north into Maryland and Pennsylvania would be wide open for another invasion.

And given the state of the army, Will thought, this thrust northward, if it came, might well be the last one of the war. One way or the other, this could be the beginning of the end.

ABIGAIL BRANNON pounded and rolled the skimpy ball of dough, flattening it out so that it would make as many biscuits as possible. She had used the last of the flour and had no idea where she was going to get more. Maybe now that part of the army was gone and the rest would soon be leaving, the civilians of Culpeper County would be able to get their hands on more supplies. Abigail didn't hold out much hope that that would be the case, but her natural faith wouldn't let her give up.

At least she and her family wouldn't starve. They had corn growing in the fields and some vegetables in the garden patch near the barn. A few hams from the previous fall's slaughtering hung in the smokehouse. They had a good milk cow, too. The Brannons would get by. This farm had supported them for many years, and it would continue to do so.

Henry and Cordelia were both working in the fields this morning, so when Abigail heard a heavy step on the front porch, she had a pretty good idea who it belonged to. Her visitor seemed to have a knack for knowing when she was alone in the house. A moment later, when the familiar knock sounded, she was sure of it. Abigail put the pan of biscuits on the stove to rise and hurried to the front door, wiping her hands on her apron as she went.

When she opened the door, a tall, broad-shouldered man in late middle age stood there, his black hat in his hands. He had thick white hair and a white mustache, and his face was rugged and tanned. "Good morning, Abigail," he smiled.

"Hello, Benjamin. What brings you out here?"

"Oh, you know me. Just making my rounds. The shepherd tending his flock, so to speak."

"Well, come in." She moved back so that he could enter the house. "It's always good to see you."

Benjamin Spanner, pastor of the Baptist church in Culpeper, stepped into the foyer. He turned his hat over in his hands, a gesture that Abigail recognized as nervousness. Why that would be the case, she didn't know. He was certainly welcome in the Brannon house. More than welcome.

She shut the door and ushered him into the parlor. "Sit down and tell me the news," she said.

"What news?" Spanner asked.

"You said you'd been making your rounds. Surely there are things going on in the county worthy of being discussed."

"Oh." Spanner sat on one end of the sofa while Abigail seated herself at the other. "I thought that you might mean the war news."

She shook her head. "I hear enough about the war from Henry. Besides, I have faith that in His own good time the Lord will help us prevail over those heathen Yankees. I'd rather hear about our friends and neighbors."

"Well, in that case . . . Mrs. Dinsmore is ailing again."

"Oh, I'm sorry to hear that! Is there anything I can do for her?"

Spanner shook his head. "No, she has her daughters-in-law there to take care of her. Her boys are still off with the army, of course." He thought for a moment. "The Satterfields have a new grandson down in Richmond. Charles's wife had a baby boy last month."

"That's wonderful news."

"Indeed. In the midst of death, there is life. It's always been that way, I suppose."

Abigail frowned. The preacher's thoughts seemed to be turning today toward the war and the army and death and dying, no matter what he started out talking about. Everyone in church had sons or husbands in the army. She supposed the weight of it all was preying on his mind. That came as no surprise, though. He was, after all, a man of God, and despite his big, rugged appearance, he had a truly gentle soul. His Christian sympathies went out to everyone with whom he came in contact. His compassion was what made him such a good minister.

"Would you like a cool glass of buttermilk?" she asked.

"That would be mighty nice," he said. "Thank you, Abby."

She came to her feet. "I'll right back, Ben."

The familiarity came easily to their lips now. At first, when Spanner had replaced Reverend Crosley as pastor of the church, they had been Brother Spanner and Sister Brannon to each other. That had progressed to Brother Benjamin and Sister Abigail, then to just Benjamin and Abigail. Now they were Ben and Abby to each other, especially in these unguarded moments when they were alone.

She would never forget the first time he had held her in his arms and kissed her. She had been shocked, but she hadn't pulled away and reproved him, as she knew she should. Instead, she had given herself over to the feelings he aroused in her, feelings she hadn't experienced in so long, it was as if they were totally new to her.

Afterward, even though they had only kissed for a few moments, she felt so guilty that she was driven almost to distraction. She had been a widow for many years; she had no business kissing a man like that, like she was some sort of brazen hussy. And him a preacher at that!

But even her late husband John had never made her heart pound so hard, as if it were about to burst out of her chest. John Brannon had been a man of strong, lusty appetites. Abigail had tolerated them because it was her duty as his wife, although their relationship had been one more of endurance than pleasure. The shocking sensation that had raced through her when Benjamin Spanner kissed her was something totally new and unexpected for her. She had sworn to herself that she could never allow such a thing to happen again.

But it had . . . more than once, in fact.

She had hoped to keep it a secret, but her children had figured it out. Shame filled her every time Henry made some laughing comment about how often the preacher came to visit, and each time she promised herself that she would tell Benjamin not to come back to the house. They could see each other in church, as was proper, but nowhere else.

Despite her resolve, each time he knocked on the door, she answered and invited him in. Although they tried to make small talk, both of them knew it was only a matter of time before they wound up in each other's arms again.

She brought the glass of buttermilk from the kitchen and handed it to him. "Thank you, Abby," he said, but he set it aside on the small table beside the divan without tasting it.

"I have to talk to you, Abby," he went on, turning toward her with a solemn expression on his face as she sat down at the other end of the sofa.

Oh, dear Lord! she thought. His expression was so serious. Abigail's heart began to pound. If he asked her to marry him, what would she say? After John's death, never in her wildest dreams had she ever imagined that she would take a husband again. She had her children and the farm. That was enough for any woman, she told herself.

And yet . . . and yet . . .

"You know part of the army has pulled out, and the rest is going soon. At least that's the word around town."

She stared at him, feeling a little stunned. He was talking about the army again. Why was it weighing so heavily on his mind today?

"There was a big battle a couple of days ago. Up around Brandy Station."

"So I heard," she said, confused by the unexpected turn this conversation was taking. "Mac was involved. He sent word that he was all right, though. The cavalry is still camped there."

Spanner nodded. "I rode up to see if there was anything I could do. Ministers are always needed after a battle, you know."

Abigail knew what he meant, certainly. There were wounded men to comfort and burial services to conduct. The army chaplains couldn't be everywhere.

"There were heavy losses on both sides," Spanner went on, his voice growing more hollow now. "I saw blood everywhere on the ground. The artillery was used, and men were . . . were blown to bits. An arm here, a leg over there . . . ."

Abigail swallowed the queasy feeling that was rising in her throat. Why was he doing this? Why was he saying these awful things when she had expected something so different? "I really don't need to hear about this, Ben," she said. "I worry enough about my boys already."

"I think you do need to hear it," Spanner said. "I want you to understand what I'm about to say to you, Abigail."

She stiffened. It was clear she wasn't going to like this, or at least he was afraid she wouldn't.

"Why don't you just go ahead and say it, whatever it is," she suggested.

He took a deep breath. "All right. Earlier you said that the Lord would help us prevail over the Yankees. Do you really believe that?"

"Why, of course! Don't you?"

"No," Spanner said. "I don't."

Abigail stared at him in disbelief. "You don't think that we'll win, sooner or later?"

"You say that as if I'm part of the Confederacy, Abby."

She began to feel hollow inside. "You're a Virginian, Ben. You have to support the Confederacy. You have to believe in the righteousness of our cause."

"I'm sorry, I truly am. But I just don't feel that way, and I can't pretend that I do any longer. I can't keep lying to you."

She shrank back against the arm of the sofa as sudden anger and revulsion filled her. "You . . . you're on the side of the *Yankees?* Like that Hatcher boy—"

"No," Spanner said. "Not like Nathan Hatcher. From what I've heard, he went off to fight for the Union. I'd never do that. I think both sides are wrong to be waging war."

"But how can you feel like that? The Yankees invaded us!"

"Only because we provoked them when the Southern states began to secede—"

"We had a right to do that! We had a right to form our own country if they were going to try to dictate to us!"

Spanner shook his head. "I'm not going to argue the causes of the war with you, Abby. The folks up north say it's all about slavery, and down here they argue states' rights. It doesn't matter." He leaned toward her, his expression intense. "Don't you see? It's all just an excuse for man to revert to savagery! In the end, it's just about the killing, and the Lord says *Thou shalt not kill.*"

Abigail wanted to clap her hands over her ears so she couldn't hear what he was saying. She had never even considered the possibility that he might be opposed to the war. Everyone she knew hated the Yankees and believed in the cause of the South. Everyone except Nathan Hatcher, and he had deserted his home and run off to the North like the despicable coward he was. How could Benjamin feel like this?

How could he do this to her?

"Get out," she whispered.

He moved closer to her on the sofa. "Abby, you don't know how hard it's been these past months, getting closer and closer to you, all the while knowing how you felt. I . . . I just couldn't lie to you anymore about how *I* feel—"

"Get out!" she screamed at him. "Get out of my house!"

Spanner's hands reached out and closed on her arms. "I swear in God's holy name, Abby, I love you—"

She pulled her right arm free and her hand flashed up and cracked sharply across his face. He didn't flinch. But a hurt that had nothing to do with her blow bloomed in his eyes.

"Abby, please . . ."

"Don't call me that," she hissed. "Get out of here, or I swear I'll get a gun and shoot you down like the traitorous dog you are."

"You can't mean that."

She stared into his eyes, and as she did so, her body filled with a white-hot pain. It was the pain of what she had lost, even though she realized now she had never really had it. For a moment that spiritual agony wracked her, but then it began to fade, replaced by a cold, slow-moving tide of rage.

"Indeed I do," she said.

Spanner pulled back from her and sighed. "I'd better go," he said. "I'm sorry, Ab—Sister Brannon."

"I'm not your sister," she said. "And I'll never set foot in that church again as long as you're there."

He stood up. "Please, don't cut yourself off from the Lord because of me."

Abigail shook her head. "The Lord's not there. Not as long as you are. He wouldn't show His face to you."

"I'm sorry you feel that way," he said as he put his hat on. "I wish I hadn't hurt you so badly. But I couldn't continue lying to you of all people."

He turned and walked out of the parlor. A moment later, Abigail heard the front door open and close. Then came the slow hoofbeats of the preacher's horse as he rode away.

"Why not, Ben?" she whispered aloud as the tears rolled down her face. "Dear Lord, why couldn't you have just kept on lying to me?"

—〜〜—

ROMAN EASED the door open, willing the hinges not to creak as he did so. If Massa Yancy had fallen asleep, Roman didn't want to disturb him. The doctoring could wait until later. Roman believed that the rest would do Yancy as much good as anything.

"What the devil do you want?" came the hoarse voice from inside the library.

Roman took a deep breath, pulled the door open the rest of the way, and stepped into the room. "Time to change that poultice, Massa Yancy."

"Later," Yancy said from the armchair where he spent most of his waking hours and many of his sleeping ones. "I don't feel like it now."

Roman hesitated. He had been willing to postpone changing the poultice for a while if Yancy was sleeping, but since his master was awake, it would be better to go ahead and get it over with. He came farther into the room. "It won't take long, Massa Yancy—"

"I said later, damn it!"

Roman didn't allow himself to feel anger at the lashing tone of Yancy's voice. At least Yancy wasn't drunk all the time anymore. Since Mister Will's visit a few days earlier, that no-account Israel Quinn and his jugs of moonshine hadn't been anywhere near Tanglewood, as far as Roman knew. When Quinn hadn't shown up to make his usual delivery, Yancy had ordered Roman to ride over to the man's place and find out why. Roman had a pretty good idea: Mister Will had paid a visit to Quinn and put a stop to his selling liquor to Yancy. But he knew if he tried to explain that, Yancy would just get angrier with him. So he lied. "I'll see what I can do 'bout that, Massa Yancy."

The first few days had been hard. Yancy had yelled and threatened and raged as the need for the whiskey almost consumed him. But now the demons that had been gnawing at him had eased up at last, and Roman was starting to have hope again.

It helped, too, that the army doctor had come by and tended to Yancy's leg. That was more of Mister Will's doing, Roman knew. The doctor had shown him how to make the poultices that would draw the infection out of Yancy's leg and had given him orders to change them several times each day.

Roman had done so, ignoring any objections Yancy might make. Yancy was too weak and miserable to do anything about it other than complain and threaten to sell Roman to Duncan Ebersole. "Now, Massa Yancy, we both know you don't want to do that," Roman always said. In the back of his mind, though, the fear lurked that Yancy might someday carry through on his threat, no matter what Mister Will had said about seeing to it that he didn't. Only a couple of days after Will had been here at Tanglewood, the army had moved out, and Mister Will had gone with them, of course. Roman wasn't completely sure he was safe from the cruelties of the Scotsman Ebersole.

He approached Yancy, carrying the bucket containing the hot, damp towels he would wrap around the stump of Yancy's right leg as a poultice. The towels were soaked in hot water in which some sort of medicine had been mixed. The doctor had given him a small bottle of the stuff and told him what to do, but that was all Roman knew. The doctor had called the medicine "carbolic acid," or something like that. Roman wished he could learn about such things. He knew how to read and write, which was more than most slaves could do, but there was so much else in the world to learn. Sometimes he stood and looked at all the books in this room and wished he had the time to read them all and study them until he understood them.

But there was too much to do in taking care of Massa Yancy and seeing that the plantation continued to run as smoothly as possible under the circumstances of the war.

"Get away from me with that," Yancy snapped, waving a hand at Roman as he approached with the bucket.

"Now, Massa Yancy, you know that the doctor said to change these poultices three, four times a day. It won't take long."

"Damn you, I said—"

Yancy stopped short as running footsteps made both him and Roman look toward the door of the library. A small black boy, the son of one of the maids, burst into the room. "Roman, they a rider a-comin'!" he said excitedly.

"Who is it?" Roman asked.

"Mama says she thinks it's that Massa Quinn."

Yancy sat up straighter. "Israel—?"

Roman set the bucket on the floor. "I'll see about this, Massa Yancy," he said as he turned toward the door.

"Blast it, if it's Israel, you send him in here! You hear me, Roman? You send him in here!"

Roman shooed the little boy out of the library and followed him into the hall. He hurried toward the front of the house.

As he stepped out onto the gallery, he saw that the visitor to Tanglewood was indeed Israel Quinn. The tall, spare, hatchet-faced white man rode up the lane and reined his horse to a stop in front of the house. He had a jug tied to the saddle and a rifle lying crosswise in front of him.

"You there, boy!" Quinn called as soon as he saw Roman. "I come to pay a call on Mister Lattimer. Come take care of this horse for me."

Roman shook his head, and when he saw the anger flare in Quinn's eyes, he said hurriedly, "Massa Yancy, he's asleep, suh. That's all I mean. I ain't meanin' to be disrespectful."

"You best watch your tongue, boy." Quinn reached for the jug and started to untie the thong that held it to the saddle. "You give him this and tell him I'll settle up with him later."

Roman risked Quinn's anger again. "No, suh, he say for me to tell you he don't want no more of that 'shine."

Quinn paused. "Is that so? Well, I reckon I'm gonna have to hear that from Yancy hisself before I take the word of a slave."

The sudden thudding behind Roman went through him with a shock like he'd been struck by lightning. He turned in time to see Yancy push awkwardly through the door, balancing on his crutches. "Israel!" Yancy called. "Thank God you've come. Don't listen to this damned darky. You're welcome here at Tanglewood any time."

Quinn looked at Roman with an expression that was half-scowl, half-smirk. "Lied to me, did you, boy? Well, I'll let your master deal with you. Was it me, though, Yancy, I'd have this black bastard whipped."

"That's exactly what I'm going to do."

Yancy's words and the look he gave hurt Roman more than any whip ever could. But Massa Yancy wasn't himself these days, Roman reminded himself. He hadn't been ever since he was hurt in that battle. And he was worse now. No matter what, though, Roman couldn't find it in his heart to blame Yancy.

Quinn swung a long leg over the saddle and stepped down from the horse. He had the jug in his hand. He lifted it and grinned. "Got some mighty good brew here, Yancy. It'll lift your spirits better than any other medicine."

"I can use it," Yancy said as Quinn came up on the gallery. "Where've you been the past few days?"

Quinn grimaced. "That bastard Brannon came by my place, threatened me if I brought you any more whiskey. Like it's any of his damned business. Anyway, he's gone now. I couldn't let him stand between a couple of friends like us."

Israel Quinn was no friend to Massa Yancy, Roman thought. And someone had to stand up to him, because Yancy certainly wasn't going to do it.

"Massa Quinn," Roman said, overcoming the ingrained urge to step out of the way and cast his eyes toward the floor. "Massa Quinn, the doctor say Massa Yancy don't need that stuff. I been doin' all the doctorin' Massa Yancy needs."

"Shut up and take care of Israel's horse," Yancy snapped. "I swear, you're as bad as some old mammy, Roman."

"Massa Yancy, I just tryin' to take care of you." Roman moved forward even more, trying to get between Yancy and Quinn. "Massa Quinn, you best go on and get out of here."

Quinn stopped in his tracks and stared at Roman. "Boy, are you threatenin' me?" he demanded, his eyes burning with fury.

"No, suh, just tryin' to make you see that Massa Yancy don't need—"

"Get the hell out of my way." As he snarled the words, Israel Quinn backhanded a fist across Roman's face. The blow was fast and hard and brutal, and it knocked Roman's head to one side. He stumbled and tried to catch himself, but Quinn kicked his feet out from under him, and Roman fell to the gallery.

Quinn started to kick him, the white man's boot heel driving again and again into Roman's side. "You black son of a bitch! You damned ape! Don't you dare sass me!"

With each word, Quinn's foot smashed again into Roman's ribcage. Pain washed over Roman, and though he struggled against it and tried to get up or at least roll out of the way of the kicks, he couldn't move. Along with the savage physical assault, Quinn rained down curses on Roman.

"Israel, no!" Yancy cried. "You don't have to do that!"

"Somebody's got to teach this darky a lesson. You can't do it no more, Yancy, so I'll do you a favor and take care of it for you." Quinn smashed one last kick into Roman's belly. "There! He won't ever dare disrespect a white man again." Quinn was breathing hard. "Let's go on inside and get out of the heat. You got to sample this brew."

That was all Roman heard before he passed out.

———※———

HE HAD no idea how long he was unconscious. All he knew when he woke up was that he hurt all over. He had never been beaten on Tanglewood, never until today. Slaves on other plantations knew what it was like to endure such punishment, but not those who lived here. Not Roman.

A groan shuddered from his body as he pushed himself to his hands and knees. His whole torso was a ball of pain. He reached out for the railing that ran along the edge of the gallery and managed to get hold of it. He steadied himself, got his other hand on the railing, and pulled himself up. Then, leaning against the railing while he breathed hard through teeth gritted tightly against the pain, he looked around.

Israel Quinn's horse was gone. It could be that one of the other slaves had put the animal in the barn, but Roman didn't think so. He had a feeling that Quinn was gone, too.

In fact, no one was in sight. The other house servants probably had seen or heard Quinn's vicious attack on him and were still hiding.

Massa Yancy! . . . He had to find Massa Yancy.

Roman took a stumbling step away from the railing and almost fell. He managed to stay on his feet and totter toward the front door, which stood open. As he went inside, he called, "M-Massa Yancy?" His voice was choked and barely audible, even to himself. He stopped and tried to take a deep breath, then winced and almost doubled over in pain. He had at least one broken rib, he decided. He pressed his arm against his side and started down the hall toward the library. That was probably where he would find Yancy.

That door stood ajar. As he reached it, Roman leaned on the jamb. "Massa Yancy?" He looked at the armchair near the fireplace. It was empty.

Then a metallic sound made him look toward the desk on the other side of the room. His eyes widened in surprise as he saw Yancy sitting behind the desk, just like in the old days.

The difference was that instead of a ledger book and a pen, Yancy now had the whiskey jug on the desk in front of him and a revolver in his hands. As Roman stared in horror, he snapped the cylinder of the weapon closed.

"M-Massa Yancy, what're you doin' with that gun?"

"I'm sorry, Roman," Yancy said. "I never should have let Quinn do that to you. There was a time I would have thrashed him for daring to lay a hand on one of my people."

Yancy's voice was stronger than he had heard it in quite some time, Roman thought, but it had a blurred quality to it, too, and he knew that Yancy had been drinking. In fact, as Roman watched, Yancy lifted the jug with his other hand and took a long swallow from it. The jug thumped back onto the desk when Yancy finally lowered it.

"Massa Yancy, you best put that gun away and let me have that jug," Roman said as he started across the room, trying not to wince or surrender to the pain. He had to be strong for his master. "I'll pour out the rest of that whiskey. You don't need it no more."

"You're right." Yancy shoved the jug away from him and lifted the gun. "This is all I need."

"Massa Yancy, where's Massa Quinn?"

"Gone. Long gone. I paid him and he left."

"You ain't got to go after him, suh. Not on my account."

Yancy had been staring at the revolver. He lifted his eyes from it and looked at Roman. "Is that what you think I was about to do? Go after Israel Quinn?"

"Massa Yancy, I don't know no more what you're goin' to do. I just don't want you to get hurt—"

Yancy laughed. "A bit too late for that, isn't it? I'm a cripple now. I couldn't go after Quinn even if I wanted to. But I don't. I wish he hadn't hurt you, but I'm greatly indebted to the man."

Roman shook his head. "Massa Yancy—"

"Israel showed me all that I'm good for now. He showed me that I'm useless. I can't even protect the people I care about. I can't do nothing."

Roman was halfway across the big room now. "Massa Yancy, that's not true."

"Yes, it is." Yancy pulled back the hammer of the revolver. "I carried this gun through all the battles I was in, but in the end, it couldn't save me. Now it can." He looked at Roman again. "I'm sorry."

"Massa Yancy, no!"

Roman lunged toward the desk, but he was too far away, too late to do any good. Yancy Lattimer pressed the barrel of the revolver against the side of his own head and pulled the trigger. The booming gunshot echoed back from the dark, leather-bound volumes that lined the room with their secret knowledge.

Chapter Thirteen

ABLACK HAZE SEEMED TO hang over Fleetwood Hill. As the group of riders drew closer, Mac saw that it wasn't haze at all. The air was filled with flies, buzzing around the feast that had been left for them by the battle the day before.

Mac's jaw clenched as he drew rein and surveyed the field along with Stuart, Lee, and the other officers. Burial details were already at work this morning, but still the ground around Fleetwood Hill was covered with the bodies of dead men and dead horses. The stench of blood filled the air along with the flies.

Stuart's face was grim. At least for today, he was no longer the laughing cavalier. The previous night he had insisted that the cavalry make camp in exactly the same spot it had occupied when the day began. That had been impossible. The top of the hill, like the slopes and the area along the river, was carpeted with corpses and the debris of battle. Faced with that grisly reality, Stuart finally had done the prudent thing and ordered his headquarters moved to Brandy Station.

Now, as he looked out across the field from the hilltop, the general muttered, "We'll get this cleaned up, and then the lads will need a rest."

Mac brushed a gauntleted hand at the flies buzzing in front of his face. Far too many of the "lads" would be resting from now on, he thought, an eternal rest.

There was movement on the field as the burial details went about their work, but Mac spotted a civilian prowling around as well. While Stuart and the other generals carried on a low-voiced discussion, Mac turned the stallion and rode over to where the man had made his way to a cluster of Yankee bodies. The Union cavalrymen lay there in shredded uniforms and torn flesh. They and their horses, which also sprawled stiffly on the ground, obviously had been caught and flayed by a bursting artillery shell.

Mac was afraid the civilian was a corpse robber, but as he came closer he saw that the man was attired in a rather expensive tweed suit and a fine bowler hat. He didn't look like the sort who would be stealing from the bodies of dead soldiers. The fellow looked up as Mac approached, revealing a lean face made to look even more narrow by bushy muttonchop whiskers.

"You shouldn't be out here, sir," Mac said as he reined in. "This is no place for civilians."

The man grunted and waved his hand toward the corpse-littered ground. "No place for these soldiers, either, by the looks of them," he said.

"Losses in battle are always regrettable."

"It's not these Yankees that bother me so much. It's all our boys who died here for nothing."

Mac stiffened. "They died for the South, sir. For their homes. Their families."

"The Cause deserves better than that prancing fop." Venom dripped from the man's words as he looked toward Stuart and the group of officers around the general. "Why doesn't he stage one of his fancy reviews now? He's got a captive audience here. These men aren't going anywhere until they're dumped in a hole in the ground."

Mac felt his anger growing. "Sir, you have no right to say such things."

"I have every right," the man insisted. "I have eyes, don't I? I was here yesterday. I saw how the Yankees surprised you boys, not once but twice. Stuart's damned lucky his entire command wasn't wiped out."

Mac didn't recall seeing the man the day before. "Just who are you?"

"Higham, from the Richmond *Examiner.*"

"A newspaper correspondent."

"That's right." Higham looked around. "And I'm going to have a great deal to write about in the dispatch I will be sending to the paper."

"You'd be well advised to write the truth."

Higham gave him a cold, smug smile. "That's exactly what I intend to do, Captain."

Mac's fury was rising. "Get off this field, sir. You don't belong here." He made an effort to control his voice as he spoke.

"On the contrary, someone has to tell the people of the South what really happened here. That's my job. You do yours, Captain, and you won't have to worry about what I might write."

Short of dismounting and thrashing the man, Mac knew there was nothing he could do. He turned the stallion and rode back to the others, but as he did so, the disdainful stare of the journalist followed him. He could feel it burning into his back.

"What was that about?" Fitz Lee asked him. "Who is that?"

"No one important, sir," Mac replied. "Just another scavenger on the battlefield."

———⟋⟍⟍———

THE BLUE RIDGE is beautiful country. The blue-green pines on the slopes of the mountains give them their name. Will had been through Chester Gap and into the Shenandoah Valley several times, and he knew that under other circumstances this would have been a pleasurable trip indeed. Even with the prospect of battle facing him, there were moments when Will looked around and relished the warm sun on his face and the mingled scent of pines and wildflowers in the air.

Perhaps it was not in spite of the coming battle but because of it that everything seemed sweeter and more beautiful, he thought as he rode at the head of his company toward the town of Winchester. He had noticed before how the threat of death seemed to sharpen a man's senses and make him more appreciative of life.

On the previous evening, June 12, Ewell had outlined his strategy to his staff and his officers. Winchester was in the hands of the Yankees, squarely in the path of Robert E. Lee's advance toward the Potomac. A considerable force, upwards of five thousand men, was supposed to be in place there, under the command of Maj. Gen. Robert H. Milroy. With an entire Confederate corps approaching, a more prudent officer might have withdrawn. Harpers Ferry lay only thirty miles to the northeast. But the scouts ranging out in front of Ewell's advance indicated that the Yankees in Winchester were staying put.

Ewell intended to come up from the south, split his forces around the town, and feint with Edward Johnson's division from the east while the main thrust of the attack would come from Jubal Early's division to the west.

On the map spread out on a table in his headquarters tent, the balding, feisty Ewell speared a finger at three fortifications on the west side of Winchester. "These forts are the key," he said. "If we take them, the town is ours."

It seemed like a good plan to Will. His only problem with it was that the Stonewall Brigade, as part of Johnson's division, would serve as not much more than a diversion to the Yankees. The men on the other side of town would catch the brunt of the real fighting.

Johnson, followed by his staff, came riding back along the column, checking on the disposition of the troops. "Old Allegheny," as he was called, was well liked by most of the men and received cheers and salutes as he rode down the line. Badly wounded in the foot during Jackson's Shenandoah Valley campaign the year before, Johnson carried a cane with him everywhere he went, even when he was in the saddle. The cane was as much a bludgeon as anything else, being a thick, heavy length of wood, and he waved it jauntily at the men as he rode past.

Not long after that, Will heard the crackle of gunfire in the distance to the north. The leading edge of the Confederate advance must have encountered Yankee pickets south of Winchester. Will motioned for Darcy to keep the men moving while he rode ahead to join the officers gathering around James Walker, the commander of the Stonewall Brigade.

A heavy-faced man with a prominent dimple in his chin, Walker was a well-respected officer and had been promoted to major general on the recommendation of Stonewall Jackson himself, who had been one of Walker's instructors at the Virginia Military Institute. Walker had not attained his position by trading on old friendships, however. Will had heard that Walker had been dismissed from the Institute by Jackson and had even challenged Jackson to a duel as a result of that disciplinary action. No such duel had ever been fought, to the best of Will's knowledge, but everything Walker had achieved since entering the Confederate army had been due to his prowess as a soldier and commander.

"Gentlemen, swing your troops to the northeast and continue to advance until you draw even with Winchester," Walker ordered now. "Then you are to demonstrate in the direction of the town."

Nods of agreement and understanding came from the cluster of officers. They saluted and rode back to their men.

The firing in the distance was more intense now. As Will rode up, Darcy Bennett grinned at him. "Are we goin' to get in on any o' that, Cap'n?"

"Not right away," Will told him. "We're veering to the northeast, then we'll turn west toward Winchester."

"Dang," Darcy said. "I was hopin' to smell some powder smoke before the day was over."

It was still possible the sergeant could get his wish, Will thought. There was no guarantee the Yankees would respond as Ewell expected them to. You never could tell what an army might do.

But if the Union commander made the mistake of concentrating on Johnson's division to the east, he would find himself overrun by Early's division in the rear. Either way, Will had a good feeling about this battle.

During the afternoon of June 13, Will's company and the rest of Johnson's division moved into position east of Winchester and slowly advanced toward the town. Reports reached headquarters that the Yankees had withdrawn from the skirmish line south of Winchester and concentrated their forces in the three forts, just as Ewell had predicted.

So far, all the elements were lining up as the Confederate commander had hoped.

The feint from the east was not totally unopposed, however. As Will and the others moved up, they encountered Federal skirmishers. The Yankees didn't seem to have any artillery on this side of town, however. The Confederate cannons sent the defenders scrambling for cover and then fleeing back toward the town itself. Johnson and his men drew steadily closer, keeping the eyes of the Yankees on them, not on what was going on west of town.

When night fell, everything was still settling into place. Will didn't bother to pitch his tent. He and the rest of the men ate their supper and then sprawled out on the ground underneath some trees. The lights of Winchester were visible a couple of miles away. Will figured that the Yankees were also peering out into the night and seeing the cooking fires of the Confederate army. About now, they'd be getting a mite nervous, he thought with a grin as he dozed off.

The next morning, Johnson's artillery came into play again, lobbing shells into the woods between their position and the town. Brigades of men marched around, creating plenty of dust and ensuring that the sound of tramping feet reached to the ears of the defenders. If they could make the Yankees believe that the whole Army of Northern Virginia was over here, so much the better, Will thought. He sensed a restlessness in his men, however. They were ready for action.

Will's own impatience grew as the sun beat down hotly and the day wore on. He wondered what Ewell was doing. Was Early's division still being shifted into position for the attack on the forts? Noon came and went, and still the men marched and postured and pretended to be threatening the town.

Finally, past midafternoon, a thunderous roar sounded in the west. As Will heard the shelling commence, he leaned forward in the saddle. Hard on the heels of the first Confederate volley came a ragged burst of return fire from the Yankee gunners. Those scattered blasts, however, were drowned out by another peal of thunder from Early's artillery.

"Take it easy, boys," Will called to his troops. Now that the full-scale attack from the west was underway, the Stonewall Brigade and the other units to the east of Winchester could stop their pretending. Instead, they now held themselves ready to move and cut off any retreat by the Yankees.

The barrage continued for ninety minutes. When it finally stopped, it was followed by high, keening yells as Early's infantry swarmed down a hill toward the forts where the Union defenders were huddled. As Will listened to the distant shouts and the rattle of musketry, he could imagine the scene being played out on the other side of town.

He wasn't the only one. Darcy Bennett said disgustedly, "Dadgum it! I wish we were over yonder and not stuck here."

"We're doing our job, Darcy," Will assured him, although he knew exactly how the sergeant felt. He felt pretty much the same way himself.

As night fell, cannon fire erupted again. Reports reached Johnson that Early's forces had captured the westernmost of the three forts and were now using captured artillery from there to blast the Federals out of the other two forts. Gradually, those forts were abandoned, too, as the last of the troops pulled back into Winchester itself.

Around ten o'clock, a messenger from Ewell galloped up to Johnson's headquarters tent and flung himself out of the saddle. Will was nearby with General Walker and some of the other company commanders from the Stonewall Brigade, so it was impossible not to overhear the message.

"General Ewell's regards, sir," gasped out the young lieutenant. "The general instructs me to tell you that the Federal forces formerly in Winchester are now retreating toward Harpers Ferry on the Martinsburg turnpike."

Sulphurous curses spilled from Johnson. The general was known far and wide for his colorful language. "We'll just have to get in front of them," he declared. He swung around, looking at the officers gathered nearby. "General Steuart!"

Brig. Gen. George H. Steuart stepped forward. A handsome man in his midthirties with sleek dark hair, Steuart had been born in Baltimore and was known as "Maryland" to many of his fellow officers. "General, I am at your disposal."

"General, take your brigade and intercept the Yankees," Johnson ordered. "My staff and I shall accompany you."

"It will be our honor, General," Steuart replied.

Johnson turned. "General Walker, your brigade will support General Steuart's."

Walker acknowledged the order, but Will felt a twinge of disappointment. Once again, the Stonewall Brigade had been cast in a supporting role rather than taking the lead. If Old Jack were still alive, that wouldn't have been the case, he thought. He had nothing against Ewell, but in the minds of the men who had followed Stonewall Jackson, Ewell would never be equal to the man he had replaced.

Walker sent the captains hurrying back to their companies. As Will came up to the campfire where Darcy was sitting, the sergeant leaped to his feet, perhaps reading on Will's face that they were about to go into action.

"Get the men ready to move, Sergeant," Will ordered. "The Yankees are running, and we have to get in their way."

"Damn well about time, Cap'n," Darcy said with a grin. He snatched his rifle from a stack of weapons and bellowed to the rest of the company, "On your feet, boys! The Yankees are rabbits, and we're the hounds!"

A corporal saddled the dun and brought it to Will. He swung up on the horse's back and watched in approval as the men of the Thirty-third Virginia prepared to move out. Only a short time later, they were ready to go, their rifles canted rakishly over their shoulders and grins of anticipation on the men's weathered faces. A midnight march like this was a challenge, but they hadn't done much more than rest all day. Will was confident that they were up to whatever was required of them.

All that remained was to wait for the order to move out. It took a long time coming.

Will's impatience grew when the order didn't come. Elsewhere in the sprawling camp that housed the division, Steuart's brigade tramped off to the north, accompanied by their artillery and by the small party composed of Johnson and his staff. Will had expected the Stonewall Brigade to move out right behind them. But still they waited for the order.

Will was never sure what had happened to delay the departure of the Stonewall Brigade. He suspected that one of the other companies was slow in getting ready. Either that, or there was a missed communication between the commanders. The reason didn't really matter, he told himself. What was important was that almost an hour passed after Steuart's brigade left before the Stonewall Brigade received the order to follow. Once the men were moving, they stepped out at a quick march, but Will feared they might be too late. By moving fast across country, Steuart might be able to get in front of the Yankees on the Martinsburg turnpike and cut off their retreat.

The question was, With only one brigade, would he be able to hold them until help arrived?

—m—

THE TURNPIKE curved to the northeast from Winchester, and running roughly parallel to it, on the south side of the road, were the tracks of the Winchester and Potomac Railroad. The first stop out of Winchester on the rail line was the tiny hamlet of Stephenson's Depot, which was nothing more than the depot itself and a couple of houses.

Also nearby, just west of the depot, was a spot where one of the smaller roads that intersected the turnpike crossed over the railroad on a bridge that spanned the deep cut where the tracks ran. The turnpike itself was only a short distance to the north.

Several hours after midnight, in response to a signal from Gen. Edward Johnson, a party of Confederate officers reined their horses to a stop on the bridge over the railroad cut. Gen. "Maryland" Steuart was with Johnson, and each man was accompanied by his staff.

Johnson listened intently, and after a few moments some of his customary curses came from his mouth. "Listen to that," he told Steuart.

Noises carried well on this quiet night. Steuart nodded as he heard low-pitched voices calling orders and the rhythmic thudding of a great many horses' hooves against the hard-packed dirt surface of the turnpike.

"Must be the Yankees, General," Steuart said. "I'll send some scouts forward to find out just how close they are."

"Better make it quick," Johnson growled. "It sounds as if they're almost upon us."

Steuart motioned a couple of his scouts forward from the mass of infantry that had halted just south of the bridge. Hastily, he gave the men their orders, and the two soldiers slipped off into the night, their shadowy forms disappearing from sight within a matter of moments.

While the scouts were checking on the proximity of the Federal force, Steuart surveyed the situation as best he could. The bridge was on a slight rise, which was why the cut had been constructed and the railroad tracks routed through it. This elevation gave the Confederates a vantage point from which they could sweep the turnpike below with rifle and artillery fire. And the banks of the cut itself would give his men shelter for any return fire, Steuart decided.

"I'd like to place my men here, General," he said, turning to Johnson.

"They're your men, General," responded Johnson. "Place 'em where you damned well please."

Steuart issued the order to one of his aides then added, "Have Captain Dement send up one of his guns."

Within moments, the infantrymen began to move up, and as they arrived at the railroad, they were directed down into the cut. The banks were steep but not impossible to descend. Soldiers slid down the south bank, hurried across the tracks, and scrambled up the north bank, stopping at the top to poke their rifles over and draw a bead on the turnpike.

In the meantime, one of the cannon was brought forward, but before it could reach the bridge, the spiteful cracking sound of rifle shots disturbed the night. Johnson, Steuart, and the other officers had withdrawn from the bridge and were sitting on their horses near the southern end. Johnson stiffened and lifted himself in his stirrups. "That'll be our scouts encountering Milroy's men. I would have preferred that Milroy not know we were here until we were ready, but so be it."

Mere seconds later, a volley of gunfire rang out nearby, followed by shouts. Bullets whined over the heads of the officers, too close for comfort. Steuart exclaimed, "By God, the Yankees are attacking!"

The Yankees were indeed pouring through the woods between the turnpike and the railroad. The Federal force was still sizable, and though it was difficult to tell in the moonlight, it looked as if Milroy had committed all of his men to the attack. Steuart twisted in the saddle and bellowed for the rest of his men to hurry into the railroad cut. To those who were already in the protection of the cut, he ordered them to fire at will. His horse reared up, startled by the sudden gunfire so close.

Drawing a tight rein, Steuart brought the animal under control. He said to Johnson, "It might be prudent for us to move to the rear, General."

Johnson lifted his cane and brandished it like a sword. "I wish I could ride amongst the blue-bellied bastards and give 'em a taste of this! But I suppose you're right, General. But damn prudence, anyway."

The division commander didn't argue further. He and Steuart moved back behind the infantry that was still flooding into the railroad cut.

Steuart looked around. "Where's Walker?" he asked. "Where's the Stonewall Brigade?"

"They were supposed to be supporting you," Johnson said. "Those were my orders. Good Lord, what's become of them?"

Steuart shook his head. "I don't know, sir. Looks like we'll have to make do without them."

The riflemen inside the railroad cut were blazing away, and their fire took a heavy toll among the Yankees. The cannon that had been brought up from the rear had reached the bridge by now. With its wheels rattling the planks, it was rolled out onto the narrow structure and turned at an angle so that its muzzle was pointed toward the forefront of the Union line. The gun crew sprang to work loading it, but before they could get a shot off, two of the men jerked and fell as bullets flew up the slope from the Yankee position. More men hurried to take their place.

A few minutes later, the cannon was ready, and it roared and belched flame from its muzzle as the gunner pulled the lanyard. The recoil sent the cannon jolting backward, toward the edge of the bridge. With startled yells, men leaped to grab the gun carriage and hang on to it as they tried to keep it from toppling off the bridge.

The gun was wrestled back into place and loaded. Another man fell, fatally wounded by Yankee lead. Moments later the cannon boomed again, sending another shell into the onrushing horde. Again the recoil sent it skidding perilously close to the edge of the bridge before it could be stopped.

"Damn it, chock those wheels!" shouted one of the officers. Then he made a gagging sound as a Union bullet tore away his throat. He spun around and crumpled, hitting the edge of the bridge and falling into the railroad cut below. Some of the men shouted in alarm as the artillery officer landed among them. It must have seemed to them that it was raining corpses.

On the far side of the cut, Johnson and Steuart dismounted and stood side by side, trying to follow the progress of the battle, which was difficult to do in the darkness that was only intermittently lit by the flashes of guns. "We're outnumbered, General," Johnson murmured, "but your men are fighting valiantly."

"Of course, sir," Steuart said offhandedly. "I never doubted that they would."

"There are only so many of those charges we can withstand. Damn it, where's the Stonewall Brigade? They should have been here by now."

On this night, Johnson was not the only one to express that particular sentiment.

WILL DISMOUNTED and led his horse because it was too dark to see in these woods. Darcy Bennett and the rest of the company crashed through the brush behind him. Somewhere up ahead, someone had taken a wrong turn, and the brigade was floundering through the countryside, searching for the fight that they knew had to be up there somewhere.

Suddenly, Will emerged from the trees and found himself on a narrow road. Confederate troops were streaming along it, moving as fast as they could. A glance at the stars told Will that the men were heading almost due north. The sky also told him that dawn was not too far off, no more than an hour.

Will swung up onto the dun, reined over to the side of the road, and waved Darcy and the rest of the men on. Now that the Stonewall Brigade had reached this road, the troops began to move faster. A few minutes later, the sounds of battle became audible over the tramping of feet.

Fighting the impulse to gallop ahead, Will stayed with his men. The sky lightened some more, and some of the stars began to fade out against the creeping grayness. Will could see Darcy's rough-hewn face better as the sergeant grinned up at him. "Sounds like the party's still goin' on, Cap'n."

"Yes, and I'm sure that the Yankees have no doubt saved a dance for you, Darcy."

That brought a chuckle from the burly sergeant. "We'll show 'em a Virginia Reel, sure enough."

As the firing grew louder, the pace of the march increased until the men were almost running. Will loosened his saber in its scabbard as he trotted the dun alongside the men. The ground rose in a gentle slope, and he spotted bursts of fire at its crest. A cannon boomed.

The orderly advance of the Stonewall Brigade turned into an all-out charge. Spreading out over a wide line, the Confederate soldiers surged up the rise, howling as they went. Will finally gave in to his natural inclination and rode ahead, and as he did so, he heard the whine of bullets in the air.

He reined in when he reached the top of the slope. He found himself on the edge of a deep gully that he recognized a second later as a railroad cut. Off to his right, the gully was spanned by a bridge. The cut was full of Confederate soldiers firing desperately at the Yankees, who looked to be no more than twenty yards away on the other side of the gully. Will's saber rasped against the scabbard as he pulled it and lifted it over his head. "Pour it into 'em, boys!"

The reinforcements opened a steady fire, sending volley after volley into the Union ranks. The Yankees, who had been in the midst of a charge, saw their line suddenly falter. More men fell than in any of the previous attacks. The cannon on the bridge roared again, and the bursting shell mowed down even more of Milroy's forces.

An officer rode up to the south end of the bridge and shouted, "Up and after them, boys!" Will recognized the voice as that of Gen. George Steuart. He hadn't seen General Johnson yet, and he hoped that Old Allegheny was all right.

Darcy Bennett slid down the bank into the cut, shouting for the men of the Thirty-third Virginia to follow him. They swarmed into the cut and up the far side, leapfrogging the exhausted men who had been holding out against the Yankee attack for several hours. Then they crashed into the weakened Federal line, and it buckled and gave way completely. The Yankees turned and ran, many of them dropping their weapons.

Will rode back and forth on the edge of the cut, grimacing in frustration. He couldn't take his horse down that steep slope, and the bridge was blocked by the cannon—and by the bodies of the fallen gunners that lay sprawled all around it. It had cost a terrible price in blood, but the gun had remained in action all through the battle.

On the far side of the railroad cut, the rout was on. The Yankees had battered the Confederate line half the night, only to be thwarted when they were convinced they were on the verge of triumph. The Stonewall Brigade had arrived in time to swing the momentum around and break the back of the Union thrust. As the sky grew lighter and the sun finally began to peek over the eastern horizon, the last of the vicious hand-to-hand fighting dwindled away. All that was left was the rounding up of prisoners and captured supplies and artillery.

Steuart rode up to the bridge again, and Will was relieved to see that Johnson was with him now. Johnson shook his cane at the routed Federal forces. "Try to get past us, will you, you miserable, double-damned Yankee bastards!"

Steuart looked at Will. "Glad to see you, Captain," he said. "I assume you're with the Stonewall Brigade."

"Yes sir. Captain William Brannon of the Thirty-third Virginia."

"You and your boys got here at a very good time. We were just about out of ammunition." Steuart grinned.

"I'll keep that to myself, sir."

"Of course, it would have been better if you boys could have put in an appearance a little bit earlier, but I suppose that was beyond your control. Do you know if anything has happened back in Winchester?"

"No sir," Will said. "I imagine General Early's division has occupied the town by now. As far as I know, all the Yankees pulled out and came this direction."

Steuart nodded. "That means there's almost nothing to stop us now. Maryland awaits us, and beyond that, Pennsylvania."

There was a wistful tone in Steuart's voice as he spoke of his native Maryland. Will just hoped the general's return to his home state was as pleasant as Steuart thought it would be.

Somehow he doubted it.

Chapter Fourteen

THE PASSAGE OF A week since the battles around Brandy Station and Fleetwood Hill had done little to improve the mood of James Ewell Brown Stuart. In fact, Mac thought as he watched Stuart pace in front of the headquarters tent, the general was more upset than ever, although he took pains to conceal how he really felt. He laughed and joked with his staff, but anyone who knew him could see the resentment smoldering in his eyes.

The *Richmond Examiner* had been the harshest in its judgment of Stuart, berating him endlessly in its columns for allowing his command to be surprised by the enemy not once but twice. In addition to the *Examiner*, other newspapers throughout the South had been less than favorable to Stuart in their reporting of the clash between Union and Confederate cavalry. Some had been downright cruel, Mac thought. Stuart tried to laugh it off, but Mac knew the criticism stung the general.

So it was a good thing that they were going into action again, Mac decided. Once they were on the move and fighting Yankees, Stuart's mood would improve.

Camp was being struck after a week in which the five cavalry brigades had done little except rest and lick their wounds. Now Robert E. Lee had need of them again. Ewell's corps, including the Stonewall Brigade, had moved out almost a week ago, soon after the Brandy Station battle. The two corps under the commands of Gens. James Longstreet and A. P. Hill were set to follow. They would cross the Blue Ridge and proceed up the Shenandoah Valley toward the Potomac River and the Maryland border.

Mac had been in attendance at the meeting earlier today at which Stuart had gathered his commanders and given them their orders. In a plan worked out between Stuart and Robert E.

Lee, the cavalry brigades would form a defensive screen along the Loudoun Valley, just east of the Blue Ridge.

If Union Gen. Joseph "Fighting Joe" Hooker did not know already that the Army of Northern Virginia was on the move, he soon would. Lee was confident that Hooker would send his cavalry northward to find out what was going on. It would be Stuart's job to keep the Federals from crossing the mountains and discovering exactly where the Southern army was and where it might be going.

Fitz Lee was still talking to the restlessly pacing Stuart, leaning heavily on a cane as he did so. Lee's bad leg was still bothering him, so Col. Thomas Munford remained in command of Lee's brigade. Munford was not the only substitute commander. Rooney Lee had been wounded during the battle near St. James Church and was out of action. His brigade was now being led by Col. John R. Chambliss.

Mac stood beside Fitz Lee's buggy, waiting for his friend and commanding officer. Lee finished his conversation with Stuart, then limped over to the vehicle and pulled himself up onto the seat. As Lee took up the reins, Mac mounted the stallion and fell in alongside the buggy.

Lee hesitated. "Mac," he said, "you've got to be my eyes and ears. I can't keep up with the brigade in this contraption . . ." He waved a hand at the buggy with a look of disdain that was the cavalryman's natural reaction to any mode of transportation that didn't involve a saddle. "So I expect you to help Tom Munford as much as you can and still keep me apprised of what's going on."

"Yes sir," Mac said. Lee was expecting a lot of him, but Mac would do his best to give the general what he wanted.

"We'll be moving out soon. Are you ready to ride?"

"Always, sir," Mac responded.

Lee grinned and flapped the reins. The team broke into a trot as Lee sent the buggy bouncing back toward his own headquarters. Mac followed, a grin on his face.

By afternoon, three of the five brigades had crossed the Rappahannock and were on their way north, following the Warrenton turnpike. General Stuart rode at their head. If his confidence had been shaken by the battles and their aftermath, he gave no sign of it but instead rode along as jauntily as ever.

The two brigades under Grumble Jones and Wade Hampton remained behind and would do so until the last of the infantry had pulled out for the Blue Ridge, just in case Robert E. Lee had need of them. Then they would rejoin their fellow cavalrymen.

That left three brigades to turn back any Yankee probes across the Loudoun Valley toward the Blue Ridge. To the east of the valley were the smaller Bull Run Mountains. There were two gaps Stuart had pinpointed as likely places for the Yankees to cross into the Loudoun Valley. One brigade would cover each gap; the third brigade would be stationed between them and held in reserve for wherever it might be needed.

Mac hoped that Fitz Lee's brigade would be assigned to one of the gaps, but they wouldn't know until the next day. On June 16, the cavalry proceeded to the vicinity of Upperville, a short distance west of the Bull Run Mountains, and made camp.

The next morning Stuart issued his orders. He and his staff would move on to Middleburg and establish a headquarters there. Fitz Lee's brigade would continue on through Snickers Gap to the small town of Aldie just beyond. Rooney Lee's brigade, under Chambliss, would have the responsibility of protecting Thoroughfare Gap. Held in reserve would be Beverly Robertson's brigade.

Mac was pleased with the orders, not because of the prospect of doing battle with the Yankees, but because he wanted to be near the center of the action so that later he could report first-hand to Fitz Lee. He rode just behind Munford as the brigade proceeded to Aldie, almost in the shadow of the rounded, wooded slopes of the Bull Run Mountains just to the west.

The townspeople who remained in Aldie came out to watch the Confederate cavalry. A few cheers went up at the sight of the horsemen with their colorful sashes and long sabers. Not everyone was pleased to see them, however. Aldie wasn't that far from the Potomac and the Maryland border. Feelings were mixed in this part of the state. Support for the Confederacy was still strong, but a significant number of civilians were Unionists.

After the sally through Aldie, Munford brought his troops back to a point just west of town then gathered his staff and the brigade commanders to issue his orders. "We'll put out pickets around the town," he said, "and establish our main camp here. If the Yankees show up, we'll be in position to turn them back."

Munford wasn't lacking in confidence, Mac thought. A good cavalry commander had to have plenty of that. Sometimes it backfired, but a supreme confidence bordering on arrogance was one of the cavalryman's greatest weapons.

As the day passed, Mac rode from picket post to picket post in a circuit that took him around the town. When he had checked with each position, he turned toward Munford's head-quarters and reported to the colonel. As the afternoon reached its midpoint, Mac had nothing to report except inactivity. There was no sign of the Yankees. He set off once again, estimating that he could make a couple more circuits of Aldie before evening began to settle in.

He was just crossing the Little River turnpike, the main road through the town, when he spotted a haze of dust to the east. Drawing rein, Mac studied the brown haze with a frown. As he watched, it coalesced into a billowing cloud, and Mac knew there was only one thing that could cause that: a large force of horsemen. As far as he knew, there were no Confederate cavalry units that far to the east.

That meant the Yankees were coming.

Mac wheeled the stallion and sent it in a gallop along the turnpike to the west. He came within sight of the village a moment later. A glance over his shoulder told him that the dust cloud was a lot closer now, and though it was probably his imag-ination, he thought he could actually hear the thundering hoofbeats of the horses. He passed one of the picket posts at the edge of the village and saw that the men stationed there were already aware of the onrushing horde. They had their carbines ready and were hunting cover. Mac waved at them as he raced past, carrying the word of the imminent attack to Munford.

He rushed through Aldie, making for headquarters, vaguely aware of the faces of the startled townspeople watching him. Behind him, gunfire began to crackle. The pickets were putting up a show of resistance, but soon they would retreat, drawing the Yankees on toward the waiting Confederates.

No tents had been set up at headquarters; instead, Munford sat at a folding table under a grove of trees next to the road. To the north stretched a long ridge, its crest dotted with haystacks, giving the scene a bucolic, peaceful air in the afternoon sunshine. Munford came to his feet as Mac galloped up, and his face radiated with eagerness. "What is it, Captain?" Munford asked. "I thought I heard firing a moment ago."

"That you did, sir," Mac replied. He waved a hand toward the village. "The Federal cavalry is in Aldie by now."

Munford clenched a fist and nodded. "Our boys will make them think they're on the run and lead them right to us." He swung around to his staff and started barking orders. Dismounted riflemen were to rush to the top of the ridge and conceal themselves behind the haystacks. They would open fire when the Yankees came within range.

The plan struck Mac as a good one. All it needed to succeed was a bit of impetuousness on the part of the Union cavalrymen.

He reached for his carbine, intending to ascend the ridge with the other men, but Munford stopped him. "Hold on, Captain," the colonel said. "You'll stay here, in case I need you to gallop back to General Stuart for further orders."

Mac acknowledged the order but his jaw tensed as he did so. He was a fair shot with a rifle—not as good as his brother Titus had been, but no one in all of Culpeper County had been a better shot than Titus—and wanted to do his part in the coming battle. Mac wouldn't have thought of arguing with Fitz Lee, and he was a little ashamed of himself for having considered it with Munford, even if only for a second.

He stood behind the colonel, holding the stallion's reins. Munford trained his field glasses on the town. After a few minutes, he said, "Here they come."

Even without field glasses, Mac could see the blue-clad riders emerging from the cluster of buildings that marked Aldie. They pounded along the turnpike toward the ridge.

Minutes later, a volley of fire rang out from the men hidden behind the haystacks. The leading edge of the Federal advance faltered. More shots sounded, raggedly now as the riflemen fired as soon as they had reloaded. Down on the turnpike, men and horses fell, and those cavalrymen who were so far untouched by the shots struggled to control their horses as the scent of blood drifted to the animals' nostrils and made them skittish.

Munford turned to the waiting commander of one of the regiments. "Now that we've got their attention, let's show them what we're made of. I want a saber charge!"

"Yes sir!" The captain snapped a salute and ran to where his men waited, ready to mount up and attack the Yankees.

Less than two minutes later, as the sharpshooters on the ridge still poured fire down on the milling Union horsemen, an entire regiment of howling, saber-waving, gray-clad cavalrymen thundered past Mac and Munford. Down the road they charged, and the firing from behind the haystacks died away as the Confederate riflemen saw that their fellows were joining the fray.

Mac clearly heard the clash of steel on steel as the two forces came together. A few pistols cracked, but most of the fighting was done with sabers. Mac had been in the middle of fights like this one, knew all too well the feeling of unreality mixed with anger and fear that came over a man as he swung his saber, blocking the thrusts and slashes of the enemy and trying to strike blows of his own. It was a hard, bloody, terrifying business, and once in the midst of it, all a man could do was try to survive the best he could.

The Confederate cavalrymen were heavily outnumbered. Although they had surprise and an unmatched enthusiasm for combat on their side, sooner or later they had to give ground. When they did, the riflemen on the ridge opened up again, preventing the Yankees from giving chase to the retreating foe. After a few minutes, the Federals withdrew as well.

"There they go," Munford said as he lowered his field glasses. "But they'll be back."

Mac agreed. The Yankee horsemen had demonstrated at Brandy Station and Fleetwood Hill that no longer would they crumble under pressure as they had in past battles. They had a confidence of their own now and what seemed like better leadership than they'd had before. That didn't bode well for the Southern cavalry, Mac thought. So far during the war, the Confederate horsemen had clearly outclassed their Northern opponents, but that might not continue to be the case.

Less than half an hour later, Munford's prediction proved to be correct. The Yankees tried another charge. Once again, the dismounted riflemen broke the back of the attack, and the mounted regiments slammed into the Yankees and forced them to retreat. The engagement was broken off again as the Federals retreated toward Aldie.

"They can keep that up all day," Munford said, "but they won't get past us."

That would depend on how many men the Union commander had in reserve and how stubborn he was, Mac thought. Although the Union losses had been heavier, the brigade had suffered casualties of its own. Some of those bodies of horses and men littering the turnpike and the surrounding fields were Confederate.

The next attack brought a new development. As the Federal cavalry charged yet again, Mac caught sight of movement to the south. "Colonel!" he said urgently. "I think they're trying to flank us!"

Munford swung around and inspected the field. "You're right, Captain. The head-on attack is to be a distraction this time. I was expecting as much."

He issued orders to one of the waiting officers, and within seconds another regiment galloped to cut off the Yankee flank attack. "Go with them, Captain," Munford said to Mac, "and let me know how we fare."

Mac swung up onto the stallion's back and raced after his fellow cavalrymen. He saw a narrow, sunken road winding through the rolling countryside up ahead, and alongside the road was a stone wall. The Yankees would have to follow that road to get around Munford's men, and if the Southerners reached that wall first and dug in behind it . . .

That was exactly what happened. As Mac watched, approximately half of the Southern riders came up to the stone wall, threw themselves out of their saddles, and flung themselves down with their rifles behind the wall. The horses were taken back down a hill, out of sight, where they were held along with the other half of the regiment, which was still mounted. Mac reined in at the top of a nearby knoll where he had a good view of both the road and the wall. A few minutes later, the Yankee cavalry came into sight, galloping along the narrow road. If the Federals had any idea what they were riding into, they gave no sign of it.

A couple of heartbeats passed, then the Confederates behind the wall opened fire. Mac's breath hissed between his teeth as he watched the slaughter, for slaughter it was. Taken by surprise, the Yankees fell in droves as the riflemen rained death upon them in the sunken road. Men and horses screamed and toppled, blood gushing from the wounds torn into their bodies by the Southern lead. The Yankee officers tried to rally their men, but it was no use. In a matter of minutes, the road was covered with corpses.

The still-mounted Confederate cavalrymen joined the battle then, swinging around the end of the wall and attacking with sabers that flashed in the hot sun. The road became a welter of blood and steel as the Southern cavalry hacked its way through the enemy.

This time, the Federal retreat was a rout. The men who survived the ill-advised flanking maneuver now ran for their lives, back toward Aldie. The Confederate commanders let them go, unwilling to split their forces any more than they already were. Seeing that for all intents and purposes this part of the battle was over, Mac swung the stallion around and galloped back to Munford's position.

He got there in time to witness a charge and countercharge along the turnpike as the Yankees continued to try to break through. Out in the lead of the Federal thrust, dangerously exposed, was a Union officer who seemed either heedless or scornful of his peril. Long yellow hair, almost as long and thick as a woman's, spilled from under his blue hat and shone in the sun as he waved his saber and urged his men on. Mac watched him for a moment, reflecting that the Yankee officer was either one of the bravest or one of the most foolhardy men he had ever seen.

The Union charge was turned back yet again. Munford looked up at Mac. "Keep your seat, Captain. I'll be wanting you to ride to General Stuart soon."

"For orders, sir?"

"That's right." Munford wiped a hand over his face, leaving trails in the dust that coated his features. Everybody and everything was dusty on this hot summer day. "We've fought splendidly and delayed the Yankees, but it's becoming obvious that there are too many of them for us to stop them in their tracks. I'd like to pull back through the gap toward Middleburg but will not do so unless and until I receive orders to that effect from General Stuart." He smiled grimly. "If, of course, the general would prefer for us to attempt to hold our lines, then we will do so, to the last man if necessary."

Mac saluted. "Yes sir. I'll tell the general."

Munford returned the salute. "Godspeed to you, Captain."

Mac wheeled the stallion around and heeled it into a run. Behind him, Munford turned back to view the clash of cavalry on the road.

———⚋———

IN MIDDLEBURG, Jeb Stuart had spent a pleasant day relaxing and talking to the ladies of the town, many of whom were friends and acquaintances. They flocked to the temporary headquarters he set up, and while that was going on, the general's staff spread out through the town, also visiting friends.

The massive Heros Von Borke was sitting on the front porch of a house, carrying on a conversation with the family who lived there, when a commotion in the street drew his attention. He stood up and went down the flagstone walk, stepping out through a gate in the white picket fence just as a frantic rider started to gallop past the house.

"Halt!" Von Borke bellowed, and he reached out with one long arm to catch hold of the horse's bridle. His strength was such that he was able to pull the animal to a stop, almost unseating the rider. "Vat are you shouting about?" the calm Prussian demanded of the panicked cavalryman.

"The Yankees are coming, sir!" the man said, twisting in the saddle to point down the road to the east, the direction he had come from.

"Mein Gott!" Von Borke exclaimed. "How did ze get on zis side of the mountains?" He shook his head, waved a big paw, and answered his own question. "It does not matter. Find General Stuart und deliver to him the bad news."

The rider raced away while Von Borke returned to stand at the foot of the steps leading to the porch. He bowed to the small assemblage. "I regret I muss take my leave zo soon, madam," he said to the lady of the house. "Auf Wiedersehen."

He swung up into the saddle and rode toward the center of town, where he knew he would find Stuart. When he got there, he discovered that the courier had delivered the message. Stuart and his staff were preparing to depart from Middleburg.

"I won't fight a battle here if I can avoid it," Stuart said. "Too many innocents would be in jeopardy. Henry," he called to his aide, Captain McClellan. "We'll withdraw to the west and rejoin General Robertson's brigade. Send word to Munford and Chambliss to converge on us with their brigades. I know my boys; they'll move so fast those Yankees will find themselves surrounded before they know what's happening to them."

McClellan nodded and passed along the orders. Men sprang to their horses to carry the word to Munford and Chambliss.

Stuart and his staff rode quickly out of Middleburg and drew up after they had gone a mile or so out of town. The general took out a spyglass and studied the situation for several minutes. "There they are," he said as blue-uniformed riders appeared in the streets of Middleburg. "I can see their flag . . . Rhode Islanders, from the look of it. No match for our lads." He closed the spyglass. "Let's find General Robertson and tell him that the Yankees have come to join our festivities."

A short time later, Stuart and his companions trotted up to the headquarters set up by Beverly Robertson. The brigadier saluted. "I've heard that Federal forces are in Middleburg, General. I'd be pleased to rout them out for you, if you'd like."

"That is exactly what I would like for you to do, General," Stuart told him.

"Do you know the size of the enemy force, General?" Robertson asked. He made a motion with his hand. "Not that it really matters."

A grin stretched across Stuart's face. "As a matter of fact, I don't. But I'm sure our numbers will be sufficient to the task."

"Yes sir." Robertson strode away to mount up.

The smile disappeared from Stuart's face as soon as Robertson had ridden away. The general displayed instead a look of concern. He had not forgotten how the Yankees had gotten around Robertson's forces at Brandy Station.

"Let us hope the general does a better job this time, gentlemen," Stuart said in a voice that only McClellan and Von Borke could hear. "Otherwise we may find ourselves in for a troublesome time."

Robertson's brigade thundered down the road toward Middleburg. The sound of gunfire followed shortly thereafter as the two cavalry forces clashed in the town.

Always restless when he was forced to wait, Von Borke decided to climb a tree to get a better view of what was going on. He pulled his bulky body from branch to branch with an agility that was surprising in such a big man.

"The Yankees are retreating!" he called down to Stuart a few minutes later. "I can see General Robertson's forces pursuing them out of the settlement."

The Rhode Islanders were outnumbered by Robertson's brigade and turned tail to run. Unfortunately for them, by this time the news of their presence in the Loudoun Valley had reached Colonel Chambliss, in command of Rooney Lee's brigade at Thoroughfare Gap. Following Stuart's orders, Chambliss was heading toward Middleburg on the same road that the Yankees were using to flee. As scouts alerted Chambliss to the approaching Federal horsemen, the colonel ordered a charge that took the enemy completely by surprise.

The rout became sheer chaos.

—◆—

PICKETS DIRECTED Mac to Stuart's headquarters. As he approached the tent erected next to the road west of Middleburg, he found Stuart sitting on a three-legged stool, tapping a booted foot in time to the music from a couple of fiddle players.

Mac dismounted and saluted as the musicians ceased playing. "Colonel Munford's compliments, sir."

"Good evening, Captain Brannon," Stuart welcomed him. "I sent for Colonel Munford earlier this afternoon. Did he receive my message?"

"I wouldn't know, sir. I've been looking for you to let you know that the Yankees have moved into the village of Aldie, but when I left we had them stopped west of there. Colonel Munford said to tell you that he doesn't think we can keep them stopped."

Stuart waved a hand. "No need for that. Our job is just to dance with the Yankees for a while, instead of letting them spy on General Lee. I'll send a galloper to tell Colonel Munford to withdraw to Snickers Gap, unless he's already done so. I thought I might need him earlier in the day, but General Robertson and Colonel Chambliss disposed of the Yankee threat. We captured nearly all of them."

"The Yankees were this far west, sir?" Mac asked incredulously. "They must have ridden a long way around, because they didn't come through us."

"Of course not, Captain. I don't know exactly how they got here, but that doesn't really matter now, does it?"

"No sir, I suppose not." Mac turned toward the stallion. "I'll take your orders to Colonel Munford—"

"Rest easy, Captain," Stuart said sharply. "I'd rather send a fresh man on a fresh horse. Supper will be ready soon. I'd be pleased to have you join us."

Mac hesitated then nodded. He couldn't refuse the general. Besides, he had ridden enough today and he was weary. Even the great silver gray stallion wasn't tireless.

It bothered him, though, that the day had been filled with fighting, and he had done nothing but watch it.

"Have a seat," Stuart said, waving to another stool, "and tell me what happened over yonder at Aldie."

Chapter Fifteen

THE NEXT DAY, JUNE 18, was something of a stalemate. Following the return of Munford's brigade, Stuart established a defensive line west of Middleburg but made no move to attack, preferring to wait for the arrival of Grumble Jones and Wade Hampton so that the command would once again be at full strength. Surely the rest of Robert E. Lee's infantry had crossed the Blue Ridge into the Shenandoah Valley by now, Stuart decided, so Jones and Hampton had to be on their way north.

The only action of the day came when scouts sent out by Stuart encountered Yankee scouts in a series of skirmishes. Mac was at Stuart's headquarters along with Munford when Lt. Col. John Singleton Mosby, whose partisan rangers had operated a great deal in this area, rode in with a leather dispatch case draped over his saddle.

Mosby saluted Stuart and handed over the case. "Thought you might find this of interest, General," he drawled. "We picked up a Yankee courier a little while ago, and he was carrying these messages."

Stuart spread out the contents. His finger stabbed at one of them. "These are dispatches from General Hooker to General Pleasanton, in command of the Yankee cavalry." The general's voice hardened as he mentioned Alfred Pleasanton's name. Stuart knew by now that Pleasanton had been behind the Yankee attack at Brandy Station. He went on, "From what I gather here, General Pleasanton's entire cavalry command is now at Aldie. Some seven thousand men."

That meant the Confederates were outnumbered, Mac thought, but not by much and only because Jones and Hampton had not yet rejoined them.

Stuart lifted his eyes from the dispatches and looked at his officers. "I won't have Pleasanton breaking through our lines, gentlemen. I simply won't have it." The anger in his voice was unmistakable. Brandy Station was a blot on his record, the only one of note in his career. It would not be repeated.

Robertson, Munford, and Chambliss nodded in agreement. None wanted to let the commander down. Mac felt his own determination strengthen as he met Stuart's steely eyed gaze.

June 19 dawned hot and clear, as previous days had been, but there was a heaviness in the air that had not been there before. A change in the weather was in the offing, Mac suspected, although he had no idea how much of a change it might be or when it would arrive.

The oppressive atmosphere seemed to make the men more tense as they spread out along the defensive line that was established on a ridge west of Middleburg. Stuart ordered the horse infantry brought up and made ready. Although there was no sign of the Yankees, the feeling was that they would be coming today.

Nervous anticipation made the hours drag by and seem to stretch out even longer. Everyone heaved a sigh of relief when the scouts finally reported that a mounted division of Federal cavalry was only a short distance down the turnpike.

Behind the Confederate line, Mac stood holding the stallion's reins, ready to go wherever Colonel Munford sent him. Munford was a good commander, but he was not the daredevil that Fitz Lee was, and as a result, he and his staff were seldom in the thick of the action as Lee had been. The frustration Mac had felt a couple of days earlier lingered under the surface. Standing apart from the battle rubbed him the wrong way.

He was becoming as addicted to combat and danger as his brother Will, he reflected as he waited for the Yankees to come into sight. Will was a natural soldier, a born warrior. In his days as the sheriff of Culpeper County, he had demonstrated flashes of that, but the war had brought out his true nature and he had flourished, coming back from several wounds that might have laid low a lesser man. Although Mac had always admired Will, he wasn't sure he wanted to be like his brother in that respect.

For all its horrors, war in its own way was seductive, and Mac wanted to be able to withstand its lures.

Still, he hoped that today's battle wouldn't bypass him entirely.

A short time later, the Yankees came down the road, and they made for an impressive sight, rank after rank of blue-garbed horsemen moving crisply along the turnpike. Stuart ordered the artillerymen to stand by to fire, but suddenly the Union forces came to a halt. The cavalrymen dismounted and drew their rifles. Teams of horses and mules hauled their cannon into position.

There would be no charge today, Mac realized, no thunder of hoofbeats, no sabers flickering in the sun. Today the cavalry-men on both sides would fight more like infantry.

"Artillery! . . . Commence firing!" Stuart shouted when it became obvious what was happening.

The Confederate guns opened up, booming loudly. The shot and shell burst among the Yankees, throwing up geysers of dirt and vegetation and sending broken men spinning through the air. Mere moments later, however, the Union gunners began a barrage of their own, and explosions ranged along the ridge where the Southerners were positioned. Small-arms fire began to rattle from both sides.

Back and forth the battle raged, shells whistling and howling through the air, bullets whining past the ears of some soldiers and thudding into flesh. Some men merely grunted as they died while others screamed as oblivion claimed them. The quarter-mile between the two fronts was a hellish wasteland of powder, lead, and flame.

The Federals tried more than once to advance and were driven back each time. But still they kept coming, and Mac began to wonder if their superior numbers were going to prevail in the end. Colonel Munford was gnawing on the same question, and late in the afternoon, after several hours of inconclusive fighting, Munford summoned Mac.

"Find out what General Stuart plans to do, Captain," he ordered. "I'm not sure we can keep this up until nightfall."

Mac led the stallion a little farther back from the line, down-slope from the crest of the ridge, then mounted and rode quickly toward Stuart's headquarters.

When he got there, he found that the general and his staff were preparing to withdraw. There was another ridge to the west, slightly higher than the one that presently marked the Southern-ers' line. Stuart indicated it with a jerk of his bearded chin.

"Tell Colonel Munford we're pulling back to that ridge," he commanded. Just then, Colonel Von Borke rode up, leading Stuart's horse, and Stuart swung up into the saddle.

Mac gave the general a salute and was starting to turn away when he heard the grisly, unmistakable thump of a bullet strik-ing flesh. Mac jerked the stallion around, thinking that Stuart might have been hit by a stray shot, but instead he saw Heros Von Borke slumping forward in the saddle, blood gushing from the back of his neck.

Stuart exclaimed and made a grab for Von Borke's arm as the massive Prussian swayed in the saddle. He missed, and Von Borke toppled off his horse, landing on the ground with a crash.

Instantly, Mac rushed to Von Borke's side, along with several members of Stuart's staff. Judging by the amount of blood and the fact that the bullet had hit Von Borke in the back of the neck, the wound looked fatal. As the men rolled the Prussian over, however, they saw that he was still breathing.

Mac whipped off his neckerchief, folded it into a thick square, and pressed it to the back of the man's neck, holding it over the wound as tightly as he could. He looked up at the others as he knelt beside Von Borke. "We've got to get him out of here."

Von Borke's horse was plunging around wildly, maddened by the smell of the blood that had splashed on it. One of Stuart's officers caught hold of the horse's ear and twisted it hard, bring-ing the animal under control again. He took the reins and brought the horse over to where Von Borke lay on the ground. Mac saw the wounded man's eyes flicker open, and Von Borke began to make feeble movements.

"Lie still," Mac told him. "You've been hit, Colonel."

Stuart looked down from horseback, his face grim with worry for his friend. "I have to see to the withdrawal," he said. "Will you gentlemen take care of Colonel Von Borke?"

The small group nodded. The man holding Von Borke's horse said, "Yes sir. We'll get him to safety."

Stuart sketched a salute and galloped off to spread the word himself that the cavalry would pull back to the next ridge. Mac glanced after the general, riding untouched through the hail of bullets that filled the air, the plume on his hat streaming behind him as he galloped along. The newspapers had cast aspersions on Stuart's wisdom, but no one who had ever gone into battle with him doubted his courage.

Nor that of the men gathered around Von Borke. While Mac held the already blood-soaked compress to the Prussian's neck, the others lifted the man's massive bulk. One of them staggered, lost his grip, and fell. Mac saw that a bullet had hit him in the side of the head, killing him instantly.

The longer they stayed here, the more danger they all were in. He added his strength to that of the others, and within a matter of moments, the semiconscious form had been lifted into his saddle. He slumped forward over his horse's neck but managed somehow to hang on.

Mac dropped the neckerchief, which was no longer stemming the flow of blood anyway, and dashed over to his stallion. As he swung up into the saddle, another officer cried out and spun off his feet, shot through the body. One of his companions knelt beside him then stood up shaking his head.

Mac leaned over and took hold of the reins of Von Borke's horse. He still had to get back to Munford and make sure the colonel knew to pull back, but he hoped to get Von Borke on his way to safety first. In the long run, it might not matter, because the wound the Prussian had suffered would surely be fatal, but Mac and the others couldn't simply abandon such a magnificent fighting man on the field of battle.

The group started off at a trot, unable to go any faster because Von Borke's seat on his horse was so tenuous. After a few minutes, one of the officers spotted an ambulance and hailed it. They rode over, and although a couple of bullets smacked into the sideboards as they loaded Von Borke into it, no one else was hit.

Mac stepped back as the driver whipped his team into a run, and the vehicle started rolling toward the rear of the Confederate lines, bouncing over the rough ground. If the wound didn't kill Von Borke, Mac thought, that wild ride just might. But there was nothing else he could do for the Prussian. With a wave to the members of Stuart's staff, he mounted again and turned the stallion toward the front.

———✺———

NIGHTFALL BROUGHT an end to the battle. Stuart's men had successfully pulled back and established a new line. Meanwhile, Pleasanton's horse soldiers relented and settled in for the evening. Both sides waited for dawn.

That evening, Grumble Jones's brigade rode into camp. Their arrival, plus the news that Hampton's brigade would be there by the next morning, buoyed the spirits of the Southerners. So far, they had accomplished the objective set out for them by Robert E. Lee: The Yankee cavalry had not penetrated the Loudoun Valley to the Blue Ridge Mountains. But the fighting had been fierce and their losses high—although not as high as the Federal casualties—and instead of moving forward, the Confederate troops had been pushed back steadily. The campaign so far had been successful but hardly satisfying.

Mac had returned to Munford's brigade without mishap and pulled back with the rest of the men to the new line. Hearing that Von Borke was in Upperville, resting in the home of Talcott Eliason, one of Stuart's staff surgeons, he received permission to visit the wounded Prussian. He knew it might be his last chance to see the foreigner who had become a friend to most of the officers in Stuart's cavalry.

Eliason was on the porch, smoking a pipe, when Mac rode up. He knew the surgeon slightly and greeted him with a friendly nod. "Good evening, Doctor," he called out. "How is Colonel Von Borke?"

The man shook his head. "Not good, I'm afraid. The bullet missed his spine, thank God, but it struck his windpipe and was deflected into his left lung. The colonel has the constitution of a horse, or else he'd already be dead. As it is, I don't see how he can last until morning."

Mac hated to hear that. "Can I see him?"

"Of course, but I fear he won't recognize you. I've had to give him opium for the pain."

Mac nodded. It would do him good to say his farewells, whether Von Borke was aware of his presence or not. Moments like this were as much for the living as for the dying.

He went into the house and found several members of Stuart's staff in the parlor. The room was filled with their quiet conversations, some regarding the day's action and some lapsing into reminiscences of experiences with the Prussian who lay in the next room.

The officers directed Mac to the small bedroom where the large man lay. When he stepped into the room, Stuart looked up from the chair where he sat at Von Borke's bedside. An open Bible lay in Stuart's lap.

"Good evening, Captain," the general said. "I was just having a word with my old friend here."

The Prussian's face was very pale because of all the blood he'd lost. His breathing was harsh and irregular, and Mac remembered what Eliason had said about the bullet in his lung. It did indeed seem that this would be Von Borke's deathbed.

"I just wanted to pay my respects, General," Mac said. "I won't intrude."

"No, that's all right." Stuart closed the Bible and came to his feet. "I have to be getting back to camp." His tone became more brisk and efficient. "There's nothing more I can do here."

The general's pragmatic attitude was just a pose, Mac thought; he could hear the pain in Stuart's voice and see it in his eyes. Stuart would miss Von Borke a great deal. He bent over his friend and kissed his pale, sweating forehead then straightened, gave Mac a nod, and left the room. Mac hesitated and patted Von Borke's leg through the covers and whispered, "So long, Colonel." He followed Stuart out of the room.

The general was in the midst of a low-voiced discussion with his officers. Mac heard enough of it to know that they were planning for the next day to be a repeat of today: The Confederates would hold the line as long as possible and then withdraw to the west if need be. As long as they could keep the Federals screened off from the Blue Ridge, they were doing their job.

As Mac rode back toward the camp, a drop of rain hit his face, then another and another. By the time he got to his tent, a steady drizzle was falling.

The change in the weather, portended all day, had finally come.

IT WAS still raining on the morning of June 20, a harder rain that fell from morning until night. The weather did not prevent Stuart from setting out his men along a north-south line about halfway between the villages of Upperville and Middleburg. Hampton's Legion had arrived as promised, so now the cavalry was at full strength once more with all five brigades arrayed against the Yankees.

Hampton confirmed the news that Grumble Jones had brought the previous evening. Longstreet's and Hill's corps had crossed the Blue Ridge and were on their way up the Shenandoah Valley, following in the footsteps of Ewell's corps, which a week earlier had reclaimed Winchester from the Federals and by now were thought to have crossed the Potomac into Maryland.

Mac knew that the Stonewall Brigade was with Ewell, and he wondered how his brother Will was doing. If there had been fighting at Winchester, Mac was confident that Will had found a way to get in on at least some of it. He hoped he hadn't been wounded again—or worse.

He wouldn't allow himself to think like that, but it was hard not to let a momentary depression creep into his mind as he sat in the rain with the other men and waited all day for the Yankees to show up. Von Borke was probably dead by now, and who knew how Will was doing? And the thrust by the Army of Northern Virginia into Yankee territory, while ostensibly a foraging expedition, was really designed to bring the Union army chasing after it so that another battle could be fought. The last battle, some of the men were already calling it. This time when the Confederate army was victorious and crushed the Union army, it would mark the end of the war. Lincoln would have no choice but to accept the peace that the Confederacy sought.

Mac had no confidence that would prove to be the case. For more than two years now, some people had thought that each battle was going to be the last one. And each time, another battle was waiting. There were moments, especially on days such as today, that Mac wondered if the war would *ever* end. He cast his mind toward the future and saw nothing but year after year of vain, futile battle, with nothing ever solved and nothing really ended.

If he had been asleep, he might have comforted himself with the thought that it was only a nightmare. But he was wide awake, and he knew that it could happen the way he visualized it. And peace would never come . . .

But on this day, neither did the Yankees. Mac had no idea why. Maybe Pleasanton just didn't want to get out in the rain.

—〰—

By SUNDAY morning, June 21, the downpour had ended, and although the roads were muddy, the bright sun promised to dry them fairly quickly.

Pleasanton didn't wait for that. Early that morning, he threw his entire force of Yankee cavalry against the Confederates. It was augmented by an infantry division that had arrived during the night.

Mac was sipping coffee next to a campfire that morning when he heard the roar of artillery and the bugle calls summoning the men to action. The rifles of the skirmishers barked and crackled. Mac gulped down the rest of the coffee, unwilling to waste any of it, then tossed the cup aside and ran for his horse.

He knew that Stuart was a deeply religious man and didn't like to fight on the Sabbath. War was no respecter of religion, however, and the Yankees were leaving them no choice. When Mac reached the front, he saw a wave of blue-uniformed infantry marching steadily toward the Southerners' line. His eyes widened in surprise at the sight of the infantry. Stuart's dismounted cavalrymen fought well, but they were no match for so many soldiers.

Mac sought out Munford, who already looked harried. "We'll have to withdraw," the colonel announced. "We can't hold them here."

"Should I find General Stuart and tell him that, sir?" Mac asked.

Munford grimaced. "If he doesn't know it already, Captain, I'd say we're in for a bad time of it today."

Moments later, a courier raced up with orders from Stuart to withdraw toward Upperville. As the retreat got underway, the Yankee cavalry suddenly put in an appearance, racing in to disrupt the withdrawal. Mac found himself cut off by two blue-clad horsemen who galloped at him with flashing sabers. He pulled his pistol and shot one of them out of the saddle then flung up his hand and used the gun to block the sweeping slash of the other man's saber. The blade clanged off the barrel of the revolver. Mac grabbed his attacker's jacket while the man was off-balance. A sharp tug unhorsed him, and as he struggled to get back to his feet, the stallion's hooves pounded him back to the ground. His screams were cut off as one of the steel-shod hooves crushed his skull.

Mac hauled the stallion around and waved to a nearby gun crew, telling them to withdraw. Bullets whipped around his head, but he tried to ignore them. If one was meant to find him, there was no way he could dodge it. All he could do was trust his fate to luck and the stallion's speed.

The horses hitched to the gun limber began moving, pulling the heavy weapon to the rear. Mac rode on along the line, shouting at the men to fall back. There would be no rallying the troops today, not against the overwhelming force the Yankees were throwing at them. The soldiers, however, insisted on making their foes pay for every yard of ground they gained.

Sensing victory within his grasp, Pleasanton deviated from the counterpunching attack underway and resorted to a frontal charge. Hampton's brigade met the oncoming Federals head-on. From a distance, Mac saw the sabers glitter in the sunlight as the Confederates threw the Yankees back.

That victory was short-lived, however. Pleasanton sent his infantry forward again, once more holding his cavalry in reserve so that it would strike what he hoped would be a deathblow. But that occasion did not arise, as the Confederates continued their orderly withdrawal. Mac and several other officers were everywhere at once, shouting orders and calling encouragement to the men. This was one withdrawal that would not turn into a rout. The Southerners might pull back, but they wouldn't turn tail and run.

Stuart's men paused briefly in Upperville, at the foot of the Blue Ridge. Looking up at the mountains beyond the town, Mac could see Ashby's Gap. Once they reached that pass, they could hold it successfully against the Yankees, he thought. Pleasanton didn't have enough men to push through.

Munford and his staff, including Mac, trotted their mounts down the street where Talcott Eliason lived. Mac drew rein as they passed the surgeon's house, surprised to see Stuart emerging from it. Munford reined in as well, and the other men followed his example.

"Colonel," the general called out, "would you detail one of your ambulances to carry Colonel Von Borke to safety?"

"Of course, sir," Munford replied. "What's the colonel's condition?"

Mac was surprised to hear that Von Borke was still alive. He had assumed that the Prussian would have succumbed to the dreadful wound by now.

Stuart smiled. "He's rallied somewhat. I believe our foreign friend simply may be too stubborn to die."

"We'll see that he's brought to safety, General," Munford promised and looked over to Mac.

"I'll take care of it, Colonel," he said without hesitation. He turned the stallion and rode off in search of an ambulance.

Less than twenty minutes later, he had found one and brought it back to Eliason's house. With the help of the driver and a couple of men, Mac loaded Von Borke onto a litter and carried him out to the wagon. Von Borke grinned wearily as he was lifted into the ambulance. "I hope zis ride iz not as rough as the last one, *ja?*" he said.

Down the street, a Yankee shell struck a house and exploded.

"We'll take it as easy as we can," Mac promised. "But we don't have any time to waste."

Bullets whined through the air, and more shells burst as the driver whipped his team into motion. Mac rode alongside, and they hurried out of Upperville. The Confederates were going to make a stand at Ashby's Gap, as Mac had suspected, and he knew that already artillery batteries were being hauled up the pass to turn back the Yankee advance.

The Federal horsemen were swarming into Upperville as Mac and the ambulance wagon raced out of town to the west, however. He knew they couldn't reach the gap before the Yankees did. They would have to hide somewhere. He waved for the driver to leave the turnpike and head south on a smaller road. After they had gone a couple of miles, Mac spotted a farmhouse that looked abandoned. Most important, there was a barn behind the house where the ambulance could be hidden. He pointed it out and told the driver to head for it.

Twisting in the saddle, Mac looked back. The air was filled with the dust churned up by the Union horses, but he didn't see any Federals at the moment. The driver hustled the ambulance into the barn. Mac rode in after it and dropped off the stallion.

"Do we take the colonel in the house or stay here?" the driver asked anxiously.

Mac swung the barn doors closed. "We're going to stay right here for the time being. The colonel might be more comfortable in the house, but not if the Yankees spot us."

Chinks in the walls of the barn admitted shafts of sunlight. Mac and his companions waited tensely, listening to the sound of rifle and cannon fire in the distance. Several times during the long afternoon, horses came close, and voices called out orders and commands. Each time, Mac drew his pistol and waited to see if they were going to be discovered. The hoofbeats moved on, however. None of the Federals stopped to investigate the seemingly deserted farm.

By evening the guns had fallen silent, and no one was moving around the barn. Mac and his companions risked carrying Von Borke into the house. They found a bedroom and laid him carefully on the bed in the darkness. The Prussian was only half-conscious. "A good fight, *ja?*" he murmured.

Mac squeezed his shoulder. "Yes, a good fight," he said. And for once, he was glad that he had managed to avoid most of it.

He wondered all night if the withdrawal to Ashby's Gap had been successful. It was the middle of the next morning before he found out. When he heard the sound of hoofbeats approaching the house, he peered past some tattered curtains and saw a Confederate patrol approaching. Mac closed his eyes for a moment and sighed in relief. Then he stepped onto the porch of the farmhouse and called to the men.

They rode over, led by a lieutenant. The insignia on his uniform told him that the young officer was attached to Hampton's Legion. "What news of the battle do you have?" Mac asked.

"The battle's over, Captain," the lieutenant replied. "The Yankees never got past Ashby's Gap, and now they're pullin' back. Looks like they're headed back to Aldie. We done fought 'em to a draw, I reckon." He frowned and asked curiously, "What're you doin' over here? You didn't spend the night behind Yankee lines, did you?"

"I'm afraid so," Mac said. He jerked a thumb over his shoulder. "We have Colonel Von Borke from General Stuart's staff in here. He's been badly wounded, but I think he'll be all right."

"Dang! You mean that big ol' German fella? I heard that Gen'ral Stuart was mighty worried about him. We'd best go tell Jeb where he's at."

Mac was too tired to say anything other than to thank the lieutenant.

The patrol wheeled their horses and galloped off. Mac put his hands on the porch railing and leaned on it, feeling weariness spread through his body. Despite being tired, he felt a sense of triumph as he looked at the Blue Ridge looming over the valley. The Federals had thrown their entire cavalry command at Stuart, as well as a division of infantry, but they had never crossed the Blue Ridge. Knowing the Union commanders, they would probably proclaim themselves the victors because they had pushed the Confederates back at every encounter, but that didn't tell the full story, Mac thought. War was a matter of objectives, and Stuart had achieved his.

And so had he, Mac thought. He was still alive.

Chapter Sixteen

GEN. ROBERT E. LEE had established his headquarters in the tiny village of Paris, west of Upperville at the very foot of the Blue Ridge Mountains. From there Lee could monitor the progress of his troops across the Blue Ridge and into the Shenandoah Valley.

On June 22, after the battle at Upperville the day before in which the Yankees had pushed Stuart's men back to Ashby's Gap, the situation had reverted to what it had been before the series of clashes. Alfred Pleasanton withdrew his forces when he found that his men and horses were simply too exhausted to continue the fight. Besides, he had several "victories" to trumpet, even though they had accomplished nothing. With the Yankees pulling back, Stuart once again established a defensive line between Middleburg and Aldie. Stuart's own headquarters were set up at Rector's Cross Road, near Middleburg.

Uncertain what to do next, Stuart sent a courier to Longstreet requesting orders. Longstreet passed the message on to Lee, and both generals responded. Lee's note to Stuart expressed concern about Ewell's corps, which was already in Pennsylvania. Ewell needed at least some cavalry with him, so Lee suggested that two brigades of cavalry should be left to guard the passes and keep the Yankees east of the Blue Ridge and the other three brigades should get into Pennsylvania as quickly as possible and link up with Ewell. Longstreet's advice was similar, with the added wrinkle that Stuart might be able to cross the Potomac in the rear of Hooker's forces, assuming that the Yankees had indeed started north, trailing the Confederate army.

Longstreet's suggestion appealed to Stuart, and after a rainy June 23, when John S. Mosby arrived at Stuart's headquarters with a scouting report that indicated that Hooker's troops were widely dispersed, Stuart was even more convinced that he should adopt this daring tactic. A year earlier, during the Peninsula campaign, Stuart had ridden completely around George McClellan's army and had won plaudits throughout the South for doing so. In fact, he had performed similar feats twice since then—the Chambersburg raid of October 1862 and the Dumfries raid in December. There was no reason to doubt that he could do it again.

Stuart was asleep that night under a tree, despite the rain, when a courier from Lee arrived. Maj. Henry McClellan took the message from the galloper. Seeing that the note came from Lee himself, he roused the general.

By the light of a lamp shielded by a piece of oilcloth under the dripping branches, Stuart read Lee's suggestion that he leave two brigades behind and start north with the rest of his men. The two brigades would follow the last of the infantry up the Shenandoah Valley once all three corps had crossed. Lee left it up to Stuart which route to follow with his other three brigades, but he was to cross the Potomac with all due speed and find the right side of Ewell's corps. Once in position, the cavalry would screen Ewell's flank and provide him with intelligence and supplies.

With a grin of anticipation on his face, Stuart turned to McClellan. "Send word to General Hampton, Colonel Munford, and Colonel Chambliss to rendezvous tomorrow at Salem."

"I believe General Fitzhugh Lee returned to his brigade today and resumed command, sir," McClellan replied.

"Without telling me?" Stuart clucked. "I'll have to have a word with Fitz about that. But it'll be good to have him back. By the way, Henry," he added, "don't open any more of my confidential messages."

McClellan accepted the mild rebuke with a nod. "Yes sir. I'll get word to the generals, as you wish."

Stuart lay back down on the ground and rolled up in his blankets once more, still smiling as he listened to the falling rain. General Lee hadn't ordered him to cross the Potomac in

Hooker's rear and ride around the Union army to join up with Ewell in Pennsylvania.

But the commanding general certainly hadn't ordered him *not* to, either.

—◆—

IT FELT awfully good to be riding alongside Fitz Lee again, Mac thought. He didn't have anything against Tom Munford; in fact, the colonel had done a satisfactory job in Lee's absence.

But the First Virginia Cavalry belonged to Fitzhugh Lee, and Mac was confident the men would perform even better with the general in command again. His spirits had risen greatly when Lee rode into the camp the afternoon before.

"How's the knee this morning, sir?" Mac asked as they headed for Salem.

Lee slapped his thigh. "It's fine," he said. "The rheumatism's all gone."

Lee's voice boomed out with its usual vigor, but Mac thought he saw a flicker of discomfort in the general's eyes. The medical problems must have improved or Lee wouldn't have been able to sit a horse, but he was convinced that Lee was still in some pain. Lee was ignoring it because he couldn't stand to be away from the brigade any longer. The thought of another officer leading his men into battle was more than he could tolerate.

"I heard that you had a bit of excitement while I was away," Lee commented. "Something about saving Colonel Von Borke's life?"

"No sir. I just happened to be where I could lend a hand when he was wounded and then later when we had to get him out of Upperville."

"One step ahead of the Yankees, from what I hear."

"It was a near thing," Mac admitted with a smile. "But what's important is that the colonel is recovering from his wound. It was bad enough that no one thought he was going to live."

"No one except Von Borke, eh?" Lee grinned. "He's tough as shoe leather, that Prussian."

Mac couldn't argue with that.

He wondered what this day was going to bring, but he was fairly sure of one thing: With three brigades gathering at Salem, they were probably going to be on the move. He was ready for that. By this time, some of the infantry was probably in Pennsylvania. Ewell's corps—including Will and the rest of the Stonewall Brigade—would need the cavalry at hand should it get into a scrape with the Yankees.

As they rode up to Salem, Mac saw six guns of the horse artillery being readied for travel. If Stuart intended to take only half a dozen field pieces, he must be planning on traveling fast, Mac thought. That was fine with him. The sooner they joined up with Ewell the better.

Stuart greeted Fitz Lee with a grin and a firm handshake. "I'm glad to see you, Fitz," he declared. "Now I'm sure we'll be able to run rings around old Fighting Joe."

"We're going *around* Hooker?" Lee asked with a slight frown.

"That's right." Stuart gripped Lee's arm. "Just like last December, eh, Fitz? The Yankees will look up in a day or two and find us closer to Washington City than their own army is. Ought to give them a bit of a jolt." Stuart laughed. "We'll race around them, raiding as we go, and then join up with Dick Ewell in Pennsylvania."

Lee hesitated then returned Stuart's smile and nodded, won over by the enthusiasm of his commander and friend.

Mac stood nearby in silence. Stuart's plan was audacious, no one could deny that, and the raid he proposed might be able to do some significant damage and capture some supplies, depending on what they ran into. But it also meant they would take longer to reach Ewell's corps. That was unavoidable with such an out-of-the-way route as Stuart proposed to follow.

Mac just hoped the delay wouldn't wind up causing any problems for Ewell and the rest of the men with him up there in the North—including Will.

So THIS was what a countryside looked like that wasn't at war, Will thought as he rode through Pennsylvania. For more than two years, battles had ranged far and wide across Virginia, and the combat had taken its toll in shattered buildings, burned fields, roads pocked with shell craters, fallen trees, and slaughtered animals. Here in Pennsylvania the fields were full of healthy crops that waved in the breeze and orchards full of trees dotted with fruit. Cattle grazed peacefully, cropping lush green grass. The air was clean, carrying no taint of smoke or death.

The Yankees who lived up here, Will thought bitterly, had no idea how lucky they had been.

But chances were, they were about to find out.

The Army of Northern Virginia's advance up the Shenandoah Valley, across the Potomac near Shepherdstown, through Maryland, and into Pennsylvania had gone as smoothly as anyone could have expected or hoped for. Since the battles at Winchester and Stephenson's Depot more than a week earlier, there had been no more clashes with the Yankees. In fact, Will hadn't seen any Union troops in that time.

Now the Stonewall Brigade and the rest of Johnson's division was approaching the town of Chambersburg, some twenty-five miles into Pennsylvania. Although the terrain was not that much different from what he was accustomed to in Virginia, Will had the distinct feeling that he was traveling through an alien land. Faces peered in fright from the windows of the houses the army passed, and it was hard to believe that little more than two years earlier, those people had been his countrymen. Now they all seemed strange and foreign to him.

Some of Ewell's corps was already in Chambersburg. Robert Rodes's division had marched in and occupied the town without opposition. Johnson was not far behind, and Jubal Early's division, traveling on a parallel road to the east, had Chambersburg as its objective, too. Once all three divisions were concentrated there, they could spread out over the Pennsylvania countryside and begin foraging operations.

Will had heard that the two corps under Hill and Longstreet were also moving rapidly and would soon be marching across Maryland if in fact they were not already doing so. But there had been no word concerning the disposition of the Federal forces. If Hooker was following the Confederate army north, as Robert E. Lee hoped he would, Will and the other junior officers had not been told. Perhaps Lee and his inner circle knew.

Darcy Bennett marched along briskly beside Will's horse, keeping an eye on the men of the company. "This here is mighty fine country," he commented, echoing what Will had been thinking a few moments earlier. "Shoot, if I lived up here and had me a farm as good as the ones we've been passin', I wouldn't go runnin' off down south to try to boss those folks around. I'd just plow my ground and grow my crops and leave ever'body else alone."

"It's too bad more of the Yankees didn't feel that way a couple of years ago, Darcy," Will said quietly. "If they had we could've worked something out."

The burly sergeant grinned. "Yeah, but think about all the fun we'd've missed."

Will heard the bleak sarcasm in his friend's voice and nodded. He looked out over the company of marching men with their tattered uniforms and blistered feet. Their faces were sunburned, and they were lean and stringy from the short rations they had been given for months now. Outnumbered and outsupplied, they had every reason to look discouraged. And yet Will saw nothing but optimism and anticipation on their faces. Another battle, maybe two, and the war would be over. They could go back to their homes and their lives. Some never would return, of course, but that was the price to be paid if the Confederacy was to survive.

Evening came as Johnson's division arrived on the outskirts of Chambersburg. The men made camp, and Ewell, Johnson, and Rodes went into conference. Early would be there the next day, and the whole corps would be together again.

From where he sat next to a campfire, Will could see the lights of Chambersburg as dusk settled in. The townspeople had only to look out their windows to view the campfires of the Confederates, hundreds of them spread out across the countryside. Will decided that he wouldn't have wanted to be one of those people tonight. He imagined there were some mighty nervous folks in Chambersburg.

"Captain Brannon?"

Will looked up and saw a sergeant of the guard standing there. He recognized the man but couldn't recall his name.

That wasn't true of the individual standing next to the sergeant. Will knew him right away, and immediately he came to his feet. "Roman? Good Lord! What in the world are you doing up here?"

The sergeant said, "Then you *do* know this darky, Cap'n? He says he's been lookin' for you."

"Yes, I know him," Will said. He stepped forward to grip Roman's shoulder. The young man looked haggard and exhausted. "I'll vouch for him, Sergeant."

"All right, then," the sergeant said. "He better stick close to you from now on, though, Cap'n. A darky wanderin' around by hisself might get taken for a runaway."

When the sergeant had moved on, Will turned to Roman. "Sit down. How long's it been since you ate anything?"

Roman sank wearily onto the ground. "I don't rightly remember, Mister Will," he said. "I think it was yesterday mornin'."

"Well, I've got a little pone and fatback. I'd be glad to share it with you."

Roman started to his feet. "No sir, I couldn't take your food away from you—"

"Sit down and eat," Will said. "That's an order, even if you're not one of my soldiers."

"No sir, but I reckon you can tell me what to do, anyway."

Will frowned, not understanding what Roman meant by that. The young man might be referring to the fact that he was black and Will was white, but Will had the sense that it was more than that.

He dug food out of his pack and passed it to Roman. The man tried to control his hunger and eat slowly, so the rations would last longer, but Will could tell that it was hard for him.

"Where's Yancy?" he asked. If Roman was here in Pennsylvania, then his master had to be around somewhere, too. Roman never ventured very far from Yancy's side.

But what the devil was Yancy Lattimer doing in the middle of another Confederate invasion of the North? That didn't make any sense at all.

"Massa Yancy . . . he . . ."

Roman had to stop and draw a deep breath, and as he did so, a chill went through Will. Even without hearing it, he knew what Roman was about to say.

"Massa Yancy's dead." Roman forced the words out.

Will bowed his head and closed his eyes as grief washed over him. Even though he'd been expecting the news, it still hit him hard. While he was sitting there like that, he sent up a brief prayer that in death Yancy could be made whole again as he never could be in life and that his soul would find peace. Then he looked at Roman and asked, "What happened? His leg? . . ."

"No sir." Roman shook his head, and his next words were as difficult for him to say as the news of his master's death had been. "He killed hisself."

Anger flared up inside Will. "That can't be!" he exclaimed. "Yancy was one of the bravest men I ever knew. He wouldn't do such a thing."

But did he really know Yancy Lattimer that well? he suddenly asked himself. They had never been friends until after the war started. He had seen Yancy's courage and gallantry in battle many times, but he had also seen how Yancy had changed after losing his leg at Sharpsburg. The Yancy who had gone into combat with him wouldn't have turned to the jug as the other Yancy had done in the past few months. He wouldn't have had anything to do with scoundrels like Israel Quinn, let alone befriend him.

"I'm sorry, Mister Will, I really am," Roman said. "I wish it was different, but I was there when Massa Yancy . . . when he shot hisself."

"You didn't stop him?"

"I tried," Roman said, sounding as miserable as any human being Will had ever heard. "I've prayed that the Lord God had made me a mite faster on my feet that day, but that just ain't the way it happened."

Will looked down at the ground. After a moment, he said, "I'm sorry, Roman. I know you did everything you could for him. And I'm sorry about Yancy. He was a good man."

"The best man I ever knowed. The way he was there at the end . . . that don't make no difference. He wasn't hisself then. I just don't pay that no never mind and remember him the way he used to be."

Will nodded. "That's right. That's just what we need to do." He put his hands on his knees and sighed. "Roman, I don't want you to think I don't appreciate it, but you didn't have to traipse all the way up here just to tell me what happened. Lord, you've come a hundred miles or more!"

"Yes sir, I did have to," Roman said, gazing at Will with a solemn and severe expression on his face. "I didn't have no place else to go."

"You could've stayed at Tanglewood. Yancy must have had heirs. He had to leave the place to somebody in the family, maybe a cousin or something."

"Yes sir, he left the plantation to his cousin up in Farquahar County, but that ain't the only bequest he made in his will. He done left *me* to *you*."

Will stared at the young man for a second, not really comprehending what Roman said. "What? Yancy left you to . . . to . . ."

"I belong to you now," Roman said. "Reckon I best start callin' you Massa Will."

"No!" Will smacked his fist against his thigh, surprising himself with the vehemence of his reaction. "No, damn it! I never owned a slave in my life, and I don't intend to start now. No one in my family ever owned slaves."

Roman shrugged. "Judge Darden took care of the whole thing. He's the one drawed up the papers for Massa Yancy. Said it was all nice an' legal." Roman reached inside his shirt and drew out a folded document. "He give me this here paper, told me to keep it with me all the time whilst I was on my way up here to find you. He said if anybody stopped me I could use it to prove I wasn't no runaway."

Will took the paper. Judge Darden was the most prominent attorney in Culpeper County, and he recognized the lawyer's signature at the bottom of the document. According to what Will could read by the light of the campfire, whether he liked the idea or not, he was now the lawful owner of the slave known as Roman. The paper included a brief physical description of the young man.

Will gave the paper back to him. "Better keep that," he said. "You'll have need of it if anything happens to me."

"You see, Massa Will? I had to come find you."

"I suppose so. You walked all the way?"

Roman nodded. "Yes sir. This here army moves pretty fast, but one fella by himself can move faster. I just hoped I'd catch up to you 'fore you started fightin' the Yankees again."

"The only battles we've had were down in the Shenandoah. It's been mighty peaceful so far here in Pennsylvania." Will rubbed his jaw, recalling how Roman had always insisted on staying close to Yancy, even when the army was going into battle. "I don't suppose there's any chance you'd go back home and wait for me there until this is all over?"

"No sir, I couldn't do that. Where would I go?"

"Back to the farm," Will said, the idea occurring suddenly to him. "Ma and Henry and Cordelia would take you in. You could live there until the war's over. And they could use another hand, I'm sure."

Roman frowned in thought for a moment before saying, "I don't know, Massa Will . . . Your ma's a fine woman an' all, but she ain't kindly disposed to colored folks."

That was probably true enough, Will told himself. "I'm sure it would be all right for a while."

Roman shook his head. "No sir, if it's all the same to you, I'd rather just stay here."

"Not as my slave."

Now Roman looked confused. "But how else—"

"As a free man. If I own you then I can, by God, give you your freedom, too."

"Manumission," Roman said softly. "Freedom. But that takes time, Massa Will. Judge Darden'd have to draw up the papers and—"

"Damn it, if I say you're free then you're free!" Will felt his frustration growing. "I'm no slave owner."

"I reckon you'll have to be until you can get back home and take care of it legal-like."

Will's jaw tightened. "The law may still say that I own you, but you and I know that's not true, Roman. And as soon as I get back to Culpeper, I'll see to it that everyone else knows, too."

Roman's voice was thick with emotion. "Massa Will, I . . . I don't hardly know what to say . . ."

"Captain," Will broke in. "You should probably call me Captain. From here on out, as far as I'm concerned, you're my civilian aide. I'll even try to get you carried on the regimental books like that."

"Civilian aide," Roman repeated. "Does the army have such things?"

A grin stretched across Will's face. "They do now."

"Well, then . . . Cap'n . . . I reckon I'm reportin' for duty."

"At ease," Will told him. "Now eat the rest of that fatback."

Chapter Seventeen

MAC YAWNED SO WIDELY he felt like his jaw was going to crack. Stuart liked these middle-of-the-night departures, but Mac didn't care much for them. He had managed to grab a couple of hours of sleep before the three brigades were roused and ordered to make ready for departure, but that was all. He was still drowsy, and he knew he might doze off in the saddle before morning.

Luckily he was riding the big silver gray stallion with its easy gait. At least if he fell asleep, chances were he wouldn't fall off the horse.

It was a little after two o'clock in the morning on June 25, 1863. About an hour earlier, the column consisting of the brigades under Fitzhugh Lee, Wade Hampton, and John Chambliss had pulled out of Salem and ridden east. They had crossed the Bull Run Mountains and were now following a road that led to the village of Haymarket, where they would take a road leading north and east. That was the path Stuart intended to follow on this fast trek around the Union army.

Riding just ahead of Mac, Fitz Lee turned. "This is going to be quite the adventure, isn't it, Mac?"

"Yes sir, I expect so. Things tend to happen wherever General Stuart finds himself."

Lee chuckled. "Isn't that the truth? And Beauty wouldn't have it any other way."

Mac hesitated momentarily. "It seems to me that we're taking an awfully long way around, though. It may take us days to reach General Ewell's corps, and they should already be in Pennsylvania by now."

"I'm sure General Ewell will do just fine without us until we get there," Lee said, "and think how surprised the Yankees are going to be when they realize what we've done."

Mac couldn't argue with that, but the problem was that their job wasn't to surprise the Yankees, it was to defeat them.

"I'd like to see the look on Joe Hooker's face when he gets the news," Lee went on. "Hell, I'd pay a month's wages just to be there and laugh at him."

Mac didn't say anything. He had better uses for his pay, such as it was, than spending it to view some general's consternation.

The hours rolled on, and not long before dawn, a forward-ranging scout galloped up to the column to report that there were Federal troops ahead. Stuart happened to be riding with Fitz Lee at the time, so Mac heard the news and Stuart's reaction to it.

"How many are there?" Stuart asked.

The scout took off his battered hat and scratched his head. "A powerful lot of 'em, Gen'ral. At least a division, maybe a whole damned corps. They's marchin' right smart up the road."

"The road we intend to use?" Stuart's question was sharp and angry.

"Yes sir."

Stuart turned to Major McClellan. "Have the guns brought up, Henry."

Mac frowned at the prospect. Surely Stuart didn't intend to take on an entire corps with only three brigades of cavalry. Although the foot soldiers wouldn't be able to move fast enough to pose any real threat to the horsemen, by the same token Stuart's force was too small to inflict any serious damage on the Yankees. Besides, Stuart's plan had been to go around the Union army, not through it.

But there was only one real commander here, and that was James Ewell Brown Stuart. The six guns of the horse artillery were brought up as Stuart ordered and placed in position on a ridge overlooking the turnpike where the Union infantry marched. In the predawn gloom, Mac could see the Yankees only vaguely. One good thing about artillery, though: It didn't require precise aim.

The cannon began to boom, lobbing their shells toward the Yankees. The munitions burst with flashes of light that showed the blue-clad troops in confusion. As the sky began to turn gray with the approach of morning, however, Mac could see the Yankee officers rallying their men and nipping any panic in the bud. The infantrymen responded, forming into their ranks. Volleys of rifle fire crashed out, and bullets raked the ridge where the Confederate artillery was placed.

Stuart turned to Lee. "Fitz, take the lead and get us around those Yankees. Swing as far to the south as you need to in order to avoid them."

Lee wheeled his horse and snapped, "Come on, Mac!"

Both men broke into a gallop. Fitz Lee waved for his command to follow him, and the gallant Virginians did so. They rode through the fading shadows of the dawn, up and down rolling hills, splashed through creeks, and pounded across open fields. Behind them came the other two brigades of horsemen, and the horse artillery brought up the rear, withdrawing from the ridge and racing after the rest of the command before the Yankees even knew they were gone.

The pace didn't really slow until midmorning, when Stuart caught up with Lee at the head of the column. Stuart had hung back to make sure there was no cavalry traveling with the Union infantry, so there would be no pursuit. Now that he was certain of that, he ordered first a slowdown then a full-fledged halt so that the horses and men could rest. They had come a good distance since leaving Salem in the middle of the previous night, and Mac estimated they were somewhere south of Manassas.

For the rest of that day, the horses cropped grass while the men ate and dozed under the shade of leafy trees. That night, everyone got a good night's sleep except for those who were on picket duty. By the next morning, June 26, when the march resumed, Mac felt considerably refreshed.

With the scouts reporting that no Yankees were nearby, the cavalry continued southeast for another day before swinging north again on June 27. As they pulled out that morning, Stuart announced, "I'd like to get across the Potomac today."

Mac agreed with that sentiment. They had done a lot of riding but weren't really getting anywhere.

By midday, following a northward course that roughly paralleled the Potomac, the column was approaching the town of Fairfax Court House. All morning, they had seen evidence that a large Federal force had moved through here ahead of them. The roads had been chopped up by the wheels of countless wagons and the hooves of the animals pulling them. Bits of gear discarded or dropped accidentally by the soldiers littered the road. Mac saw leaky canteens, broken belts, boot heels, ammunition pouches, a broken axle, a campaign cap with a large hole torn in its crown, and other debris left behind by a passing army. One thing about war, he mused, it damned sure wasn't neat.

So they had seen with their own eyes plenty of proof that the Army of the Potomac under Joe Hooker was taking the bait and moving north toward Pennsylvania. It would have been good to pass that information along to Ewell, Mac thought—if they had been anywhere close to Ewell themselves. As it was, they were even farther away from the Army of Northern Virginia than the Yankees were.

Wade Hampton's brigade was in the lead at the moment, and as they rode into Fairfax Court House, gunfire suddenly erupted. A small group of Yankee cavalry spurred their horses forward and charged the Confederates. For a few minutes, men hacked and slashed with their sabers and fired at each other at almost point-blank range. Then the Yankees who had survived the foolhardy charge turned and fled. Lee's column, with Lee and Mac at its head, arrived in the settlement in time to see the last of the Federal troopers racing away with some of Hampton's men in hot pursuit.

At a hastily called council of war under the trees on the courthouse lawn, Hampton noted, "Well, they know we're here now, if any of those Yankees got away."

"We're here *now*," Stuart corrected. "In a little while, we won't be. An army is a large and ponderous creature. The Yankees won't try to turn theirs around just because of us."

"We can't turn back, anyway," Lee commented. "We've come too far now."

Stuart nodded. "Exactly. We'll proceed to Draneville then cut east to Rowser's Ford. Even if the Yankees are guarding it, I suspect any force there will be small and easily overwhelmed. I plan to sleep tonight in Maryland."

The delay at Fairfax Court House was a short one. The cavalry pressed on, reaching Draneville by the middle of the afternoon and then riding east to Rowser's Ford. As Stuart had predicted, there were no Yankees to be found at the crossing. However, the Potomac River was running a bit higher than usual due to the recent rains.

Stuart, his generals, and their staffs sat on horseback on a small knoll overlooking the ford. "We can get the men across," Lee commented, "but the artillery will be another matter."

"I won't leave the guns behind," Stuart said after a moment's thought. "Do the best you can, gentlemen. We shall all cross over the river."

A chill went through Mac at those words. Stonewall Jackson had said something very much like that in the moments just before he died. Mac thought it was just a coincidence, but the sentiment Stuart expressed was similar enough to make Mac worry about its being a bad omen. He told himself that superstition had no place in something as practical and pragmatic as a maneuvering military force . . . but he still seemed to feel a tingling in his bones, and the hair on the back of his neck bristled for a second.

The fording of the Potomac commenced. The horses were able to swim across the swollen river, but not without difficulty. Their riders slipped from the saddle and held tightly to the reins, letting the horses pull them to the other side of the swiftly flowing stream.

Mac and the stallion made the crossing with less trouble than the others. The Potomac's current was no match for the horse's great strength. All Mac had to do was hang on. It was almost dusk when they emerged dripping from the water.

Hours more were required for the rest of the column to cross, and it was an even more arduous task to get the guns across. The last of Stuart's men finally trudged in their sodden uniforms onto Maryland soil long after midnight.

Fording the Potomac had taken a lot out of the men and the horses. Wisely, Stuart ordered another rest, so the three brigades camped on the banks of the river to dry out and recover some of their strength.

Hampton was the first to move out the next morning toward Rockville, a few miles to the east. The other two brigades followed later, with Stuart accompanying Fitz Lee at the head of that part of the column. Gunfire crackled in the distance, making both officers lean forward eagerly in their saddles. "General Hampton must have run into some Yankees," Lee said. Mac could hear the thirst for action in the voice of his commander and friend.

Stuart nodded. "I expect we'll hear from him soon."

Indeed, before long a messenger from Hampton came galloping up the road toward this main body of the Confederate cavalry. The courier reined in, saluted, and reported breathlessly. "General Hampton sends his compliments, sir. He said to tell you that we have engaged and defeated a small Federal force in Rockville."

"Prisoners?" Stuart asked.

"Pretty much all the Yankees who aren't dead, General. But that's not all."

"Well, get on with it, son," Stuart coached when the courier paused briefly.

"General Hampton said to tell you that a Union supply train is on its way toward the town from the southeast. Our scouts spotted 'em a little while ago."

Stuart's eyes widened in surprise and anticipation. "A supply train?" he repeated.

"Yes sir, a mighty big one. At least 150 wagons, one of the scouts said."

Fitz Lee let out a low whistle. He said to Stuart, "I might remind the general, we packed three days' rations for this trip—and we left four days ago."

Stuart laughed. "So we did. I think it's only fitting that the Yankees feed us for a while, don't you?"

"Those were my thoughts exactly, General," Lee replied.

"There's, uh, one other thing, sir," the messenger ventured. "There's some sort of girls' school there in Rockville, and the young ladies are mighty anxious to meet you, General."

"Why didn't you say so in the first place?" Stuart demanded with another laugh. He waved the men ahead. "Come on, Fitz!" And with that he put the spurs to his mount and charged ahead in a gallop.

Yankees to fight and pretty girls to fawn over him, Mac thought. Jeb Stuart didn't need much of anything else.

But Mac had to admit that his own pulse quickened and throbbed in anticipation as he joined the headlong charge toward Rockville. The roofs and steeples of the town came into view only a few minutes later. The column barely slowed as the two brigades rejoined Hampton's Legion, and then Stuart's whole command was charging out of town on the road that led southeast to Washington.

The first wagons in the supply train were less than a mile away. The cavalrymen topped a rise and saw the wagons spread out in a long line ahead of them. The Yankee soldiers driving the wagons saw the gray-clad horsemen, too, and a sense of panic suddenly gripped the wagon train. Drivers whipped their teams and tried frantically to turn the vehicles around. Some went off the road and bogged down in soft ground. Others made the turn successfully and started racing back toward Washington. The supply train had only a small escort of Union cavalry, making it painfully obvious that they hadn't expected to encounter three brigades of Southerners out here.

Rebel yells ripped out as the charging riders swarmed around the fleeing wagons, easily brushing aside the Yankee defenders. Mac and Fitz Lee took off after one of the wagons. The general was grinning broadly, having the time of his life. The rheumatism that had threatened to cripple him was forgotten for the moment. He rode ahead, urging every last bit of speed from his horse. For once his mount outstripped even Mac's stallion.

Lee drew up alongside the left side of the wagon then forged ahead, pulling up next to the galloping team. As the general came abreast of the lead team, he leaned over in the saddle and reached for the halter, intending to pull the team to a stop.

Mac raced up alongside the wagon, following Lee, and saw the Yankee soldier on the driver's box drop the reins and jerk a pistol from its holster. Lee had his back to the driver and had no idea what was happening.

Mac's right hand flashed across his body and ripped his saber from its scabbard. He swerved the stallion dangerously close to the spinning front wheel of the wagon and slashed at the Yankee with the saber. The blade sliced across the man's wrist. He screamed as blood spurted, and the pistol slipped from suddenly nerveless fingers. Clutching his injured wrist in his other hand, the Yankee screamed again as he lost his balance and toppled forward, falling off the box and under the hooves of the team. His scream was cut short.

From the corner of his eye, Mac saw the wagon lurch as the wheels passed over the body of the Yankee. He pulled away from the vehicle as Fitz Lee finally got a good hold on the harness and began hauling the team to a stop. When the wagon was finally halted, Lee looked around and saw that the box was empty. "What happened to the driver?" he asked.

Mac shrugged. He had acted to save the life of his friend and mentor and would have done it again in a second, but he didn't particularly want to dwell on what had happened. Nor did he want to examine the bloody heap on the ground that had once been a man.

At Lee's suggestion, Mac tied the stallion to the back of the wagon and climbed onto the box to drive it back into Rockville. Before he got the wagon moving, though, Lee rode up alongside and looked to the southeast along the road.

"You know what's down there, don't you, Mac?" he asked.

"Yes sir. Washington."

"Probably no more than three or four miles away. My God, we could be there in less than an hour. What do you think old Abe Lincoln would do if we came cantering up on the White House lawn?"

"I imagine he'd be a mite surprised," Mac said.

"If we could get our hands on Lincoln . . . we could do it, you know. We'd have to move quickly, before the Yankees knew what we were up to . . . but we could end the war, right here and now . . ."

Lee's excitement was vaulting and soaring, Mac saw. "I reckon General Stuart's waiting for us back in town." It would be better to remind Lee of his duty rather than letting him dwell on some crazy sortie into the enemy's capital that would probably get them all killed.

Lee sighed then nodded. "You're right, of course. Better get this wagon turned around and headed back into Rockville."

As he started toward Rockville, he saw that his comrades had captured well over a hundred of the wagons and had made prisoners of the Yankee wagoneers. The wagons that they hadn't been able to grab had overturned, spilling their contents all over the road. It was quite a successful raid.

But Mac saw Fitz Lee look back over his shoulder toward Washington. "Still, it's something to think about," he muttered.

That was all too true.

REPLACING A commander as beloved as Stonewall Jackson had to be difficult, Will thought as he watched Gen. Richard Ewell confer with Generals Rodes, Johnson, and Early in front of the headquarters tent in the Chambersburg camp. Ewell had a good reputation, but this was his first command after returning from medical leave following the loss of his leg. Not only that, he found himself in charge of an entire corps in the largest operation yet conducted by the Army of Northern Virginia. He had to be feeling a great deal of pressure to perform well.

The meeting broke up, and the three divisional commanders spread out to issue orders to their subordinates. Eventually the word came down to the company commanders. Rodes would push northeast to Carlisle, perhaps even penetrating as far as Harrisburg, the Pennsylvania capital, if circumstances allowed. Early's division would march due east through Cashtown and Gettysburg and on to York, gathering up provisions and supplies as they went. Johnson's division would be split: The brigade commanded by George Steuart would move west to Greencastle and McConnellsburg, also in search of supplies, while the division's other units, including the Stonewall Brigade, would accompany Rodes to Carlisle. Ewell himself would ride with Rodes.

Will was a little surprised that Ewell would scatter the corps so much. Here in enemy territory, it seemed to make more sense that the Confederates remain concentrated, so that they couldn't be cut off from each other. But the decision was not his to make, so he passed along the order to Darcy Bennett to get the men ready to march.

"Yes sir, Cap'n," Darcy said crisply enough, but he hesitated before turning away to carry out the order.

Will asked, "What is it, Darcy?"

"Well, sir . . . ," Darcy tugged at his beard. "Some of the fellas ain't real comfortable havin' that darky around."

"You mean Roman?" Will asked, surprised. He glanced over at the young man, who was gathering up and packing away

Will's gear in preparation for the move. If Roman heard the exchange between Will and Darcy, he gave no sign of it. "Why should he bother anyone?" Will went on. "Other officers have servants with them."

"You may not know it, Cap'n, but there ain't but one or two men left in this company who ever held any slaves. Most of 'em are farmers like you and me who never had either the money or the need for any field hands. I reckon they think you're puttin' on airs by havin' a darky to do for you."

"It wasn't my idea for Roman to come up here from Culpeper," Will said, trying to control the irritation he felt at this development. "You know he belonged to Captain Lattimer."

Darcy nodded. "Yes sir. And Cap'n Lattimer left the boy to you in his will. I understand all that. It's some of the other fellas who don't."

"Then it's up to you to make them understand. And for what it's worth, Roman is a slave in name only. As soon as we get back home, I'm going to have manumission papers drawn up and give him his freedom."

"Is that right? Well, it's good to know that, Cap'n. The men have always thought of you as one of them, even though you're an officer. They'll be glad to hear you ain't decided to act like some fancy planter."

"Not hardly," Will said, thinking of Duncan Ebersole. He didn't want to be like Ebersole in any way, shape, or form, and that included owning slaves.

Darcy went to supervise the company's preparations for pulling out, and Will walked over to Roman. The young man looked up him. "I got all your things ready to go, Cap'n."

"Thanks, Roman."

"I'll go saddle your horse now." Roman started to turn away then paused. He reached into the ragged burlap pouch that was slung over his shoulder, in which he carried his few belongings. "Brought something with me you might remember, Cap'n," he said as he brought out a small wooden box.

Will recognized it right away. He held out his hand. Roman gave him the box, and Will opened it, revealing a set of small but finely carved wooden chessmen. The box itself formed the chessboard. "I've missed our games," Will said with a smile.

"I reckon that belongs to you now, too," Roman said, "even though Massa Yancy didn't say nothin' about it in his will."

Will closed the box and fastened the catch. He shook his head as he held the box out to Roman. "No, you keep it," he said. "You carved the pieces. It's rightfully yours."

"Law says the master owns whatever the slave makes."

"Virginia law." Will grinned. "We're in Pennsylvania now. Besides, you won't be a slave much longer."

Roman hesitated then took the box and slipped it back in his burlap pack. "Thank you, Cap'n," he said softly. "For this here chess set . . . and everything else."

Will nodded. He and Roman understood each other.

It was a damned shame too many other people in both the Union and the Confederacy couldn't say the same thing.

Chapter Eighteen

WHERE WERE THE YANKEES?

That was the question Will asked himself as Rodes's division and the two brigades from Johnson's division marched toward Carlisle. He knew that the main body of the Army of the Potomac was either still in Virginia or on its way through Maryland, but he hadn't expected to find Pennsylvania so devoid of Union troops. They hadn't even encountered any militia. Did the Yankees think themselves so powerful that they were immune to invasion? Were they so arrogant as to believe they could shed blood throughout the South and not risk having it spilled on their own homeland?

And yet it was true that the Northern civilians had little or nothing to fear from the Confederate army. No force led by a gentleman such as Robert E. Lee was going to make war on innocents. The Southerners would fight like demons against enemy troops. They would confiscate whatever supplies they needed, and they would destroy rail lines, bridges, and whatever else they could in order to make it more difficult for the Union to wage war on them. But the civilians here in Pennsylvania or anywhere else the army might end up were in no personal danger.

The troops marched into Carlisle and found it defenseless. Some of the citizens peered fearfully from the windows of their houses while others who were more sympathetic to the cause of the South came out to greet them. A few young women even offered flowers and lace handkerchiefs to the marching soldiers, who grinned broadly as they accepted the tokens.

There was an unused U.S. Army cavalry barracks at Carlisle. Ewell knew it well, because he had been stationed here before the war. Will saw the pride on the general's face as the Confederate flag was lifted over the barracks. Ewell cleared his throat, which seemed to be choked with emotion, then called for the commander of the cavalry brigade attached to Rodes's division, Gen. Albert Jenkins.

"General, I want you to take your men and scout toward Harrisburg," Ewell ordered, "with a view toward whether or not it would be feasible for our forces to capture the town."

The man saluted. "Yes sir. It will be our honor." The cavalry under Jenkins would continue the Confederate thrust deep into Yankee territory.

Will wished he could go with them. He was not about to abandon his company, however.

The next day, June 28, passed peacefully while the forces in Carlisle waited for word from Jenkins. Will played chess with Roman, setting up the board on a folding table. Darcy sat nearby on a stump, watching intently. "I figure if I keep an eye on you fellas, one o' these days I'll get the hang of that game," he said.

"I'll be glad to teach you how to play, Sergeant Bennett," Roman offered.

Will was reaching for one of the pieces. He paused to watch Darcy's reaction. For a second, the big sergeant stiffened, clearly surprised at the idea that a black man could teach him anything and not too pleased by it, either. But then a thought occurred to him. "Might not be a bad idea. Seems like you've won more'n half the games I've seen you play with the cap'n here."

"I do my best," Will said with a frown that he didn't really mean. He moved one of his rooks.

Roman immediately slid one of his bishops across the board. "I reckon that's checkmate," he said.

Darcy nodded. "There you go. Just what I was talkin' about."

Will couldn't help it. He burst out with a laugh.

Jenkins and his cavalry rode back in on June 29. Will stood nearby as Jenkins made his report to Ewell, explaining that he and his men had ridden to within four miles of Harrisburg. "We camped there last night," Jenkins explained, "and thought to get even closer today, but we ran into several groups of Federal cavalry instead."

That news caught Will's attention. Finally, proof that there were a few Yankees left in Pennsylvania.

"We skirmished with them several times near the Susquehanna River," Jenkins said, "then broke off the engagement and returned here. General, based on the resistance we encountered, our army can take Harrisburg. There'll be a fight, of course, but I'm confident that we will emerge victorious."

Ewell nodded, and Will could almost see the thoughts going through the commander's bald head. The state capital would be quite a prize. Not enough to make the Yankees capitulate, of course, but it would be that much extra bait to draw out Hooker and the Army of the Potomac, not to mention putting added political pressure on Abraham Lincoln.

"Thank you for your report, General," Ewell said solemnly to Jenkins. "I shall give it the utmost consideration."

Ewell was a cautious man. Will knew he wasn't going to jump into anything too hastily. And once they were committed to attack Harrisburg, there would be no turning back. It wouldn't hurt to ponder the matter for a little while, Will supposed.

But later in the day, a courier arrived in Carlisle, galloping into town with his uniform and his horse coated with dust from the road.

He brought a message from the commanding general.

THREE DAYS earlier, the division under the command of Jubal Early had passed through the community of Gettysburg, a settlement in the midst of fine farming country that was the junction point for nine roads. The town was defended by a small group of militia, none of whom had been in the service for even a full week. In fact, they had arrived in Gettysburg only the night before. For novices in the art of war, however, they proved to be quite astute and immediately recognized discretion as the better portion of valor.

They ran like rabbits at the first sign of the Confederate division bearing down on them.

Early, a man not noted for his sense of humor, was moved to observe about the Union militia, "It was well that the regiment took to its heels so quickly, or some of its members might have been hurt."

It was Early's intention to accumulate a good deal of supplies for his troops while in Gettysburg, but he found that the local merchants had had enough warning of his impending arrival to conceal most of their goods. Unwilling to take the time necessary to tear the town apart in a search for provisions, Early ordered his men to move on. As they were pulling out, though, he called a courier over to him.

"Ride on back to Chambersburg. Hill ought to be there by now," Early said, referring to the corps commanded by A. P. Hill. Early spat in the dust of the street. "If his boys' shoes are as worn out as ours, he might want to send some men to Gettysburg. I'm told they've got a whole factory here that doesn't make anything except shoes!"

The young lieutenant snapped a salute. "Yes sir! I'll carry the message to General Hill. Any word for General Lee?"

"Just that we're goin' on to York."

That was what Early did, briskly covering the thirty miles from Gettysburg to York and arriving there on the evening of June 27. Again, the small garrison of Union troops protecting the town proved to be no resistance at all. This time, however, the Yankees surrendered to Early rather than fleeing.

The next morning, as the Confederates marched through the town, several of the officers under Early's command were moved to make speeches. One of them, Gen. John B. Gordon, sought to reassure the nervous civilians that they were in no danger from the Army of Northern Virginia. A young woman stepped out of the crowd and handed Gordon some flowers, a gesture that drew cheers from the passing troops. Gordon, a dashing Georgian, smiled at the young woman, swept off his hat, and bowed to her. As he did so, he noticed that there was a folded piece of paper stuck amidst the stems of the bouquet. He moved on with his men, waiting several discreet minutes before opening the paper to see what the young lady had written to him.

This was no love note, he saw to his surprise. Instead, it was a detailed description of the Federal militia that was defending Wrightsville, the town where Early planned to go next.

Immediately, Gordon sought out Early and showed the note to him. Early scanned the information and grunted. "All right, General," he said, "since you were made a present of this intelligence, your brigade can lead the way to Wrightsville. We'll take the town without much trouble, I expect. There's a bridge there over the Susquehanna that I want." Early clenched a fist. "If we can get across the river, we can come at Harrisburg from the southeast at the same time General Ewell's comin' in from the southwest."

"Yes sir," Gordon agreed. "It sounds like a fine plan."

Early handed the note back to Gordon. "At least something good may come out of the way you fellas like to speechify."

With Gordon's brigade taking the lead, Early's division raced on to Wrightsville. The information in the mysterious note concerning the Yankee militia proved to be right. There were enough of them in Wrightsville to put up a fight, but Gordon shared Early's confidence that the defenders were no match for the Confederate army. The Yankees were still vastly outnumbered here.

But as the initial skirmishing began to break out, Gordon noted clouds of black smoke rising on the other side of the town, about where the bridge over the Susquehanna was located. With apprehension growing inside him, he sent scouts circling the community to see what was burning. When they reported back to him a short time later, his fears were confirmed. The Yankees had set fire to the long covered bridge, destroying it rather than letting it fall into Confederate hands.

When Gordon relayed this news to Early, the crusty old general cursed in frustration. "Without that bridge, we can't do a damned bit of good here, and I'm not going to waste any more troops and ammunition rootin' out those militiamen. We'll go back to York and wait to see what General Ewell wants us to do next." He grimaced and added, "I reckon you can save that pretty little note as a souvenir, General."

"Yes sir," Gordon agreed.

The note itself was in the handwriting of a woman. Whether it had been written by the young lady who gave him the flowers, or by someone else, Gordon never knew.

A day later, it didn't really matter, because a galloper arrived in York from Chambersburg, and he brought new orders from the commanding general.

THE OTHER two Confederate corps, those of Gens. James Longstreet and A. P. Hill, had followed Ewell up the Shenandoah Valley, across Maryland, and into southern Pennsylvania. It had been a long, hot march, so brutally hot that some men had died from it. Those who survived were covered by a layer of dust so thick it was like a second skin. But they had reached their objective, and by June 29 both corps were camped east of Chambersburg, on the road that led to Cashtown and Chambersburg.

Longstreet brought more than a corps of men, however. He brought news that Robert E. Lee desperately needed to know.

Several weeks earlier, Longstreet had taken it upon himself to send a spy into Washington. The man was known only as Harrison, and although Longstreet referred to him as a scout, it was clear that his mission was espionage. He was to remain in Washington until he uncovered information he deemed important enough to bring to Longstreet. Unwilling to give anyone the exact details of the Confederate plan of march, especially someone who was going into the heart of enemy territory, Longstreet had left it up to Harrison to locate the army, assuring the spy that it was large enough the task shouldn't be too difficult. On the night of June 28, Harrison finally caught up to Longstreet as the corps was moving into its camp near Chambersburg.

At first the pickets were reluctant to take Harrison to Long-street's tent. The spy was dirty and dressed in torn clothing. In fact, Harrison was taken first to Lt. Col. G. Moxley Sorrel, Long-street's chief of staff, and he had to convince Sorrel of his identity before he was allowed to speak to the general. Once he had done so, however, Longstreet wasted no time in sending him on to report directly to Lee.

Harrison's information was that the Army of the Potomac had begun to move north from Virginia, swallowing the bait dangled by Lee's invasion of Pennsylvania. Not only that, but the Yankees had moved quickly enough so that by now their entire force was most likely north of the Potomac and coming in this direction toward Lee.

Lee was as reluctant to accept Harrison's story at face value as the sentries had been, but it had been a week since he'd had any word from Stuart's cavalry. Without any intelligence from the cavalry, Lee was in the dark, and Harrison's report was the first ray of light since the army had entered Pennsylvania.

Summoning Longstreet and Hill, Lee discussed the situation with them and reached the conclusion that he could no longer afford to have his army scattered across southern Pennsylvania from McConnellsburg in the west to York in the east. "We must concentrate in this area," Lee declared. "Send word to General Ewell, General Early, and General Steuart to retire to Cashtown immediately."

Cashtown was east of Chambersburg, about halfway between that town and Gettysburg. Lee had studied the maps and knew it was a central location where all of his troops could come together again.

"We'll be ready by the time Hooker gets here," Longstreet confidently vowed.

In the corner of the tent, Harrison looked up from the tin plate of rations he had been given. "Excuse me, sir," he said, "but General Hooker's not in command of the Union army anymore. He was when they started out, but on the way up here I heard that he'd been replaced."

"Who is in command now?" Lee asked.

"Meade. George Meade, I think."

—◊◊◊—

WILL WELCOMED the return to Cashtown. The fact that the army was on the move again instead of just sitting in Carlisle boded well for action. Of course, like everyone else he had expected that they would head for Harrisburg next, in an attempt to capture the Pennsylvania state capital, instead of going back in the direction they had come from.

"What you reckon is goin' to happen, Cap'n?" Roman asked as he brought up the saddled dun for Will to mount. Darcy was forming the company into its ranks and preparing them to march.

Will thought about it for a moment as he took the reins from Roman. "The only reason I can see that we're backtracking is that the Yankees are about to show up somewhere down south of here. General Lee must have gotten word that they're moving closer to our position there."

Roman nodded solemnly. "There'll be fightin', then."

"I expect so."

"Your brother, Mister MacBeth, where's he at?"

Will could only shake his head. "I don't know. When we left to come up here to Carlisle, it had been several days since I heard anything about the cavalry. They were supposed to join us when we got to Pennsylvania. I have to admit I'm getting a mite worried."

"Don't you worry none 'bout Mister MacBeth, he'll be all right, Cap'n," Roman said. "Long as he's got that big horse of his'n, ain't nobody goin' to hurt him."

Will grinned as he swung up into the saddle, remembering the things Mac had said about the stallion in the past. Mac was about halfway convinced there was something magical about that animal, like it wasn't really a horse at all but some sort of spirit creature instead. Will had never been a superstitious man; he didn't believe in such things.

But he believed in speed and strength and instinct, and Mac's stallion had those things in abundance. "I imagine you're right," he said to Roman. "My brother and that horse of his make a pretty good team. I expect he'll be all right in any scrape as long as they're together."

A few minutes later, the order came to move out, and the Stonewall Brigade, along with the other elements of the Confederate army that had made this foray into northeastern Pennsylvania, turned its face south again.

AFTER CAPTURING 125 wagons and approximately four hundred Yankee prisoners the day before on June 28, Jeb Stuart was faced with the decision of what to do with these spoils of war. He wanted the wagons, especially the supplies they contained. The food would fill the bellies of his men, and the bags of grain that were also found in some of the wagons assured that the horses would eat well, too. But he didn't have any use for the prisoners, and so he paroled them and headed north again, using all the daylight that was left to get as far into the Keystone State as he could—and hopefully link up with Lee's army.

By nightfall, the cavalry had reached the settlement of Cooksville, twenty miles from Baltimore and almost due west of that Maryland city. As they made camp, Mac worried about the fact that they were still in Maryland instead of across the border in Pennsylvania. In a week's time, the cavalry had covered less than half the distance Mac had hoped they would have traversed by now.

"Why the frown, Mac?" Fitz Lee asked that evening as they sat next to a fire with their supper.

"I was just thinking about the rest of the army, General," Mac replied. "I don't much like the idea of their marching around up there in Pennsylvania without us along with them to cover their flanks."

"We've been through this before." Lee's sharp tone showed his slight irritation. "General Stuart knows what he's doing."

"Of course, sir. I never doubted that."

It was true, Mac thought: Stuart knew exactly what he was doing. He was trying to carry out another daring raid so that people—and the newspapers—would be talking about that instead of what had happened at Brandy Station. As those thoughts went through his head, Mac felt a twinge of guilt at the disloyalty he was showing to General Stuart.

Stuart by example had showed the world what a fantastic body of men the Confederate cavalry was. He had been firmly on Mac's side during the tension with Jason Trahearne, even though his duty had compelled him to act impartially. The general exemplified more than anyone else except Robert E. Lee and the late Stonewall Jackson the combination of Southern gentleman and brilliant military tactician.

But even a man such as Jeb Stuart could make a mistake, Mac thought grimly, and in abandoning the rest of the Confederate army during its invasion of Yankee territory, he was convinced that Stuart had made such a mistake.

The next morning, June 29, the cavalry pressed north toward Westminster. The pace was slowed by the captured wagons, but Stuart was unwilling to leave them behind. Along the way, Fitz Lee ordered some of the men to fall out and destroy some of the tracks belonging to the Baltimore and Ohio Railroad. Mac joined in the effort, using the stallion's strength to help pull up the tracks. Once the tracks had been dragged off, the ties were levered out of the roadbed, piled up, and set afire. The sections of steel track were thrown onto the blazes so that they softened from the heat and bent out of shape. The Yankees wouldn't be able to use them again.

The railroad wasn't the only thing to be disrupted. Troopers threw ropes over telegraph lines and pulled them down from their poles. Some of the poles were chopped down and burned, and the wire was cut everywhere possible. This sort of interuption of travel and communication was a specialty of the cavalry. It would be a long time before everything could be put back to normal in central Maryland.

Late in the afternoon, as the column approached Westminster, two companies of Federal cavalry suddenly appeared and charged the startled Confederate horsemen. The Yankees were vastly outnumbered, however, so the element of surprise wasn't nearly as effective as it would have been had the two sides been more evenly matched. From where Mac drew rein and watched the brief clash with Fitz Lee, the battle was nothing more than some stirred-up dust, the winking of sunlight on steel, and the shouts of men.

The Yankees fought well, but the odds were against them. In less than half an hour, those who had not been killed or captured had fled. A satisfied Stuart waved the column on. The Confederates didn't stop for the night until they reached the small town of Union Mills, just five miles south of the Pennsylvania border. Stuart sent scouts ahead to check the road between Union Mills and Hanover, Pennsylvania, the next community of any size to the north.

Mac was with Fitz Lee and the rest of Lee's staff that evening as they met with Generals Stuart and Hampton, Colonel Chambliss, and their staffs at the headquarters tent that had been erected for Stuart. On a map, the general pointed out their position as the officers gathered around him.

"We are here, gentlemen, and this is the Susquehanna River." He traced a line on the map about fifty miles northeast of Union Mills. "If all has gone well for General Lee and his troops, I suspect they have reached the Susquehanna by now and have perhaps even captured Harrisburg. We shall proceed in that direction and will probably encounter their right flank within the next twenty-four to forty-eight hours."

If the army has taken Harrisburg, thought Mac, it hadn't done so without a fight. And that meant Will had gone into battle again. At this point, Mac didn't know what to hope for.

The generals were still discussing the situation when Major McClellan was called away for a moment. When he returned, he reported, "I'm sorry to interrupt, sir, but some of the scouts have returned with news."

"Very well, then, let's hear what they have to say," Stuart quickly ordered.

One of the scouts who strode up to the gathering in front of the general's tent was Corporal Hagen. Mac had been on several reconnaissance missions with the massive corporal in the past, and he realized now that he greatly missed being on his own and riding through the open countryside with only one or two companions. Scouting was a dangerous business, to be sure, but it also had its compensations, especially for a man like Mac who had never quite been comfortable in the company of thousands of soldiers.

"How does the road to Hanover look today, Corporal?" Stuart asked.

"The road to Hanover ain't the one you got to worry about, General," Hagen replied. "It's the one that turns off up ahead a ways and runs over to the west."

Fitz Lee put his finger on the map. "This one?" he asked Hagen. "The road that goes to Gettysburg?"

"Yep, I reckon. Anyway, it's full of Yankees."

"That close to us?" asked a member of Hampton's staff, a slight edge of nervousness in his voice.

"Yes sir. From what we seen and heard, I'd say there's a division of Yankee cavalry on that road, 'bout seven miles from here. They're bedded down now, but they was movin' in a fair hurry when we first spotted 'em."

Stuart frowned. "It's doubtful the Yankees would have that large a cavalry force on the move without having their infantry close by, too."

Mac wasn't so sure about that. Stuart had more than half a division under his command here at Union Mills, and the rest of the Confederate army wasn't anywhere near, at least as far as Mac knew. It wasn't his place to say anything, though.

Stuart turned and peered off into the night, first one way and then the other. A faint smile was on his face as he stared into the darkness. "I wonder just how many of them are out there. They could be all around us."

Several of the officers frowned in concern, but Stuart didn't seem overly worried, just curious. He would fight the whole Union army if he had to. He might even prefer it that way.

The general turned and looked at the others. After a moment he laughed softly. "You'd better get a good night's sleep, gentlemen," he said. "You never know when you'll have the chance for another one."

Chapter Nineteen

MOVING A DIVISION AND a half of infantry plus a few cavalry regiments was not an easy thing. The men under Generals Rodes and Johnson marched steadily all day on June 29 but by evening had not yet reached Chambersburg. They made camp, confident that the next day they would rejoin the rest of the Army of Northern Virginia.

Will sat beside his campfire that night with Roman, but they weren't playing chess. Rather, Will stared into the gently leaping flames and pondered the battle to come. For surely, there *was* going to be a battle. Lee would not have ordered his forces to concentrate unless the Yankees were somewhere nearby.

All day long, as he rode beside the marching men of his company, a cold feeling had come upon him. He had never been one to brood about the dangers he faced as a soldier. He had learned as a lawman before the war that it did no good to worry about what might happen. You just prepared as best you could and went ahead and did your job, and whatever happened, so be it. But there was something different about the uneasy sensations he had felt today.

He had heard others talk of knowing they were going to die in an upcoming battle. They wrote letters of farewell to their families, entrusted tokens to their friends to be taken back home and given to grieving wives or parents or children. That sense of fatalism sometimes grew so strong it was almost paralyzing. Men had trouble moving because they were convinced that death was just ahead for them. Often, they were right.

But not always. Will recalled many instances where men had been so convinced their number was up that they had gone to their fellow soldiers, saying, "When I'm gone, you take my boots . . . and you, my ammunition pouch . . . and you, my saber . . . ," only to come through the battle unscathed and have to admit with a rueful but relieved grin that they were going to need their gear for at least a while longer. He had witnessed, too, plenty of occasions when a man seemed to feel that he was going to live forever and would be struck down with a mortal wound an instant later.

There was no way of knowing. That was all there was to it. You just never knew.

So why did he sense this terrible foreboding tonight?

"Cap'n Will, you got the darkest frown on your face I ever did see," Roman said.

Will looked up from the fire and chuckled humorlessly. "Just thinking about the future . . . or the lack of it."

"You shouldn't ought to be doin' that," Roman said with a shake of his head. "One thing you learn when you a slave: You just wastin' time worryin' about tomorrow. You got to worry about today. You live from mornin' to evenin', and then you sleep, and when the sun comes up, you do it again. What's it say in the Good Book? The sun goes down in the evenin', but it always comes up the next mornin'. 'Clesiastes, I think it is."

Will nodded, remembering the sermons Reverend Crosley had preached at the Baptist church back in Culpeper. Will had never been one to draw much comfort from the Scriptures, but somehow the words that Roman spoke made him feel better. He was worrying for nothing, he told himself.

"I think I'll turn in," he said. "Thanks, Roman."

"Whatever I done, you're mighty welcome, Cap'n. Good night."

"Good night, Roman."

—⁂—

DESPITE GENERAL Stuart's advice, Mac didn't sleep particularly well that night. He tossed and turned restlessly in his bedroll, and when he finally did doze off, his slumber was haunted by dark dreams punctuated by what seemed to be gun flashes.

The next morning a cup of the bitter brew made mainly from crushed grain and passed off for coffee revived him somewhat. He was at least relatively alert as the column resumed its northward trek. When they reached Hanover, Mac thought, they would be at last in Pennsylvania.

Stuart sent Lee's brigade off to the left to cover that flank. There were Yankees in that direction, they knew from Hagen's report. Of course, there might well be Yankees to the right, too, but they couldn't know that for sure.

With Lee's brigade forming a screen to the west, the brigade led by Colonel Chambliss took the lead. Behind them the captured wagons rattled and creaked along the road. Bringing up the rear was Hampton's brigade. All in all, it was a formidable force in motion.

At midmorning, as Chambliss's riders cantered into the edge of Hanover, Federal cavalrymen appeared in the road ahead of them. Chambliss didn't hesitate, figuring it was better not to give the Yankees a chance to charge. He sent the Second North Carolina Regiment thundering forward in an attack.

Riding off to the left of the column, Lee's brigade heard the sharp popping of gunshots. Lee lifted a gauntleted hand, halting his men. "Blast it! Chambliss must have run into trouble when he rode into town. Go find out what's happening, Mac, and let me know."

Mac had anticipated the order. He was already wheeling the stallion in that direction. After acknowledging the order, he and the silver gray stallion sprang away in a gallop.

The wind was strong in Mac's face as he raced toward Hanover. He reached up with his free hand and tugged his cap tighter on his head. Within minutes he came up to the edge of the column and spotted Stuart and several aides galloping toward the front. Mac fell in with them.

The general glanced over and grinned at him. "Yankee cavalry in town!" he called over the pounding of hoofbeats. "Chambliss is giving them battle!"

The buildings of the town of Hanover were only a couple of hundred yards ahead of them, the streets filled with a milling mass of blue and gray riders. Abruptly, the Confederates turned and began streaming out of the town, pursued closely by the Yankee cavalrymen. The Federals outnumbered the Southerners by a great deal, Mac saw to his dismay. Chambliss's men were in full retreat.

Stuart and his companions brought their horses to a halt as the fleeing horsemen streamed around them. "Stop!" Stuart shouted to them. "Rally up, boys! Rally up!"

The troopers ignored him, if indeed they even heard him over the thunderous hoofbeats of their horses and their own pounding hearts. In frustration, Stuart shouted to one of his officers, Lt. William Blackford, to rally the retreating cavalrymen. But there was nothing Blackford or anyone else could do to stop them, and more important, by this time the Yankees were practically on top of Stuart and his entourage.

A short hedge ran alongside the road. Stuart turned his horse and kicked it into a run toward it. Seeing what he was trying to do, Mac and Blackford followed. If they stayed on the road, they would be overrun by the Union cavalry. They had to take their chances in the fields on the edge of town.

Stuart put the spurs to his animal and hauled back on the reins. The horse lifted and sailed over the shrubbery. Mac and Blackford came right behind. The silver gray stallion cleared the hedge with no difficulty. So did Blackford's horse.

No sooner had the stallion's hooves thudded onto the ground than Mac spotted at least two dozen blue-clad riders galloping toward them. The group of Yankees was flanking the main body in pursuit of the fleeing Confederates. Stuart and his two companions had jumped almost into the middle of them! At first the Yankees began to shout at them, calling on them to halt and surrender.

Surrender was never an option for Jeb Stuart. He put his horse into a run, heading across the field away from the Yankee cavalry. Mac and Blackford followed. Pistols cracked, and Mac heard the uncomfortably close whine of a bullet near his head.

The grass was high, but it didn't slow the horses. Mac and Stuart rode almost abreast, with Blackford just behind. Mac could tell that the stallion wasn't running at top speed. If he had wanted to, he could have pulled ahead of the others and left them behind, but he didn't ask that of the stallion. He wasn't going to abandon Stuart to the Yankees.

Suddenly, a dark line across the field in front of them caught Mac's attention. As they came closer to it, he saw that it was a small creek running through a gully that was several feet deep and at least fifteen feet wide. If they slowed to make their way carefully down the creek bank, the Yankees would catch up to them. There was no doubt of that in Mac's mind.

Stuart had seen the creek, too. He raked his horse with his spurs and called out to it for more speed. The general intended to jump the gully.

As their options flashed through his mind in less than a second, Mac knew that Stuart was right. Leaping over the gully was their only chance to escape.

They were on top of the gully in a matter of seconds. Mac let the stallion edge ahead at the last moment, knowing that the horse could make the jump. The other mounts were less likely to balk if they saw the stallion leap successfully over the gully. A slight tug on the reins was all it took to send the stallion soaring into the air.

Even as he jumped, Mac glanced over and saw Stuart close beside him. The general's horse had left the ground a fraction of an instant after Mac's. To an observer it must have been a beautiful sight, the two magnificent animals flying through the air, their riders straight in the saddles.

Then they were down, the silver gray animal cleared the gully with six feet or more to spare. Stuart was also safely on the far side of the creek, and a second later, so was their companion, whose horse also made the jump successfully. All three of them reined in and looked around to see the Yankee cavalrymen slowing as they approached the gully. Clearly, none of the Federal horsemen were willing to risk their horses—and their lives—in such a daring leap.

But they still had carbines, and bullets sang around Stuart and his companions as they wheeled their mounts and rode away. None of the shots found their mark. Stuart roared with laughter as they made their getaway.

The general led them in a loop, circling back to the hills southeast of Hanover. There they found the rest of the column regrouping after Chambliss's men had been driven out of town. Hampton had come up to reinforce Chambliss, and the Yankees had broken off their attack and returned to Hanover. That didn't mean they wouldn't be back later.

"Tell Fitz to come on in," Stuart ordered. "We'll bring up the artillery in case the Yankees try to attack again before he gets here. Once we're all together we'll figure out what to do next."

Mac nodded, but as he did, he thought that such indecisiveness was unusual in Stuart. Men who had been under his command for a while expected him to devise brilliant tactical maneuvers on the fly, as he had done so often in the past. That was happening less and less often these days, Mac thought as he rode in search of his brigade.

Stuart still had his moments, of course. Mac knew he would never forget the wild ride across the field and the leap across the gully. During that instant they had been in the air, when he had looked over and seen Stuart there beside him, a laughing grin on his face, that picture had been imprinted on his brain like a daguerreotype. It was the perfect image of the Confederate cavalryman, the Southern cavalier.

Mac had the sudden sensation that, for good or ill, when this war was over, the world would never again see the like of James Ewell Brown Stuart.

THAT SAME day—the last day of June 1863—on the road between Cashtown and Gettysburg, a brigade of Confederate infantry from Gen. Henry Heth's division of A. P. Hill's corps was marching along in the sun, many of the men no doubt thinking of the shoes they had heard rumored to be in Gettysburg. Hardly a man in the ranks had shoes. And those who did had shoes with holes in them. Some were more hole than shoe.

The brigade was led by Gen. James Johnston Pettigrew, who hoped that outfitting his men with new footgear would raise their spirits even more. Morale was already higher than it had been for quite a while, no doubt because the troops had been eating better in recent days. Living off the fat of the land in Pennsylvania was considerably easier than it was in Virginia. The war had stripped away too much of everything that was good about Virginia and much of the rest of the South. That was why it had to be over soon, while there was still something worth fighting for.

As the brigade approached Gettysburg, Pettigrew and a few members of his staff rode ahead to make sure the way into town was clear. The general reined in at the top of a rise and took his field glasses from a pouch strapped to his saddle. Before he lifted them to his eyes, he swept his gaze across the landscape spread out in front of him.

Gettysburg was a beautiful spot; there was no denying that. The good-sized, prosperous-looking community, filled with sturdy brick buildings and well-kept residences, was surrounded by fertile fields and thickly wooded hills and ridges. From his vantage point, Pettigrew could see several of the roads leading into town. Picket fences ran alongside them and also separated the fields. Large farmhouses and barns dotted the green landscape. On a shallow ridge just on the outskirts of town stood a large brick building with a white cupola on top of it. A school of some sort, by the look of it, Pettigrew judged. To the south of town rose another ridge, crowned at its southern tip by two hills. An even higher hill sat off to the southeast.

Satisfied by his survey of the surroundings, Pettigrew concentrated his attention on Gettysburg. He lifted the glasses again and focused on the town, searching for any sign of Federal troops. A few townspeople were moving about the streets, but they all seemed to be civilians. He saw a wagon or two rolling along, but no artillery or ambulances or anything else that looked even vaguely military. Gettysburg was drowsing under the summer sun.

A haze of dust in the air drew the general's attention to a road that ran parallel to the ridge south of town. He swung the glasses in that direction, and after a second the view sprang out at him in sharp relief. He stiffened as he saw a column of blue-clad horsemen riding toward the town.

"Yankees!" he said as he lowered the field glasses. They were moving fast toward Gettysburg.

Pettigrew turned to one of his staff. "Have the men pull back." The brigade was atop the ridge by now, in full view of anyone in town who cared to look in that direction. No doubt some had. As soon as those Yankee cavalrymen arrived, they would hear from the townspeople about the Rebel soldiers just outside of town.

The North Carolinian grimaced. He could push on into Gettysburg, but a single brigade of infantry was a poor match for a large force of cavalry. He was unsure just how many Yankees were moving into the town, but it was a large number. He wasn't going to throw away the lives of his men without clear orders to do so. He had come to Gettysburg for shoes, not bullets.

WITH HIS brigade waiting on the road some four miles west of Gettysburg, Pettigrew rode back to Cashtown to confer with Heth. No sooner had he begun his report about the Federal cavalry he had seen moving into Gettysburg than the corps commander, Gen. Ambrose Powell Hill, rode up.

Hill cut a dashing figure, sometimes wearing a bright red shirt into battle even though it made him a better and more tempting target for the enemy. Now he swung down from his saddle and listened intently to his generals' report.

When Pettigrew finished, Heth turned to Hill. "What is your opinion of the situation, General?"

"My opinion is that the enemy is still encamped at Middleburg," Hill replied bluntly. He looked at Pettigrew. "I mean no offense, General, but I suspect what you saw was just a routine Yankee patrol."

Pettigrew's jaw tightened. He knew quite well what he had seen, and it was considerably more than a patrol. But these men were his commanders, and he could not contradict them. Instead he inclined his head and said nothing.

Heth nodded. "Then if there is no objection, General, tomorrow I will take my men and get those shoes."

"None in the world," Hill said.

—⟋⟋⟍—

THAT NIGHT, far to the east, Jeb Stuart's men were once more on the move. After the clash that morning, Stuart had decided to leave Hanover to the Yankees. The column turned east instead.

That move took them away from the rest of the Confederate army, rather than toward them, Mac thought with increasing frustration. Somewhere off there to the west or north was his brother Will, and Mac knew he wasn't going to feel better until he was sure that Will was all right. Even if they went into battle, it would be better if they could go together.

Before morning, however, Stuart turned north again, which eased Mac's mind a little. At least they were going in the right general direction now, and with each mile they penetrated farther into Pennsylvania.

It was slow going. The mule teams of the captured wagons were hard to handle. They had had no grain for several days, and their hunger made them even more balky than usual. It was not just the mules that were hungry and exhausted. Stuart's men and horses were reaching that point themselves.

The general sent out scouts to search for the army, but as each man rode back, he reported no luck. Stuart's impatience grew. As the sun rose on July 1, 1863, the Confederates neared the small town of Dover. The general ordered a halt so that everyone could rest and scouts and foragers could ride into Dover to seek out any provisions to be had there.

This mission was also unsuccessful, but one of the men brought back some news. Only a couple of days earlier, at least a division of Confederate infantry had been seen in Carlisle, some thirty miles to the northwest.

Mac's spirits took a leap when he heard that. He had no way of knowing if Will was part of that division, but he hoped that was the case. If it was, the Brannon brothers would soon be reunited, because Stuart quickly decided to push on to Carlisle. Surely there would be rations there, and he and his men could link up with the Army of Northern Virginia.

The ground between Dover and Carlisle still had to be covered, of course, and that wasn't as easy as it sounded. The mule teams continued to balk, and the weariness of men and horses slowed the column as well.

Mac leaned forward in the saddle as he rode with Fitz Lee. The general smiled over at him. "No need to be anxious," Lee said. "We'll be there soon."

"It can't be too soon for me," Mac said. "I just hope that if Will was there before, he still is."

"He probably is if Uncle Bob hasn't pushed all the way to Harrisburg. What a plum that would be, to capture a Yankee state capital!"

A plum, perhaps, but not one easily plucked from the tree, thought Mac. The Pennsylvania militia, not to mention any units of the regular army that happened to be up here, would mount a stiff defense before they would surrender Harrisburg.

The day dragged on so that it was the middle of the afternoon before the column approached Carlisle. As it did, a rider
came back along the line and found Fitzhugh Lee. "General
Stuart wants you and Captain Brannon to report to him at the
head of the column, sir."

"Thanks, son," Lee said. He turned to Mac. "Wonder what
the general wants with us. Only one way to find out, I suppose."
He urged his mount forward, Mac following on the stallion.

Stuart greeted them with a smile and an upraised hand.
"We're near Carlisle," he said, "so I was wondering if I could
borrow Captain Brannon, Fitz. I want a fast rider in case the Yankees are waiting for us."

"Of course, General," Lee replied. "I'm sure Mac would
rather reconnoiter than plod along with us. Right, Mac?"

"I'll do whatever you say, General." Mac's answering smile
was a clear enough indication that he was glad to get the new
assignment, however.

"Take Corporal Hagen with you," Stuart suggested. The big
man sat nearby on his horse, a grin on his bearded face. He was
ready for some action, too, Mac thought.

The two riders descended the hill toward Carlisle. Mac kept
a close eye on the settlement, watching for any sign of the
enemy, so right away he saw the artillery detail that suddenly
wheeled a piece into the road and pointed its gaping muzzle
toward them.

"Whoa!" Mac called as he reined in. "Corporal, do you see
what unit that is?"

"Looks like Yankee militia," Hagen rumbled. "And they're
loadin' that thing."

Mac took out his field glasses to study the town as the
Yankee gunners executed the intricate drill to prepare their
weapon for firing. He saw quite a few uniformed men forming
into ranks that spilled from the side streets. If the Confederate
army had been here, it was gone now and had been replaced
with what looked like two brigades of Yankees.

"Uh, Cap'n, we might ought to light a shuck out of here," Hagen suggested.

Mac trained the glasses on the lone cannon and saw the gunners ramming home the shell. "I think you're right." He wheeled the stallion and urged it into a run. Hagen was right beside him.

Behind them, the cannon roared. Mac heard the high-pitched whine of the shell screaming through the air toward them. It slammed into the road and burst about fifty yards behind them, doing no real harm but making the men urge their mounts on to greater speed.

Everyone had heard the blast of the cannon. As Mac and Hagen galloped up, Stuart and Lee frowned with concern. "From the looks of you boys, those weren't our people waiting for you in the town," Stuart observed.

"No sir," Mac reported. "I estimate at least two brigades of Union militia have occupied the town."

"Only two brigades?" Stuart's eyes brightened. "Not enough to stop us."

Probably not, thought Mac, but the Yankees had more than enough men to make an attack on the town very costly for the Confederates. Especially considering that half of the men were dozing in their saddles, even after the cannon shot. A fella could drive himself only so far, Mac told himself, and then his body just wouldn't do it anymore.

"I want to call on the leader of those Yankees, whoever he is, to surrender," Stuart said. "Someone will have to ride down there under a flag of truce."

"I'll do it," Lee said immediately.

Stuart thought about it for a second then nodded. "When they see that a brigadier general has come to negotiate with them, they'll take us seriously."

"I'll go with you, sir," Mac offered.

Lee smiled. "I'll be glad for the company. See to the rigging of a white flag."

Minutes later, the small party was ready to go. Hagen also insisted on joining them. He carried the pole to which a piece of white cloth had been attached.

The three rode slowly toward Carlisle, passing what looked like a military barracks on the edge of town. Mac tried not to stare at the cannon, but he had a hard time keeping his eyes off the weapon. The Yankee gunners stepped back, honoring the truce, but it would take only seconds for them to have it ready to fire again.

Several horsemen rode out to meet Lee, Mac, and Hagen. They wore the uniform of the Pennsylvania militia, and as they came closer, Mac could see that the man in the lead was glowering. When the two groups were only a few yards apart, the men reined in. Lee saluted and addressed the Yankee commander. "General Fitzhugh Lee, at your service, sir. I bring you the compliments and best wishes of General Jeb Stuart, Confederate States cavalry."

"I don't recognize any such thing," snapped the Yankee. "I'm General William F. Smith. Tell your General Stuart that he is not welcome in Carlisle."

"Now, General," Lee said smoothly, "there's no need for trouble here. We have three full brigades and a battery of artillery. We seek no prisoners, only supplies."

"You'll have to fight for 'em," Smith replied.

Lee eased forward in his saddle. "That will mean casualties on both sides, General. It's unavoidable."

"You can avoid 'em by going the hell back where you came from, you damned Rebs!"

Mac saw Lee's back stiffen. Lee didn't like taking that kind of talk, but he was under a flag of truce and had no choice. "Is that your final word, sir?" he said. "You refuse to surrender?"

"You're damned right I do."

"Very well. I shall convey your answer to General Stuart."

"You may convey it to the devil for all I care!" snorted the militia commander.

Lee turned his horse and trotted back to the ridge. Mac and Hagen followed, with Hagen bringing up the rear so that the white flag was the last thing the Yankees saw. As they approached the crest of the slope, Mac saw that the artillery had been brought up. All six guns ominously poked their snouts over the top of the ridge.

Shaking his head, Lee reported. "General Smith of the Yankee militia refuses to surrender the town, General. He told me that if we want provisions, we'll have to fight for them."

Stuart's mouth tightened with anger under his beard. "All right, if that's what he wants, that's what he shall have." He turned in the saddle and called to the gunners. "Gentlemen, you may fire at will!"

Within moments, the cannons began to roar. From his vantage point, Mac saw the shells crash into the streets, scattering the Yankee troops. Some of the shots hit the buildings. Mac saw a tall chimney explode from a direct hit. The lone Yankee cannon tried to reply, but several shells fell around it, damaging it and routing the gunners.

Stuart pointed to the abandoned barracks. "Fire that building. I want a nice blaze that everyone in town can see."

Soon flames were leaping from the roof of the building, dancing high in the air that rapidly became clogged with billows of black smoke. While the blaze was going on, the bombardment continued.

Mac watched the destruction so intently that he was unaware that Stuart had come up beside him until the general spoke to him. "I have another job for you. I've already spoken to General Lee concerning it, and he has given his blessing."

"We are all yours to command, General."

"Be that as it may . . . ," Stuart smiled faintly then went on. "I'm sending out scouts to search for the rest of our army. I'm growing a bit worried that we haven't encountered them yet."

A bit worried was an understatement as far as Mac was concerned. He wanted to find out what had happened to the rest of the army and where they were now, so he was hoping that Stuart's next words would be what he anticipated.

"I want you to serve as one of those scouts, Captain."

Mac nodded. "Yes sir. Shall I leave right away?"

"As soon as possible. I'm sending you all out by different routes. I want you to ride south from here, toward the town of Gettysburg." Stuart hesitated then said with emotion, "Find our army, Captain. Find out where it is and what has happened to it, and then ride back here to tell me posthaste."

"Yes sir," Mac said. "I won't let you down."

He hoped he would be able to keep that promise.

Chapter Twenty

I T WAS RAINING LIGHTLY around Gettysburg on the morning of July 1, 1863. Not long after dawn, shots suddenly broke out west of town on the Chambersburg pike. Heth's brigade, on its way into Gettysburg to get the shoes that Pettigrew had failed to obtain the day before, had encountered Union cavalry. The exchange of fire was sharp and vicious. Heth's men found themselves on the top of a ridge that ran north and south. To the east, across a small valley formed by a slow-moving creek, the Federal forces held another ridge. The shooting died away for a moment as Yankee and Confederate faced each other across that shallow valley, and for a moment it was as if the world were holding its breath.

Then the firing began again, and the battle commenced.

———∿∿∿∿———

AT LEAST the clouds overhead meant that the sun wasn't blasting down so unpleasantly, Will thought as he and his troops moved along the road from Carlisle to Chambersburg. While the men were tired after their efforts of the day before, this morning's march hadn't been too strenuous.

The column was smaller today. Quite early in the morning, Ewell had received word from Hill that Yankee troops had been spotted in Gettysburg the day before. As a precautionary measure, Ewell had ordered Gens. Robert Rodes and Jubal Early to march their divisions directly toward Gettysburg. Ewell would proceed with Gen. Edward Johnson's division to Cashtown, where they were supposed to join Robert E. Lee.

Despite the overcast, Will's mood was lighter. The grim feelings of the day before had faded. Roman walked alongside Will's horse, keeping up a running commentary on the countryside through which they were passing, and Will found himself smiling and occasionally laughing as he talked with the young man.

He had been a fool, he told himself when he remembered the bleak thoughts that had run through his head. Roman was right: A man could live only one day at a time.

THE RIDGE occupied by Heth's forces was known as Herr Ridge. The creek was Willoughby Run. The ridge on the other side of the stream was McPherson's Ridge, named after a farming family that lived there. Heth could see those things on the map he studied, and he could look up from the map and see the Yankees on McPherson's Ridge. If there were Union forces up there, it was fairly certain there were Yankees in Gettysburg itself, as well. Pettigrew had been right.

Faced with a situation like this, right or wrong didn't really matter. It was what it was, and it had to be dealt with.

Heth turned to an aide. "We'll push on and occupy the town."

The firing intensified. Two brigades faced the Yankees, one north of the turnpike under the command of Gen. Joseph R. Davis, whose uncle was the Confederate president, and another to the south commanded by Gen. James J. Archer. Archer's men were from Alabama and Tennessee and had been seasoned in battle. Davis's troops were greener, and so was Davis himself. But they all followed orders and surged down Herr Ridge, charging toward Willoughby Run.

Two Yankee brigades opposed them, arranged north and south of the road as the Confederates were, but those Federal brigades were smaller than their Southern counterparts. Heth was throwing over seven thousand men against fewer than three thousand. The Yankees were outnumbered more than two to one and would have to have help from Gettysburg if they were to turn back the Confederate attack.

Both Federal brigades were dismounted cavalry armed with carbines. Outnumbered they might be, but they had the natural advantage of all defenders: The other side had to come to them. Blistering fire from their carbines raked Heth's troops and brought the advance to a stop.

Reinforcements were on their way to the Yankees, not only from Gettysburg but from other units of the Army of the Potomac in the area. Gen. George Meade, now in command of the Union army after having replaced Joseph Hooker, had no intention of fighting a general engagement at Gettysburg. Unknown to Meade, Robert E. Lee felt the same way. But once the battle was underway, both men felt that they had to support their troops in the field.

Several brigades of Federal infantry that were headed toward Gettysburg from the south left the road and started across the fields toward the ridges west of town, not bothering to enter the settlement itself. This cross-country maneuver brought them to McPherson's Ridge at midmorning, just in time to relieve the exhausted and battle-scarred cavalrymen who had been holding back the Confederate tide.

Among the reinforcements was the famous Iron Brigade, known to the Southerners by its tall black felt hats, which the Confederates had seen before at Antietam Creek. One sight of the black hats was enough to tell Heth's men that they weren't facing a poorly trained, poorly equipped militia. Just the opposite: The Iron Brigade was a salty veteran outfit that had dealt out plenty of punishment to the Army of Northern Virginia in previous clashes. When they found themselves flanked by these Yankees, it was too much for the attacking brigade under Archer. They crumbled, allowing the Federals to swarm over them and even to take Archer prisoner.

At the other end of the line of battle to the north, something of the opposite situation was developing. Despite their lack of experience, Davis's troops were performing well and managed to flank the Yankees. The order came for the Federal troops to fall back to Seminary Ridge, so named because the Lutheran Theological Seminary—the large brick building with the white cupola that Pettigrew had observed the day before—had been erected on it.

Not all the Union regiments received the order as they were supposed to, however. As a result, one group was left behind in a wheat field, nearly surrounded by Confederates, as the rest of the brigade retreated.

Seeing what was going on, some of the Yankees who had been fighting south of the turnpike turned to help their fellows, and their fire forced the pursuing Confederates to seek the cover of a nearby railroad cut. This attempt by the Yankees to shore up their right flank seemed at first to backfire, because the Southerners now safely in the railroad cut were able to send volley after volley of deadly fire crashing through them.

Facing destruction, the Yankees followed the only course left to them. They attacked, charging the railroad cut. With each step, more men fell, chopped down by the Confederate bullets. But despite the devastation, the Union charge never broke, and the Yankees reached the cut and used gun butts and bayonets to drive the Confederates back from the rim.

Now the tables were turned yet again. The Southerners trapped in the railroad cut had no choice but to surrender. Those who made it out fled toward the Confederate rear. Davis's brigade had fought well and seemed to be on the verge of victory, but then bad luck and overconfidence had snatched it away from them. What was left of the brigade pulled back to Herr Ridge and regrouped with the survivors from Archer's debacle south of the turnpike.

As the eerie quiet that always followed a battle settled down west of Gettysburg, a grim-faced Henry Heth looked at his bleeding, battered men and realized that they probably weren't going to be getting any shoes today.

"WHAT THE hell?" Will muttered as Ewell's corps came within sight of Chambersburg. The column gradually slowed to a stop because there was no place for them to go. The roads ahead were clogged with wagons.

As the men of the company shuffled about nervously, unwilling to stop now that they had come so far, Sgt. Darcy Bennett walked over to Will's horse. "What's all that, Cap'n? Circus come to town?"

"Not unless General Longstreet's the ringmaster," Will muttered as he squinted into the distance, trying to make out the flags that flew over the wagons. "I believe that's his corps up ahead of us."

He also saw General Ewell's buggy rolling toward the town, but its progress was slowed and finally stopped by the congestion in the streets. Ewell finally gave up, had a horse brought to him, and mounted awkwardly because of his missing leg. He was strapped into the saddle, then started making his way through the crowd of wagons on horseback, obviously looking for Lee or Longstreet or anyone else who could tell him what was going on and what to do next.

Time dragged by, and Will's impatience grew. He thought he knew what had happened. Longstreet's corps had reached Chambersburg just ahead of Ewell and had passed on through to start toward Cashtown. The supply train, coming up last, was stalled for some reason, blocking the roads. What Ewell's command needed to do, Will thought, was to forget about the roads and cut across country. They could get ahead of Longstreet's wagons that way. It would be harder to keep the division together, but they would just have to manage. Otherwise they might be sitting here all day, wasting their time while a battle was going on elsewhere. He didn't know that that was the case, but the edginess he felt told him it might be.

"You know, Cap'n," Darcy said, rubbing his bearded jaw, "we're all hurryin' toward Gettysburg. You reckon the Yankees are, too?"

"Could be," allowed Will. "If they're close enough."

"Sounds to me like there's goin' to be a tussle."

Will shrugged. "I can't believe General Lee would want to fight a battle with our army scattered out all to hell and gone." Most officers wouldn't have dreamed of saying such a thing to a subordinate, Will realized, but he wasn't regular army, never had been and never would be. He spoke his mind to his friends, and that certainly included Darcy.

"What a fella wants ain't always what he gets," the burly sergeant added to Will's observation. "Could be we ain't goin' to have much choice. Sometimes the fight finds you, 'stead of t'other way around."

Will had to nod in agreement. The underlying purpose of this invasion of the North was to draw the Army of the Potomac into one final clash so that they could be destroyed.

God help us all, Will thought, *but we may be about to get what we came for.*

GENERAL HETH'S fingers tightened on the hastily scrawled message he held in his hands, but he was able to stop short of crumpling it. "General Hill has been taken sick," he said aloud to the circle of staff officers surrounding him. "He will be remaining in Cashtown. But he says that he is sending General Pender to help us."

That assistance could not arrive soon enough for Heth. He was eager to attack again, feeling that this morning's defeat had been a personal failure for him. He had thrown more than twice as many men at the Yankees as they had, yet they had repulsed the attack. True, they had been reinforced, and rather heavily at that, but Heth didn't care. There was still a stain on his record that could only be wiped out by victory.

He would wait for Pender, but he hoped the wait would not be a long one.

—m—

DURING THE lull in the fighting, the Yankees reestablished their defensive line along McPherson's Ridge, both north and south of the turnpike. The northern end of the ridge merged with Seminary Ridge to form Oak Ridge, which extended a good distance to the north before terminating in Oak Hill.

The Yankees were taken by surprise when Confederate gun crews suddenly appeared on Oak Hill, wheeling artillery into position. The Southerners had taken advantage of the cover offered by the woods to conceal their approach to the hill. Within a matter of moments, their big guns began to boom, and the startled right end of the Union line found itself under a screaming bombardment.

At about the same time, Gen. Robert Rodes and the men under his command were marching rapidly toward Gettysburg from the northeast. Having been detached earlier in the morning from Ewell's column along with Early's division, Rodes had pulled ahead and was now nearly at the town.

Down on the Chambersburg pike near Cashtown, in a small stone farmhouse with a tumbled-down picket fence around its yard, Robert E. Lee had made his headquarters, and from there he was trying to coordinate the actions of his far-flung army. He had received word from Ewell that Ewell's corps had been split, and that Rodes and Early were taking a more direct path toward Gettysburg. Lee sent a courier in search of Rodes and Early, telling them that while he approved of Ewell's tactics in dividing the corps, he did not want to bring on a full-fledged battle until Longstreet's corps and the rest of Ewell's command were ready to take part. That courier found Rodes as the mustachioed general was approaching Gettysburg.

Rodes scanned the landscape with his field glasses as excitement welled up inside him. He could see the Yankee line west of Gettysburg, with its northern end being assaulted by Confederate artillery. None of the Federals seemed to be paying any attention to the northeast. They were just sitting there, one of the most tempting targets Rodes had ever seen.

But Lee had said not to bring on a battle. Rodes's fingers tightened on the field glasses. To attack or not to attack?

By early afternoon, Rodes could no longer stand the temptation. He sent his men forward to slam into the battered Union right flank.

The attack proceeded raggedly, however, with some regiments being held back and others charging haphazardly. Not only that, but the delay while Rodes wrestled with his dilemma had allowed the Yankees to reinforce their line, and Rodes was unaware of that fact. Withering fire from a Federal brigade concealed behind a stone wall along the Mummasburg road slashed into the Confederates as they charged down from Oak Ridge. Their losses were so heavy that they had to pull back immediately. The advance was shattered almost before it began.

Nearby, the scene played itself out again as another Confederate brigade, with its flank exposed because of the failure of their fellows to advance, veered into an ambush. More Yankees were hidden behind another stone wall, and when they finally raised up and opened fire, they were shooting at almost point-blank range into the shocked Confederates. Blood fell on the ground like rain as the bullets tore through the close-packed ranks of Southerners.

On the other side of the ridge, one of Rodes's brigades tried to circle around to hit the Yankees head-on, but again the advance was blunted with heavy losses for the Southerners. The staggered punches being thrown by Rodes were not working. Everywhere he tried to strike, the Yankees seemed to be waiting for him.

But Early's division was coming up quickly now in support. The battle could still be won. And farther to the west, atop Herr Ridge, someone new had come onto the scene. Unwilling to remain at his headquarters while artillery thundered to the east, Robert E. Lee had come to watch the battle for himself.

—ᛟ—

AT CHAMBERSBURG, orders finally filtered back through Ewell's column. The corps was to proceed through the town and onto the road running toward Gettysburg.

"Dang it, Cap'n," Darcy complained when he heard of the order. "It'll take us all afternoon to get through them damned wagons."

"I know," Will said, nodding slowly. The sun was out now, cooking the landscape. Will sleeved sweat off his forehead, missing the cool overcast he had enjoyed earlier in the day. "But there's nothing else we can do."

"Some of the fellas are sayin' they've heard rumors there's already fightin' goin' on over yonder at Gettysburg. They want to get there and do their part, Cap'n. You sure we can't sort of sneak off and find us a better way?"

Will thought about it for a moment, actually considering the idea of disobeying orders and taking out across country with his company. That would probably get him court-martialed . . .

But not until after the battle. By then it might not matter.

In the end, the devotion to duty and the chain of command that had been instilled in him over the past two and a half years won out. "I reckon we'll stay with the Stonewall Brigade," he said. "Sorry, Darcy."

The sergeant grimaced and walked off muttering. Will grinned humorlessly. That was just like Darcy, getting impatient because he had to wait for the chance of getting himself killed. Of course, he understood the way Darcy felt. Will felt the same way himself.

"An army's a mighty strange thing, ain't it, Cap'n Will?" Roman asked. "Y'all hurry from one place to the other, then you wait around for a spell, then you hurry again."

Will laughed, and this time there was humor in it. "That's pretty much right, Roman. And I'm afraid right now we're in for more of that waiting."

GENERAL HETH looked up to see the lean gray-bearded figure striding toward him. He came to attention and saluted. "General Lee, sir," Heth said.

"At ease, General," Lee said quietly. Across the valley, along the base of McPherson's Ridge, fierce fighting was going on, and both men could hear the boom of artillery, the rattle of muskets, even—and this might have been his imagination, but Heth thought not—the cries of dying men.

"General Pender is here, sir," Heth said. "We'll be attacking soon." He had spent the past hour struggling to get what was left of his command in some sort of order, waiting at the same time for Pender's force to arrive. Now that Pender was on hand and ready to enter the battle, Heth was more eager than ever to get back into action.

Lee shook his head. "No, I am not prepared to bring on a general engagement today." His voice was so soft as he spoke that Heth had to lean toward him to make out the words over the distant clamor of battle. "General Longstreet is not up."

"But, sir—"

"That is my decision, General." Despite his quiet tone, Lee's words held an edge of sharpness.

"Of course, sir," Heth replied. He would follow his commander's orders, whether he liked them or not.

Yet a few minutes later, the situation began to change. Lee peered curiously at the dust in the air beyond the right end of the Union line. The early morning drizzle had long since stopped and the sun shone hotly again. There hadn't been enough rain to properly lay the dust on the roads. The only thing that could kick up that much of it, Lee knew, was a large force of men on the move. Rodes was already engaged. If someone else was coming in, it had to be Early.

When a courier galloped up a short time later, confirming Early's arrival on the battlefield, Heth's impatience grew even stronger. He looked at Lee, thinking that surely the commander saw the same things he did. Rodes's attack was not going particularly well, but it was keeping a sizable chunk of the enemy force busy despite that. To the south, Hill's artillery was bombarding the Yankees, and Hill was also extending a skirmish line toward McPherson's Ridge. Now, with Early joining the battle at the far end of the Federal line, all that was lacking was an attack straight down the Chambersburg pike, an attack that Heth and Pender stood ready and willing to provide.

"General," Lee said, "you have permission to move against the enemy."

Heth snapped a salute and an acknowledgment. As he turned away to give the orders that would launch the attack, he snatched up the hat he had been wearing earlier. It didn't fit him very well, so his clerk had modified it by rolling up papers and stuffing them in the sweatband to make it tighter. Heth jammed the hat on his head and strode toward his horse, barking orders as he went.

Within minutes, fresh brigades were streaming down the slopes of the ridge toward Willoughby Run, where some of the Federals were concentrated. Pender's men took the lead, since they had been spared the previous fighting. The troops who had survived the battle earlier in the day followed in support. The clash was vicious, but the Federals' Iron Brigade, despite its staunch defense of the Union line, was forced to pull back into the woods on the other side of the creek.

As the Yankees retreated, Heth rode across Willoughby Run. He knew he shouldn't be so close to the front, especially not on horseback. Yankee sharpshooters had a habit of aiming at horsemen, knowing them to be officers. But Heth was gripped with such eagerness, he couldn't hold himself back. He sensed triumph, and he wanted to see it for himself.

The bullet struck him in the head like a hammer blow, and as he reeled out of the saddle and fell into darkness, he was certain that his eagerness had just killed him.

EARLIER IN the day, the Yankees had dug some earthworks on Seminary Ridge, near the Lutheran seminary, and as the tide of battle swung against them, they retreated toward those earthworks. If they had had a chance to settle themselves behind those fortifications, they might have had a chance to put up a better fight.

As it was, the Confederates under Gen. William Dorsey Pender didn't give them an opportunity. Pender's men swarmed up the ridge and overran the Union position, capturing it in a burst of terrible carnage that saw men dying by dozens with every passing heartbeat.

The Yankees were retreating all over the field now, turning and running back toward Gettysburg as they broke under the assaults of Early, Rodes, Pender, and Hill. Fleeing soldiers in blue thronged the streets of the town, and Gettysburg's terrified inhabitants huddled in their houses, waiting to see what was going to happen next.

No doubt many of the townspeople feared that the Confederates were about to sweep through the community like a conquering horde. These Northerners had been told over and over what barbarians the Rebels were, and they expected no mercy, only pillage, rape, and murder.

South of town, at the northern tip of the long ridge that ended in two rocky, wooded hills, stood Evergreen Cemetery, its entrance marked by a huge arch made of red brick that also served as the gatekeeper's quarters. The ridge, and especially the cemetery, drew the Yankees as they retreated from the Confederate onslaught. The ridge could be defended; in fact, one Federal regiment had been up there all day, erecting earthworks around the cemetery's archway. There were fences and tombstones to provide cover, so the idea began to spread through the dispirited Yankees: There among the dead, they would sell their lives, if need be.

Command of the Federal forces in the field had changed hands several times during the day as officers were killed or injured. Now it had devolved upon Gens. Winfield Scott Hancock and Oliver O. Howard. Although there was friction between the two men, they knew they were facing defeat and death if they failed to work together. As they stood atop what was called on some maps Granite Ridge and on others Cemetery Ridge, they looked around and made it official. This was where the Army of the Potomac would make its stand.

—⟋𝔪⟍—

WILL COULD hear the firing now. The afternoon had been interminable: The column had spent hours stopping and starting and winding its way through the wagons in Chambersburg and on the road to Gettysburg. Finally, though, they had passed through Cashtown. As they came closer to Gettysburg, the roar of cannons became audible first, followed by the crackling and popping of rifle fire.

They were nearly there, Will thought. The battle was *right up there.*

And yet the order to move into position for an attack did not come. He knew he shouldn't leave his men, but Will's impatience could no longer be restrained. He rode toward the front to see what was going on.

The column was swinging around to the north of the town he saw as he reined in. That put the battle off to his right. He squinted through the dust and smoke in the air and saw the long ridge south of Gettysburg. There was movement up there, and even at this distance, Will knew that he was seeing the enemy.

Rattling of buggy wheels caught his attention, and he looked around to notice that Ewell's little vehicle was rolling toward the rear of the column. The general had been up at the front but was now leaving. Will frowned. Did that mean the corps wasn't going to attack?

Slowly, the sounds of battle to the south and west of the town died away as Ewell's corps moved to the north of Gettysburg. As hours passed and dusk approached, Will began to seethe. They had come all this way, spent two hard days on the road, and now it was all over before he and his men even got to strike a blow for the Cause?

By the time evening settled down, the corps had bypassed Gettysburg entirely. They camped to the northeast of the town, along the York turnpike and the Gettysburg and Hanover Railroad. Most of the men were silent as they sat around their fires and gnawed their meager rations. They didn't know the details, but they knew they had missed something today. If they had gone into battle, many of them would have died, but a sense of disappointment nevertheless hung over the camp anyway.

Will's bad leg ached from all the time he had spent in the saddle, and he limped as he returned to his tent from a meeting of the brigade's officers. Roman was sitting by the fire. He looked up with concern as Will sat down and sighed. "What's wrong, Cap'n Will?" he asked. "That leg o' yours hurt pretty bad?"

"Not as bad as knowing that we could have made a difference today, and we didn't," Will said as he looked at the leaping flames. "General Gordon wanted General Ewell to push on through Gettysburg and capture those hills south of town, but Ewell wouldn't do it. Said that General Lee's orders left things to his discretion, and he wouldn't go on without direct orders." Will's right hand clenched into a fist. "Damn it, if Jackson had been here—"

He stopped. Thoughts like that wouldn't do any good. Stonewall was dead, and the brigade he'd left behind had to follow the orders of another man now. But it would have been different . . . it would have been . . .

Will took a deep breath. "General Hill declined to attack that ridge south of town where the Yankees forted up, too. He said his men were too tired. Hell, everybody's mad at Hill and Ewell both. What if the Yankees bring up more reinforcements tonight?" He took off his hat and ran his finger around the sweatband, then gave a grim chuckle. "General Heth almost got himself killed today. A ball hit him in the head and wounded him pretty bad. But it would've killed him, they say, if he hadn't stuffed a bunch of paper in his hat to make it fit better."

"Lord have mercy," Roman said. "Fate takes some mighty strange twists and turns, don't it, Cap'n?"

"That it does." Will put on his hat, thumbed it to the back of his head. "So here we sit, with the Yankees huddled down there on those hills, and those poor bastards probably don't have any more idea what tomorrow is going to bring than we do."

Quietly Roman said, "I reckon they know what it'll bring for some of 'em, Cap'n, and you do, too."

Will couldn't disagree with that, and as he nodded, he felt the darkness slipping down over his soul once again, coating it like black ice.

Chapter Twenty-one

MAC YAWNED HUGELY AS the stallion trotted down the road. He stiffened in the saddle as he saw lights up ahead. At first they seemed no more than the winking of fireflies, but as he drew closer, he realized they were campfires. He had seen enough army camps to recognize one now. He reined in and looked in awe at the way the lights spread across the horizon, almost as far as he could see in each direction.

He had found an army, all right. The question was, which one was it?

There was only one way to find out. He heeled the stallion into motion again. Mere minutes later, figures stepped into the road in front of him and issued a challenge.

As he pulled the stallion to a stop, Mac saw four men confronting him. All carried rifles, and the weapons were pointed straight at him. Confident that he had recognized a southern drawl in the voice that had called out, he responded, "Captain MacBeth Brannon, First Virginia Cavalry. I'm looking for General Robert E. Lee. I have a message from General Stuart."

"Come a mite closer," ordered the picket. "Yeah, I reckon you're one of us, all right." He lowered his rifle, and the other men did likewise. "Go on ahead."

Before riding on, Mac asked, "Do you know where I can find General Lee?"

"Naw, I don't know where his headquarters is. This outfit belongs to Gen'ral Ewell."

Mac felt his heart jump. "What division?"

"Gen'ral Early's."

"Do you know where General Johnson's division is? The Stonewall Brigade, in particular?"

The soldier pointed to the east. "Over yonder a ways, I think. But I thought you was lookin' for Gen'ral Lee."

"I am," Mac said, and he was glad he had been reminded of his duty. He wanted to find Will, but he couldn't yet, not until he had found General Lee—and maybe not even then, depending on the circumstances. Stuart had told him to deliver the message and get back to Carlisle as quickly as possible.

More sentries stopped him farther down the road, and they took him to a tent where several officers were huddled around a map. Mac recognized Gen. Jubal Early. The general was taking swigs from a flask and frowning darkly as he studied the map. When Mac was brought in, he snapped, "What the hell is it?" clearly annoyed by the interruption.

"Got a courier here from General Stuart, sir, looking for General Lee," the guard explained.

"Oh." Early's irascible attitude eased a bit. He looked Mac up and down. "Cavalryman, are you?"

"Yes sir."

"Where in blazes have you been the past week? What's wrong with that idiot Stuart? Don't he know there's an invasion goin' on?"

Mac's lips thinned. He didn't like hearing anyone talk about General Stuart that way, but his reaction was tempered by the fact that he didn't agree entirely with the way Stuart had led the cavalry since leaving Virginia, either.

"If you would tell me where I can find General Lee, sir, I have an urgent message to deliver to him," Mac said, ignoring Early's harsh questions.

Early took another swig of whiskey and waved his other hand vaguely toward the west. "He's over on the Chambersburg pike somewhere, I reckon. Last I heard, that's where his headquarters is."

"Thank you, sir." Mac saluted.

Early returned the salute carelessly and snapped, "Go on, get out o' here, Captain."

Mac left and was glad to do so. He wasn't sure what had happened here today, but he suspected there had been a battle. As he rode through the Confederate camp, he was sure of it. He came to a large tent that had been set up as a field hospital, and as he did so, a man stepped out of the tent carrying a wicker basket. He went to the side of the tent and upended the basket, dumping out amputated arms and legs, the pale dead flesh splattered with blood. There was already a large pile of similar extremities next to the tent.

Mac shuddered at the grisly sight and rode on. There had been a fight, all right, he thought. He didn't know who had won, but obviously there had been plenty of casualties.

It took him half an hour to search through the camp that stretched north and west of Gettysburg before he was directed to the small, ramshackle farmhouse on the Chambersburg turnpike where the commanding general was pondering the day's events with a view toward tomorrow. As Mac drew rein in front of the house, he was surprised to see a familiar face emerge. "Major Venable?" he inquired.

Maj. Andrew Reid Venable was Stuart's assistant adjutant and also one of the couriers who had been sent out to find the Army of Northern Virginia. He grinned up at Mac. "I see you've been successful in your mission, too, Captain Brannon."

"Yes sir. May I take it that you've spoken with the commading general?"

The smile disappeared from Venable's face. "Indeed I have. I'm about to ride back to Carlisle right now with orders for General Stuart."

"May I accompany you, sir?" Mac offered.

Venable shook his head. "No need for that. Remain here and get some sleep tonight. You're liable to need it when the rest of the boys get here tomorrow morning." Venable grimaced, no doubt realizing that he had just revealed some of the orders he was carrying for Stuart. "Keep that under your hat, Captain."

"Yes sir." Mac hesitated. "You're certain . . ."

"Stay here," Venable said. "That's an order, Captain."

"Yes sir." Now Mac could find Will with a clear conscience.

Venable reached for the reins of a horse tied to the picket fence around the yard. Mac asked, "Sir, if you don't mind telling me, what happened here today?"

Venable jerked the reins free and swung up into the saddle. "We ran right into the Yankees," he said. "There was a lot of fighting here, west of the town, but we finally pushed them back to a long ridge to the south." The major jerked his chin in that direction. "They're hunkered up there now, just waiting for us, I suppose."

"By chance, do you know if the Stonewall Brigade was in the fighting, sir?"

"That's your brother's outfit, isn't it?" Venable shook his head. "I don't know the details, Captain. If you're thinking of trying to find him tonight, that's probably a good idea."

Mac didn't have to ask what he meant by that. With the Union army still close by, daylight would probably bring more fighting. If Will were alive, now was the time to see him.

"Thank you, sir. Good luck."

Venable turned his horse. "And to you, too, Captain."

Mac sat there for a moment while the major rode into the night. He thought about the struggle that had taken place today. From the sound of it, the Confederate army had won the day, yet the battle might be far from over. Would it have been different if the cavalry had been here?

As he pondered these things, he heard a footstep on the porch of the farmhouse. Mac looked up and saw a figure standing there, silhouetted by the light of a lamp in the house. The man was in shirt sleeves, and he could discern the man's short, gray beard.

"Good evening, Captain," Robert E. Lee called.

Mac stiffened in the saddle and saluted as crisply as he had ever done before. "Good evening, sir!"

"At ease," Lee murmured. "You're a cavalryman? Another of the boys General Stuart sent to find me?"

"Yes sir."

"I wish you all had found me sooner . . ." Lee waved a hand. "But what's done is done. I've already given orders for General Stuart to Major Venable."

"Yes sir. I spoke with the major as he was leaving."

"Are you going back to Carlisle tonight as well?"

"No sir. Major Venable ordered me to stay here. I . . . I have a brother in General Ewell's corps."

"Then by all means you should go to him," said Lee. "Good night, Captain."

"Good night, sir."

Mac rode away from the farmhouse, leaving Lee standing there, a tired old man with his coat off. He couldn't begin to imagine the sort of burden that Lee was carrying on his shoulders. Thousands of men lived or died—mostly died—according to that man's orders, and the hopes of the Confederacy rose or fell depending on what he did.

Fervently, Mac hoped that no such burden was ever placed on *him*.

—⁂—

WILL HAD turned in for the night and was dozing in his tent when Roman shook his shoulder. "Cap'n, they's somebody here to see you."

Suppressing a groan, Will sat up and swung his legs off his cot. He was fully dressed except for his boots, jacket, hat, saber, and pistol. Expecting that some orderly had brought new orders for him, he snapped, "What is it?"

A man stuck his head into the tent. "Is that any way to greet your brother?"

"Mac!" Will's head jerked up, his weariness vanishing in an instant. He sprang forward, grabbed the newcomer in a bear hug. "Mac!" he exclaimed, pounding him on the back.

Mac was hugging him just as hard and pounding him. Roman stood to one side. After a few moments, Will stepped back and put his hands on Mac's shoulders. "Yeah, it's really you," he said. "What the hell are you doing here?"

"Looking for the army." Mac chuckled. "I'd say I found it."

"Where's the cavalry?"

"Up at Carlisle. They'll be here tomorrow, more than likely."

"Roman, light a lantern," Will said. "Mac and I have a lot to talk about."

Mac looked over at the young man. "Roman? I thought that was you. Why are you here?"

"It's a long story," Will answered. "What it boils down to is that Yancy's dead and Roman is staying with me now."

Mac's face was solemn in the yellow glow that filled the tent as Roman lit the lantern. "I'm sorry to hear about Yancy," he said. "I know what a good friend he was to you, Will."

"This damned war—" Will broke off the words with a shake of his head. He hooked a stool with his foot and pushed it toward Mac. "Sit down and tell me what you've been up to since we all left Virginia."

For the next half-hour, the brothers caught up on everything. Mac described the long ride around the Union army, Will spoke of the battles at Winchester and Stephenson's Depot and the trek across Maryland and into Pennsylvania. He concluded, "We got here too late for the battle today. I reckon it's not really over, though."

"That agrees with what I've heard," Mac said. "The Yankees are up on some ridge south of town—"

"Cemetery Ridge. There's a good-sized hill between here and there called Culp's Hill, so you can't really see the ridge from here. Reports say there are a lot of Yankees up there, though." Will's mouth was a grim line. "If they'd thrown us into the fight late this afternoon when we got here, Culp's Hill and the ridge would be in our hands now, and we'd have busted the whole damned Yankee army in half. We could have ended it today, Mac . . . but we didn't."

"I guess the generals figure we can end it tomorrow."

Will shrugged. "Maybe. I hope so. Reckon we'll see."

"You hear anything from home?"

Will shook his head. "Not a word. We won't be getting any letters while we're up here. I expect everything's all right. At least there's no fighting down there now."

"It's all up here for sure," Mac said with a grin.

"That's right. You say the cavalry's going to be in on the fighting tomorrow?"

"That's what I figure."

Will was sitting on the cot. He stretched his bad leg out in front of him, easing the ache in it. "Well, the army's pretty much all together again," he said quietly. "We missed a chance to end it today, but like you said, there's still tomorrow. You going to stay here tonight?"

"If you don't mind."

"I'd like that," Will said. "I'd like to talk awhile longer . . . about home."

NEITHER OF them got much sleep that night. They talked until long after midnight, laughing as they recalled the humorous things that happened in any family, growing solemn as they remembered the times of loss and hardship. When they finally dozed, it was only fitfully, because Mac and Will both knew that the morning would bring more fighting.

Will was awakened early by Roman. He looked over at Mac, who was rolled up in a blanket on the ground and still asleep. Will dressed as silently as he could and left the tent, emerging into the predawn grayness.

The brigade's officers were gathering at General Walker's tent. Will joined them, and during the brief meeting, he gleaned a better understanding of the situation.

The Yankees were concentrated on Cemetery Ridge, their exact numbers unknown. They were also on Culp's Hill, the tall, wooded knob that stood between Ewell's corps and the main body of the Union army. The Union line as Walker indicated it on the map was shaped like a fishhook, with the shaft running north and south along the ridge then curving around Culp's Hill. Of necessity, the Confederate line was also curved in the same shape to confront the Yankees. The Stonewall Brigade was at the far end of the "hook," anchoring the terminus of the Confederate line.

Walker's finger stabbed at Culp's Hill. "Although I have not yet received our orders, gentlemen, I am certain this will be our objective today," he said. "If we can take this hill and situate our artillery atop it, we will have a commanding field of fire."

Will saw the logic in that. As the meeting broke up and he started back to his company, though, he paused to look at Culp's Hill in the distance across a field. The sides of it were steep and covered with woods and rocks. Getting up those slopes wouldn't be easy, especially with a bunch of Yankees up above trying to stop them.

When he got to the tent, Mac was awake. "I'd better ride back to General Lee's headquarters. I'm sure that's where General Stuart will go when he gets here."

"Have some breakfast first," Will suggested. "It'll be short rations, but . . ."

Mac nodded, seizing the chance to spend a little more time with his brother. "Thanks."

All too quickly they had munched on some hardtack and gulped down steaming cups of the bitter brew that passed for coffee. The camp was full of activity now. No one knew when the orders would come for the division to move up, but everyone wanted to be ready when they did.

Finally, Mac took a deep breath and extended his hand to Will. "Good luck out there today," he said.

Will took his hand. "Good luck to you, too." Without releasing Mac's hand, he pulled him closer and embraced him for a long moment.

When they parted, Mac swallowed hard. "I'll see you when this is over."

"Count on it," Will said. He summoned up a grin.

Roman had taken care of Mac's stallion, the horse proving to be more tolerant of being handled by him than by most people other than Mac. Now the young man brought the animal over to Mac already saddled and ready to go. He patted the silver gray flank. "This is some mighty fine horse, Cap'n Mac."

"He is, isn't it?" Mac said as he took the reins and swung up into the saddle. He returned Will's grin, gave him a jaunty salute, and turned the horse to ride away.

As man and horse departed, Will prayed that he wasn't seeing his brother for the last time.

ON THE other side of the Confederate line, Robert E. Lee had left the farmhouse and moved up to Seminary Ridge to get a better view of the situation this morning. Looking across the lower ground to Cemetery Ridge through field glasses, it seemed to him that the Federals were clustered at the northern end of the ridge, on the hill where Evergreen Cemetery itself was situated. The ridge narrowed as it ran south toward the two hills at its lower end. Lee saw no enemy movement on that part of the ridge or on the hills themselves.

Although surrounded by his staff, Lee stood alone as he studied the terrain. Shortly thereafter, James Longstreet arrived and walked ponderously over to join the commanding general. Longstreet again argued that the army should swing around to the Federal left and get between Meade and Washington City. He continued to contend that if the Confederates threatened Washington, Meade would be forced to pursue them. On those terms, the Army of Northern Virginia would be in the better position of picking the ground for the coming fight. In that scenario, the Confederates would be cast as the defenders and the

Yankees would be forced to take the offensive, instead of the other way around as it was now.

Lee had heard all of Longstreet's arguments and remained unconvinced that he should change his orders for the upcoming fight. For indeed he had come to Pennsylvania to fight. Even though he hadn't expected it to come about in this particular place and in this fashion, running away from a fight rubbed him the wrong way. As he looked across at Cemetery Ridge, it seemed to him that the enemy was primed for destruction.

A. P. Hill arrived, still under the weather but unwilling to withdraw completely from the conflict. He sat down with Lee and Longstreet on a log. The three men talked in low voices for a few minutes, and to any observers it must have seemed a strange sight. Three men—two middle-aged and the other growing elderly—chatting amongst themselves and, in the process, perhaps deciding the fate of a nation.

Longstreet's voice grew louder, but Lee remained quietly insistent. His plan called for two of Longstreet's divisions to move to the south and advance across the Emmittsburg road, take the two hills at the southern end of Cemetery Ridge, and attack the Yankees at the northern end of the ridge. Hill's divisions under Gens. Richard H. Anderson and William Dorsey Pender would move in from the west at that point, so that Cemetery Hill would be under assault from two directions at once. It was a plan that could work, but the outcome was by no means certain.

Almost as an afterthought, Lee outlined his plan for Ewell's corps, which would move toward Culp's Hill on the other side of Cemetery Ridge at the same time that Longstreet launched his part of the attack. Lee wanted to capture Culp's Hill, too, knowing that a Confederate presence on that commanding eminence would make it easier to take Cemetery Hill.

"I shall go and tell General Ewell myself," Lee said. He stood up and dusted the seat of his trousers. He called for his horse and rode down from Seminary Ridge, heading through

Gettysburg in search of Ewell. If all went well, by the time he got back the attack would be underway.

—✵—

WILL STOOD in the ravine, peering over the rim at the thickly wooded hill. It looked so close he felt like he could spit that far. But every so often he saw movement on the knob and knew the Yankees were there. The field between the ravine and Culp's Hill would seem a whole lot wider to a man who was trying to cross it under fire.

The morning had passed peacefully, and now the sun stood almost directly overhead. Tension gripped the soldiers spread out through the ravine and across the terrain facing the hill. Everyone expected orders at any second commanding them to move against the enemy. So far, nothing had happened anywhere on the battlefield. It was quiet, and occasionally Will heard a bird singing in a tree.

He hoped it flew away before the air was filled with canister, grapeshot, and bullets.

In the meantime, he waited, reaching down from time to time to rub his leg.

Roman was back at the camp. He hadn't wanted to stay behind, but Will had insisted. Darcy Bennett was near Will's side, though. "I ain't ever goin' to get used to this waitin', Cap'n. That's always been the worst of it, all the way back to that first brawl at Manassas."

"A necessary evil," Will said. He kept his eye on the hill but glanced up at the sun.

"Necessary, maybe, but that don't mean I got to like it," Darcy complained. "I'd rather be fightin'."

Will grinned. "And that's exactly why we keep winning battles, Sergeant."

"Damn right." Darcy spat. "You think them Yankees up there want to be there? No sir, they'd rather be home, wherever that is, thinkin' about how much better they are than us poor ignorant Southern folk. They thought we'd just roll over like a hound dog and let them tell us what to do. Well, I reckon they never figured we'd be up here in their own backyard one of these days. You figure they wish they'd never started this war?"

Will just shook his head and didn't say anything. He didn't know about the Yankees . . .

But he wished the war had never started, and he wouldn't have minded being home right now, either.

LEE WAS deeply troubled when he returned from his meeting with Ewell and found that the attack on Cemetery Ridge had not yet begun. Longstreet was having trouble moving his men into position. Some of them had not yet arrived, and others were unable to use the route that Longstreet had planned for them to take in their approach to the Emmittsburg road because they would be seen too easily and might alert the Yankees to what was about to happen.

Such delays were inevitable in preparing for battle, Lee supposed, but they were still galling. The enemy was there, waiting for him to strike. He planned to oblige them.

Some time after noon, Stuart arrived at the Lutheran seminary with a few members of his staff.

MAC WAS sitting on the front steps of the seminary building, which faced across the lower ground toward Gettysburg and the ridges and hills to the south of town. Discovering that Lee had moved his headquarters here overnight, Mac had waited on the grounds throughout the morning, knowing that Stuart could show up at any time. His arrival, of course, depended on when Major Venable had reached Carlisle and how fast Stuart had moved toward Gettysburg. Mac came to his feet as he spotted the small group of riders approaching the seminary. There was no mistaking the man who rode in front, the plume on his hat waving gaily in the wind.

Lee too saw the newcomers approaching and walked out to meet them. Mac moved behind the general, wondering if Fitz Lee would be with Stuart, but he didn't see him, which meant that Fitz was probably still with the brigade, which was likely also to be on its way toward Gettysburg.

Stuart reined in and dismounted, offering a salute to General Lee. "Well, sir, here I am," he announced gregariously.

Lee raised his hand, but not to return Stuart's salute. For an awful instant, Mac thought that Lee might slap Stuart. Then, slowly, the commanding general lowered his hand. "Yes, and where have you been? I have not heard a word from you for days, and you are the eyes and ears of my army."

Stuart's lips tightened under his beard, and his eyes glittered with both hurt and anger. Demonstrating an effort to control himself, he said, "I have brought you 125 wagons and their teams, General."

"And what good are they to me now?" snapped Lee.

Stuart stood there silently, clearly unsure what to say in the face of Lee's great anger. Mac looked at the faces of the staff officers who had accompanied Stuart. Their expressions were a mixture of respect for General Lee and anger and dismay at the way the commander of the army was talking to their general. Everyone looked uncomfortable. Mac certainly felt that way.

Suddenly, Lee gave a little shake of his head and emitted a sigh. "Let me ask your help," he said. "We will not discuss this matter further. Right now, help me fight these people." He gestured toward the ridge in the distance where the Yankees were dug in, and Mac was struck by how thin and almost transparent the skin of the general's hand was. Lee's vitality made people forget that he was an old man, but at moments such as this, his age seemed more pronounced.

"Of course, General," Stuart said without hesitation. "Myself and my men are at your disposal."

Lee shook his head again and gazed into the distance. "It may be too late," he said. "It all depends on what General Longstreet does."

Chapter Twenty-two

MIDAFTERNOON CAME AND STILL Longstreet had not launched the attack. Determined to surprise the Yankees, Longstreet had his divisions take a longer but less visible approach to Cemetery Ridge. While that was going on, unknown to any of the Confederate commanders, Union artillery and infantry had been moved onto a slight elevation west of the ridge, a flat-topped height that was used as a peach orchard. To the southeast of the orchard was an area where large boulders were clustered like toys thrown down carelessly by a giant child; the locals called the place Devil's Den. The smaller of the two hills at the southern end of Cemetery Ridge, known as Little Round Top, was almost due east of Devil's Den and some five hundred yards away. The low ground between held a small meandering creek called Plum Run. Unlike the rich farmland that surrounded Gettysburg for the most part, this region where the Federals had taken shelter after being routed by the Confederates on July 1 was rugged terrain that wasn't good for much of anything.

Except defending.

—⁂—

MAC RODE back to join the rest of the cavalry with Stuart's party. He was happy to see Fitz Lee again, and Lee pumped his hand and slapped him on the shoulder. "Did you see my uncle?" he asked brightly.

"Yes sir, several times," Mac replied. "He's quite an impressive man."

"People get the wrong idea about him sometimes, because he talks quietly and looks like a professor. They don't see the iron that's in him."

357

"Then they don't look closely enough, General, because I had no trouble at all seeing it."

Lee laughed. "Beauty tells me we may not get in the fight today after all."

"There may not *be* a fight," Mac said with a shrug. "Everyone thought our attack would be underway by now."

He should have known better than to say such a thing. Less than twenty minutes later, from the cavalry's position on Seminary Ridge, the roar of the artillery and the crackle of rifle fire suddenly filled the air. In the valley to the east, Longstreet's divisions were finally going into action.

THE ATTACK up the Emmittsburg road was supposed to be led by Gen. John Bell Hood, but the canny Hood had spotted the Yankees in the peach orchard and knew that it would be suicide for his men to advance directly in front of them. Three times Longstreet tried to prevail on Hood to follow Lee's plan of attack, but finally Hood disregarded the orders and sent his troops charging toward Devil's Den and the rocky hills beyond. They met with savage resistance from the Yankees.

Hood was wounded early in the battle, his arm badly injured by a bursting shell. His men continued on, fighting their way step by step and foot by foot to Devil's Den. It was a hellish scene of hand-to-hand carnage amidst the rocks, but gradually the Confederate troops seized the upper hand. They pushed on past Plum Run, through what would come to be called the Valley of Death, and though the ground was soon covered with dead and dying men, the Southerners arrived at the base of the largest hill and started up.

There were no Yankees waiting for them at the top of the slope, and although it was a hard climb, the Confederate soldiers reached it successfully. Here on this high and rocky point, they rested for several minutes while their commander, Col.

William C. Oates, pondered his options. If he could find a way to get cannon atop the hill, the Yankees would never be able to dislodge him.

Before Oates could put that idea into action, new orders arrived. He was to abandon this position and ascend the smaller hill just to the north across a shallow saddle of ground. Oates was not terribly pleased with the decision, but orders were orders. He led his men toward the smaller hill, picking up reinforcements as he went—bloody, smoke-grimed men who had fought their way through Devil's Den and across Plum Run—and reaching the base of it, the Confederates started up again.

This time the Yankees were waiting for them.

—∿—

ON AND on the firing sounded in the distance, across the ridge, and Will cursed in frustration as he lowered his field glasses.

"See anything, Cap'n?" Darcy Bennett asked.

"Not with that damned hill in the way," Will said, gesturing toward Culp's Hill. Beyond it, he could see a small section of Cemetery Ridge, and he could see as well the grayish black haze that hung in the air above the ridge. Those were clouds of powder smoke, he knew, generated by all the shooting that was going on. It sounded as if all of Longstreet's and Hill's divisions were engaged in the fighting.

But not Ewell's corps, though. The men just sat on their rumps, waiting while somebody else did all the fighting.

Will looked along the line and spotted General Johnson in conference with some other officers. Old Allegheny had an impatient air about him; he was speaking sharply and gesturing from time to time with quick motions on his hands.

Finally, in response to orders from Johnson, all four batteries of artillery under Maj. Joseph W. Latimer were brought to the front and positioned on a small knoll. Someone called it Brenner's Hill. Minutes later, these cannon began to thunder, and the earth trembled under Will's feet as shells cascaded down on Culp's Hill.

The barrage drowned out the sound of firing in the distance, so Will had no idea what was happening on the other side of Cemetery Ridge. But the bombardment boded well for this side of the battle, he thought. Usually when the cannon were brought into play, it was to soften up the enemy for an attack by the infantry.

The Yankees weren't just sitting on Culp's Hill taking the punishment, however. They had artillery of their own on the summit, and soon those big guns began to roar their defiance. Shells screamed down around the Confederate batteries, killing some of the gunners and horses and damaging some of the Southerners' big guns. For two hours, both sides lobbed shells back and forth, until finally the Confederate artillery had to withdraw. The situation had simply gotten too hot for them to stay where they were. Only four cannon were left behind to provide covering fire for the infantry's advance.

The time was now, Will knew. A runner brought orders along the line. Will listened carefully but didn't particularly like what he heard. The brigade led by Gen. John M. Jones would be first to attack, followed by the brigades of Col. J. M. Williams and Gen. George H. "Maryland" Steuart. The Stonewall Brigade would be held back until last.

Will gritted his teeth but nodded his understanding of the orders. The runner moved on. Darcy, however, had overheard the orders. "Damn it, Cap'n, why're they holdin' us back?"

Will could only shake his head. "I don't know, Darcy. But I imagine there are enough Yankees up there to go around."

It was late afternoon by now. The Confederate skirmishers moved out, charging from the ravines and gullies that had sheltered them and running across the fields toward a creek that flowed along the base of Culp's Hill. Bullets whined through the air around their heads. From time to time, a man would stop, drop to his knee, take aim, and fire toward the summit of the hill before reloading and running forward again. Other times when a soldier stopped, he fell where he was, not to rise again.

One by one the companies started toward the hill. Will drew his sword and waited his turn. He would be on foot for this charge; the dun was back with the rest of the brigade's horses, well behind the lines. The company to the right moved out, and then it was finally time for Will and Darcy and their men to move forward into battle.

Only two more companies were to the left. Will's company was almost as far in that direction as it could go and still be part of the Confederate line. As they began to advance, the remaining two companies did likewise, the soldiers running into the field and keening the distinctive Rebel yell.

Suddenly, from the right, gunfire poured into the charging Confederates. The light had begun to fade a bit with the advancing of the afternoon, so Will was able to see the muzzle flashes of rifles from the corner of his eye. Something plucked at his right sleeve as he waved the saber over his head, urging his men on toward Culp's Hill. He heard men scream, heard the rattle of shots, and swung in the direction of the unexpected attack. To his surprise, he saw Federal troops charging into the right flank of the Confederate thrust. He didn't know where they had come from, but if they weren't stopped they would cripple the attack on Culp's Hill.

"Darcy!" he shouted. "To the right!"

"Whoo-eee!" Darcy bellowed as he turned and saw Yankees less than two hundred yards away. "I thought all the fightin' was gonna be over with 'fore we got there! Come on, boys!"

He charged toward the enemy, rifle held slanted across his chest. This would be hand-to-hand fighting, rifle butt against rifle butt, bayonet against bayonet, just the sort of fracas that Darcy liked the best. A huge grin stretched across his bearded, homely face.

He had gone less than ten yards when his head jerked and he spun off his feet.

Will saw Darcy fall, but there was nothing he could do about it. The Union and Confederate lines were closing too fast.

He switched his saber from his right hand to his left, drew his pistol, and emptied it into the mass of blue-clad soldiers. No time to reload, he thought. He jammed the gun back into the holster and waded into the melee, hacking right and left with the saber.

Will experienced the same sort of feeling that he always did at moments such as this. For all of its vast sweep and scope, there were times when war became intensely personal. Everything in the universe boiled down to Will, the blade he held, and the enemy he faced. He cut, thrust, sliced, grabbed hold of a uniform and hauled its owner aside, twisted, stabbed, punched with his free hand, drove his elbow into a man's side, lifted his knee into a groin, felt the warm splash of blood as his saber opened a man's throat, looked into the dying eyes of an enemy with two feet of steel in his vitals. The work was hard and brutal and dirty, and Will smelled the stench of death and felt the dark wave of it roll over him . . .

The Stonewall Brigade repulsed the Federal thrust on its right, but the action delayed it so that the brigade had no chance to join in the general attack on Culp's Hill before night fell. Up ahead, at the base of the hill, Steuart's men had captured a line of breastworks. Many of the Northerners had been captured, along with a Yankee flag. Although the Union soldiers still held the top of the hill, as darkness settled the Confederates were in firm control of the bottom. They would keep up their fire long into the night, determined that the Yankees wouldn't pass a restful evening.

Back in the field where the Stonewall Brigade had been attacked, Will walked unsteadily through the dusk. His bad leg throbbed, and he was covered with cuts that stung wickedly. His right cheek was dotted with powder burns from a Yankee pistol that had gone off almost right in his face. A second later, he had driven his saber through the throat of the pistol's owner.

He was looking for someone now, and in the fading light, he found him. Sgt. Darcy Bennett lay on his side, his rifle underneath him. Will knelt and put a hand on Darcy's shoulder. Gently, he rolled Darcy onto his back.

The grin of anticipation was still on Darcy's mouth, frozen there by death. Just above his left eyebrow was the black-rimmed hole where a Yankee bullet had bored into his brain. Will had caught a glimpse of the bloody ruin at the back of Darcy's head where the projectile had burst out of his skull. He didn't need to see more than that.

At first Will was numb as he stared down into the dead face of the man who had fought beside him for more than two years, the man who had been his friend, the man who had saved his life more than once. *Hell*, Will thought, *the way he watched my back, he probably saved me more times than I'll never know.*

A shudder went through Will, and for the first time in longer than he could remember, he felt tears run down his cheeks, cutting trails in the grime left by dust and powder smoke. His hand shook as he reached out and closed Darcy's eyes. Then he slumped forward over his friend's body and his back heaved as he cried in a way he hadn't thought he was capable.

That was the way one of the men from his company found him later. The young private got Will to his feet and led him toward the rear. Will had gone only a few yards when his mind, stunned by anger and grief, realized what was happening. He pulled away from the soldier's hand on his sleeve.

"I have to find the rest of the company."

"Battle's over for today, Cap'n," the man said. "You come on back to camp with me, get somethin' to eat, maybe rest a little."

Will pulled his gun, and the soldier's eyes widened as he tensed. He relaxed slightly as Will began to reload the weapon. "Got to find the company," Will said again. He put the pistol back in its holster and started toward the base of Culp's Hill, where the Confederate line was now formed. "The battle may be over for now, but there's still tomorrow."

And the Yankees are still up there, he thought as he lifted his eyes for a moment to the dark wooded hill looming over the corpse-littered fields.

—m—

WILL GATHERED up as many men as he could find and reported to General Walker.

"Glad to see you, Captain," Walker said as he took off his hat and ran a hand over his balding head. "How did your company fare?"

"We lost our sergeant and half a dozen other men," Will said.

"I'm sorry to hear that. Still, I'm told that you handled the attack on our flank with great courage. They might have damaged us badly if not for you and your men, Captain."

If that was supposed to make him feel better about Darcy's death, Will thought, it wasn't working. Right now he wondered if any of the fighting was worth it. He felt the loss of Darcy because the sergeant had been his friend . . . but every man who had died on the hill and around it today had been a friend to someone. Friends, brothers, sons, fathers . . . Will forced those thoughts out of his head. He had killed over a dozen men today; he didn't want to consider how many widows and orphans he had made in the process.

Walker was sitting on a large rock beside the creek at the base of the hill. He nodded toward another rock. "You don't look so good, Captain. Perhaps you'd better sit down and rest for just a moment."

Will decided that was a good idea. He sank down on the rock. After a moment he asked, "Have you heard how the fight went on the other side of the ridge?"

With a sigh, Walker said, "Not well. We were able to take the larger and southernmost of the hills, but when our forces tried to move to the smaller one they found the enemy waiting for them. They were repulsed with great loss of life on both sides. I've heard that they call those hills Big Round Top and Little Round Top." Walker shook his head. "Many good men died today on Little Round Top. Our boys were atop it, but only for a moment before they were pushed back."

Will shook his head. He wasn't too familiar with the terrain over there, but he knew that taking the high ground was one of the keys to winning any battle.

"The Yankees pushed out a salient into a peach orchard just west of the ridge," Walker continued, "and of course we tried to cut them off. We nearly broke through their line there, but they held us off until their reinforcements arrived." Walker's voice became hollow with regret. "It was attack and counterattack through the wheat fields and the peach orchard. We broke them ... my God, we broke them ... why didn't they collapse? Somehow they held. Somehow ..."

Walker took a deep breath. "General Early tried to take Cemetery Hill itself. I was told that again our boys fought their way to the top, only to be flanked and forced back. So close, Captain. We came so close."

"Yes sir," Will said softly.

A volley of rifle fire from nearby crackled through the night. Will heard more shots coming from up above on Culp's Hill. He thought he heard the whisper of bullets through the leaves of the trees over his head, but he wasn't sure. After a few minutes the shooting died away.

"We're in for a night of that," Walker said when silence had fallen again. "If you can find a chance to sleep, Captain, you should do so. Tomorrow we'll be going up the hill."

"Yes sir," Will said, but sleep was the last thing he wanted right now. Exhausted though he was, he was afraid that he would dream.

And if he dreamed, he knew his slumber would be haunted by the dead face of Darcy Bennett.

DURING THE evening of July 2, following the orders given to him by Robert E. Lee, Stuart moved his cavalry around to the far left flank of the Confederate line.

Fitz Lee was with Mac when the orders came for the men to remain in their saddles until further notice, so that they would be ready to pursue and harass the enemy if the Yankees tried to withdraw overnight to the east.

Mac didn't think the Yankees were going to go anywhere, not dug in the way they were on those ridges and hills where they had all the advantage. Yet he had heard the reports that came in during the afternoon and evening and knew that despite heavy Confederate losses, the Federals had been hit hard, too.

He didn't know anything about General Meade, who was now in command of the Army of the Potomac. Maybe Meade would surprise everyone and decide to make a run for it.

"I'm not sure this is a good idea," Fitz Lee said as he and Mac sat on their horses at the front of the brigade.

"What's that, sir?"

"Staying mounted all night. The men and the horses are too tired for this. How effective are we going to be tomorrow without some rest?"

Mac frowned. He didn't know what Meade was going to do, but Fitzhugh Lee certainly had surprised him just now. Lee had always been one of Stuart's staunchest supporters, but now he was questioning one of Stuart's decisions. Maybe Lee had seen some of the same things in Stuart that Mac had seen in the past days: the indecisiveness, the stubbornness, the need to do everything in a grand style rather than in a manner that would be most likely to ensure victory.

Lee suddenly wheeled his horse. "Come on, Mac," he said. "I'm going to talk to the general."

Mac rode alongside him as they went in search of Stuart. They found the general a short time later, sitting on horseback and gazing off toward Culp's Hill and Cemetery Ridge.

Lee saluted Stuart. "Begging your pardon, General, but it seems to me a good thing that the men might be allowed to rest for a bit."

The unusual stiffness and formality in Lee's voice surprised Stuart. "What's that, Fitz?"

"I think it would be a good idea to let the boys rest, General, rather than staying in their saddles all night."

Slow hoofbeats signaled the arrival of more men riding out of the darkness. In the light from the moon and stars, Mac recognized them as General Hampton, Colonel Chambliss, and a newcomer to Stuart's command, Gen. Albert G. Jenkins. Jenkins was in charge of the cavalry brigade that had accompanied Lee's infantry through the Shenandoah Valley, Maryland, and on into Pennsylvania. With Stuart's arrival today, Jenkins's brigade had been placed under his command, too.

"Good evening, General," Hampton said in his deep, stately, stentorian voice.

"Hello, Wade," Stuart replied. "Have you boys come to plead the case for your troops, too?"

Hampton and his companions glanced at Fitz Lee. After a moment, Hampton said, "If you mean do we think they need some rest, General, then you are correct. I believe we should station a sufficient number of pickets to keep an eye on the situation and allow the rest of the men to sleep."

"That seems to be the consensus," Stuart said. "Very well. Issue the necessary orders, gentlemen."

Hampton and the others, including Lee, saluted and thanked the general.

"No need for thanks," he said. "Tomorrow will be a busy day, and the men and horses should be as fresh as possible."

Lee and Mac rode back to the brigade, where Mac took care of giving out the orders. Men sighed in gratitude as they dismounted and eased weary muscles.

"No fires," Lee added. "There's no need to announce to the Yankees exactly where we are."

Mac looked toward Culp's Hill, looming darkly in the night. He had heard that the efforts of Johnson's division to capture the hill today had been unsuccessful. He couldn't help but wonder how Will had fared in the battle. Mac was very glad that he had been able to spend some time with Will before the fighting. If he had been able to, he would have ridden there tonight in search of his brother. His duty was here, though, with the rest of the cavalry. Any reunion with Will would have to wait until after the Yankees had been dislodged from their perches on the ridge and the hills.

The stallion bumped Mac's shoulder with his nose, breaking into his reverie. Mac grinned. "You're right. Let's get that saddle off of you so you can rest, too."

Chapter Twenty-three

THE FIRING AROUND CULP'S HILL continued nearly all night, not going on constantly but too frequent to be called sporadic. Will sat down on the ground with his back against a tree and rested for a while, but he kept himself from falling asleep. It would have been difficult to relax enough to sleep anyway, because every so often he heard a thud and felt a faint vibration in the tree trunk as a bullet struck it. That didn't make for a very restful situation.

Finally, the shooting stopped, and silence settled down over Culp's Hill. Will slipped into a dazed state, not asleep but not fully awake, either, although his eyes were open and he was peering down the slope at the creek.

The eastern sky had begun to turn gray with the approach of dawn when suddenly he was jolted out of his stupor by an explosion that caused the ground underneath him to shake. Hard on the heels of that blast came another one. All through the woods, men sprang to their feet, crying out in fear and confusion. Another explosion slammed into the Confederate line, then another and another.

The Federal batteries atop the hill no longer had a good angle at which to target the Southerners. So the Yankees must have moved some cannon around to the Baltimore pike to command a better field of fire, Will thought. He clapped his hat on his head and shouted to the men, "Take cover! . . . Take cover!"

Men dived behind the Yankee breastworks and into the trenches they had captured the previous evening. Others hunkered between fallen trees or simply hugged the ground, trying to make themselves as small as possible. Will raced along the line and saw that his men had placed themselves in whatever shelter they could find. No one would be safe from a direct hit, but perhaps not too many of them would be cut down by shrapnel or flying debris.

A shell hit a tree trunk and burst a short distance to his right. The explosion was close enough to throw Will off his feet. He sailed through the air and crashed to the ground with several other men. One of them made a hideous gagging sound, and when Will pushed himself up on his elbows and looked at the man, he saw that a jagged piece of wood nearly a foot and a half long had been driven through the soldier's throat. The last of his life's blood bubbled out as the man pawed feebly at the wooden shard. He stiffened, and his arms fell to the side.

Will felt a stinging in the back of his right shoulder and reached behind him with his left hand to discover a smaller piece of wood lodged in his own flesh. He pulled it free and tossed it aside. That made the wound hurt worse, but he forced himself to ignore the pain.

"Stay down," he said calmly to the men around him. "Keep your heads down. The Yankees can't keep this up forever."

He hoped that was true. He had no idea how much ammunition the Yankees had. From the very first day of this war, they had been better supplied than the Confederate troops. There was no reason to think things were any different now.

The sun rose and spread light over the blasted landscape. It was another hot, clear summer day. Birds should have been singing and bees buzzing. But the only things taking flight today were bullets and cannonballs. The sharpshooters on top of the hill opened fire again, raking the Confederate line and adding the threat of bullets to the bombardment. Some of the trees toppled from the explosions, and as Will looked along the slope, he saw leaves swirling down everywhere, cut loose from their branches by flying lead. The leaves were still green, rather than brown or red or gold, or else it would have looked like an idyllic version of autumn along the base of Culp's Hill as the leaves floated and looped and settled gently to the ground.

The sun rose higher. How long could they endure it? Will wondered. And yet where could they go?

Forward, he realized. Forward was always the answer.

The order came at last. Shrieking out their defiance, the Southerners surged up out of the captured trenches and headed for the top of the hill. Will went with his company, saber in his left hand, pistol in his right.

The slope was steep. His boots slipped from time to time, and he had to sheath his saber so he could use one hand to keep his balance. The men around him yelled and whooped. Will added his voice to theirs, bellowing, "Come on! Up, boys, up!"

Bullets rendered the air around him. He saw muzzle flashes coming from behind a large deadfall above him on the hill. He paused and squeezed off a couple of shots, saw the lead chew splinters from the top of the fallen log. He didn't really expect to hit any of the Yankees behind it; he just wanted to make them duck long enough to give his men a chance to get there. But one of the blue-clad soldiers suddenly stood up, swaying as blood welled from a hole in his forehead. His arms jerked spasmodically as he died and toppled to the side.

Will never stopped moving. He climbed higher as some of the men in front of him reached the deadfall and threw themselves over it. Rifles rose and fell as bayonets and rifle butts did their deadly work. By the time Will reached the fallen log and climbed past it, the Yankee skirmishers who had hidden there were all dead, hacked and battered into bloody rags that looked only vaguely human.

When the hammer of Will's pistol finally clicked on an empty chamber, he didn't take the time to reload it. He picked up a fallen rifle, fired it on the run, dropped it, and picked up another that had slipped from the lifeless hands of its former owner. Proceeding in that fashion, he made his way higher and higher until he could see the crest of the hill. Some of the Southerners had already reached it and were clambering past it. As Will paused to look up at that goal, he saw several men fall backward toward him, driven off the rim by heavy Federal fire.

The Yankees were waiting up there, Will realized. They had fought to keep the men of Johnson's division from reaching the top of the hill, but it didn't really matter. There were even more Yankees poised to pick off any soldier who poked his head up.

But lower down on the slope, the cannon fire was still crashing among the trees, so they couldn't retreat. Will's brain was growing battle-numbed, but he understood that much. He and his companions could go up to death or down to death, but either way, that was all that awaited them.

A huge anger began to grow inside him. They had fought so hard, so well, for so long. They had won battles they weren't supposed to win, defeating enemy forces that were larger—sometimes more than twice as large—and better armed and equipped. They had dared to hope that the justness of their cause would carry them to victory against great odds. For a time that victory had seemed to be within their grasp. Now . . . now it was slipping away. One more battle, the men had said on their way up here to Pennsylvania. One more fight, one more defeat for the Yankees, and they would give up. They would see they had been wrong. It was almost over, and when it was they could all go home . . .

One more battle.

It was no high-pitched, keening Rebel yell that came from Will's throat as he threw himself up the slope once more. Instead it was a hoarse, inarticulate shout of rage. The power of that shout reached out to the men around him and drew them with him, and together they went up the hill and over the crest. Bullets fanned the air around them, but they no longer cared. In their hearts burned the bitter blaze of men who knew they were about to die.

A hundred yards away thousands of Yankees crouched behind breastworks that had been erected over the past two days. The volley of fire that roared from their rifles swept the rim of the hill. The leading edge of the Confederate advance was blasted back, but as each man fell another took his place . . . until finally there were no more to continue the charge.

Will had taken only two steps when he felt the hammerblow on top of his left shoulder. The impact turned him so that he was sideways to the Yankees. A bullet burned along his back, then something struck him on the right hip and drove him back over the crest of the hill. He fell, out of control, and tumbled down the slope, crashing into tree trunks, bouncing off, feeling the brush clawing at him, gradually slowing him down. He wasn't sure how far he rolled down Culp's Hill. When he came to a stop, he just lay there, breathing hard, fighting against the pain that filled his body. He was too stunned to do anything else.

When his brain finally began to function a bit better, he tried moving. His left arm was numb and would not respond, but his right seemed to work all right. He was lying on his left side. The worst pain was in his right hip. He moved his hand there, expecting to find that a Yankee bullet had torn his flesh and shattered the bone. He thought he would discover that his trouser leg was soaked with blood.

But there was no wound that he could find, only a tear in the broad leather belt that supported his holster. He realized that the bullet must have glanced off something, spending most of its power, before hitting his belt hard enough to knock him down but not hard enough to penetrate the thick leather. Still, the blow had been like a sledgehammer. The rest of the damage he felt, except for his left shoulder and the bullet burn on his back, had been done on his wild plunge down the steep hill.

With a grunt of effort, he rolled onto his right side so that he could push himself into a sitting position. His left arm hung limply. He turned his head, saw the blood on the torn shoulder of his uniform. Surprisingly, there wasn't much of it. He pulled the jacket and shirt aside and saw that the bullet had clipped the top of his shoulder. The bone might be broken; he wasn't sure about that. Somehow, the wound had deadened all the nerves in his arm, making it hang uselessly at his side. The feeling might come back to it later. He hoped so.

Will twisted half around to look up at the crest of the hill. Bodies covered the slope. Even where he was now, farther down, he could have reached out and touched three dead men.

A few soldiers were still struggling to reach the top of the hill, but most of them were pulling back now. A young lieutenant stopped beside Will and shouted over the roar of gunfire, "Do you need help, Captain?"

Will reached up to him. "Give me a hand."

The two men clasped wrists, and the young man hauled Will to his feet. "We have orders to withdraw across the creek, Captain!" the lieutenant said.

"Go on." Will waved his good hand. "Fall back!" He turned and raised his voice so that others could hear him. "Fall back!"

Stumbling, Will started down the slope. He limped heavily from the pain in his right hip. Around him, others began to retreat, too. He felt hollow, burned out by the fires of rage that had carried him to the hilltop, only to be driven back down by enemy fire. Now there was nothing in him but ashes, and he moved awkwardly, jerkily, his muscles working but not his brain.

Thankfully, the shelling from the Yankee cannon had lessened, and one by one, company by company, regiment by regiment, the survivors of the battle for Culp's Hill staggered back through the creek and across the fields that bordered it. Behind them, gunfire continued as the Yankees harried the stragglers.

One of the men left behind was a young soldier of the Second Virginia Infantry named Wesley Culp, a native of Gettysburg who had moved to Virginia several years earlier. His uncle owned the hill on which he had died.

—◊◊◊—

MORE THAN a mile away, at the Lutheran seminary, Robert E. Lee had been surprised as well that morning by the sounds of battle coming from the Confederate left. He climbed to the building's cupola and trained his field glasses on Culp's Hill. The plan he had formulated the day before, after the attempts to take Little Round Top and Cemetery Hill had failed, called for Longstreet and Ewell to attack in unison today. Longstreet was to aim his corps at the center of the Federal line on Cemetery Ridge, and Ewell was to target Culp's Hill and the Union right flank. Clearly, a battle was already underway over there. Lee's white-bearded face was grim as he lowered the glasses. The day was barely started and already his plan was ruined.

Longstreet was waiting in front of the seminary when Lee descended from the cupola. Without waiting for Lee to speak, Longstreet began: "General, I've had my scouts out all night. You still have an excellent opportunity to move around to the right of Meade's army and maneuver him into attacking us."

For a long moment, Lee just stared at the man he had referred to in the past as his strong right hand. Then he pointed in the direction of Cemetery Ridge. "The enemy is there, General, and I intend to strike him."

Longstreet looked down, clearly conflicted in what he felt, torn between his loyalty to Lee and what he regarded as a grievous mistake being made by the older man. Finally, he lifted his eyes to meet Lee's level gaze. "General Pickett's division is on its way here now. His men are fresh. I would like to wait until he arrives to begin our assault."

Lee considered the suggestion. George E. Pickett's men had spent the past two days guarding the army's supplies at Chambersburg rather than being bloodied and battered in the futile attacks against the Federal line. Today's action would have more chance of succeeding if there were fresh troops in the vanguard.

With a curt nod, Lee agreed to Longstreet's plan. "Pickett will lead the charge," he said. "I want Heth with him, as well as Pender and Anderson just behind . . . Do you see those oak trees?" He lifted his hand and pointed.

Longstreet squinted toward Cemetery Ridge. The small copse of trees stood alone on the crest. There were no other trees around it.

"I see them," Longstreet said softly.

"There is our objective. Our men will keep their eyes on those trees and proceed toward them, and we will win the day."

"Yes sir," replied Longstreet. There was nothing else he could say.

"CAP'N WILL!"

Roman leaped up from where he had been sitting under a tree. He ran forward to meet the bloody figure who limped toward him. Will's uniform was splattered with blood in several places, and something was wrong with his left arm.

"I'm all right, Roman," Will assured him. "Just a little banged up."

"The battle? . . ."

Will just shook his head.

"Come on over here," Roman said as he put an arm around Will's waist to support him. "You got to sit down and rest."

Will leaned against the tree while Roman went in search of a canteen. He brought one back a few minutes later and handed it to Will. Water had never tasted any better, Will thought as he gulped it down his smoke-seared throat.

"We best find a doctor for you—" Roman began.

"I'm all right," Will cut in, lowering the canteen from his mouth. "I fell down the side of that damned hill. That's how I got most of these cuts and bruises."

"What about your shoulder?"

"A Yankee got lucky. I'm pretty sure the shoulder's not broken, though. My arm just got knocked crazy somehow. If you can fix me up a sling, that's all I need."

"I reckon I can do that," Roman said with a worried frown, "but I still think I ought to fetch a doctor."

"No," Will snapped. "Our sawbones can tend to the ones who really need them. Just get me that blasted sling."

Roman nodded, seeing that it did no good to argue.

He tore a strip of cloth from the bottom of his shirt and tied it around Will's neck, then gently placed Will's arm in the makeshift sling. Will grunted. "Must be getting better," he said. "That hurt like hell."

Roman hunkered beside him. "Wasn't sure I was ever goin' to see you again, Cap'n. When you went off yesterday and never come back, I didn't know what to think."

"The attack didn't start until late, and then the Yankees flanked us . . ." Will frowned as he tried to get the details of the past twenty-four hours in their proper order. His brain was working better now than it had been when he came down off Culp's Hill, but his thinking was still a little fuzzy. He said, "Darcy . . ."

Roman looked around. "Where is Sergeant Bennett?"

"Dead."

Roman stared at him for a second then whispered, "Oh, dear Lord. I'm sorry, Cap'n Will. I am surely sorry."

"And he didn't even go down fighting. He died before he got there. Damn it. Darcy would have been happier if he'd gone with his bayonet in some Yankee's guts—" Will stopped short and laughed, a harsh, ugly sound. "What the hell's wrong with me? What does it matter how he died? He's still dead. He doesn't give a damn now."

"Cap'n Will . . . you don't need to take on so—"

A new voice called out. "Captain!"

Will looked up to see General Ewell on horseback, strapped into the saddle with his wooden leg dangling on one side of the horse's body. He was alone, which was strange considering that a commanding officer was nearly always surrounded by his staff.

Will got to his feet as quickly as he could, given his injuries, and saluted. "Captain Will Brannon, sir," he said, knowing that Ewell wouldn't know who he was.

"Captain Brannon, are you badly injured?"

"No sir."

"Do you have a horse?"

"Yes sir."

Ewell nodded. "Good. I need someone to ride over to General Lee's headquarters and tell him what happened here this morning. I want him to know that it was the Federals who commenced this battle, not our men."

Will wasn't sure why that would be important for the commanding general to know, but it wasn't his place to question a general. "Yes sir, I can do that."

Roman looked like he was about to speak up. Will figured he wanted to say that the captain was in no shape to be carrying messages around the battlefield. Giving Roman a sharp look to keep him quiet, Will asked, "Is there anything else, sir?"

"No, Captain." Ewell sighed. "Just tell General Lee that we did our best."

Ewell turned his horse and rode away slowly, pausing to check on some other men who were straggling back from the unsuccessful battle at Culp's Hill.

Will said to Roman, "Get my horse."

"Cap'n, I don't know—"

"I have my orders, damn it, and so do you! Get my horse."

Roman stiffened and looked at him defiantly. "Thought you said you wasn't goin' to treat me like no slave."

For an awkward moment, Will couldn't say anything. Then, as he started to turn away, he muttered, "You're right. I'll get the horse myself."

"Hold on, hold on," Roman said quickly. "I'll get that horse saddled and ready to go for you, Cap'n Will. But there's just one more thing . . . I'm goin' with you."

"Fine. I'm too damned tired to argue with you."

Roman hurried off to fetch the dun, and Will stood there, his arm in the sling, his right hand braced against the tree. When he looked up at Culp's Hill, he saw how the terrible shelling and volley after volley of rifle fire had destroyed the forest of oak trees on its slopes. Some of the trees were shattered, others had been blown over, and all of them were stripped of their leaves. Bare branches clawed at the sky like skeletal fingers, as if the dead men who lay so thickly around them were reaching up futilely for heaven.

A wave of dizziness went through Will, and his fingers tightened on the rough bark of the tree. He couldn't give in to the pain and exhaustion, he told himself. He had orders to carry out. He still had work to do.

MAC LISTENED to what sounded like thunder, even though the sky was clear. He knew all too well what it was: The big guns were firing again. He didn't know if the rumbling came from Union or Confederate cannon or both, but it didn't really matter. The battle was underway again this morning.

Stuart's cavalry trotted along the York turnpike, four brigades strong, counting Albert Jenkins's men. Mac knew that despite their impressive numbers, they might be limited in what they could accomplish today. Even after spending the morning looking for ammunition, they were dangerously low on firepower. Mac had heard that Jenkins's men had only ten rounds apiece. The other brigades weren't in much better shape.

Following Stuart's orders, the cavalry was moving so far to the left of the Confederate line that they were now in the rear of the Union army. Mac had overheard the discussion between Stuart and the other generals that morning. He knew that General Lee planned to attack the Yankees in the middle of Cemetery Ridge today. Although Stuart hadn't been specific about his own plans, it seemed likely that Stuart was positioning them to hit the Yankees if they fled from Lee's attack. Either that, or they were going to strike the rear of the Federal line at the same time as Lee was assaulting the front.

With a wave of his gauntleted hand, Stuart led the horsemen off the turnpike and onto a smaller road that ran across some fields to a thickly wooded ridge. The cavalry ascended to this ridge and halted while they were still in the concealment of the trees. Mac and Fitz Lee dismounted and moved forward to the edge of the woods, staying far enough back in the shadows underneath the trees so that they couldn't be seen easily. Stuart and the other commanders were doing the same thing, studying the terrain spread out before them.

Mac's pulse quickened as he spotted the Federal cavalry in the fields below. They were close enough that he didn't need field glasses. The Yankees were out in the open, not hiding at all, and there looked to be several brigades. Their numbers, Mac thought, would match up fairly evenly with those of the Confederates. The Yankees didn't seem to be going anywhere. They looked almost like they were waiting for something.

"Bring up one of the guns from the horse artillery," Stuart ordered quickly.

While the cannon was being set up, Mac took out his field glasses. A mile away across the open country, Cemetery Ridge was plainly visible, along with Culp's Hill to its northeast. The distance was too far for Mac to be able to make out any individuals, even with the field glasses, but he could see the haze of smoke floating over Culp's Hill. That must be where the battle was centered this morning. He frowned in thought, knowing that Ewell had been scheduled to attack Culp's Hill at the same time that Longstreet was to advance on the middle of Cemetery Ridge. Something must have happened to disrupt the timing of the attack. Over on the ridge, things seemed to be quiet, despite the fighting on the hill.

Will was there somewhere, Mac thought as his fingers tightened on the glasses. He knew his brother well and knew that he would be in the middle of the assault on the hill if possible.

They had both come through so much in these past two years. Will had been wounded several times, while Mac was practically unscathed. The odds were stacked against both of them and getting worse all the time. With each passing battle it was more likely one or both of them would be severely injured or even killed.

Mac lowered the field glasses and sleeved the sweat from his forehead. It wouldn't do to think too much about the odds.

When you were in the army, you had to consider the chances of your side winning, not of your own personal survival.

The cannon had been rolled into position just in front of the trees and was ready to fire. Stuart strode forward to stand near the big gun and direct its aim. "Up a bit more," he said to the soldier adjusting the elevating screw. "There. Ready, gentlemen? Fire!"

The cannon roared and rocked back on its carriage. As the echoes of the blast began to fade, the whine of the shell could be heard then a sharp explosion as the projectile burst in the midst of the Federal cavalry below. The Yankees had begun scurrying for cover at the first sound, but the shell blew several horses and riders to the ground anyway.

Stuart had the gun crew adjust its aim and ordered another shot. Again the shell did a little damage, but not much. Over the next quarter-hour, the pattern was repeated several times more. Mac wondered if the series of shots was designed to give some sort of signal to Robert E. Lee, letting him know that Stuart was in place on this side of Cemetery Ridge.

Whatever the purpose, the barrage stirred up a hornet's nest among the Federal cavalry. The blue-clad horsemen pulled back out of range but did not flee the field completely.

"General Jenkins," Stuart said, "dismount your men and have them advance to those fences. I want to hold the fences and that barn."

Within minutes, Jenkins's troops were moving down the ridge toward the fences and the barn Stuart had pointed out. The men broke into a run and threw themselves behind the fences as they got there.

The Union commander reacted as Stuart must have known he would. He sent three brigades of cavalry forward, accepting the challenge that the Southerners had thrown down. As the Yankees thundered toward the fences, their artillery also began to fire, the shells arching over the charge to fall around the barn now occupied by Confederate troops.

"Fitz," Stuart said quietly as the scene developed, "I want you and General Hampton to be ready to ride when I give the word. You're to stay out of sight in the trees until then, however."

"Yes sir, General," Lee said. He looked at Mac and nodded. Both men mounted their horses and drew their sabers. All along the line, metal rasped on metal as more sabers were drawn.

Jenkins's men began to fire, their carbines cracking wickedly. The volleys tore into the Federal charge and slowed it, but Mac knew how low on ammunition they were. Within minutes they ran out, and between the Union artillery and the onrushing cavalry charge, Jenkins's men knew they had no choice. They did the only thing they could: withdraw as quickly as possible toward the shelter of the trees atop the ridge.

They had served their purpose, however, and drawn out the enemy. Poised in the trees, the brigades belonging to Lee and Hampton waited for the order to charge. When it came they burst out of the woods and galloped down the slope, streaming toward the Yankees.

Mac was near the front of the line, the stallion racing alongside Lee's horse. He found himself shouting out the Rebel yell along with the other riders. A moment such as this was no time to think. A man could only act.

Shells from the Federal artillery began to slam into the Confederate charge. Men and horses went down, but those who didn't never slowed. On they came, down the ridge into the field, sunlight glittering on the drawn sabers.

Suddenly the Federal forces veered apart, leaving a few regiments to face the Confederate charge head-on while the others spread out to flank the onrushing Southerners. Mac caught a glimpse of the officer leading the Yankee charge, who seemed fearless despite being outnumbered. His long yellow hair was almost as bright in the sun as the polished steel of the sabers, and in an instant Mac remembered seeing him at Aldie as well.

Then, with a terrible crash, the two lines came together, and Mac lost sight of the Union officer. Horses rammed together, knocking each other down so that their riders were spilled and trampled in the melee. A few guns barked, but mostly it was saber play as the sides met and fought, and the air was full of the ringing of steel on steel.

The orderly ranks of charge and countercharge disintegrated and within seconds the field was utter chaos. Mac found himself between two Yankees, desperately jerking his saber from side to side to fend off their blows. The stallion saved him by throwing itself into the horse to the left, knocking it back several feet, giving Mac the respite he needed on that side to turn the other way and dispatch the Yankee to his right with a saber thrust through the shoulder. Then Mac was able to swing around and meet the threat from the left as that Federal cavalryman came at him again. Mac deflected the man's saber and flicked the point of his own blade across the Yankee's throat. Blood geysered.

Mac wheeled the stallion and spotted General Hampton nearby. Hampton was also trying to defend himself against two enemies, but he wasn't as lucky as Mac had been. One of the Yankee blades caught him a glancing blow on the head, knocking his hat off and opening a gash. Blood welled from the cut into Hampton's eyes, momentarily blinding him.

With a shout, Mac sent the stallion lunging toward the general. He swung his saber and struck one of the Yankees from behind, the blade cutting so deeply into the man's neck that it grated on bone. Mac jerked the saber free as the Union cavalryman toppled out of the saddle. Meanwhile, Hampton ducked under a slashing blow from the other Yankee and then spitted him on his saber.

Hampton wiped the blood from his eyes and nodded his thanks to Mac. "Better get back to the ridge, General!" Mac shouted to him above the clamor of battle. Then there were more Yankees to fight off, and Mac was too busy defending himself to see if Hampton took his advice or not.

Quickly, it became apparent that the Federals' tactic of splitting the attacking force had proved to be successful. The Union horsemen on the flanks of the Confederate charge closed in, and the Southerners were pinched together. Mac hacked his way through the dust and confusion and death, looking for Fitz Lee. When he found him, Lee was calling for his men to fall back.

Lee was ordering his men to retreat, but as usual he was in no hurry to do so himself. He and Mac fought side by side as the surviving members of the brigade began making their way toward the ridge. Finally, as Mac cut down one of the Yankees and Lee drove his saber into the chest of another man, the general shouted, "We'd better get out of here!"

Mac couldn't have agreed more. He hauled the stallion around, and he and Lee pounded off through clouds of smoke and dust. Bullets whipped around them as the Yankees realized they were trying to escape. Mac bent low in the saddle to make himself a smaller target.

They reached the slope and started up it toward the trees at the crest. More dismounted cavalrymen had come forward to kneel behind the fences and provide covering fire for the retreat. Mac and Lee jumped their horses over one of the fences and finally reached the top. They reined in and turned to watch as the rest of the Confederate artillery joined in the fray and battered the Union lines, preventing the Yankee cavalry from pursuing the men who had fled back to the ridge.

Blood pounded inside Mac's skull as he sat there and tried to catch his breath. Everything was pretty much as it had been before the battle, he realized. Stuart's cavalry still held the ridge and the fence line and the barn, but the Yankees were still sitting there across the way, blocking any advance from this direction toward Cemetery Ridge.

Mac wiped the blood off his saber then slid it into its scabbard. He dragged the back of his hand across his mouth and sighed. "Did we do any good?" he asked.

"We did all that was possible," Fitz Lee said. "But I don't suppose we'll really know what we accomplished until we hear from Uncle Bob."

Will was still somewhere over there, beyond that distant ridge, thought Mac as he lifted his eyes toward the Yankee stronghold.

ROMAN TROTTED alongside Will's dun as the two men moved through the streets of Gettysburg. The town was gripped by an eerie silence and seemed deserted except for the Confederate troops under Early and Gordon, who were waiting there in reserve should they be needed later in the day. No doubt many of the civilians had fled, Will thought, and those who remained behind probably had huddled in their cellars for the past three days, wondering if their world was about to come to an end.

Will's nose wrinkled in disgust as he and Roman started out of town toward the Lutheran seminary. Two days earlier, as the Yankees were driven back through Gettysburg to their current position, there had been heavy fighting along here, and many corpses of Union soldiers still lay where they had fallen. The heat had done its grisly work, causing a terrible stench to hang over the entire area.

"I thought I'd seen some bad things in my life," Roman said as he ran beside the horse, "but I never seen anything like this, Cap'n Will."

"It's even worse than Sharpsburg," Will agreed. There had been huge losses in that battle, but it had lasted only a day. This great conflict had been going on for more than forty-eight hours so far, with no end yet in sight.

His body still ached miserably from the punishment it had received. His left arm continued to be numb most of the time, although occasionally it tingled and sharp pains lanced through it. The actual wound on top of his left shoulder burned like fire. He should have had Roman clean and bandage it, he thought, but there hadn't been time. He could have it tended to later, he told himself.

388 • *James Reasoner*

They left Gettysburg on the Chambersburg pike. Will reined the dun to a halt and climbed down. "What's wrong, Cap'n Will?" asked Roman.

"I can walk the rest of the way," Will said. "The seminary's not far. I can't ask you to run like that in this heat, Roman."

With a shake of his head, Roman protested, "It don't bother me none, Cap'n. You should ride—"

"Here," Will broke in as he thrust the reins into Roman's hand. "You lead the horse." He started striding along the pike.

Roman followed, hurrying a little to catch up. They walked along under the midday sun until they reached a smaller road that turned off to the left and led up to Seminary Ridge. The sides of the road were littered with dead men and dead horses. Will kept his eyes fixed grimly on his destination, not looking at the death and destruction around him.

As they approached the seminary, Will was surprised to see a civilian there, a tall, lean man in a brown tweed suit and a black hat. The man had just emerged from the building, and when he saw Will and Roman, he asked, "I say, Captain, have you seen General Lee or General Longstreet?"

The man's accent was like nothing Will had ever heard before, even though he had no trouble understanding him. "I'm looking for General Lee myself," Will replied.

The civilian proved not to be a civilian at all, despite his garb. "Colonel Arthur Fremantle of Her Majesty's Coldstream Guards, Royal Army, and unofficial representative of Her Majesty, Queen Victoria, to the Confederate States of America."

Will shook hands with him. "A Britisher, huh?"

Fremantle laughed. "I 'reckon,' as you Southerners might put it. And you are . . . ?"

"Captain Will Brannon, Thirty-third Virginia Infantry. On a mission for General Ewell to General Lee."

"Then by all means let us find him. Come along, Captain."

As they walked in front of the seminary building, Will gave in to his curiosity. "How did you come to be here, Colonel?"

"As I said, I'm observing the conflict unofficially. Came by ship across the Atlantic and through the Gulf of Mexico to a charming village in Texas called Brownsville. A bit of a tropical paradise, that. Then up through Texas and across Louisiana on a wagon train full of supplies bound for Vicksburg. You lads have been importing English weaponry in that fashion. Seems appropriate that you import an Englishman as well, eh?"

Under other circumstances, Will probably would have felt an instinctive liking for the garrulous Englishman, but right now he hurt all over and had his mind on the battle. He didn't pay much attention as Fremantle continued to talk.

Suddenly, the British colonel was silenced by an overpowering roar of artillery. What sounded like every big gun in the Army of Northern Virginia began to blast away from farther south along the ridge. The barrage continued, shaking the ground under Will's feet and assaulting his ears. It was the most awesome bombardment Will had ever heard, and he would have just as soon missed it.

Soon clouds of smoke floated thickly over the ridge and drifted into the valley to the east of it. Will, Roman, and Fremantle moved along, and as he looked out over the lower ground through gaps in the smoke, Will thought he could tell that the majority of the shells were aimed too high. They seemed to be passing over the crest of Cemetery Ridge, missing the Federal troops that were massed along the edge of the ridge and at its base.

Not all the shells went astray, however. One of them struck a Federal ammunition caisson, causing a tremendous explosion. Loud cheers went up from the Confederate gunners at the sight of smoke and flame rising into the sky.

Even as the barrage continued, rank after rank of Southern soldiers moved out of the woods along Seminary Ridge and started toward Cemetery Ridge, color-bearers leading the way. From their position about halfway along the ridge, Will and his two companions watched as thousands of men in butternut and gray advanced toward the enemy. They marched crisply, rifles held at the ready. Will knew he had to be imagining it, but he thought he could hear the flags fluttering and popping in the wind that blew the clouds of smoke across the field.

The Federal artillery came into play, shells screaming and whistling down among the marching Confederates. Men fell to the blasts, but the rest surged on, moving faster and faster. There were gaps in the line indicating that three divisions were charging Cemetery Ridge, but as they went across the open field the groups moved closer together, centering themselves and aiming at a small grove of trees on the opposite ridge. The field was not flat but had a slight rolling quality to it, so that the ranks wavered up and down as the men passed through the depressions. That motion made them look even more like a gray wave rolling toward the distant ridge.

The Emmitsburg road was bordered by plank fences, and that slowed down the advance for a few moments while the men in the front ranks climbed over and knocked down the fences. Then the Confederate tide rolled on, undeterred. It left behind the men who had already been wounded, some of whom managed to get to their feet and stagger or hobble back toward Seminary Ridge.

The message from Ewell was meaningless now, Will realized. Utterly meaningless. The main attack against the center of the Federal line had been launched, and nothing could call it back.

Fremantle took out his field glasses and trained them on the advance. "That's General Pickett's division there on the right," he said. The Confederate artillery was falling silent now, so the men could talk again. "Generals Garnett, Armistead, and Kemper, from left to right. Splendid fellows. Splendid. Over there on the left of the advance, Pettigrew and Trimble. Straight as an arrow, eh?"

Actually, the brigades were still converging toward the center, Will thought. But in a way, Fremantle was right. They might be moving at an angle, but they never wavered. Each brigade pushed on ahead, letting nothing stop it from reaching its destination.

But the Federal artillery was now taking a terrible toll. The soldiers who had not yet been hit had to step over or onto their fallen comrades to continue the advance. They were leaving too many men behind, thought Will, too many bloody shapes sprawled in the dusty fields. But as the faint sound of Rebel yells drifted back to the observers on Seminary Ridge, the Southerners broke into a run, charging right into the solid wall of bullets that came from the Union troops concentrated along the base of the ridge.

Will lifted his field glasses to his eyes and trained them on the ridge. He saw that a pole fence ran along the base of the slope, and behind it, rocks had been piled to form another fence. It was in poor condition, having collapsed in places, but it still provided good cover for the Yankee riflemen who crouched behind it and poured fire into the charging Confederates.

"My God," Fremantle said softly as he watched the carnage. "Such valor. I've never seen its like."

Will saw an officer atop a black horse waving his hat over his head to urge on his troops. Off to the right, another officer who was on foot had taken off his hat, stuck it on the end of his saber, and was using it as a makeshift guidon. Both men, and the troops who followed them, were not far now from the stone wall. Will saw that the fence jogged back, forming a right angle, and he wondered if that might not be the target at which the Confederate leaders were aiming. If they could break through the line there, and hold the ground they gained . . .

Smoke scudded across the battlefield, and for a moment Will couldn't see anything. Then it cleared again, just in time for him to see Confederate troops rolling over the stone wall in the angle of the fence. The hand-to-hand fighting was fierce just beyond the wall. Will watched an officer carrying a flag clamber over the stone barrier, only to fall. But a heartbeat later, the flag rose again, snatched up by one of the other Confederates.

"How can they keep fightin'?" Roman said. "They's torn all to pieces."

Will saw a riderless black horse dashing around in a frenzy and wondered if it belonged to the officer he had seen earlier. He couldn't see the man anywhere else. Nor could he spot the officer who'd had his hat on his sword. In that maelstrom of death, no one was immune, certainly not the leaders who bravely put themselves in the forefront of the attack.

More and more of the gray-clad attackers poured over the wall. Long minutes passed as the grim struggle continued. By now, Will thought, the corpses had to be so thick on the ground that men would have a hard time standing up. And once a man fell, chances were he would never be able to get to his feet again. Despite the heat of the day, Will felt cold as he watched the battle. He knew all too well how those men felt, the anger and terror and sorrow they were experiencing at this moment as they fought tooth and nail for their lives, their lungs clogged and their eyes burning from smoke, the coppery scent of blood filling their nostrils as it washed around their ankles in a floodtide, the shrill cries of dying men that assaulted their ears, the pain that engulfed their bodies as bullet or bayonet drove into them, the longing for home and family as men fell, the tears that welled from their eyes as they felt their lives slipping away . . .

Will lowered his glasses. He couldn't watch any more.

For twenty minutes, the Confederates held the ground they had gained on the other side of the stone wall. Then Federal reinforcements arrived, and the Southerners were thrown back. Those who couldn't get across the wall were slaughtered. And just like that, the attack was over. Men broke and ran, trying their best to get back across the fields filled with blood and corpses to the relative safety of Seminary Ridge. They had thrown everything they had at the Union line, and that line had stretched and bent and cracked . . . but it had never broken in two. Somehow, it had held and then grown stronger, and the charge led by Pickett's division was a failure. To some, enamored of the great courage displayed, a glorious failure perhaps—but still a failure.

Colonel Fremantle muttered, "I must find General Longstreet." He hurried on, and after a moment Will and Roman went after him. Wherever Longstreet was, General Lee would probably be there, too, and Will could ask Lee if there was any message he should take back to Ewell.

They found Longstreet sitting dispiritedly on the top rail of a fence. "You saw, Colonel?" he asked Fremantle.

"Indeed I did, sir. I saw unimaginable gallantry in that field today."

"It didn't get us anything," snapped Longstreet. "Except for a lot of good men dead."

Retreating soldiers covered the slopes of the ridge now, many of them wounded. Some used their rifles as crutches while others were so badly hurt they had to be carried by their less-injured comrades. Will saw very few men who weren't bleeding from some sort of wound.

General Lee rode up, unmistakable on his gray horse. The lines on his weathered face looked deeper and more finely drawn than ever. As the wounded men stumbled past him, he spoke to some of them, congratulating them on their efforts. "It's my fault, all my fault. Don't you worry, you did fine, son. I brought us to this. All my fault."

The pain in the old man's eyes was so overwhelming that Will couldn't bring himself to approach him. What could be said at a time like this? Nothing could soften the blow of what had happened here today.

"Come on," Will said softly to Roman. "Let's get out of here." He wanted to get back to what was left of his company. When he was mounted, he held his hand down to Roman. "Swing up here behind me."

Roman hesitated. Will knew that no white man would have ever offered to let him ride double before. Roman probably couldn't even conceive of such a thing. But after a moment,

Roman took his hand and climbed onto the dun's back behind the saddle. Will heeled the horse into a trot along the ridge, then cut through Gettysburg and headed for the place where he had left Ewell's division, north of Culp's Hill.

In the distance, shots still popped and cracked as skirmishers clashed here and there. The shooting wouldn't completely stop until nightfall, Will thought.

But when darkness finally settled down over this bloody landscape, then men would pause and draw deep breaths and give thanks that they had lived through another day. The really lucky ones would fall into a dreamless sleep, where for a time, battle would be far, far away . . .

That was what he was thinking when the bullet slammed into his chest and knocked him out of the saddle. He felt himself hit the ground, heard Roman cry out, "Cap'n Will! Cap'n Will!" but it was almost like everything was happening to someone else. He knew he should be in pain, but even the aches he'd had earlier seemed to have gone away suddenly. He felt nothing except an overwhelming sadness.

He wasn't sure if he was sad for himself, or for everyone who had come here to Gettysburg in this hot July.

Chapter Twenty-four

M AC WAS TRYING TO fight off a sense of panic as he rode toward Seminary Ridge along with the other members of Fitzhugh Lee's brigade. It was the morning of July 4, and the cavalry was moving into position to provide an escort for the supply wagons and the numerous ambulances carrying Confederate wounded. Since the disastrous attack on the center of the Federal line the day before, Robert E. Lee had been making plans to withdraw his army. The supplies and the wounded would go first, with the cavalry protecting them, while the infantry would continue to hold Seminary Ridge in case Meade should decide to attack. Rumors were flying to that effect, so there was a sense of desperation in the air as the Confederates pulled back from Gettysburg and the area north and east of the town to concentrate on the Chambersburg pike west of Seminary Ridge.

Mac's unease was not born of a fear that the Yankees would try to attack while the army was battered and exhausted. He had been searching for Will ever since the cavalry had returned to the area the day before, and so far he hadn't been able to find his brother or anyone who knew anything about him.

Ewell's corps, including the Stonewall Brigade, had withdrawn to the vicinity of Oak Hill, northwest of Gettysburg, about ten o'clock the previous night. Mac had gotten Fitz Lee's permission to look for Will. He had found the Thirty-third Virginia—what was left of it—and spoken to several men who told him that Will had survived the final attack on Culp's Hill but had vanished sometime after that. No one knew where he had gone or what had happened to him.

With tens of thousands of corpses scattered across the landscape, Will could be lying dead anywhere on the battlefield, Mac thought. Darcy Bennett, Will's sergeant and friend, was out there somewhere. Several members of Will's company had told Mac about the sergeant's death.

Now the cavalry had a job to do again, and Mac was terrified that he would have to leave Gettysburg not knowing what had happened to Will.

He couldn't desert his duty, though. With the army in such terrible shape, getting back across the Potomac wouldn't be easy, especially if the Yankees tried to stop them. The cavalry would be needed every step of the way.

Mac, Lee, and the other horsemen rode up to the long column of wagons as midday approached. In the distance, clouds were forming in the sky, and Mac heard a far-off rumble of thunder. A good soaking rain might be just what Gettysburg needed right now, he thought. It might wash away some of the blood.

Some . . . but not all.

Fitz Lee headed for the front of the column. Mac went with him, riding past the line of ambulance wagons. Suddenly, from one of the vehicles, a voice called out. "Cap'n Mac! . . . Cap'n Mac!"

Mac reined in sharply, thinking that he recognized the voice. When he turned in the saddle, he saw the young slave called Roman looking at him from the driver's seat of the wagon.

Lee noticed that Mac had stopped, and the general turned back. "What is it, Mac?" Lee asked.

"General, that slave was with my brother—"

"Go see about him," Lee said without hesitation. "You can catch up with me later."

With his heart pounding heavily, Mac urged the stallion over beside the ambulance. "Roman!" Mac said. "Where's Will?"

Roman jumped down from the box and hurried to the rear of the wagon. "Back here, Cap'n!"

Mac swung down from the saddle and looped the reins over one of the wheel spokes. He fought back the fear that threatened to engulf him. If Will was dead, he wouldn't be in an ambulance, Mac told himself. They buried dead men.

Roman pulled aside the canvas flap over the rear of the wagon. Mac saw that half a dozen wounded men had been loaded into the ambulance. One of them—

God, one of them was Will.

Mac saw his brother's face, pale as death, as Will lay on a pallet on the wagonbed. Bloodstained bandages were wrapped around his chest and his left shoulder. His chest rose and fell in a ragged rhythm, and even above the hubbub surrounding the column, Mac could hear the harshness of his breathing.

"I would've come an' tried to find you," Roman said, "but I couldn't leave Cap'n Will."

"How—" Mac had to stop and swallow hard before he could go on. "How badly is he hurt?"

"Mighty bad. Shot right through the chest, he was. But the doctor said this mornin' it's a good sign Cap'n Will ain't died yet. He might pull through, the doctor says."

"He'll pull through," Mac said, determination in his voice. "I know my brother."

But as he climbed into the wagon and moved carefully past the other wounded men to kneel beside Will, the pallor of his brother's face made Mac less sure of that. Judging by those stains on the bandages, Will had lost a lot of blood.

Mac became aware that Roman was hunkered beside him. "What happened?" he asked in a quiet voice.

"We was takin' a message to Gen'ral Lee from Gen'ral Ewell 'round to Seminary Ridge. Never got to deliver it before the attack, and after that Cap'n Will didn't think it mattered no more. We started back toward where his soldiers was, and . . . and this bullet come out of nowhere and knocked him right out of the saddle. He was bleedin' mighty bad, front and back both. I tore off pieces o' my shirt and wadded 'em up and held 'em on the holes while I got him up on his horse and brought him here."

Mac looked over at Roman. The young man was considerably smaller than Will, and Mac knew it must have been quite a job lifting him into the saddle. "You saved his life."

"I knew Massa Yancy would've wanted me to look out for him. That's why he fixed it so's I'd be with Cap'n Will."

Mac put a hand on the young man's shoulder and squeezed. "Thank you, Roman," he whispered. "My family and I owe you more than I can ever say."

"Don't you worry none 'bout that, Cap'n. Let's just get Cap'n Will home—"

Will's eyelids fluttered open, and he croaked, "H-home?"

"That's right, Will," Mac told him. "We're taking you home, Roman and I."

"M-Mac?"

"It's me, Will. I'm with you. You'll be all right."

Slowly, Will lifted his right hand. It shook from the strain, but he managed to raise it several inches from the wagon bed. Mac took hold of it, and Will's fingers clenched tightly on his. Even as badly shot up as he was, Will still had the strength to clasp his brother's hand.

The strength of the Confederacy, Mac thought, and he held on tight as Will sighed and closed his eyes to go back to sleep.

—⟋⟍⟍⟋—

Gettysburg . . . fought the Yankees there . . . Gettysburg . . . lost nearly half the army . . . Gettysburg . . . what'll Lee do now . . . Gettysburg . . . Gettysburg . . .

The whispers ran through the barracks at Camp Douglas as the rumors spread that hot July. Even as the Confederate prisoners devoted most of their waning energy to sheer survival in hellish conditions, they found the time and strength to talk about what had happened at some little town in Pennsylvania called Gettysburg. Nobody wanted to believe it had been as bad for the Confederates as the gloating Yankee guards made it sound, but one thing was certain: The battle had been a defeat for the Southerners. The Army of Northern Virginia had been thrashed so soundly that President Lincoln was said to be furious that Meade hadn't pursued it and wiped it out. That day was coming, though, the guards boasted.

"Pretty soon there won't be no damned Confederacy for you Rebel bastards to go back to, even if we wanted to let you go, which we don't," Sergeant O'Neil taunted the prisoners.

Titus Brannon and Nathan Hatcher stood near the deadline and gazed out over the hellhole that had been their home for more than half a year now. Pitching his voice low so that it couldn't be overheard, Titus muttered, "If we're goin', it's got to be soon, while there's still something to go back to."

"I don't know . . . ," Nathan said.

"I do." Titus looked him square in the eye. "I'd rather die than spend any more time cooped up in here than I have to."

"But how? How can we get out?"

As he thought of Miss Louisa Abernathy, a thin smile curved Titus's lips. "I reckon I may know of a way."

—◆—

ABIGAIL BRANNON enjoyed hanging up the wash, even on a hot day like this. Maybe even more so than on other days, because the heat made the wet sheets and clothes seem even cooler. She moved along the clothesline with her basket, humming a hymn under her breath. She missed church, missed singing the old hymns and hearing the gospel preached. She never would have thought she could go this long without attending a service. But she couldn't go back while Ben Spanner was there. She just couldn't. He would have been too painful a reminder of what had happened.

Hoofbeats made her look up from what she was doing, and she said aloud, "Speak of the devil." The Reverend Benjamin Spanner rode into the yard between the house and the barn.

Abigail stepped around her basket and walked toward him as he got down from his horse. Trying to sound polite but firm, she said, "You're not welcome here, Mr. Spanner—"

She stopped at the look on his face as he turned toward her. Something was wrong, terribly wrong. His face was bleak and hard, but worst of all, she saw sympathy in his eyes.

"Abigail," he said, "where are Henry and Cordelia?"

"They're . . . they're working in the fields." She took a step toward him and lifted a hand. "What is it, Ben?"

"We've had some news in town. Bad news. Vicksburg surrendered to the Yankees."

Abigail caught her breath. Cory was in Vicksburg, along with the girl he had married and what was left of her family. She knew that the Yankees had had the town on the Mississippi River under siege for weeks. She had hoped and prayed that somehow Vicksburg's defenders would be able to turn away the invaders, but if what Ben was saying was true, that hadn't happened.

"I know you have a son there," Spanner went on. "They say there was some fighting, and the Union forces under General Grant shelled the town heavily. But at least it's over now, and you can hope for the best for Cory."

Abigail closed her eyes for a moment and then nodded. "Yes, you're right," she said. "I'll pray for his safety and for those who are with him." She looked at Spanner again. "Thank you for riding out here to tell me, Ben. I . . . I suppose I can allow you that much forgiveness."

"That's not all the news, Abigail."

The words were a fresh blow. Abigail lifted a hand to her throat, wishing she could tell him to stop, to just turn around and ride away. She didn't want to hear any more.

"Right around the same time that Vicksburg surrendered, there was a big battle up in Pennsylvania," Spanner went on. He wiped the back of his hand across his mouth. "A really big battle at a place called Gettysburg. The Confederate army got whipped. They're supposed to be on their way back here now, the ones who made it through the fight. What we heard . . ." He stopped, unable to go on for a couple of heartbeats. "What we heard was that half the army got killed. Now, I don't know if that's right, Abby," he added quickly, "but . . . it's what we heard in town today."

Stunned, Abigail felt tears well from her eyes and roll down her cheeks. She put her hands over her face and shuddered. Spanner stepped forward and put his arms around her to comfort her, and although she had sworn she would never let this man touch her again, she did not pull away. Instead, she huddled against him and wailed.

They stood there like that for a long time as Abigail Brannon cried for her children.